M. ANDERSON

A Fire in the East

Knights of the Fallen Realm: Book II

First published by Anderson Books 2020

This novel is entirely a work of fiction. The names, characters and incidents portrayed in it are the work of the author's imagination. Any resemblance to actual persons, living or dead, events or localities is entirely coincidental.

Photograph by Dean Stewart Photography

First edition

ISBN: 978-1-7331908-2-4

Editing by S. Jean Brenner
Cover art by E Book Launch

This book was professionally typeset on Reedsy.
Find out more at reedsy.com

I

Part One

1

Alex

My name is Alex Winters, and I'm about to die.

To be fair, it is the fifth time I've died since breakfast, and the forty seventh time this week, so it's routine.

I look up at the servo just before the fireball leaves its mouth. The little robot is floating about five feet from the floor at the other end of the practice chamber. I'm not sure if someone is directly controlling it, or if it's under the effect of a spell, but I can't worry about that. I need to concentrate on the massive fireball flying towards me.

I can do this. I. Can. Do. This. Once the fireball leaves the servo's mouth, I'll have fifteen seconds to glimmer. Concentrate. Ten. Concentrate. Five. Concentrate. Is that burning rubber?

And... that'll make six.

Being dead isn't that bad, I guess. I mean, without the pain dampening spell my instructor has on the servo, it would be a lot worse... It's just like being in the DMV with the lights off and you're not sure how many people are ahead of you in line. I see the light before I feel it, and the spell envelops me like a warm familiar (way too familiar) blanket. I slowly come back to my senses and look up to

3

see Marin looking down at me.

"Forgot to glimmer again?" He asks with a smirk.

"Didn't forget, just can't. Also shut up. Also, thanks for saving me again," I say with an eye roll.

"Seriously, Alex, between you keeping me busy bringing your sorry self back from the brink twelve times a day, and the Domesticants casting mending spells on your robes every time you get blasted, you're keeping half the Sanctum employed." As he speaks, a smile lights up his face and his green eyes dance with laughter.

Urgh. I hate Marin. He's so smug, but also correct. I'm a mess. I grunt in response and make myself feel better by punching him. He might be a better Magi than me, but his reflexes still suck.

"That's about enough for this morning, let's go get lunch! Lunch makes everything better!" Marin says with gusto. As he takes one final chuckle at me, he adjusts his robes. He keeps his white hair short and orderly, aside from a cowlick he can't even seem to manage.

I take one last angry look back at the servo which is still floating harmlessly in the air, just waiting to devour me with another fireball. It's been a week and I still don't feel any better at casting spells than when I got here. If anything, I feel twenty times worse. But Marin's right, lunch makes everything better.

As we leave the hall I stop at a mirror on the wall and rearrange my robes. Aside from being one size too big (and the steaming holes from aforementioned fireball robot of doom) I just can't ever seem to get them right. As I fidget with my robes, my hair falls out of the tight bun and cascades around my shoulders. I don't like keeping my hair back that tight, but since I arrived a week ago, I've had little choice.

"Your hair is too long. If we must let a female study with us, the least you can do is not remind us of it," was the first thing the Grand Esoteric said to me upon arrival. This would be the friendliest thing he would say to me. There were about twenty different things I wanted to say in response, but Kyria's swift kick to my shins kept them in check. So, I just curtsied instead. God, I miss her and Ahrun. It's only been a week since they left, but I feel like I've been on my own for a month.

"You look fine," Marin says.

"Fine, let's go. But let's make this quick," I say back to him as I rearrange my robes one last time.

We start down the hallway and after a series of quick lefts and rights we arrive at the latchkey. As we get closer, I can feel its energy pulsing. The first thing I learned about the Magi was they're a bunch of sexist pigs, except for Marin, which is probably why he doesn't have any friends and never gets to sit at the cool Magi table at lunch. There doesn't seem to be much of a reason for their idle distaste for women, but I get the sense that this has been the status quo for a long time.

The second thing I learned about them is they are lazy. There are sets of ornate staircases running throughout Sanctum, but they never get used except by the Domesticants. Everyone else just uses the latchkeys, their name for a portal from place to place. I guess I understand it, but honestly, some of these Magi could stand to use the stairs once in a while.

As I pass the threshold of the latchkey, I feel myself getting pulled inside of it. It's something like when we used the waystone to get here, but a hundred times smoother. We arrive on the other side, just outside the dining hall. I grimace and adjust my robes one last time. I hate this.

The angry stares and silent judgments wash over me, and by extension, Marin, the moment we walk into the hall. It's been a week and they aren't any friendlier and this isn't any easier. I make my way into line behind Marin, who seems perfectly pleasant and unphased by all of it. Lunch today seems to be some kind of pulled chicken and bread. On the other side of the Magi, a half dozen Domesticants move food about and prepare plates. It's the only time I get to see women using magic. These types of tasks is the only application fit for a woman's abilities, or so they tell me. Like I said, sexist pigs.

I get my food and follow Marin to a seat. He's trying to talk to me about some fancy incant he's working on, but I can't concentrate. All I can feel are the eyes all over me and it's making my stomach churn. Besides demeaning women, the Magi don't seem to mind objectifying them either.

"Can we go?" I ask Marin. A sheen of icy panic coats my words.

He looks at me and raises an eyebrow. "Sure, we can."

I want to tell him thanks, but first I just want to get out of here. My head is buzzing and all I can focus on is the feeling of eyes and the snide whispering all around me. I get up and start walking out of the hall when I see a pair of boots in front of me. Looking up, I see the boots belong to Caiaphas, Magi prodigy and just about the biggest jerk in Sanctum, which is impressive all things considered.

"And where does it think it's going?" Caiaphas asks. He directs his attention and his words to Marin. He's been tormenting me since I arrived, but he's also maintained his steadfast policy of never talking directly to a woman. Something about it being a waste of his time.

"I'm leaving. Something about your presence just makes everything taste rotten. Must be a coincidence," I say back.

"Someone needs to teach this creature some respect for the way things are around here," Caiaphas replies with a sneer. He's looking at me like I'm covered in sour milk, but that's just the way he always looks at me.

"Try. It." I say, doing my best to keep my voice calm and measured.

"With pleasure," he says, and begins chanting an incant.

He's quick, and his incantations are spot on. His goons clear away from him and I see arcane energy surging. Runes appear on the floor around him and the spell is nearly complete. The runes hiss and pop, steaming with intense heat, and I can tell it's a flame incant. Doesn't matter though. His spell might be quick, but my fist is quicker. I bring a right hook crashing into his jaw that sends him sprawling backward over a nearby dining table. A bowl of mashed potatoes erupts and covers his torso as he crumples on the other side. The hall erupts in laughter. As much as they hate me, I'm sure they hate Caiaphas more. Aside from his goons, I never see him talking with anybody (well, not counting the massive quantities time he spends sucking up to the instructors).

I turn and leave the hall, but with Marin in tow. Neither of us can contain our laughter, but I feel something in the back of my head and dodge right as a pillar of flame shoots past me. I whip around and see an angry, mashed potato covered Caiaphas readying another incant. To be fair, I think it's a good look for him, but he's not getting another cheap shot off. I tackle him with a flying leap and lift my fist to strike him. I can't bring it down and I look up to see my entire hand engulfed in blue energy.

This isn't good.

"Alex Winters," a loud voice booms. It's coming from a simulacrum in the corner. Creepy little eyeless creatures that act as a P.A. system throughout Sanctum. "The Grand Esoteric summons you to his chambers. Now."

Before I can react or even say anything to Marin, I feel myself being pulled into a latchkey that just formed several inches above my head. The energy pulls me up into the portal and I feel myself falling for what seems like a while.

The chamber's stone floor greets my butt with a firm hello and a dull ache. Pulling myself back up, I attempt to put myself together a bit before he sees me, but it's too late. Turning around in a swiveling chair worthy of a James Bond villain, the Grand Esoteric clears his throat, and it feels like all the air just got sucked out of the room. I rise to meet his gaze and it's uncomfortable. Out of the hooded cowl of his flowing blue robes, his eyes are picking me apart, examining every flaw and failing down to my most elemental core. Intellect and malice are doing a tango in his eyes and it's hard to tell which is winning, but his gaze conveys a singular message effectively: You are not welcome here, and you are nothing but a disappointment.

On the bright side though, by some miracle, my robes look half decent. That's something, I guess.

2

Kyria

I t had been a week, and Kyria was missing the Magi. Granted, she had tried to kill them a half-dozen times, and if it wasn't for the guiding hand of Ahrun, she might have succeeded. That they would have summoned immense arcane power and fried her to a crisp were less important details. Still, she would take another day dealing with those sexist pigs (a phrase Alex taught her that she found delightfully accurate) over wandering through the jungle. And then there was Ahrun.

She and the Paladin only recently saw eye to eye after some early disagreements, but in the week since they left Alex at Sanctum, their relationship had disintegrated rapidly. Kyria knew Ahrun was a valuable ally in the fight against the court, but all the same, she wished more and more than a large bug or lizard might crunch him up or slurp him down for lunch.

Ahrun's smooth voice interrupted her thoughts. "This way," he said, pointing farther up the trail. He held a map in his hand.

"How do ya know tha's the right way?" Kyria asked. He hadn't led them astray yet, but it irritated her that he needed to explain himself.

She also needed a break from walking, but there was no way she'd admit that to him.

"Well, if you'd look at the map, it..."

"I don' want ta look at yer stupid map. It jus' some trick o' those lousy wizards ta get us out o' their hair while they play some magic an' witch poor Alex's brain. I still say we should 'ave stayed with her."

"As we discussed, we need to follow this lead," Ahrun said, his voice steady and even. "If it pans out, it would be a..."

"Bloody miracle, tha's what. Anyway, I don' trust yer eegit map, and I don' trust yer sense o' direction, but far be it from me ta stop ya."

Ahrun sighed.

"So, jus' keep goin' on down that fool's path. Maybe we'll find a lost treasure ship and be able ta bribe the Court out o' Aquillon."

Ahrun said nothing but kept walking. Kyria sighed and followed. She felt a twinge of guilt for how she spoke to him, but she hadn't gotten over the fight yet.

"I don' care, we're no' leavin' Alex here with these cretins," Kyria said, her voice barely below a shout.

Ahrun looked down the hall and saw several Magi staring daggers in their direction.

"Can you contain your ire for even a moment? We are guests of Sanctum and we need to carry ourselves well. We may well need the Eastern Watch as allies in the war to come, so if you could avoid burning this bridge while we're standing on it, that would be excellent," Ahrun said. He rubbed his temples as he finished.

Kyria conceded the point and lowered her voice. "I know yer hot on this map they gave ya, but whose ta say it's accurate, or even that this dragon exists at all?"

"If there is even the smallest chance that the Mistress of Scale still draws breath, we must find her. She is the single best chance, outside of Alex, of defeating the Court. Besides, we need to be accommodating to the wishes of the Magi." As soon as he said it, he knew it was a mistake. He could see the geyser of anger on Kyria's face about to erupt.

"Oh, I see, so we should accommodate them by removin' my offensive female presence from the honourable gentleman here? Is tha' it? Kyria asked, her voice shaking. "Or maybe ya want me ta join their little commune o' woman servants? That might be better?"

Ahrun stammered, trying to undo the damage. "That's not what I meant at all. Please don't..."

"Oh, I knew well what ya mean't. So fine, 'ave it yer way, we'll go lookin' for this mythical dragon o' yers, but don' speak to me, or I'll make sure I'll be the only one who ever speaks ta tha' scaly beast," Kyria said. She turned and stormed away, throwing a book at his head as she went. He dodged it and shook his head, sighing. A thousand years and you still do not understand how to talk to women, he thought to himself. He hoped the journey would allow her to focus on something else.

It hadn't. As Kyria walked each mile deeper in the jungle, all she could think about was how irritated she was, with Ahrun, with this fool's errand, with all of it. And she missed Alex. Her friend had been the glue holding the group together, another expression Alex taught her on their journey, and now, without her, Kyria was just irritated, and directed most of it at Ahrun.

A crash in the jungle interrupted Kyria's muttering and fuming. She saw Ahrun drop prone below a line of bushes and shrubs, and she followed suite. She held her breath and waited, watching the tree line with intent.

After several moments, the jungle exploded as a gargantuan creature breached the tree line ahead of them. It looked like a great hippo, like the kind she had seen in river deltas on Aquillon, but ten times the size. Great tusks, sharp as swords, gleamed in the sun that shone down through the canopy. From the top of its head, massive globe-like eyes swiveled back and forth, attempting to ferret out whatever it had heard. Hardened skin covered the whole of the beast, like great flaps of impenetrable armor.

Kyria glanced across the thicket to where Ahrun stooped down, sitting so still he would have blended into the greenery if not for his long, black traveling cloak. She caught his eye and gave him a questioning look. He responded by signaling for her to wait. It wasn't her nature to hide from things, but she figured there wouldn't be much of a fight between her and the creature, and she wanted to maintain her long-standing policy of not becoming anything's lunch. Or dessert.

After several agonizing minutes had passed, the creature turned left and walked in a different direction, apparently satisfied that nothing edible was in the thicket. Reaching the tree line, it continued to walk through the trees, pushing them aside casually as if they were stalks of wheat it was pushing past.

Kyria stood slowly, waiting for the beast to leave, and took a step. As soon as she took it a sound caught her ears and a sea of panic flooded over her.

A twig under her foot snapped with a loud pop that reverberated through the clearing. She waited, praying the giant death hippo had gone far enough away to not hear the sound, but the furious roar on her left told her otherwise. Ahrun looked at her and seemed to do his best to suppress his annoyance. She'd apologize later, but for now they just needed to run.

They looked around and found a small path between the trees that led out of the clearing. Ahrun moved to inspect his map, but Kyria swatted it away.

"There's no time ya eegit, jus' run!"

Ahrun said nothing and ran towards the path, followed closely by Kyria. They arrived at it just as the creature burst into the clearing with an equally massive crash. Looking down, the creature's eyes spotted them and it bellowed with primal fury, and charged. The earth shook with every step it took, and Kyria barely kept her balance. She and Ahrun ran as fast as they could, but the creature was gaining ground, quickly.

As they ran along the path, the hippo closed the distance and was right behind them. It brought one of its towering legs down with a shattering sound, and the impact of the hoof knocked Ahrun and Kyria cleanly off their feet. It swept Ahrun out of the path of the monster's fury, but Kyria wasn't as fortunate.

When she re-gathered her senses, Kyria looked up to see a hoof the size of a small house coming down on her. She stood up and tried to move out of the way, but she was still dazed from the impact before. She moved to avoid where she thought the hoof would come down, but she was too slow. She had nearly cleared it when she felt Ahrun grab her arm roughly and pull her clear of the hoof. Kyria stood up, surprised and grateful not to be dead, and she saw Ahrun standing just on the outer edge of where the hoof was about to strike.

As it hit, it shattered the earth and sent Ahrun flying headfirst into a tree. His body hit the ground with a thud and he slumped over and did not stand back up. Kyria sprinted over to him, dodging in and out of the legs of the death hippo. She reached his body and took a moment to check if he was alive.

He was.

Kyria grabbed his arms and pulled him deeper into the jungle, trying to get out of the line of sight of the titanic beast. The hippo searched around frantically, bringing branches down as its head crushed through them. Kyria managed not only to avoid them but also pulled Ahrun's body clear of any falling debris. She felt the creature's eyes settle on them and it roared before leaning down to go for the kill. Kyria was trapped by its legs on both sides and braced herself.

Death never came, though. As she waited to be slurped up by some tongue or impaled on one of the huge tusks, she thought to herself it was taking a while. Looking up, Kyria nearly squealed with delight to see a massive lizard wrapped around the hippo, biting and pulling at the hippo's throat. The hippo bucked and stomped wildly, but the lizard held on, its legs and tail, locking the hippo in a vice grip. The lizard finally pulled the hippo into the clearing and Kyria began pulling Ahrun's body as far away as she could from the death match between the monsters.

Once she got a fair distance from the path and from the creatures, she collapsed next to Ahrun and sobbed as she felt her heart thundering in her chest. Kyria closed her eyes and offered a silent prayer to whatever great, forgotten god ruled over these creatures, and then drifted off, despite her best efforts not to. She would handle everything else later, but for now, just not being in a death hippo's stomach was plenty good enough for her.

Test

3

Alex

I t seems like an eternity before the old man speaks a word, but as soon as he does, I'd just as soon go back to the tense silence.

"If you're seeking to prove me right about your kind, female, you're doing an excellent job," he says. His words are tight and punctuated, like he can't spare even an idle moment between words.

"In my defense," I say. It's hard to find my voice. I've talked smack to demon lords, gods, and monsters, but I find it hard to talk back to him. Which is weird, because I hate him more than any of the aforementioned nasties.

"There is no defense for you," the old man says, cutting me off. "I knew it was a poor idea to accept you into our ranks. There is a reason we do not accept your kind. I suppose it's not entirely your fault, there is a hard limit on the capabilities of a female."

His voice is dripping with contempt and superiority. I've never wanted to punch someone in the face this badly. Ok, that's a lie, but this jerk is top five for sure.

"When you arrived, my first thought was to reject you. But I sense the power in you, and your Paladin friend is right, there is an air of destiny about you," he said.

That was the nearest thing to a compliment I've heard the old man give. "But your presence here is becoming more taxing that it seems to be worth. I should throw you and your meddlesome mother out, but she's another matter entirely."

I clench my jaw. If there was one person, I'm angrier at than this old bigot, it's my mother.

"Still, there may yet be some time for you to be of use. The Trials approach. You know this?"

I nod.

"Good, it's nice to see that some information can stay in that skull of yours. Well, we will let the trials decide if you're worth keeping around or not. If the information your mother provided me is accurate, getting through the trials should be no trouble at all. We will see. But in the meantime, if you engage in any more hostilities with my students, your friend Marin will pay the price," he says. His words linger in the air, becoming more threatening by the second.

"But Caiaphas started it!" I say, my voice quaking with outrage.

"I don't care what he or any other student says or does to you. As your superiors, it is their right and I will not interfere with that. You will hold your tongue, and your fists, in check. Am I clear?"

I'm clenching and grinding my teeth so hard I'm worried I might break a tooth.

"Well?"

"Clear."

"Clear, what?"

"Clear, sir."

"Good. Now get out of my sight and continue preparing for the trials. You'll need all the time you have, I'm sure." As he speaks his upper lip curls back into a sneer that I can just make out behind his beard. I say nothing, but my mind is a flurry of curses and anger. I really hope he's not psychic. Scratch that, I hope he is.

I turn and leave his office as fast as possible. Marin is leaning against a wall outside, leafing through a book on applied ice magic. He looks up with a pleasant smile that vanishes as soon as he sees my face.

"It went that well, huh?" he asks with a smirk.

"Just peachy," I say, rolling my eyes at him. "I think I might have a new best friend." I make a gagging noise and Marin chuckles. I like his laugh. It's like water gurgling in a brook.

"Well good. For a minute there I thought you were in real trouble or something. Well, we better get back to it. The Trials are in two days.". A serious look creeps across his face.

"Don't remind me," I say with a dejected sigh. I've been here for a week and I can't even glimmer, which is a simple teleportation spell that anybody should be able to master. I haven't been able to do anything since I got here, actually. It's like my powers ditched me. Now I have to compete with novices that have been studying for a year for a few spots at chauvinist Hogwarts.

Marin seems to notice my mood shifting even worse and clears his throat. "Let's go up top. Get some air." He says.

My gut reaction is to say no, go back to my room and wallow, but that doesn't seem helpful. I need to clear my mind so I can get back to practicing, and Marin has a way of calming me down. I also haven't seen the sky in two days.

"All right, let's go then. We can't be too long, though. I've got a date with a floating fireball robot."

"Well, let's hurry then," he says.

It doesn't take long to get to the correct latchkey. It was a tricky process to figure out. When I first arrived, I ended up landing in at least three bowls of soup and was nearly gobbled by some hideous pig monster on floor four hundred and fifty-seven because I got my latchkeys mixed up. I still miss Thistle. I'd give anything for him to see this place. I miss his stories, his snoring, his over-the-top gallantry.

We jump in the latchkey, and moments later we're on floor eight hundred. Sanctum isn't really that tall, mind you, it's just a series of pocket dimensions. Stairs link some stories, but not others, and some staircases are just a never-ending loop. Marin told me it's a defense mechanism. It's nice to know I'm safe from demon attacks, even if I'm surrounded by sexist wizards. Plus, the stair loops have turned out to be a great running zone since, shockingly, the Eastern Watch isn't big on gyms or cardio.

Turning the corner, we see the door leading to the roof, but I also see her. My mother is waiting at the end of the hall. Marin gives me a nervous glance, but I wave for him to go, and I'll catch up. He walks past her and goes out onto the roof, leaving the door cracked slightly. I walk up to her, and every muscle in my body is straining against me. I don't want to talk to her, but here she is.

"Can we talk?" She asks. I see tears welling in her eyes, and there's a part of me that wants to forgive her. Most of me just wants to walk away.

"I have nothing to say to you." My words are cold and detached, and it barely feels like I'm speaking.

"Alessandra, please, I can't apologize enough. You have no idea how sorry I am."

"You're right. I don't. But it doesn't matter now. I have trials to prepare for, and you're not helping, so just leave me alone."

"Please, I…"

"Don't."

I walk past her and slam the door as I hear soft sobbing. Part of my heart is breaking and just wants to call her mom and rush to her, but the bigger part of me can't forgive her. I walk over to Marin, who is throwing rocks over the side of the tower.

18

I've been up to the top of Sanctum a few times now, and I can't get enough of it. As I walk towards Marin, the wind catches my hair and blows it out of its tight bun, lifting it to dance on the wind. I catch it and pull it back, but it's nice to feel free for a moment. I also find the height of the tower exhilarating. It's hundreds of feet high and there's no railing on the sides, but I find something about that fact liberating. As much as might get blown off the tower at any point, it's nice to be somewhere where no one is trying to restrict me.

Marin throws one last rock over the side and turns to me with a sad smile.

"Still not getting along, huh?" he asks.

"What gave it away?"

"Well, the shouting for a start, but I found the door slam to be a nice touch. Very subtle."

"I was shouting?"

"Yup. It was loud. If there was anything on this floor but overflow storage, you might have scared people."

I grunt in response. I'm not sure what I'm supposed to say.

"At least she's trying…" Marin begins.

"Trying to what? Make up for the fact that she abandoned me on Earth? Then brought me back to Aquillon when she figured it would help her?" I realize I'm yelling at him, but I'm having a hard time controlling my temper.

"I think it might be more complicated than that," Marin says. His voice is smooth and even. Credit to him because I'd be shouting at myself by now.

"How is a mother abandoning her child and husband on a different planet complicated? It's just horrible."

"I'm sure she had her reasons. And she called you back, at significant risk to herself and others. When they found out Grandstaff helped her, they stripped him of his rank and sent him to work in the archives.

I don't think he's coming back anytime during this millennium."

I feel a twinge of guilt. Soon after arriving at Sanctum, my mother told me about Grandstaff, the old man who brought me to Aquillon. She then told me the rest, and I haven't been able to forgive her.

"But it was for her own purposes. If she hadn't found that scroll in the archives, she would have never brought me back. She was happy to let me rot on Earth, by myself, until she needed something. That's not what a mother does. It's not..." Hot tears are streaming down my face and I can't even bring myself to say more. Marin puts his hand on my shoulder and gives it a squeeze. As friendly as he is, he's not big on hugs.

"We don't need to talk about it anymore, if you don't want to. Just relax. We came to get your mind settled out before training, and those tears won't save you from the servo."

I take a deep breath and try to focus. Looking up at the sky helps. I see the cosmos and all the stars shining down and there's a moment of peace. There's a soft glow lighting up the plateau for miles, and a cooling night wind dances playfully over the silent hills and distant rolling mountains. Just on the edge of what I can see, the barrier separating Sanctum with the jungles of the Wyld Places shimmers against the night sky.

I can't forgive my mother, but I won't worry about that for now. For now, I just need to glimmer. If I can figure that out, the rest should come. At least, that's what I'm telling myself, anyway.

4

Kyria

B y the time Ahrun regained consciousness, night had fallen. Kyria had started a fire from loose timber. There was more than enough in the hippo's wake. It wasn't overly cold, but the firelight made her feel better about being deep in an unexplored jungle filled with monsters. The fire might also attract said monsters, but for all she knew, they could see in the dark, anyway. If she was getting eaten, she'd prefer to see the beastie first, if only to give it a good smack in the mouth before it gulped her down.

Ahrun groaned and rolled into an upright position. It took him several moments to assess the situation, and he looked at Kyria, a dazed expression on his face.

"Mornin' sunshine," Kyria said to him.

"Good to know you don't hate me enough to let wild animals eat me," Ahrun said, chuckling to himself.

"It was close, but I figured ya might be good ta keep around, at least for a few more days."

"I know you had your," Ahrun paused, "reservations about coming with me, but I appreciate it. Aside from saving my rump, I appreciate the company. The world was a lonely place for a long time. I'm glad it isn't anymore."

"Don't ya get all sappy on me now, Ser Fancy Britches. As Alex says, the jury's still out o' whether I'm keepin' ya or no.'"

"Well, I hope I'm able to convince you my company yet bears some merit."

"Let's jus' get some shuteye," Kyria said. She rolled over onto her bedroll and closed her eyes. She was feeling less irritated with him, but that may have just been sympathy since the hippo had nearly crushed him.

Kyria woke up the next morning to the buzzing of the jungle. Since they had started out on their journey, she had gotten little sleep. Between the symphony of discordant noise from the jungle and the general feeling of unease created by the constant threat of death, her sleep schedule wasn't exactly normal. The first thing she saw was Ahrun studying the map. She sighed and cleared her throat.

"So, any fresh revelations on yer map o' wonders?"

"Actually," Ahrun said without looking up, "we may owe our monstrous hippo friend a debt of gratitude. It's path of destruction has revealed a marker."

"A what?"

"A marker stone. Legends say that when the last of the dragons was exiled here by the foul magic of the Court, she left marker stones along the path to lead any of her children to her. Our destructive friend seems to have unwittingly revealed one."

"I thought the dragons were a wee bit o' fantasy invented to sell relics an' tha' sort o' junk?" Kyria asked.

"Not so. My order did extensive research during the Fall about their whereabouts. There wasn't much, but there was some evidence to suggest that they existed."

"An' we're lookin' for the queen o' these scaly beasts?"

"Yes, a being known as the Mistress of Scales."

"An' what makes ya think she'll help us as opposed to eating us or fryin' us ta a crispy morsel?"

"Nothing at all," said Ahrun in his most chipper voice.

"Grand, jus' grand," Kyria said. "Well, I suppose we better get this expedition o' lunacy movin' along then."

Ahrun nodded, not pushing his luck any further. This was the most optimistic Kyria had sounded about their mission since they left Sanctum. It was also the first time she had pressed him for details, which he took an excellent sign of her general outlook on the mission.

They broke camp and made their way to the marker stone. Kyria asked Ahrun where it was, but it wasn't hard to spot. A hundred yards from their campsite, a massive stone stuck out of the forest like a sore thumb. It was so huge, Kyria was dumbstruck they had missed it. As she approached it, she felt smaller and smaller, until finally she was standing before what seemed to be a miniature mountain, carved by sizeable claw marks.

Runic symbols covered the face of the stone, each as beautiful and gracefully carved as the last. They were complete gibberish to Kyria, who looked to Ahrun.

"No, I don't read dragon, if that's what you're wondering," Ahrun said with a coy smile.

"What kind o' Paladin are ya then?"

"One who doesn't read dragon, it would seem."

"Well, I guess you'll 'ave ta do then," Kyria said, punching him in the arm.

"I can't decipher the runes, but I can use this as a point of reference for the map, so it's not a total loss," Ahrun said, rubbing his shoulder.

"Well, in tha' case, I guess ya can stay another day," Kyria said.

Ahrun pulled out his map and referenced the surrounding area. The map didn't mean much to her, but he seemed to put things together in his mind. He occasionally stopped and mumbled to himself before going back to look at the map. After twenty minutes (Kyria's rough estimation) he looked up and spoke.

"I believe we need to go this way," he said, pointing down the path that the behemoth had created.

"Well, then follow the map an' the magic rock we shall," Kyria said with a disingenuous courtesy.

They continued up the trail for the rest of the day, and as they went, Ahrun seemed to put more and more pieces of the puzzle together. By sun-down, they had discovered the second of the marker stones. Ahrun found a climbable path to the top of the stone and established a camp at the top. Kyria left him to it and strolled into the deeper brush with a hunting bow, looking for dinner. They were still relatively flush with supplies from sanctum, but fresh meat was always better than rations.

As she pressed deeper into the jungle, Kyria was left alone with her thoughts. She missed Alex, and would have given anything to have her friend there, but in her heart, she knew Ahrun was right. There was something special about Alex, and only the Magi could help her tap into it. Kyria was just happy they had made it to Sanctum at all.

As she walked, she reflected on their journey to Sanctum. It felt like a lifetime ago, even though only a week had passed. In the back at her mind a dull ache still pulled at her, like something scratching at her. She knew what it was, but didn't want to think about it. She still saw Rex in her eyes when she slept, and Thistle was never far behind. Even with all they had accomplished, defeating the Court seemed as impossible a dream as ever, but she wasn't ready to give up yet. She'd fight them until her last breath. Kyria owed Thistle and Rex a debt that she couldn't repay, so she'd keep fighting, no matter what. More than that, somewhere in her, a little girl just missed her dad. She missed his voice, his warm laugh, and the way his eyes lit up when he looked

24

at her. She felt tears welling in her eyes and she willed them away.

"No tears, girl," she told herself, "tears don' catch supper, an' tears don' keep ya breathin'."

Shaking off the emotions, she focused on the hunt. Dropping below a nearby bush, she waited until a fat rabbit hopped out of a nearby shrub. She smiled and knocked her arrow.

Once she had cleaned the rabbit, she returned to the stone and ambled her way up the rock. She was panting by the time she reached the top.

"I'm no' sayin' I don' appreciate the strategic placement o' yer camp, but gods alive, Ahrun, I'm no' a billy goat."

"You seem to have managed admirably," Ahrun said with a smirk.

"Jus' cook the bloody beast," Kyria said, tossing the rabbit's carcass to him.

Ahrun didn't argue and went about spearing the rabbit on a skewer and roasting it. In no time at all the meat was sizzling and they chowed down. When she finished eating, Kyria laid back on her bedroll and looked up at the stars. Even through the light of the fire, the stars radiated down with pure brilliance. In the distance, she heard colossal beasts moving in the forests and all around her life teemed unbound.

"So, what exactly do ya plan ta say ta this queen o' dragons?" Kyria asked Ahrun.

He sighed. "I haven't thought that far."

The remark surprised Kyria, but she tried to hide it in her voice.

"So, the man with the plan's jus' wingin' it," she said.

"I suppose so, I'm just trying to stay one step ahead of everything out here. I'm sure I'll know which words are right by the time we arrive."

"An' when might that be?"

"Soon, several days perhaps. I believe I have discovered a pattern in the marker stones. If I am correct, the resting place of the Mistress of

Scales should be somewhere in those mountains to the east." Ahrun motioned to the east, and Kyria looked. From atop the stone, she could make out the inky silhouette of a mountain range.

"All right. Well, tha's a start, anyway. I'm goin' ta sleep. I'll take second watch."

Ahrun nodded.

Kyria closed her eyes and drifted off to sleep, peacefully, for the first time since they had left Sanctum. It seemed like an eternity had passed when she awoke to sunlight and the sound of rustling trees. As she opened her eyes, she saw Ahrun gazing at something. Sitting up, she saw what he was looking at.

Towering over the treetops, a bird with a long neck and bright azure feathers looked down at them intently.

"Buaaak?" it squawked.

"Any chance ya speak bird?" Kyria asked.

"No better than I speak dragon, I'm afraid."

Kyria sighed. She was far too busy to be eaten by over-sized poultry.

"Blast it. This is gonna ruin my entire day," she muttered as she rolled over and stood, standing face to face with the mega chicken.

5

Alex

It's been a day since I spoke to the Grand Esoteric. Twenty-four hours, or just about, which is the time I have left to figure out what's wrong with my powers and get ready for the trials.

And what a fun twenty-four it's been. I spent most of yesterday and last night getting incinerated by the flying fireball robot. No matter how hard I tried, I couldn't glimmer anywhere. Not twenty feet to the end of the hall, and under the robot. Not ten feet, just in front of the robot. Not even one foot, to die in a slightly different spot, for the sake of variety. Nothing. No glimmering. I only have twenty-four hours until I make an absolute fool of myself, and get thrown out of wizard school, and doom the rest of Aquillon to another thousand years of suffering at the hand of the Court.

It's been a blast.

The only bright spot might be Marin. He's been patient, kind, encouraging, and calm. I don't know what I would do if I had to do this alone, although admittedly I don't think I'd be any worse at this; I'm not even sure that's possible. He's been getting me back up every time, and he's even eased up on the wise cracks and smarmy remarks. He's just been there, and since my friends are off on a wild dragon chase, having at least one friend is invaluable.

We're walking down the hall to the practice chamber, steering clear of every other student. I can't afford any more trouble with them, and I don't even want to think about what they might do to Marin if I get caught up in anything.

We enter the practice chamber and I glance up at the robot. It sits there, looking at me with the same blank expression as always. That almost makes the fact that it keeps burning me to death worse. At least if it had a face, I might get angry at it, and channel that towards some kind of response.

I get into my normal stance as the robot fires itself up. The mouth of the servo opens up and I see the fire forming. In a matter of seconds an enormous ball of burning death is flying across the room and I breathe deeply, trying my best to focus on anywhere else. Ten seconds, then five, then one, and I brace myself for death. But it doesn't come.

When I open my eyes, I see Marin running over to me with an enormous grin on his face.

"You did it! You glimmered!"

"I did?" It doesn't feel like I did, but I look around and sure enough, I'm all the way across the room. I can see where I was standing, and the giant charred marking on the ground where the fireball hit. I laugh and I can't stop. Before I can stop myself, I'm jumping up and down and squealing in joy. I haven't felt this good about anything, well, ever.

After several more minutes of celebrating my senses come back to me, and I speak. "So, what now? What else do I need to learn for the trial?"

The look on Marin's face isn't good. "I won't lie to you, you're still far behind the curve. We've got work to do and not much time to do it. We should be able to do the rest on the roof though. Should be less likely to get distracted up there."

I'd love for him to be more cheerful, but the truth is what I need right now. If I'm not ready, I need to be, or as close as I can manage. I only get one shot at this, and other than Marin, literally every other Magi wants me to fail. I'm thinking they're not big on re-dos and makeup tests.

We get out to the roof as fast as possible and Marin shows me spells. First, he shows me how to incant. Some spells you can just cast by thinking about them, like glimmering. Others are much more specific and require chants, or specific hand movements. Now that I managed a glimmer, everything else seems easy. I pick up fire magic easily, which makes sense. On my journey over here I cast a few fires incants without even knowing how. Fire magic is more emotional, and less logical, so it makes more sense to me. As far as ice incants go, I can't summon much more than an ice cube.

By the time the dinner bell rings, my arms are sore from incanting, and I can barely hear my voice from all the spell casting. I've never felt more confident, though. From what I understand, a prospective candidate for Sanctum only needs to know glimmering and a few offensive incants to make it through the trials. It's mostly to make sure that the innate ability in a student isn't just a fluke. The trials aren't normally a big deal, since the order allows Magi students to retest every decade. Not for me, though. Aside from the fact I don't have a decade, the Grand Esoteric made it perfectly clear I only get one shot. If I fail, I'm out, no matter what that scroll my mother found says.

We make our way back to the dinner hall and pick up plates to go. It's the last dinner seating, so there isn't much to pick from, but there are very few idiots to contend with. I'm so focused on my mashed potatoes and steak tips I don't even notice my mother standing at the end of the line, pouring water.

"Good luck tomorrow," she says.

I look up and mumble, "thanks," before making my way back to a bench. Marin follows and falls in beside me.

"She's trying," Marin says, nudging me in my arm.

"I said thanks," I say, giving him a sour look.

He just raises one eyebrow, which is Marin's way of saying you're full of crap and you know it.

"I know that, but I'm busy enough getting ready for the trials tomorrow. I can deal with my mother after that."

He says nothing but sighs. I know I'm being insensitive. He doesn't even have a mother. He was abandoned five hundred years ago in the streets. The Magi sensed his ability and portaled him to Sanctum, where he's been ever since. He doesn't look five hundred, but neither does Ahrun. The Eastern Watch put a time-field around the tower. Time still passes normally, but people don't age here. They just watch the world turn. Wherever Marin's mother is, she's long dead. I feel like a world class jerk.

"Sorry, I know it's a sore subject."

He shakes his head. "I forgave my mother years ago. You can't live for eternity with hate in your heart. At some point it's just a distraction. What your mother did is terrible, but she's still your mother, and once she's gone, you don't get another one. Just something to think about."

I don't know what to say, so I just stuff my face with mashed potatoes. They just taste sad and lonely now. Stupid Marin. I really don't like how wise and sagely he is sometimes. I guess that's what five hundred years of life does for you.

I finish my sad potatoes and head back to my room. Marin says goodnight and jumps through a latchkey. I won't see him again until the trials. I'm making my way down a long hallway (fun fact, all the hallways in Sanctum are obnoxiously long), when I see a cracked door and hear voices. I recognize both. My mother and the grand old idiot are yelling at each other.

"Enough, Tamsil! You have tested my patience enough with this girl. This ends tomorrow."

"Fallstaff, I know what I read, and so do you. She is a child of prophecy. We cannot intercede." Her voice is strong and authoritative. I've never heard her like this.

"How dare you speak to me like this?" Fallstaff growls.

"We aren't out there in front of your puppets. You know I'm right, even you cannot deny the power you see within her. She has a destiny that we cannot thwart. Her presence here should be proof enough of her abilities. It takes even skilled Magi years to learn how to use a waystone."

"I will not speculate on what the girl may or may not have done. I will see for myself. If she fails the trials, we will tolerate her presence here no longer. Prophecy does not guide the Eastern Watch, I do. Now get out."

There is a hesitance in her voice when she replies. "Very well, but you are wrong. She will show you that she is worthy of being here." I hear her moving towards the door and I duck inside a nearby latchkey. My heart is pounding. I didn't know what my mother had shown the Grant Esoteric to get me in, but now I do. I remember Ahazi mentioning something about a prophecy, but it's all too crazy to comprehend. I can't worry about this right now. I have to focus on the trials. Nothing else matters.

I make my way back to my bedchamber and after an hour of rolling around; I slip into sleep. Tomorrow will be a long day.

We don't have to report to the chamber of trials for another hour, but I've been up for two. Last night was one of the few restful nights I've had since arriving at Sanctum, and I feel ready. My arms still feel like they're made of stone, and they ache something fierce, and I don't have any idea what I will face in the Trials, but I'm ready.

I leave my bedchamber and Marin is leaning against the wall playing cat's cradle with a line of energy he conjured up. He's good at conjuring things, especially illusions, which is the school he chose. That being said, he's terrible at cat's cradle. If I planned on staying around longer, I'd commit to a school of magical study, like he did, but I'm just here to learn as much as I can and get back in the fight.

"Morning, sunshine," Marin says with a coy smile, finally giving up his losing battle with the line of energy. As soon as he drops it, the line fades into nothing.

"Yup. I feel good, I feel ready."

"Well, that's good. We should get to the chamber. Nobody likes to be the last one in a trial. Waiting for everybody else to finish can mess with you."

I nod and we start down the hall. A series of latchkeys later, and we're standing outside the Hall of Trials. The hall is a narrow, cylindrical shaped room with bench seating raised up against the walls. A long, thin strip of ground leads out to a circular platform. I haven't seen an extensive amount of Sanctum, given that I haven't been here too long, but this place is a total mystery. Initiates (their name for newbies like me) are forbidden from even being on the same floor as the Hall of Trials. Every magus has to pass a trial if they want to move up in rank. The Eastern Watch isn't big on paper tests, I guess.

I look at Marin and take a deep breath. Despite feeling confident earlier, I'm feeling the shadows of doubt nipping at my brain.

"You'll be brilliant. I know it."

"Thanks, I…"

Before I can finish my thought, he scoops me up in a bear hug and shoves me through the door. I find my place in line and fix up my robes as the door closes behind me. The last thing I see is Marin's smiling face. His eyes sparkle with humor and I'm feeling a little better. If he thinks I can, so do I. He's been here for five hundred years, and

I'm just shy of two weeks. What do I know?

I am the last one in line. I have no idea what time the other initiates showed up, but I'll assume it was disgustingly early and I'll take a good night's sleep over a choice spot in line.

It's several very interesting hours before my turn finally comes.

Ok, I lied.

It's not even interesting. I watch one by one as the initiates leave. None of them bother speaking to me, and even the ones that look crispy around the edges (I'm assuming they have fireball robots in there) somehow give me condescending sneers. I can hear them talking about me as they leave the waiting room, but I can't focus on those idiots. I need to stay focused on the trials.

The door to the chamber opens slowly, and I walk inside. The chamber is a large circular platform, divided into rings. Each ring is five, maybe six feet apart, but they are wide enough to stand on, or run around. All around the room, servos hover in the air. Some I recognize as coming from the Flame Adept School. Others I don't. I'm assuming they come from various other schools. Inbetween the rings, a large chasm drops off into a shadowy abyss. I'm really hoping those are illusion incants.

As I walk into the outermost ring, the door slams behind me and I see the sides of the room light up. Surrounding the platform, a dozen yards out, I see hundreds of magi sitting in bleachers extending upwards to the edges of the room. In the center of the circular rows, I see the Grand Esoteric sitting on a raised dais. My mother is standing by his chair, looking around nervously.

Fantastic, I have an audience. My heart thunders, and it's everything I can do, just to keep from throwing up. They all have the same smug look on their faces; they're just waiting for me to fail so that they can get back to lunch. I'm getting terrible flashbacks of the arena in Alcrest. My mother smiles at me, but it's not helping. I spot Marin in the crowd. I don't know how I spot him, but I do. I can see his smile, and his green eyes are twinkling at me. It settles my nerves a little to have at least two friendly faces in the crowd.

"Come forward, initiate, and be judged." Falstaff's voice booms throughout the chamber and the other Magi quiet down.

I walk forward and I see the servos coming online. It doesn't take long for the fireballs to fly my way. I concentrate on the center ring and will myself there. I open my eyes and I'm standing there, watching the fireballs fly harmlessly into the far wall. There's a small murmuring from above. Falstaff shifts in his seat. I feel a burst of confidence and satisfaction just knowing I've already made it further than they thought I would. I hear this hiss of another set of servos and the room's temperature drops a few degrees. No resting on my laurels. I need to stay in this.

The servos from the frost cult are powering up, and two beams of cold energy shoot out towards me. I glimmer across the room, but the servos just turn and follow me. I have to do something else. I see the flame servos recharging for another round and I have an idea.

At the moment right before the fire servos let their fireballs go, I glimmer across the room, right beneath the flame servos, and look up. The frost cult servos are following me. I wait until the last moment and glimmer straight up. The timing works perfectly. The beams of frost slam into the flame servos and the fireballs consume the frost robots, and both fall into the abyss below. I concentrate on the center ring and glimmer there, barely landing on my feet.

The audience is dead silent, so I'm assuming that's the closest they'll get to a round of applause. I turn to Falstaff and take a bow. I know I shouldn't, but I can't help myself. I'd make other gestures, but they wouldn't know them, anyway. I look up and he's furious, but he says nothing. I'm calling this round a win, but I hear more servos powering up, and I know I'm not done.

I hear a popping sound at the end of the arena and turn. It's easy to guess which school this servo is from. Servos, I should say. Facing me are twenty identical looking metal men, all heavily armed with scimitars and heavy spears. Since I'm fairly sure spontaneous welding isn't a school of magic the Eastern Watch offers, this must be illusion magic, which means only one of these is real. Unfortunately, they're all moving forward towards me, and I don't really want to figure out which one it is at the end of one of their pointy swords. I dig deep in the admittedly shallow bag of tricks Marin could teach me, and I've got an idea.

Once they've surrounded me on the circular inner platform, I do my best attempt at an air incant and it pushes me a few feet off the ground. Once I'm above them I focus on a strike and start mouthing the words to the only earth incant I know. It's not widely used by most magi because they view earth incanting as magic fit only for brutes, but it'll work for me. I chant the last words and I feel myself rocketing, first, towards the ground at the center of the platform. My fist strikes it with enough force to break my hand, but the magic cushions the blow and the force extends outward into a shock-wave. I look around quickly and all the metal men are exactly where they were before. All except one.

One automaton is trying to regain its balance at the edge of the ring, and I know I've found the real servo. I don't give it time to react and I run at a dead sprint towards it, charging a flame knife incant in my arms as I run. It's amazing to me how much magic I can summon after spending a week studying and failing at one trick. That's a mystery for another day, though. For now, I need to go melt the tin man before he cuts my heart out.

I get to the servo quickly, and it can't react to my speed. A long, blade shaped, molten blaze extends a foot from my hand. I quickly thrust it into the servo's chest. It hisses as the metal chassis pops and melt. Before long there's just a steaming metal slag heap in front of me, and by now even a few magi applaud quietly. An icy stare from the Falstaff silences the applause.

I'm standing in the center of the rings, wheezing. I've no idea what trials everybody else faced, but I'm feeling good about myself. Some magi even look impressed, despite their best attempts to hide it. I wait several more minutes, and there's nothing. No sounds, no servos. Nothing. I turn to face the old man, and he's beyond furious. His face is scrunched like a prune, and just about the same color. I'd kill to have a mic to drop right now.

"So, did I pass?" I ask. My voice is hoarse and strained. I forget how much energy magic drains.

"You pass when I say you pass," Falstaff says. "And you will not pass, except through me."

My mother and several others, including Marin, stand up.

"Grand Esoteric, she has passed her trials. More than any other initiate today," my mother says.

"Silence!" As Falstaff speaks, he waves his hand and an invisible force slams into my mother. My blood boils. I know I can't win against him. I know I'm still angry at her, but nobody hurts my mom. I might not have forgiven her yet, but she's family.

"Touch her again, and give you a molten blade instruction up close," I say. My voice is a deadly storm of rage, and I can barely contain the power swelling inside of me. I see Marin trying to wave me off, but I'm not backing down.

"Then you accept my challenge? Good, I know you are a fraud, and even if these machines could not prove it, I will. Come female, show me this power you claim to have," Falstaff says with a snarl.

Falstaff sheds his robes, revealing a fairly muscular build. He grips a staff in his hands and leaps down, landing on a nearby ring, and turns to face me.

36

"Today, you will know genuine power."

I don't even bother responding to his monologuing, and I summon fire. I'm angrier than I've been in a while, and emotion is the best kindling for fire magic. I send several small fireballs toward him, which he easily dodges. He responds with a massive wall of ice that cascades across the room. I barely glimmer above it. I send a couple more fireballs his way, but he evades them as easily as the first time. He keeps throwing ice magic at me and it's getting closer, and I'm getting slower. I'm exhausted beyond imagining. I can't stop.

We continue our lethal dance across the rings of the arena, but I'm getting no closer to making a dent in his defense. I finally think I have him when I glimmer behind him, but he turns, expecting my move, and catches me in the ribs with his staff. I double over in pain, and taste blood in my mouth.

Before I can stand up, I feel energy surround me, and I can't move. I fight it as much as I can, but I know he's won. I'm levitated upwards until I'm hovering in the air at eye level with the Grand Esoteric. He smiles at me, but it's not a friendly smile. It's the smug smile of a man who cheated and got away with it. He knows he rigged the test, but it doesn't matter.

"I commend you for trying, but you just weren't worthy. Your kind never are. You may take your leave and trouble us no further."

"You lying, cheating son of a…" I can't finish because I feel my jaw clench shut forcibly. He won't even let me defend myself. Coward.

"Grand Esoteric Falstaff," it's Marin's voice. "This is deeply unfair, and against regulation. We have never intervened in an initiate's trial before. The girl has proven herself by an even more rigorous standard that any other initiate today. She has earned her place here!" His voice trembles, and it's not the calm and collected Marin I know. He's furious.

"Sit down, Adeptus Marin. What I do with your pet is none of your

37

concern. You have no right to speak."

There is a murmuring among the other magi, and they exchange glances at one another. If I take any consolation because I'm about to be thrown out, it's because it seems the decision isn't a unanimously supported one. Falstaff is growing nervous and angrier. I can feel it in the energy field surrounding me.

"Adeptus Marin, I banish you for inciting treason against the Eastern Watch!" His voice is manic now and doesn't sound in control of anything. "Leave or die."

"I will take my leave with her, but you know I'm right. They do too."

Falstaff drops me and looks down. His expression is pure disdain and disgust, but somewhere in the corners of his eyes, I see a specter of fear.

"You have an hour to get out of Sanctum. After that, I'm turning the servos loose on you."

All I can do is smirk as I look around at the steaming remains of the servos. I think about making a snarky comment, but he seems dangerously unhinged at the moment, and I'm not looking to get my mind melted or fried. Whatever else he may be, Falstaff is a powerful magus.

I run as quickly as I can back to my room and gather what few possessions I can. I find my traveling clothes and put them back on, and pull my hair back into a ponytail, and put my Red Sox hat back on. I'm still boiling with anger, and I have no idea where I'll go now, but my hat makes me feel a little better at least. As I turn to leave my room, I see a spectral image of Marin hovering near the door, and I almost scream.

"Good god, Marin. What is wrong with you? Are you trying to give me a heart attack?"

"There isn't much time. Don't wait for me. I'll meet you outside Sanctum underneath the third statue on the right. I have a plan, but I have to hurry."

"Ok, and Marin, thanks. You didn't have to take up for me like that. I'm sorry you got banished over it."

He smiles and shrugs, "I'm not. Some things are worth fighting for." His image vanishes and I'm left smiling, despite myself. Gathering the last of my things, I find my way to the door. They have opened it for me, as if I needed any further reminder of the message that I'm not welcome. Near the door, my mother is waiting for me.

"I'm so sorry about all of this. I had hoped we would have more time to talk,"

"About this prophecy? Left that detail out, did you?" I know what I'm saying isn't entirely fair. I haven't exactly given her many opportunities to talk. My face softens. "I'm sorry, I know I've been harsh. Thank you for sticking up for me the way you did. I'm sure you will catch flack for that."

She shakes her head. "It doesn't matter. What I did was wrong, but I'm more worried about you. Where will you go?"

I shrug. "Not sure yet, but Marin seems to have a plan. That's good enough for the moment."

"Good. Here, take this," she hands me a full satchel, "I swiped as much food from the kitchens as I could. I love you. I hope you know that."

I say nothing back to her. I can't say that. Not yet, anyway.

"Ok, I have to go. Thanks for everything. I think we'll be seeing each other again," I say to her. This feels like a hugging moment, but I just settle for a pat on the shoulder, and I'm through the door. I hear the door slam shut behind me, and the sound echoes across the plateau, as if to punctuate my banishment. I make a few rude gestures behind me at the door as I walk away. I'm not sure if anyone is even watching, but it makes me feel better.

As I walk farther from Sanctum, the adrenaline fades and feel fear rising in my throat. I really don't have a plan at all, but at least Marin is coming along with me. Aside from Kyria and Ahrun, there isn't anyone I would rather have beside me. Well, there is, but he's not here anymore. Marin is an excellent runner up though. I arrive at the statue and take a seat, waiting for Marin, and I feel as alone as that day I fell headfirst in that sea a lifetime ago.

6

Kyria

"Bwaaaack?" the mega chicken repeated its question. Sadly, neither Kyria nor Ahrun spoke mega chicken or any other relevant dialect.

"Ahrun, do ya 'ave an idea or two?"

"Just don't make any sudden moves."

"Aye, I know that ya eegit." Kyria said, rolling her eyes.

Despite mocking his advice, Kyria was following it. She stood up slowly, not breaking eye contact with the gigantic bird. Its neck was as wide as she was tall, and she was fairly sure it could fit both her and Ahrun in its great beak. She instinctively put one arm out with her hand pressed down.

"Nice, birdie, good birdie, we're no' enemies. Nor food, ya great feathery dolt," Kyria said. She willed her voice to be syrupy sweet, and the bird cocked its head at her. It was considering what she said, or it was considering whether to eat her now or save her for a snack later. Kyria continued to move closer to the bird. Ahrun was shaking his head vigorously, but Kyria had a gut feeling and she followed it. Worst-case scenario, she'd be bird food. Granted that was a fairly bad worst case, she didn't see any other choice.

"Now hold yerself, ya big fluffy. I'm goin' ta call ya Harold. Is tha' alright, Harold?"

"Back." Harold cocked his head to the other side as it considered. "Bwaack."

"Good, we're agreed then, Harold. So, I've a proposition for ya. Ya don' eat us, and we'll no' kill ya. I've got somethin' better, anyway."

Kyria stooped down slowly and pulled out a bag of road biscuits. The Magi had given them to her as what she could only assume was a practical joke. They weren't edible. Not to humans anyway. Maybe birds like them. She put several in her hand and held it out.

Harold leaned in and sniffed. He opened his beak and extended a long, thin tongue which coiled around Kyria's arm. She held down breakfast as it tried to come back up from the smell wafting out of Harold's gullet. His slimy tongue slithering around her arm wasn't helping either. It gathered the biscuits into its mouth and gulped them down. Kyria held her breath (and her breakfast) as she waited to see what Harold's opinion of the biscuits was.

"Bwaaak!" Harold crooned excitedly. He leaned his head down and Kyria scratched his head.

"Tha's a good boy, Harold. Very good chicken."

She looked over at Ahrun, who looked on, dumbfounded. He was doing his best not to erupt with laughter and clapped slowly. Kyria did her best to take a bow, while still scratching Harold's head.

"So, we 'ave a giant chicken. What ta do now?" Kyria asked.

"Well, it's not a horse but,"

"I like where yer mind is, good thinkin.'"

Kyria backed up and Harold nudged her impatiently with his beak. She threw a few more travel biscuits into his beak and he gurgled happily. Kyria turned and put one hand down to the base of the stone. Harold seemed to comprehend what she was on about and he lowered his head.

"Bwaaak?"

"Aye, Harold, good chicken. That's what I needed," Kyria said, keeping her voice even and sweet.

She shook the jitters out. Despite her newfound friendship with Herald, she wasn't entirely sure he wouldn't try to eat her for this. Only one way to find out, she thought to herself. She walked to the end of the stone and turned. Harold watched her intently. Beginning with a run, she launched herself over the top of Harold's head. It took her several moments to steady herself (Harold's wild flailing didn't help), but she eventually got ahold of two large feathers from the root and used them as makeshift reigns to settle the bird down.

Using her newfound mount, she lowered Harold's head so that Ahrun could get on. He packed up the camp and turned, eying the beast for a while before climbing on.

"You're the craziest girl in Aquillon, or the bravest," Ahrun said, trying not to look down.

"Can't I be both?" Kyria said with a manic laugh, "both is good."

By the time Kyria had sufficiently figured out how to move Harold in all four directions, Ahrun had emptied his breakfast over the side of the bird three times and was an unpleasant shade of yellow. Harold seemed unbothered and shook his bright feathers around happily. Kyria was doing fine. She didn't handle well with boats, but transport via giant bird wasn't phasing her in the slightest.

Besides being quick, Harold could cut a direct path through the dense undergrowth of the forest. By the end of the day, Ahrun had located several more marker stones. Kyria gazed at each of them in silent awe. Each was as massive and intricate as the last, with great claw-carved runes covering each. Just thinking about the creature who could have carved them sent chills down her spine. She really hoped Ahrun had a plan for what to say to this dragon when they found her. They made camp on the last stone that night. Harold curled into a ball and fell asleep after Kyria fed him the last of the biscuits. Kyria figured nothing would come near them that night, as the sound of Harold's cooing echoed throughout the clearing.

Kyria looked beyond the end of the tree line and saw the outline of the mountain range they were rapidly approaching. She knew she needed sleep, but several hours of tossing and turning made her increasingly frustrated. She looked over and noticed Ahrun seemed to have similar problems.

"Can't sleep?" she asked him.

"It is evading me, for whatever reason. My mind is restless."

"Still tryin' ta figure out what ta say ta an immortal dragon that could use ya for a toothpick jus' as soon as talk ta ya?"

"More or less."

"So, what are ya gonna say?"

"I'm hoping to appeal to her better nature. The dragons have been gone a long time. No one knows how long, but if I can leverage her hatred of the court, I should be able to convince her to help."

"Aye, could work. An' if she's chummy with the Court?"

"Well, then we'll most likely be eaten alive, or possibly roasted to a crisp. Or both I should think."

"Cheery. Let it never be said o' Ahrun that he lacked a positive outlook on life. If I make it out, I'll make sure they note tha' on yer gravestone."

"Much obliged, M'lady. Your generosity is boundless."

"Aye, it is. An' I'll do ya one better. I've dubbed ya, Ahrun the Chipper. Ya can add it ta yer list o' titles and accolades."

"Ah yes, I think that is what I was always missing. Something to make my illustrious title more personal. I shall return the favor then, and dub thee Lady Kyria, the generous."

"Ah, thank ya, m'lord." Kyria stood and gave as prostrate and humble a bow as she could manage. She couldn't keep her straight face anymore though and fell over on her side with laughter. Ahrun joined her in a deep-bellied laughter that continued for a while. It felt good to laugh. There had been little laughter since the Court killed Thistle, and Kyria let the humor wash over her and just enjoyed the moment.

Moments later, drowsiness washed over Kyria like a warm blanket and she felt her eyelids growing heavy. Ahrun put out the fire and starlight flooded their camp. Kyria let herself fall into a deep sleep. As she slept, a smile crept across her face. Tomorrow there would be dragons and possibly fiery death. For tonight, though, there was laughter and friendship. That was enough for now.

Kyria felt the mountains before she saw them. After a hearty breakfast and a concert of what she could only discern were mating calls from Harold, Kyria and Ahrun set out to leave the jungle behind. As they neared the tree line, Kyria felt an oppressive heat consuming the surrounding air. The Wyld Places were tropical, muggy, and pretty much intolerable most of the time, but this was different. The heat was dry and hot and permeated the air like a presence all its own. This heat was alive, and it was not friendly. When Harold timidly poked his head beyond the tree line, Kyria saw the source of the devilish warmth.

The thick jungle foliage had ended, but by no accident. For miles surrounding the mountain range, the land was charred and black. The skeletons of trees haunted the landscape and everywhere Kyria looked, pockets of flame consumed large plots of land. The flames danced in the wind definitely, as if to dare the rain to challenge it. Marker stones stood at intervals for several miles before the foothills of the mountain range, but even without them it was clear enough to Kyria that this was a land ruled by a dragon.

The mountains themselves were tall, jagged things that reached towards the sky like fangs. No snow, or even ice graced the top of them, and even from this distance Kyria could see a great cavern yawning at the top of the tallest mountain. She looked over to Ahrun.

"Let me guess, the beast makes it lair atop tha' peak in a shadowy cave o' death?"

"So it seems."

"An' we 'ave ta climb those mountains, hopin' all the while tha' the scaly devil don' char us to ashes just for the impudence o' climbin' them? "

"You seem to have hit it dead on, my dear," Ahrun said, grinning at her.

"Grand. It might be nice o' the beast ta just eat us at the foothill. Save me the climb."

"No such luck, I think. Upwards and onwards, as Thistle would say."

They shared a sad chuckled and Kyria attempted to move Harold onward. Harold had other ideas. As soon as they cleared the tree line and he saw the mountains, Harold shook and shivered uncontrollably, and let out a lengthy series of terrified "Bwaaaks".

Kyria figured he had been around long enough to know that this patch of earth was not friendly territory for giant, tasty looking birds. Kyria relented and got Harold to let them down to the ground.

"Ya been a dutiful boy, Harold."

Harold cocked his head to one side. "Bwaaak?"

"Aye, I'm talkin' about ya. I've no more biscuits, I'm afraid."

"Bwaaak…"

"Ya gotta go now boy or the beast atop that mountain's goin' ta eat both of us, an' tha's no good."

It seemed like Harold agreed. He gave her one last affectionate nudge and lick, much to Kyria's chagrin and Ahrun's amusement, and tramped back into the forest. Kyria was sad to see him go, but not having a giant bird wandering around behind them seemed like a safer bet for not getting eaten.

Kyria and Ahrun struck out into the charred wasteland, and the heat only became more oppressive. By the time they had reached the foothills, Kyria's face was blistering and her lips cracked, and her throat burned with thirst.. As they journeyed deeper into the mountains, the fire became more and more prevalent, and by the time they reached the foot of the great mountain, the living flames nearly surrounded them.

"What is this stuff?" Kyria asked as they began the climb through a steep path that led upward toward the summit.

"Dragon fire. There are legends of it. The fire from a dragon's throat can consume anything and lives long after they breathed it. Take care to avoid it. If it catches you even a little, it will consume you."

"I figured tha' much ya dolt," Kyria said, rolling her eyes.

As they climbed, the footing got worse and worse, until finally they faced a rock wall that led straight up. Kyria emptied her pack. She had rope, and a few daggers, which was enough. After a brief time, she had rigged up a climbing gear, and she offered it to Ahrun. He eyed it and the rock.

"Are you sure there isn't some other way? I'm not much of a climber, and I'm not much for heights either."

"Ah, so we finally find somethin' mighty Ahrun the Chipper is afraid of?"

"It's not information I pander about, but no. I take no joy in heights or lofty explorations. If I must, I will amble my way up."

"Aye, ya must."

Ahrun shimmied his way into the harness Kyria had made for him and looked up at the rock wall with a shudder.

"Ah gods, yer a bigger chicken than Harold. I'll go first and secure some foothold for yer ladyship," Kyria said with a magnanimous bow and curtsy. She began making her way up the rock face, finding hand holds. She hammered her daggers in here and there, creating a series of ropes to climb up. After a while of climbing, she reached the top. Looking up, she spotted a series of narrow paths that led up the side of the mountain towards the summit. After several near-death experiences, and some swearing from Ahrun (Kyria nearly fell off the cliff in shock), Ahrun managed his way over the top of the rock wall.

"Well, as Alex likes ta say, I've got good news, an' bad news."

Ahrun grunted.

"The good news is tha' yer up the rock wall. The bad news is tha' we have ta work our way up tha' pleasant little path."

Ahrun looked up at the "pleasant little path" Kyria was referring to. It was not pleasant. Or little.

The path curved an edge around the tip of the mountain, getting slimmer and more narrow as it went. Near the summit of the mountain, it was little more than the width of a plank. It wasn't clear who, or what, had made the path, but it was not meant to be an easy climb.

Ahrun sighed, shook his head.

"Nothing for it then. Upward and onward."

"There's the spirit, my brave Sir!" Kyria said, clapping him on the back.

They made their way up the path, and once they had made it halfway, even Kyria was glancing down nervously. The path was a sliver, and only wide enough for one foot turned sideways at a time. Kyria gripped the rock wall behind her so hard it hurt her fingers. But the alternative was a very long fall with a quick stop. Even Kyria couldn't bring herself to look down, and Ahrun looked like he might throw up if it wouldn't have sent him careening over the edge.

After what seemed like an eternity, they made their way around the last bend and stepped into the clearing at the top of the mountain, both breathing deep sighs of relief. Ahrun vomited over the side of the plateau. He hadn't judged her too hard for throwing up on Sullas's ship, so she returned the favor, patting him on the back. Once he had sufficiently recovered, they turned and took in their surroundings.

The top of the mountain was cleared and flattened into a wide semi-circle, leading up to a mammoth cavern. The stone there was different. It was smooth and glassy, and all a black obsidian color. The cave itself was as tall and wide as the surrounding platform, and dark. The daylight made its way only up to the edge and did not proceed farther inside, as if even the light paid respectful fear to the creature that dwelled within. Looking at each other one last time, Kyria and Ahrun approached the cave.

They were nearly at the entrance when a deep rumble echoed over the rocks. From within the darkness, two great yellow eyes opened and regarded them coldly. They were like twin lanterns shining out of the darkness. Below them a great mouth, filled with teeth, each one the size of a grown man, opened, glowing red. A deep voice bellowed from the mouth, and Ahrun and Kyria dropped to a knee, eyes down-turned. The rocks roared with the voice and the mountain shook with each word.

"It is many thousands of years since a human befouled my mountain's steps. You've come a long way, just to die."

7

Alex

I t's been three hours, and I'm still waiting for Marin. By the time I see Sanctum's doors open in the distance, I'm getting nervous.

"Come here often?"

I yelp and turn. I see Marin smirking at me. He must have just glimmered here from somewhere down the road. I know there's a hard distance limit on where you can glimmer, but we hadn't gotten that far in wizard class when I got kicked out. "Yeah. All the time. Where else does one go when one has been disgracefully banished from an ancient order of wizards?"

"Who knows?"

"Seriously, though, do you know? I didn't have much time to plan before they gave the not-so-subtle boot. I'm hoping you had better luck?"

"I did, but lets go for now. I can fill you in on the way. I'm not sure we're alone out here."

We both glanced upward at the statue of an old man with a staff bestriding a hilltop. On closer inspection, it seems to be in the likeness of Falstaff. I definitely wouldn't put it past him to have incanted this with a surveillance spell. Beyond that, the statue's just creepy.

We set out, following Marin's lead. We're walking for now, but every now and again we glimmer a short distance, so long as the destination is visible.

"So glimmering has a hard limit?" I ask, as we walk between jumps.

"All incants do. Magic is a complex ecosystem of rules and laws, much akin to laws of nature or physics. While it might seem like incants are breaking those laws, they follow their own laws. To glimmer successfully, by which I mean not teleporting yourself inside a tree, you have to be able to see the target your jumping towards."

"So that's why a waystone might not work unless it was somewhere high up, with good visibility?"

"Yes, that is true. Why do you ask?"

"No reason," I say as I whistle. In my head I'm making a mental note to apologize to that waystone, if I ever see it again. We're several miles from Sanctum now, so I turn to Marin. "So, as much as I enjoy aimlessly wandering, do you care to reveal your fantastic plan?"

"You sure you want to know? I thought we could wander for a little while longer. I felt like we were really getting into some quality wandering!"

"I'd agree with you, except we're alone in what I feel has to be the most hostile environment on Aquillon. I need a plan to get back into the Eastern Watch and hone my skills so I can defeat a court of rampaging demons and save the world. That's two things."

"Well, splendid news then, because my plan will help with all of that. We will find the Path of Flame." He waits patiently for a moment and then looks crestfallen. "Oh, right, you wouldn't know what that is."

"I'm guessing it's not a relaxing hot spring with all you can eat cheese fries?"

"I'm afraid not, also, what's a cheese fry? Never mind that. The

51

Path of Flame is almost more of a legend than a place. No magi have ever set foot on it, and no one who went looking for it has ever found it. The reason for my delay," he paused and opens his traveling bag, revealing several old books, "is these. They contain all the knowledge us have about the Path of Flame within these volumes."

"And what exactly do we gain from going finding this place? The last time I went looking for anything in the Wyld Places, it almost killed me. Several times."

"That is less clear, but all the preliminary research I could do says that the path reveals what is within. I believe the Grand Esoteric did not banish you for being a woman. I think he feared what you might become, but I think we will need whatever lies on the Path of Flame to find out what that is."

"And do we know where this magical place is?"

"The Eastern Marches, close to the ruins of the Foxes' Den, which I heard is a smoking ruin these days."

"You can thank an army of angry goat-men for that," I say with a cheerful smile. "I've got some friends in that neck of the woods, or I should, if they've made it. But how are we getting there? I don't even know where Sanctum is, so how are we supposed to get anywhere else? I don't imagine the Magi make the best cartographers given their aversion to cardio and walking."

"Yes, we're not big on maps, but I have a plan for at least getting back to the Foxes' Den, and we can foot I but I don't know if you're going to like it."

"Don't tell me…"

"I'm afraid so."

"Look, unworthy mortal," I hear its voice before I see it, and I feel a headache coming on. The waystone floats out of Marin's bag and fixes me with a death stare. "I'm not any more thrilled about this than you are. I did you and your brute friends a favor, and I've been nothing but the laughingstock among my fellow artefacts since. You're lucky I'm indebted to your friend here for some measure of coin, otherwise I'd not even consider assisting you!"

I look over at Marin. "What? How? Coin?"

"Don't ask," he says, rubbing his forehead, "long story."

"Alright," I say. "Well, let's get this over with then. The sooner we can teleport out of here, the sooner we can be free of this annoying pebble."

"The sentiment is mutual, rabble rouser," the waystone said, rolling its eyes.

It takes a longer time than I'd like for the waystone to set up a portal. It claims something about atmospheric interference (the sky is so clear I can literally see space), but after a couple hours, the glowing portal is standing before us, ready to use. Marin pockets the waystone, which shrinks down to accommodate him, and jumps through first, and I follow, moments later. It takes a little longer to get through to the other side than I'm used to from the latchkeys, but this is a much greater distance, and has to cut through whatever strange protective field the Eastern Watch incanted on the plateau surrounding sanctum, so I'll cut the waystone some slack.

I step through to the other side, and for once, the scene on the other side is pleasantly calm and nothing is on fire. Yet anyway. My settings are familiar to me, and I'm surrounded by rolling farmland, and in the distance, the ruins of the Foxes' Den are still steaming. That brings a smile to my face. But that's not what's bringing a smile to my face.

All over the fields teams of former slaves are plowing and planting. It hasn't even been a month, but they've set up huts and tents all over, forming small communities in tight circles. Children are running and screaming everywhere, but not in terror. The sound brings a smile to my face, and I tear up. I wipe them away before Marin can see. This might be the first place since Felwind where there seems to be genuine happiness.

We walk down the hill we arrived on and as soon as we're close, people come towards us. As they recognize me, they cheer, and by the time I'm in the center of their farming huts, I'm beet red. The spotlight has never been my scene. An old man walks towards us and the crowd parts. I recognize him as the old man who tried to convince the slaves to return to the pits. He's not glaring at me, so I'm assuming he's come around to being free.

"Our greetings, Alex of Vandlehaven. Your return honors us," he says, taking a deep bow.

"I'm happy to be back," I say. My voice is shaky. Although I rescued them, I don't really feel worthy of anyone's admiration.

"Come, we will host you for a banquet tonight. You will stay with me." His voice doesn't suggest that he'd take no for an answer, so Marin and I follow him up to a hut in the center of the village. As we walk, Marin is smiling, and I'm just trying to not make eye contact. There's so much love and reverence in the eyes of the people I pass, and I don't really know what to do with it. As we walk, I also see men and women in orange robes, and I grit my teeth. Foxes. It seems the Akari didn't quite finish the job. I hate them, but if these slaves learned to forgive and forget, I can't say anything.

We arrive at the old man's hut, and he hurries us inside. The inside is modest with few decorations or possessions. In the center is a bedroll, and a hole at the top allows light down from the ceiling. Despite the oppressive humidity outside, the hut is cool enough. He gives us water in stone bowls from a bucket. I drink it and let the heat of the day roll off me.

"What brings you back to us, Alex of Vandlehaven? We thought you went for good, though we rejoice in your return," the old man says.

"How do you know my name?" I ask.

"Since the fall of the den, there was much talk of the flaxen-haired maiden who freed us. Some of our brothers and sisters are recently arrived from the west, where tales of your adventures and victories against the court have spread like wildfire." His eyes light up as he speaks.

"What victories? I spent the last two months running for my life," I said with a chuckle.

"The Lady of Deep waters has not come on land again since you smote her in Vandlehaven, and the Lady of Hunger has not stirred from the Sea of Shadows either. Even in cities controlled by the Court, they speak your name in the shadows, and the demons fear it. There is a restlessness in every province, and the Court fears an insurrection," the old man says.

My heart catches at the news and the hint of a smile rolls on my lips. If Aquillon is rising and throwing off its chains, it's nice to think I had a hand in it. Even nicer to think about the Court being nervous.

"I see. And you? I remember you being a big fan of your fox buddies and their allies. What changed?"

"And for that shame hangs upon my head like a heavy crown, but I am trying to make amends."

"I never got your name," I say.

"Esmander Thalton," he says.

"Well, I guess you know mine, but it's Alex Winters. This is my friend, Marin."

Marin waves and gives a cheesy smile. For a five-hundred-year-old man, he's goofier than a fourth grader.

"It is an honor to have you here, but what business could you have in this corner of the world?"

Marin speaks up. "We're looking for the Path of Flames. I believe it to be somewhere within the Eastern Marches."

"I have never heard of such a thing, but most of us are transplants to this region. I hail from the Sarahan Foothills myself, though it is many years since I have been home. The Marches are my home now," Esmander says.

"Is it safe here? Will the Court return?" I ask.

"Unlikely," Esmander says. This is the province of the Lord of Wrath. His Akari stalk the hills and jungles, killing most things on sight. Since the Akari destroyed the Den, I don't believe any other Hand has sent foot soldiers here. I believe the Lord of Wrath thinks us dead, otherwise he would have returned by now".

"And if he does?" Marin asks.

"Then we will do what we can," Esmander says, "but for now we are safe. The Akari are unpredictable so we will hope they stay far away, pestering others. So, how can my people help? You have but to ask."

"We could use shelter for a few days. It will take time to pour through these volumes and find a more exact route to the Path of Flames," Marin says.

"That is the least we can do."

Esmader leads us out of the hut and into the village. He guides us to an empty hut, and we put our things down. We roll our bedrolls out and Marin opens his books and gets to work. I ask if I can help, but he shakes his head.

"These books are ancient, and not especially intuitive. You could explore the ruins of the Den. There may be supplies or maps that survived the siege." I'm sure this is Marin's super pleasant way of telling me to buzz off and let him study. I don't argue and I leave to go explore.

I'm impressed with how much the slaves have been able to accomplish since I left them a little over two weeks ago. They've slowly repurposed the farms, turning them into whatever they need. Some they kept as farms, but others have been made into housing, or water reservoirs. Their understanding of architecture and agriculture is astounding, but I guess that's the advantage of having a population that came from all over Aquillon.

After an hour of wandering, I've made my way to the ruins of the Foxes' Den. The great red brick structure is a shell of itself, with only the bottom floor and the pits remaining somewhat intact. The upper floors are mostly a smoldering mess. I'm not sure what I'm supposed to find in all of this, but if I'm not careful about my footing, it won't matter. Plenty of deathtraps around this steaming ruin.

I slowly enter the main hall. The stench of death permeates the place and I nearly lose my lunch several times. Bodies litter the entryway where the Foxes made their last stand against the Akari. Not all of them, though. Blood trails off into the woods near the entrance where animals must have pulled the bodies. The ones that remain aren't in great shape and are in various stages of decomposition. I'm near the end of the hall when I feel someone, or something lurking behind me. I turn, but the sun is in my eyes, and I don't see the punch that lands in my ribs. I collapse.

"I was hoping you might drop in." It's hard to hear the voice through the pain in my ribs, but it's venomous and dripping with hatred. And it's familiar. I look up to see the icy smile of a middle-aged woman, and I remember. I remember that sneer looking up at me from the pit we climbed out of all those months ago and watching her feed those slaves to the jungle. I remember my promise to kill her.

The Akari had killed everything with a pulse in the Den, but not her. Stupid goats. Esmader was right about them being unpredictable. I have to give him that one.

8

Kyria

The titanic dragon poked her head out of the cave and fixed Kyria and Ahrun with a deadly stare.

"I suppose I should thank you. My food rarely makes the effort to come to me."

"Don' ya want ta at least know our names?" Kyria asked, trying not to sound indignant.

"Food doesn't need names, in my experience."

With no additional warning, the dragon's head lashed out of the cave and snapped its jaws at Kyria. She dodged the strike and felt the creature's fiery breath on her. As the dragon withdrew its head into the cave, the sun caught its crimson scales and the rocks around the cave were showered in a deep red light.

"My dear food, that was insensitive, don't you think?" The dragon asked in a deep rumble.

"Ya will have ta pardon my poor manners. I'm no' real keen on becommin' yer dinner," Kyria replied.

"I hardly think you will ever amount to much of anything more

58

honorable than being eaten by the last dragon on Aquillon. Now sit still!" The dragon commanded as its head snapped forward. Kyria expected this and leaped out of the way, narrowly missing the dragon's fangs.

"Honorable dragon, we came here in peace, to seek your aid. We..." Ahrun didn't get far with his plea when the dragon's claw exploded from the darkness of the cave and nearly decapitated him. He dropped prone, and the claw passed over him before retracting into the cave.

"Enough of this, I grow tired of your antics, food. If you will not behave and be eaten, I will have to teach you some manners," the dragon said.

The earth rumbled as the magnificent creature stood up and began walking out of the cave. Kyria and Ahrun took shelter behind nearby rock outcroppings. As she cleared the exit of the cave, the scale of the dragon awed Kyria. It stood the height of fifty men or more, and twice as long. Each of its shining talons rocked the earth as they tapped impatiently, and two gargantuan horns protruded from the peak of its head. Yellow eyes, ancient and fierce, scoured the plateau for any sign of their prey.

"You could have been so kind as to just be eaten, but you had to put up a fight. Now I will have to char you to cinders for your arrogance." The ground shook with each word the dragon spoke, and the air crackled with heat. The dragon crouched down and opened its jaws. There was a moment where all of creation held its breath, and then the beast let forth a pillar of fiery death. Flame engulfed the platform and slammed into the rocks Kyria and Ahrun hid behind. The heat burned Kyria's skin, and she felt her eyes drying out. Every breath she took was on fire.

"So, what's the plan?" she asked Ahrun.

"I'm afraid I have little relevant experience here. I suppose run and hide is as good a plan as any."

"As much as I hate runnin' away, I'm inclined ta agree with ya. But we need ta distract the beast, unless yer more fireproof than ya let on."

"Afraid not; just as flammable as the rest. Have anything in mind?"

"Well, this beast has ta tire o' shootin' flames, eventually. Tha' sword o' yers still come back ta ya when ya throw it?"

"It does."

"Well, let's make this dragon play dodge. Should catch it off guard, at least."

Ahrun nodded, and they waited. Kyria figured it was the best plan they had, and if the beast kept up the pillar of fire much longer, they'd be dead, anyway. After several more agonizing minutes there was a break in the flame and Ahrun didn't hesitate. He jumped out from behind the rock and threw his sword as hard as he was able at the dragon's head. It seemed to roll its eyes and snapped the sword out of the air with a lightning quick movement of its claw.

"Really, human? You think you're the first tiny knight to hurl at sword at me? I don't even know what you… wait a moment. I know this blade," the dragon said.

Ahrun paused and waited. Kyria came out from behind the rock, looking around. She was grateful they weren't dead yet, but not entirely sure why.

"This blade," the dragon said, "where did you get it?"

"It has always been mine," Ahrun said.

"That's impossible. I know well the order that forged this weapon, and they are dead and gone. A pity, they were perhaps one of the few groups of worthy humans ever to walk these lands."

"You speak of the Order of the Seventh Dawn, and I am Ahrun, last of its paladins."

"Then retrieving this won't be hard," the dragon said and dropped the blade. Ahrun held out his hand, and the blade hummed as it shot back towards him, landing in his outstretched palm.

As it settled in his hand, the dragon relaxed a bit and lowered its head.

"An unexpected turn of events, I must admit. I thought I had seen the last of your kind vanish from this world. Very well, I owe a great debt to your order. I will hear your words, and not eat you, and I will consider my ledger cleared."

"That is gracious of you, oh noble dragon," Ahrun said, bowing.

"Spare me your platitudes, human. My ears are old and have heard such things from more impressive men than you," the dragon said, rolling its eyes.

"Very well, we come seeking aid from you. You know well the scourge of the Court of Hours, and their reign."

The dragon's nostrils flared, but it said nothing, so Ahrun continued. "We would enlist your aid in our fight against these vile demons. Come back to Aquillon with us and help us rid this world of their evil."

"Foolish humans, to have come so far for this. I would not aid you even if I could. Your memories are brief, but mine is not. I remember a time when dragons and humans walked in covenant. It did not end well. If that is all you came to pester me about, begone from my mountain and take your lives as my parting gift to you."

Ahrun sighed and took another bow before turning. Kyria was not so quick to leave, and Ahrun realized what she was about to do, but was too late to stop it.

"Listen, hear ya great scaled beasty," Kyria shouted at the dragon. Ahrun turned as quickly as he could, but could not prevent her from shouting out what would probably be her last words. "I did no' come all this way, nearly be eaten by a giant chicken, an' then sent home by ya. I'll no' take nae for an answer, now yer goin' ta help us get rid o' these infernal demons, or so help me gods I'll stay on this mountain until I skin ya, or annoy ya ta death."

The dragon cocked its head to one side, as if unsure of what to do.

"You're a funny little insect. I've heard many braver men make bolder claims. Tell me, before I reduce you to ash and bone, why would I do as you ask?"

Kyria could feel the heat coming from the back of the dragon's mouth and saw the glow of flames. Still, she stood tall and answered.

"Because ya live in this blasted world, same as we do, an' you've got a duty ta defend it! Roast me if ya must, but I'm nae leavin' this rock without yer help." Kyria finished her fiery appeal and planted her feet, awaiting what she assumed would be an unpleasant and crispy demise.

But it never came.

Instead, a low rolling laughter echoed in the cave and across the platform. Kyria opened her eyes (which she had instinctively closed) to see the dragon's head thrown back in laughter.

"You may be the first human to make me laugh in, well, ever. I'll spare your life for providing me with some much-needed amusement. But I can't help you," the dragon said as a serious look passed back over its face.

"An' why no," Kyria asked. She probably shouldn't have pushed it with another question, but she was feeling lucky.

"When the Court arrived during the fall, I met with the Lord of Long Shadows. He demanded my allegiance, and I refused. I promised not to intervene on either side, but that wasn't good enough. He enlisted the aid of a powerful foe and banished my children to another realm. I haven't seen them in the thousand years since," as the dragon spoke, Kyria could almost swear she saw a tear forming in one of its great eyes.

Ahrun spoke up. "How is it you were not banished, along with your flock?"

"Scale, a group of dragons is called a scale, boy. We are not chickens and you would do well to remember that if you wish to continue breathing," the dragon said. "As for your question, he couldn't. We dragons are as old as the world itself, and woven into the fabric of it, so to banish it, the Hand of Seven used the blood of an ancient one, the beings that first walked the world when the ground steamed under new stars. Profane magic, but effective. I presume he did not have enough left to banish me."

"Then why not take your vengeance on him?" Kyria asked.

"When you are as old as I, you learn to avoid petty emotions like the need for revenge. He won, and I lost. It is as simple as that. Now go. There are no dragons here that will aid you, myself included. Begone!" The dragon slammed its fist as it spoke, but Kyria didn't budge.

"Surely there must be some way ta bring your children back? A spell, nae matter how powerful, must be able ta be undone," she said.

"Persistent as you are annoying. I like you, girl. Sadly, it is impossible. I have the raw power to reserve the spell, but not the components. I would need the blood of an ancient one," the dragon said.

"Nae problem then, we'll just go an' get some," Kyria said with a nonchalant shrug.

"I'm afraid it's not that easy. There is only one creature who has enough, and even I would not challenge him. Braga, the Eater of Light. He is the last of the ancient ones. He killed his brothers and drank their blood to grow strong. If there is any blood left, he will have it."

"Well then, I guess we better go an' pay this Braga a visit," Kyria said.

"You mean it, don't you, human? Very well, I won't stop you since it is no great loss to me if he kills you. Still, I suppose I have something invested in your success. I will tell you that if you go charging into Braga's lair, you will die. He is a keen hunter and his power gives me pause for concern. Seek Fogu, an old spirit of the mountain. He dwells in the peak's shadow and owes me a few favors. He should be able to mask your scent from Braga, for a price."

"What price?" Ahrun asked.

"That is for you to ask and find out, food. Now go, I must hunt soon, and you have already wasted too much of my time. Come back if you retrieve the blood, or do not come back at all."

At that, the dragon stood up and walked fully out of the cave. The earth shook with its size, and Kyria was stunned by how great a creature the Mistress of Scales was. It made her even more nervous that they were now tangling with a creature even the dragon wanted nothing to do with. Kyria and Ahrun held onto the rocks around the cave as the dragon took flight, and a hurricane of winds swirled in the updraft. With astounding speed, the creature was off, and before long it was a distant speck on the horizon.

"So, I guess we need ta go an' find this Braga," Kyria said.

"I fear we may have encountered him once already," Ahrun said.

"Ya don' mean…"

"I'm afraid so, the beast we encountered in the nest on our search for the waystone. I cannot imagine two creatures of such power and evil existing, even in the Wyld Places."

"Fantastic. I was really itchin' ta see that beasty again. Ya jus' made my day."

"Anything for you, Kyria the Generous," Ahrun said with a smirk and a bow.

Kyria grumbled some unmentionable things at him and they climbed down from the peak, on their way to see Fogu, and most likely meet with an unpleasant end. Whatever sense of victory she felt for strong arming a dragon, Kyria couldn't summon much enthusiasm as she marched down the mountain towards what was sure to be her doom. At least she had company to be doomed with, though. Like Alex told her once, there was always a silver lining.

9

Alex

I roll to my right just quick enough to avoid Valari's boot heel that comes crashing down only inches from my skull. Jumping to my feet, I pull my sword, and my battle senses come rushing through me like a wave. Marin told me that some magi, more combat oriented ones, experience this. It's called war-sight, and it enhances my reflexes and reaction times, and helps me understand various martial weapons, which explains my affinity for swordplay in the last several months.

"Couldn't you have just gone down with your horrible ship, Valari?" I ask. It's a serious question. I don't have time for one more idiots trying to get even. I left a whole tower of them back at Sanctum.

"You took everything from me, and I will return the favor," she says. There's the same manic look in her eyes I remember seeing when she flung those slaves down a ravine.

"I don't really have time for this, so if you're going to kill me, I suggest you and your goat-men get on with it. I'm pretty booked up for the day as it is."

She doesn't waste more words and lunges at me with her pair of long knives. I leap back, parrying, as the spark of steel flies in my face. Even with my war-sight, it's hard to dodge, but I'm keeping up. I'd just as soon glimmer out of here, but I can't. It's that same buzzing I remember the last time I squared up with this witch. Like flies swarming As she waits to ready her next set of attacks, I see it. A small charm hanging off her neck that radiates amber energy. I'm sure she's a better swordsman than me, but if I can get that necklace away from her, I've got a shot.

"Why even toy with me? Why not have your stupid goats kill me?" I ask, hoping to distract her long enough to get that necklace. The goats bray with what sounds like irritation.

"Oh no, I'm going to kill you myself. They follow strength, and I'm the alpha here. I don't need these stinking animals to kill you."

I roll my eyes. Classic villain oversight. Not very original, but it's helping me, so I don't mind. I've bided my time long enough, and I think I have a plan. I lower my sword and assume a defensive stance, lowering it a bit too much, and feign an opening. Valari sees it and takes the bait. She rushes with a flurry of attacks and I let her just close enough and swipe the necklace. It's a delicate thing, and I don't have any issues crushing it in my hand before she realizes what's happened.

The buzzing stops and I glimmer away, far out of her reach. I land on top of a ruined column, and it takes Valari several moments to realize what had happened.

"What... where did you... you coward. Couldn't finish your own fight without your cheap tricks?" I will not let her bait me. "Very well then," she continues, "Akari, kill her." She points at me with a knife and waits. Nothing happens. Several more moments pass and she looks more and more nervous. "What are you waiting for, you filthy animals? Kill her!" She is speaking with more emphasis now, but it doesn't matter. The goat-men aren't moving.

"I don't think they follow you any more. You said they follow the strongest, and well, I don't know how to break this to you but..." A white sheet of fear passes over Valari's face as she realizes I'm right. The goat demons are looking straight at me, as if awaiting orders. I ignore them and return my attention to Valari. She charges at me, but I glimmer away from her attack and send a burst of energy towards her. It slams into her and throws her to the ground, and she loses grip on her blades. I hold my sword to her throat, and she stares up at me, hatred and defiance flickering in her eyes like dying candles.

"Do it, girl, you've beaten me. I have nothing left so take my life and be down with it." Even to the last her voice is a simmering cauldron of disdain and arrogance. I want to kill her. There's some grim part of me that wants to lop her head off, and maybe I should. But I can't. No matter how much I hate her, no matter what evil she's done, I can't make myself strike the killing blow. Call me weak but the Court of Hours has done enough killing. I don't need to add one more body to the pile.

"Get up. Turn around. Walk away. And never let me see you again." Valari stands and turns. As she leaves the ruins, heading towards the jungle, she turns.

"Remember what I told you, Winters. Your compassion is your weakness. If we meet again, do not expect me to return the favor."

With that, she's gone. She vanishes into the thick verdant jungle beyond the ruins of the Den. There's a huge part of me yelling, "You idiot!" I hope I did the right thing, but I can't dwell on that. I've got two pet goats to deal with. I turn back to them. They're still waiting attentively, axes at one side.

"I don't suppose you have names?"

They just make random bleating noises. I don't know what I was expecting.

"Ok, well, I'm calling you Bob, and you're going to be... Steve". Sue me, I'm not feeling the most original and nobody told me this morning I'd have two pet goat-men by mid-afternoon. "Here's what I want you to do. You're going to drop your weapons. You don't need those anymore." Bob and Steve exchange what I can only guess are skeptical glances, but they drop their axes all the same. I'm the Alpha, and what I say goes, I guess. "You're going to stay here while I go looking for some information, and then you're coming back to the village where I will find work for you."

They look excited at the mention of work.

"Not killing people," I say with an eye roll.

A look of disappointment passes over their faces, but I give them a glare. "Just stay here, and I'll be back soon."

They snort, apparently unhappy, but unwilling to buck the alpha. I turn and glance behind me after a moment, and they are still waiting patiently. Back to exploring.

I take an hour to explore what remains of the ground floor of the Foxes Den. Not much is left, mostly smoking rubble, but right as I'm about to give up and head back, I stumble upon a door on the ground. At first I just think it's an unhinged door, blown clear of some upper floor, but as I examine it closer, it has hinges and a lock. It seems like either a bomb shelter or a cellar, and I'm hoping for the latter. I'm in no mood to deal with a bomb-shelter full of fox guards. Here goes.

After several moments of not being attacked by fox-masked bad guys, I'm sure this is a cellar. Everything else around me is charred, broken, or otherwise useless, so this is the most useful clue I've found so far. I summon a little ball of light in my palm and descend slowly into the shadowy basement.

The stairs lead me down several flights before a landing opens up into an enormous room. I see scrolls lining the walls, and dusty tomes packed tight together on ancient bookshelves. It doesn't look like anyone's been down here in some time. I never took the Foxes' Guild for particularly literate folk, so I'm a little surprised. Looking around at the massive collection, I don't even know where to begin.

After what I can only assume is an hour of filtering through dust-filled financial records, I stumble on what looks like it might be historical records. It takes a moment for the Aquillonian writing in each to shimmer into English, but I'm quickly reading through histories of Aquillon. They all record various parts of the last thousand years, but any sections pertaining to what happened before the Fall are blank. They're not even destroyed or torn out, they're just hundreds and hundreds of blank pages. Whatever the Court did to seal off everyone's memories of before the Fall, it seems to have affected books. Why they did it isn't clear, but whatever it was, it was effective.

I'm about to give up halfway through my third reading of a record of droughts in somewhere called the Sarahan Foothills when I hear a low cough from somewhere near the back of the room. I draw my sword with a quick motion and ready myself for battle. From under a giant stack of scrolls, an old man wanders over to me. He looks like he's in his mid-seventies, and he's wearing the orange robes of the Foxes. He doesn't look threatening, but I'm not taking any chances.

"That's far enough, buddy," I say, using my sword to point out an invisible line that I'd prefer he not walk passed.

"You're not the cleaning slave," he says with a look of confusion.

I look up and down at myself and then at my sword. "What gave it away?"

"Ah, well, no matter. I suppose you don't have my tea either?" he asks with a hint of hope in his voice.

"Fresh out of tea at the moment." I'm not sure if he's senile, or just playing dumb as part of a longer con that ends with a dagger in my throat. I'm not falling for that.

"No tea? Then I suppose the sounds I heard a while back must have been some army destroying the Den and burning everything to the ground?"

"Yes?"

"Good. Then I'm free."

"Wait, you're not a Fox?"

"I was, once, but the Foxes Guild has, or had I should say, a not-so-subtle way of demoting people who asked too many questions about where the money was coming from, and what kind of work we were employed in."

"I see. So, where does that leave us?"

"Well, I suppose you could kill me, if you wanted to. Or you could let me go. I'm partial to one option, but I won't try to sway you. Do what you will." As he speaks, his eyes drift over the books, as though taking them all in one last time.

"I'm definitely not killing you, but as for letting you go... I'm less sure about that. How do I know you won't try to reform the Foxes and come back here later?"

"You don't, but if I had that kind of sway with them, I don't imagine they'd have sent me down here to be their librarian. It's useless anyway. No one ever came down to look at my books, so I don't know what help it was keeping them organized. I suppose they just didn't have any use for me, but lacked the stomach to kill an old man."

"Surprising."

"They weren't all evil, you know. And we weren't always evil. The Guild started with good intentions, as all things do. Money has a way of corrupting things though, and in the end they fell under the sway of coin and their demonic masters."

I contemplated on the ex-foxes I had seen in the village who were determined to turn over a new leaf. Maybe there was some truth to what the old man was saying. "Well, I have an idea mister..."

"Long-leaf. Reginald Q. Longleaf."

"Alright, Mr. Long-leaf, here's what I'm thinking. I need information, and I also need some assurance you're not just playing the helpless old man card to get out of your just comeuppance. So, you give me the information I'm looking for, and agree to help the former slaves rebuild. I have a feeling they could use someone like you. Fair?"

He pauses for a moment, as if pondering a wide variety of options. "Fair," he says. "What information exactly are you looking for?"

"I'm looking for the Path of Flame."

A surprised look passes over his wrinkled brows. "That's a new one. I haven't heard of a soul who sought the Path in millennia or more. Why do you seek it?"

"Not that it's any of your business, but I'm a Magi, and I need to prove myself."

Reginald chuckles. "Something tells me you already have. But if you're a girl trying to become a magus, you will need to do more than prove yourself. I've known a few magi in my days. They passed through the Den occasionally. Not the most open-minded folk."

And understatement of the year award goes to Reginald Q. Long-leaf.

"Well, I'll tell you, but you may wish I hadn't. The Path of Flame isn't something to be taken lightly, and I doubt you'll survive it."

"Just give me the information. I can handle whatever it is."

"So young and impetuous. Many a young Fox went searching for the Path to gain power among the guild. You are not unlike them. None returned."

I ignore his warning and wait. If this Path of Flame can make me powerful enough to smack around the Grand Esoteric, I'm all in, even if it kills me.

"Very well. Near the northern edge of the Marches is a mountain. It has no name a human tongue could produce, but you will know it when you come to it. That is all my records tell, but there are other legends. I may or may not have omitted them when I told the young Foxes where to go, but you seem nicer, and you haven't killed me, so there's also that."

"The legends?" I ask.

"They tell of a guardian of that place. A being of ash and flame. Only the worthy may step foot on the mountain. I'm imagining that's why none of the Foxes ever came back," Reginald says with a grim chuckle.

"What is the Path?" I ask.

"The only record I have says that it is a place where the worthy are tested, and their true nature comes to bear. I know nothing beyond that."

"Alright, well that takes care of the information part," I say, "and now the other bit. Let's get back to the village."

By the time we resurface, the sun's burnt orange fire is fading into the eastern sky. To my pleasant surprise, I find Bob and Steve exactly where I left them. Collecting my odd little group of acquaintances, we start back for the village.

By the time we arrive, the stars are just starting the glimmer in the violet expanse above me, and I'm met with an understandable hostile reaction by the village guards.

A guard barks questions at me. "Why are you bringing those demons here? And who is the old man?" Fair enough, I have to admit.

"Hear me out. They're friends. Right, guys?"

The goat-men do their best friendly bleating, but it's not much different from their "We're going to kill you and burn down your village" bleating. The guards aren't convinced and don't lower their spears.

"Look, I know it seems suspicious, but they're on our side. You have my word."

The line isn't nearly as effective as I'm hoping for, but I see help is on the way. Walking down the hill to the guard post, I see Esmander with a perplexed look on his face, and Marin is barely keeping the laughter under control.

"Winters, where have you been, and who in the name of Aquillon are you bringing to dinner?" he asks. Despite my disappearance, he seems to be in his usual cheerful mood.

"I found new friends!" I say with an enormous grin. And by friends, I mean two goat-demons and an old librarian, but if I've learned anything on Aquillon, it's that friends will come from the most unusual of places. Sullas taught me that. Esmander sighs and waves the guards off, and my band of misfits follows me up the hill and into the village. From the strange and vaguely terrified looks I'm getting from the villagers, I have some explaining to do.

10

Kyria

G etting down the mountain proved just as dangerous and no more fun than climbing it had been. After an afternoon spent clambering down cliffs and narrowly avoiding long falls with pointy rocks, Kyria and Ahrun made camp at the base of the mountain. A long crag ran from the base of the mountain, weaving in and out of the foothills, and it seemed as good a place as any to begin their search. Not in the dark, though.

Kyria looked down over the edge of the geological scar and marveled that they hadn't spotted it on their way up the mountain. To be fair, they had been otherwise occupied with not dying, which seemed a decent excuse for their obliviousness. The crag was deep but narrow, never opening larger than the width of a man, and it extended many meters down into darkness. The wind howled through its twists and crevasse, creating a haunting sound.

"Thas' a cheery lullaby," Kyria said. "Should be marvelous fun ta sleep tonight."

"Look on the..." Ahrun began.

"Don' say it."

"Bright side."

Kyria sighed

Ahrun continued. "At least we didn't get eaten by the dragon, and we've made good our escape from the treacherous peak!" There was a pluck to his voice that Kyria found nauseating, but also slightly endearing. She didn't comment on his peppy outlook on the situation, electing instead to fix him with a death stare.

"You don't scare me, Kyria Killburn, I once saw you hug someone. You're not all steel and nails, despite your best efforts to prove otherwise." He grinned at her and narrowly dodged a pebble she threw at him.

"Excuse me if I don' see the bright side o' escapin' one scaly beastie only ta be gobbled up by another! This plan o' yers is daft, and I'm regettin' more an' more ever signin' up for it," Kyria said. She threw her hands in the air and made an exasperated sigh. She found the paladin annoying, but more than that she found herself unable to stay mad at him for long, which she found even more annoying.

"You could always return to Sanctum? I'm sure they have a need for a scullery maid," Ahrun said.

She paused for a moment and stroked her chin. "Nae, I'll be passin' on tha' fine opportunity. Besides, ya would be dead ten times over if no' for me."

"I can't argue that point. And I never got a chance to thank you for coming with me. This is a dangerous mission, and I can't make any guarantees of the outcome. You are a brave woman, Kyria, and I'm all the safer to have you by my side."

The fire crackled as the silence between them grew and breathed, like an animal in the dark.

"Well, I'm off ta sleep then," Kyria said, letting Ahrun's last remark go unanswered. "Ya can take first watch."

"Very well," Ahrun said.

Kyria rolled over, facing away from Ahrun and the firelight, and the ghost of a smile was on the edges of her lips as sleep crept into the back of her brain.

The morning came, and Kyria was slow to wake. Sunlight from the west poured over the hills, and she sat up, wiping the last of sleep from her eyes. Ahrun was grilling meat from a fresh kill in a frying pan they had swiped from the kitchens of Sanctum before they had been vigorously shooed out.

"What happened?" Kyria said, still groggy as reality came back into focus.

"You seemed like you needed sleep, so I took the second watch. I was fortunate that this bird flew a little too low, and now we have breakfast."

Kyria suppressed her appetite. The roasting bird looked delicious. She shot Ahrun a nasty look. "I don' need ya doin' me any favors. It was my watch, an' yer nae good ta me if ya fall asleep in the middle o' battle. Don' do tha' again, or I'll beat ya senseless, ya hear me?"

Ahrun threw up his hands in surrender. "I offer breakfast as tribute for my egregious error, m'ladyship!"

Kyria wanted to argue more, but she was too hungry. She nearly attacked the steaming drumstick, and the two ate breakfast in silence. After they cleaned up and broke camp, Kyria studied the crag.

A single path down into the crag led to a narrow walkway that meandered in and out of natural openings in the rock wall. Every hundred feet, the walkway would open up to a platform of sorts, but then continue down into the depths until she couldn't see any farther.

"So, where do ya suggest lookin' for this Fogu character?"

"It's hard to say, the Mistress of Scales didn't exactly shower us with pertinent details. Fogu could live anywhere down there," Ahrun said.

"Yes, it is hard to say. Fogu is feisty!"

Kyria and Ahrun exchanged puzzled glances, as the statement did not come from either of them. It came, rather, from somewhere closer to the ground. As they looked down, a small creature, roughly the height of Ahrun's boot, peered back up at them and waved. Kyria nearly yelped and jumped back. She held it together on the general assumption that unknown entities in this part of Aquillon should not be spooked by sudden movement, lest they produce enormous sets of teeth, acid breath, or some other unpleasant implement of doom.

Upon further observation, the shrimpy creature looked like an overly large mushroom made of stone had sprouted hands, legs and something that resembled a face which for the moment was smiling at them. Kyria took this as a positive sign and returned the greeting, waving at it.

"Ya alright then?" she asked the mushroom-man.

"Yes yes, hulking beast!" Kyria grimaced at its description of her, but from the perspective of a knee-high mushroom creature, she supposed it made sense. The mushroom-man continued. "You are seeking Fogu?"

"Aye," Kyria answered.

"Most glorious news then, hulking beast! I am also on my way to seek council from the wise Fogu. Perhaps we may journey together?" Every word from the creature's mouth seemed to bounce from one to the next, like a nursery rhyme. Kyria looked at Ahrun, who shrugged with an amused grin.

"I don' see why no'" Kyria said.

The creature jumped up and down and squealed.

"This is most magnanimous news hulk beast! May I ask your names?"

"I'm Kyria."

"And I am Ahrun Valheim, last of the..." Ahrun began.

"Last o' tha's enough information for now," Kyria cut him off with an annoyed look. Ahrun had an unwelcome habit of revealing a little too much information, and she didn't trust this mushroom creature just yet, no matter how adorable it might be.

"Splendid! Then we will travel the road of this glorious land together, and we shall seek Fogu the Wise!" Saying this, the mushroom creature began walking down the narrow path into the crag. Kyria and Ahrun scrambled to follow it as it moved at a rapid pace, despite its stubby little legs.

"We did no' get yer name earlier friend," Kyria said as they walked. The path down into the crag was narrow, but still a peaceful walk compared to the path to the summit of the dragon's mountain.

"I am Takram. Are we friends?"

"Well, we just met my little fellow, but you seem agreeable company to keep. Consider us friends," Ahrun replied before Kyria could say anything.

"Most wonderful. Takram is friends with Ahrun and Kyria!"

"Aye, most wonderful. I've always wanted a friend like ya," Kyria said, glaring at Ahrun. He ignored her.

"So tell me, Takram," Kyria began.

"Friend-Takram," Takram interrupted.

"What?"

"Now that we are friends you will call me Friend-Takram, and I will call you Friend-Kyria! It is how these things are done!"

"Aye, my apologies, Friend-Takram. As I was sayin', what business brings ya to this Fogu?" Kyria asked, trying her best to hide the rising tide of exasperation in her voice. There was a reason her superiors had never left her to watch the children of the Guard.

"I am seeking wisdom. Fogu is wise and solves many problems. He is also fabulously wealthy, with great stores of gold from deep within the ground. Perhaps that is why you adventurers seek him?" Takram asked.

"Nothing of the sort, Friend-Takram. We also seek council from the wise Fogu. We mean to sneak into the lair of a great beast, and must mask our scent," Ahrun answered. Kyria was impressed with his diplomacy. Everywhere she had been, Ahrun seemed to make friends.

"Oh, this I am sure Fogu will help with! Friend-Ahrun and Friend-Kyria will be most pleased by his aid!"

They continued along in silence for a while, much to Kyria's relief, and they finally took a rest at one of the platforms. It seemed out of place with the natural formations of the crag, as if someone had formed it deliberately. Kyria thought it odd, but everything in this part of the world was odd, so she let it go.

Before long they were on their way again and traveling quickly into the depths of the canyon. Kyria peered over the edge and the crag seemed to extend forever down into night. The sky seemed a distant memory, and even the sunlight overhead barely lit the way.

"An' how long now, Friend-Takram, before we meet Fogu?" Kyria was suspecting a trap.

"Not long now, I..." Takram never finished his sentence as a dangerous step caused him to fall over the edge. Kyria's reflexes kicked in a moment sooner than Ahrun's and she leapt to catch him, grabbing his foot a moment before he tumbled off the edge. In her haste, however, she had miscalculated and barely had time to grab the side of the path. Ahrun dropped his pack and gripped her hand.

"Could ya be a dear and pull us up?" Kyria asked, trying to hide the panic in her voice. Takram must have been made of very dense stone, because it was all Kyria could do to keep her hold on his foot.

"I am trying, but something is weighing you down!" Kyria could see the sweat pouring down Ahrun's face, and every muscle in his arms bulged to keep ahold of her.

"You may let me go, Friend-Kyria," Takram said cheerfully. "I cannot ask you to die for me!"

"Non-sense, I'm no' lettin' go o' ya. Now hush!" Kyria replied with a stern look downward. Ahrun was struggling to keep his footing, but his iron grip on her hands never wavered. With a last struggle, Ahrun lost his footing, and the group fell into the crag.

Kyria's mind flooded with panic, but as they fell, she saw the walls around her move until they formed a gigantic hand, made of stone. The hand reached out and scooped them up, pulling them through the rock wall, which seemed to shimmer and melt as the hand moved through it. It seemed to defy all logic, but the three of them sat in the stone palm, and it sailed through the stone wall as easily as a ship through water.

Finally, the hand reached an enormous cavern where it reached out and deposited them on a rocky island that floated above a great void in the earth. All around the cave the glowing light of bioluminescent mushroom lit up the chamber with a firefly warmth, bathing the rocks in soft greens and violets.

Kyria turned to Ahrun and before she knew what she was doing, wrapped him up in a hug and began crying and laughing all at once. Her senses soon flooded back to her and she rid herself of him as the post-doom hysteria wore off. She was grateful that the soft light of the cave hid the flush in her face. She focused instead on finding her little friend.

Looking around the platform, she saw him seated on a throne that had grown from the rocks. He smiled at her and beckoned her over. She and Ahrun made their way across the platform.

"Hello Friend-Ahrun, and Friend-Kyria. You have proven yourselves worthy companions. Now, tell me what business you have with Braga, and why I should help you."

11

Alex

It takes at least an hour to convince the villagers not to kill Bob and Steve, and vice versa. I kinda get where the villagers are coming from. When I first met Sullas, the muradae that transported me across the Heart of Storm to the Wyld Places, my reaction wasn't much better. Trust is hard to come by where demons are concerned.

After brokering a kind of truce, I sit down with Esmander, Marin, and Reginald in his hut. Bob and Steve are waiting patiently outside, as though they are worried that the villagers might turn on me. Their loyalty is endearing.

"So… now that that's dealt with," Esmander motions outside, "tell me some good news. Were you able to find any information on what you were looking for?"

"Better, I found Reginald here. He told me where to find the Path of Flame. He also said he might join your village Esmander," I reply.

Esmander eyes Reginald skeptically, but finally he shrugs. "He's not the first Fox to join us. We'd appreciate your knowledge. Not many of the villagers have any book learning." Reginald nods at him and then looks to me.

"Are you sure about this, my dear?" he asks. "We could use you in this village, and I fear if you leave for that mountain, you aren't coming back."

I shake my head. "I'm afraid so. I have unfinished business with the Eastern Watch, and I'm going to have to find the Path to handle it. Thanks for looking out for me though."

"As for the goat-men," Esmander says.

"Look, I know it might not seem smart to keep formally evil goat-men around, but if not for a formally evil eel-demon, we wouldn't be having this conversation. Besides, you could use the muscle," I say, hoping to reassure him.

"Very well, they can stay. I hope I'm not making a mistake."

So do I, I think to myself.

Marin speaks up. "So, where are we headed?"

"To a mountain north of here. Perhaps three days or four day's journey if you make quick time," Reginald says.

"That makes sense..." Marin says, trailing off. He rifles through his pack and pulls out his books. Opening one, he flips to a page full of writing, with a picture of a volcano. "I've been reading all day while you've been off goat-herding,".

I roll my eyes and stick my tongue at him. He ignores me and continues. "Our records tell of the mountain itself, but not its exact location. Just knowing that it is to the north should allow me to find it on our maps." He produces a small stack of scrolls from his bag.

"Not that I'm complaining, but how much stuff did you steal?" I ask.

"I believe you once told me to, 'go big or go home,'" he says with a smirk. "I figured I'd go big since I can't really go home, what with the stealing and what not."

"Well, we'd better get some shuteye then," I say. Marin and I thank Esmander and go back to our hut. Bob and Steve follow and post themselves at the front of the hut. Once we get settled in, I'm trying to go to sleep, but my mind is too busy. Apparently Marin isn't doing much better at sleeping because I see him tossing and turning in his bedroll.

"So, do you really think I can get through this Path of Flames?" I ask. It's an honest question, and I'm hoping Marin will give me an honest answer. I know I've been through a lot in the last few months, but the more I hear about this Path, the more I'm not sure if I'm coming out the other side or not.

"Can you? Yes. You're the girl who fell through time, after all. I wouldn't have gambled five hundred years of work at Sanctum away if I was worried about you making it through the Path. There was a part of me that wanted to let you get banished and not do anything about it."

"Thanks..."

"It would have been easier." He dodges the boot I throw at him and smirks. "But there was a larger part of me that wondered what we Magi have been doing all these last thousand years since the Fall, and why we never did more to fight the Court. Even we don't remember what happened before the Fall began, but perhaps things would have turned out differently if we had done something. When you were banished by the Grand Old Idiot, I figured it was fate offering me a chance to answer that what if. Besides, I like you. It would be a shame if you got yourself roasted alive or eaten by a giant worm. Gods know what might become of you if I weren't around to chaperone."

I laugh, despite myself. That's Marin. Serious and pondering moral dilemmas one moment, cracking jokes the next.

"Why didn't the Magi help during the fall?"

"I'm not sure. That's a secret Fallstaff keeps very well guarded. He's one of the few magi around then."

"And what of this guardian of ash and flame? What if I'm not worthy?"

"My dear Ms. Winters, do you really think you'd still be here if you weren't?"

I don't have a response, except for hiding my blush in my bedroll.

"What say we give this sleep thing another go?" Marin asks.

"Fine by me. Goodnight." I close my eyes and sleep eventually works its velvet claws into my brain and I let the world fade.

The morning comes quickly, and a bit too early for my taste (I got used to sleeping in during my brief stay at Sanctum). We pack our things and make ready to travel. Bob and Steve are still waiting outside our hut. I don't think they've slept. Do demons sleep?

"Alright, guys. I'm leaving, but you need to stay here." They eye each other nervously. I'm not sure if they're wondering what the villagers will do with them, or they're pondering just how much killing they can get away with while mom is away. "I've made arrangements with the village for you to stay. You will be farmers now, not killers. Am I clear on that point?"

They bleat what I assume is goat-demon for, "Fine, whatever, mom. You're ruining our lives." They're not happy with me, but they stay put as we walk away. As we reach the northern edge of the village, Esmander meets us, and hands us a small satchel.

"Just some supplies, and a few canteens of water," he says, answer the confused look I give him.

"You didn't have to," I say.

"Nonsense. We wouldn't be here, or be free to give you the supplies if it weren't for you. That is a debt we will spend our entire lives trying to repay, but I doubt we will," he says.

"So, have you figured out a name for this little commune of yours?" I ask Esmander.

He ponders for a while and shakes his head.

"Well, how about New-Boston?" I ask.

"What's a Boston?"

"The greatest city in the world," I say, grinning from ear to ear. "Home of the Bruins, the greatest hockey team in the world."

"Well, I have no idea what hockey is, but New-Boston is as good a name as any. Good luck in your ventures, Alex Winters. I don't know if we will ever meet again, but the village of New-Boston will always be behind you."

Marin and I shake his hand and we begin our journey out of the village and on an old cart path that leads north. As the village fades in the southern horizon, I feel alone again, despite Marin's comforting presence. The wilderness quickly takes over and before long, the landscape isn't much different from the Wyld Places. Huge vistas of raw, uncontaminated wilderness engulf everything around us, and we're just small specs in the untouched wilderness.

As I stare across the rolling jungle plains, it reminds me how much I miss Ahrun and Kyria. The world was still a terrifying place when they were with me, but at least it wasn't lonely. Still, I have Marin and that's something. But he can't replace Ahrun and Kyria. Nothing can. I hope they're alright. As the miles roll into each other, I can't help but wonder where they are, and if they've found their dragon yet. Hopefully if they have, Kyria hasn't got herself eaten by it. I love that girl to death, but she is mouthy.

12

Kyria

"What do ya mean, ya were testin' us, ya daft hunk o' fungus?" Kyria shouted.

Ahrun was trying to make her see that yelling at the being that had most recently saved her by pulling her through a stone wall with awe-inspiring earth powers was a losing strategy, but he wasn't making much headway.

"Well, Friend-Kyria, I had to be sure that you were good people. Fogu has been around for many years. Many bad people come to Fogu seeking advice. I had to be sure you were not bad people," Fogu said.

"And we appreciate that, Lord Fogu," Ahrun said, giving Kyria a pleading look. "But perhaps my friend meant to say, the extremity of your test startled her. We nearly died."

"Death is the greatest equalizer of false truths. This is how all who seek my wisdom are tested. The test is simple, succeed, and I grant you an audience, fail and you die. As a nature spirit I find beauty in simplicity," Fogu said. His voice had not changed; still airy, but the depth of his words showed the spirit's age. Kyria was still fuming, but she conceded the point. They needed Fogu's help, and yelling at him would not serve that end, no matter how much better it made her feel.

"Fine, let's get on with it then," Kyria muttered.

"Good, then we are agreed. Come Friend-Kyria, Friend-Ahrun, tell me what you have come here to tell me," Fogu said, listening intently.

"We've come ta find Braga, Eater of Light. We need the blood of an ancient one, an' I hear he's got a whole heap o' the stuff," Kyria said.

"Ah, you've come on behalf of the Mistress of Scales, then?" Fogu asked. Kyria and Ahrun exchanged surprised glances. "Do not be so surprised, friends! The old dragon may be the queen of the skies, but she still makes her home on a mountain. There is nothing a stone sees or hears that does not come back to me."

"Yes, we're here on her behalf. Why even ask what we're here for if you already know?" Ahrun asked.

"I wanted to see if you would tell the truth. Normally I wouldn't help you steal anything from Braga," Fogu's face looked twisted and nervous as he spoke, "but I owe a great debt to the Mistress of Scales and I would welcome a chance to clear that debt."

"So then," Kyria interjected, "how do we go about sneaking into this beasty's lair?"

"That will not be easy. Last time you tangled with Braga, you invaded one of his oldest nests. He did not know your scent then, but he will know it now. The lair you seek is his most prized, where he keeps the blood of the ancient ones. He guards it jealously and tolerates no trespass."

"What is this blasted blood, anyway?" Kyria asked.

"This world existed long before your kind walked it. Before even the Gods, or the Court of Hours. There were creatures here long before memory gave birth to story. The ancient ones were the first ones. The first to crawl from a primordial cauldron and gaze at stars that no man would see for a hundred thousand years. Braga is the last of them. He hunted his brothers and sisters to the point of extinction, and drank their blood to give him a long life, and power beyond reason. Their blood has power to do, or undo great magic," Fogu said.

"So, how much do we need? The Mistress was sparse on details," Ahrun asked.

"A small vial should do. Take more than that and Braga will sense its absence," Fogu replied. "And do not harm Braga. He is beyond your or even my power to vanquish. For this you will need great stealth. I know of something that might work, but..." Fogu , trailed off while scratching his chin. As he did the cap of his mushroom-like head shook back and forth, releasing little spores which fell to the ground. His eyes shimmered and shifted from color to color.

"If it keeps us from bein' gobbled up by the beasty, we'll take it," Kyria said.

"This is old magic. Powerful, but old. And old magic costs. I can hide you from his scent, but there is a price you pay, at least temporarily," Fogu said.

"And what might this price be?" Ahrun asked.

"It doesn't work like that. You agree and I will work the magic. You will know the price soon enough."

Kyria spoke before Ahrun had time to consider. "We'll do it!"

Fogu nodded and lead them to the center of the platform. Kneeling, he blew, and a wind filled the chamber, swirling stones and dust from the surrounding rocks into the void below. As the wind died down, Kyria looked and she saw that hidden underneath the rubble was a massive circle of carved runes and symbols. There were several circles and Fogu beckoned her and Ahrun onto them. Ahrun turned to Kyria.

"Is this really a good idea? We don't even know the price."

"If it gets rid o' the Court, no price is too high. Besides, ya have me, silly knight. Yer gonna be fine," she said, waving off his concerns. She wished she felt as confident as she sounded, but she had meant the first thing she said. No price was too high if it meant ridding her home of the demonic Court.

"Now it begins," Fogu said. His voice was serious now and had lost all its jovial bouncing. He raised his hands over the runes and they glowed an iridescent green and otherworldly blue. They lit up the cave and danced on the rocks, and Kyria's eyes grew wide as she watched the haunting light show. Without warning, energy erupted from the rocks and engulfed Ahrun and Kyria. It was a warm and slightly tickling feeling that passed almost as quickly as it had begun. Kyria turned to Fogu to speak, but he put up a hand and signaled for her to stop.

"I told you there was a cost, but as you pay it the spell works. Do not speak a word, for the moment you utter the sound, the spell will fade as quickly as the words fly from your lips," Fogu said. His voice was a stern warning, not open to compromise or question.

"And I suppose I shouldn't open my eyes then?" Ahrun said.

Kyria looked, and she saw Ahrun blindly feeling about the air.

"You suppose correctly," Fogu said.

Kyria made a gesture towards Fogu, and he seemed to interpret its meaning.

"The spell will hide you from Braga's scent. You should be able to sneak into his lair and get what you need."

"Why, pray tell, did this spell take our sight and voice? Seems a poor design? I feel we might have better luck roughing it on our own," Ahrun said.

Kyria gestured vigorously towards Ahrun, signalling her agreement.

"The spell doesn't just hide your scent. It hides everything about you. No being in the heavens or of Aquillon could find you by any means. I can no longer feel your essence, even as connected to the soil as I am. This is powerful magic, but the cost is the thing you treasure most. You are old and have seen much of the world. Your sight the lifeline to your memory," Fogu said. Turning to Kyria, he continued, "and you are a fiery rabble rouser. Your voice is your power. The spell can only hide your essence if you give up that which is most precious to you; what makes you… you. As long as you pay the spell's cost, it will shroud you."

Kyria made some more disgruntled hand gestures which Fogu chose not to interpret, or if he did, he did not respond to them. "Ah, and one more thing, friends. The magic is a tandem binding. It only works if you stay close to each other. A couple hundred feet or fewer should do the trick," Fogu added.

Kyria rolled her eyes and Ahrun spoke up with another question.

"And how are the blind man and the mute maiden to make our way to this wretched beast's lair?"

"I will take you to the edge, but no farther. I have interfered enough already," Fogu said, looking around as if someone was listening to everything he was saying.

Kyria let out a silent, exasperated sigh, but Ahrun bowed. "Then that is all the aid we can ask of you, kind sir. Take us to the lair of Braga!"

Kyria rolled her eyes. He was so irritatingly pleasant about things. He said "the lair of Braga" as he might say "the meadow of daisies and pleasant ducks," and she internally grumbled to herself. His pep would get them killed. For now though, she had to worry about conducting him or he'd get himself killed, and she was not about to have that on her conscience.

Without waiting for further prompting, Fogu extended a hand and a small pillar of fluid earth pulled itself out of a nearby wall and he directed Kyria (and, by extension, Ahrun) to it. Kyria helped guide him onto the platform. As soon as she stepped into it, the moving ground sealed itself around her boots, like quicksand that had hardened to stone. She looked up at Fogu, who was waving at them as they departed.

"Goodbye Friend-Kyria and Friend-Ahrun. I doubt we will see each other again, but on the off chance you survive and you're ever in my part of the world, please pop by! I would relish the company."

Kyria gave him a dismissive wave and Ahrun bowed once more, this time nearly bowing his way off the pillar, but Kyria's firm hand and the floor-cement kept him from tumbling to his doom. As the pillar neared the wall, there was a shimmer, and the wall melted away, revealing a long canal that ran endlessly through the stone. The rocky pillar moved faster and faster through the canal, and Kyria looked around in wonder at the stone melting before them.

"I'd ask what's moving us, but I doubt you'd have the hand gestures to explain it," Ahrun said. Kyria responded by punching him in the arm.

After some time traversing the depths of the ground, Kyria felt the pillar move upwards. They continued to ascend until finally they shot through the ground and the pillar receded, leaving them on solid earth with sun and sky extending for miles overhead. It took Kyria a moment to get her bearings and finally take in her surroundings. They were on a lush plateau, atop a hill overlooking a valley that sloped down before them. There was only one discernable trait of the land that made it any different from any other stretch of jungle in the Wyld places, but it took Kyria and Ahrun several minutes to take in the scale of it.

At the edge of the valley, something had dug a massive crater out of the ground and it dropped off steeply into darkness. It ran several hundred feet in all directions and around it; the ground was black and dead. Nothing grew and long, dark tendrils extended through the ground like veins leading back to the heart. The ground pulsed with foul energy and even from this distance it was hard to breathe. From the top of the pit, Kyria saw something she recognized. Spines shot out of the edge of the crater and they rose and fell as Braga breathed, a great demonic mountain range of gleaming death. The creature seemed to encompass the entire circumference of the pit and Kyria had trouble staying on her feet, its presence was so oppressive.

Before them stood the home of Braga, Eater of Light. Kyria took a deep breath. The longer she looked at the rising and falling of the creature's spines, the more she plunged into a river of icy fear. Her heart raced, her knees trembled, and she couldn't even scream. In front of her was an ancient god of death, old as the world, and she was just a tiny creature with no hope of victory. This time, there was no silver lining.

13

Alex

I t's been three days, and I think we're finally starting to make some headway.

"So, if the puck exceeds the line beyond the net before any player is close enough, icing is called by the zebras?" Marin asks.

I should probably clarify my statement. We've been lost for hours, but he's close to understanding hockey, so there's a silver lining, I guess.

"You've got it. That's pretty much the last rule you need to understand in order to watch hockey."

"Clever game. And it's played on ice you say? By men on blades that glide over it at incredible speeds? I don't know if I could do that with magic, much less by myself. Mighty men, these Bruins must be!"

"They are, I grew up watching them. And some women are playing, so the sport's only getting better!" I say. I tried skating once. They were doing an open skate on Boston Common Frog Pond once and after what I can only assume was a drunken ballet of dangerous swerving and near-death collisions, I never skated again. Based on this brief, but horrifying experience, I never tried hockey.

Focusing back on the task (not getting more lost or eaten by anything) I look at Marin. "So, are we any closer to finding this mountain? You'd think a mountain would be easier to spot."

"Well, we don't exactly have much of a vantage point, but I suppose it's another good chance to try your anti-ground incant," he says.

The magi of the Eastern Watch excel at many things (mastering the arcane, scientific research, repressing women, etc.) but coming up with original or clever names for their incants isn't one of them. The anti-ground incant is one I've been trying to master for a while, and it literally does what it says. If cast successfully, it will repel you, with as much force as you like, away from the ground. It's not flight per-say, but it's close, and that was enough to get me to study it. The only issue (and the reason most Magi never bother to learn the incant) is the even practicing can be lethal. Use too much force and you'll find yourself shot up, hundreds of feet in the air, falling to your death unless you can glimmer mid-air, which even advanced magi struggle with. None of the above has stopped me from trying.

We round the bend of the path we've been following for an hour (Marin seems sure he's on to something) and take pause. There are a few things you need to test an anti-ground incant, and this place has them. For starters, you need a wide-open space free of pointy rocks or sharp sticks. Check. You also need a clear sky, so as to not slam into rocks and go splat. Check.

Marin takes my pack and I try to clear my mind, which is easier said than done. The jungle hums and buzzes around me like a living organism, and it's becoming harder and harder to concentrate. The heat doesn't help. I hated how cold the stupid magi kept Sanctum all the time, but it made incanting much easier. Finally, I'm able to clear my head and empty myself of everything but the thought of leaving the ground. I focus all of my attention on escaping it and throwing off the rocks and dirt around me like shackles.

I feel my power rushing towards the thought and I almost lift upwards, when a nearby parrot squawks. For the fraction of a second I hear the noise, it's long enough to get me to think of the ground again and I feel my face slam into the dirt. Marin rushes over, but I can tell he's trying hard not to laugh. Despite the pain, I have to chuckle at the mental image of myself face-plating into the ground. Fortunately for me, this soil is softer than normal and I felt nothing broken. I'm not even missing any teeth.

"Well done! That's exactly what the anti-ground incant is supposed to do," Marin says with a grin. "You must bring that technique back to Sanctum when we return. It might make some older Magi more down-to-earth, as you say?" Before I can even respond, Marin is rolling with laughter from his own joke. I pull myself and spit some dirt out of my mouth before responding.

"Yeah, yeah, yuck it up. Whenever I figure this out, I'm going to launch myself to the deepest part of the nearest ocean and send you for a swim. Maybe the chilly water will clean out whatever brain is left between those ears of yours."

He ignores my jab and continues. "So, any more exciting dirt adventures today or are you through?"

"I'm going to keep working on it. I'm not letting this stupid dirt win."

"Excellent! I'll make lunch. I love lunch and a show!"

He runs away just fast enough to avoid the swift kick to his butt I try to deliver. I ignore him and focus, but I'm not upset he's working on lunch. I'm starving and he's an excellent cook. Incanting on an empty stomach isn't always the most successful, anyway. From what I can figure out, any magus can incant any spell, but what takes hundreds of years of training is being able to do it when the conditions are less than perfect. Marin could probably conjure up a grilled cheese sandwich in the middle of a hurricane if he needed to. Yum grilled cheese. Ok, I definitely need to get back to work.

Even after lunch, my next several attempts all suffer varying degrees of failure. Marin has taken to giving them ratings by having a glowing number hang over his head after each one. I haven't made it past four. I don't think I have any more in me, which sucks because I was really hoping to at least make a six. I dig down and focus. I'm mentally and physically exhausted. The greater the incant, the greater the strain it takes on the caster. I think there's one more attempt in there somewhere. Focus, Alex. I do my best to isolate just the need, just the desire to be away from the ground. Nothing else.

I look back to see what rating Marin has given this attempt and all I see is blue sky and jungle tree line. Looking down, I nearly scream when I see Marin a hundred feet below me jumping up and down and clapping his hands. He's shouting something.

"Mole-cat?" I say down to him,

"Mountain," he yells back, lingering on each syllable.

I give him a quick thumbs up and move around. I'm not rising or falling, but moving side to side comes easily enough. I just lean my head in the direction I'd like to, and off I float. With a flourish of hand gestures, I command my body to do a complete circle. It responds so quickly I nearly miss what I'm looking for. It rushes past my view and I turn around again, this time stopping as the speck comes into view, and I'm left staring at a towering peak in the distance. At the top of it fires burn and shoot into the sky, and I see trails of molten fire snaking down the mountain.

Around the base of the volcano, rivers of molten fire snake their way around the clearing. The jungle is clear for at least a half-mile in every direction of the burning peak. The peak of the mountain glows an eerie red, but smoke never comes from it. At the base of the volcano I spot an enormous gate, and I see a road leading up the side of the peak. The entire plateau is glowing and I see huge runes of fire etched into the ground between the rivers of lava.

I point and wave and begin trying to lower myself. Coming down from an anti-ground incant is just about as hard as coming up. I focus on the ground, but gently, careful not to put too much emphasis on the thought. I descend slowly, and as I do, I see the volcano quivering like a mirage, and by the time I'm at the level of the treetops, it's completely vanished. I get the rest of the way down and Marin runs up to me.

"Well, what's the view like up there? Good news, I take it?" he asks.

"Well yes, and no. We're close. Like, very close, but the lower I got the harder it was to see it, until finally it shimmered away, so I'm not sure if it's really there or not."

"Hmm, let me see if our records have anything to say about this," Marin says as he walks over to his books. After several minutes of leafing through one of them, he stops and squints at something. "Here," he says, bringing the book over to me. "Read this."

I focus on the words, all written in Aquillonian, but eventually they shimmer and shift to English.

"Find only the mountain shall those of truest sight, for hidden beyond reach it lies, but from birds to skies, and opens doors at night."

"They couldn't have been clearer?" I ask.

"Look this was written by Graystaff the Riddler," Marin says, "We're lucky it isn't written backwards. What direction was it in?"

I point to the north-east.

"All right then, I suggest we make our way there and see what there is to be seen." I can't argue the point, so we pack up and head out.

It doesn't take us long to reach where the trees should end, but they keep going. It makes no sense. This entire area should be flat and full of fire, not trees. I stop walking and Marin turns to me.

"This is where it should be. The start of it anyway. I think we need to wait," I say.

"For?"

"Night. Your book said the door opens at night. What if the only way it opens is at night? Like a portal or something, but you have to be in the right place to see it. We've been sleeping at night, so even if there was a portal, we wouldn't have seen it."

"Alright, Winters. I trust you. So we wait."

If anybody is wondering whether waiting for hours on end in a steaming jungle is fun, I'll save them the trouble. It's not. Merrin and I pass the time chatting and I practice some light incanting, but mostly we're just waiting and sweating. Thankfully, the sky turns orange-pink and I can feel the last moment of daylight slipping by, and finally it's night. The stars are shining down through the treetops and there's a deathly silence all around us. It's too quiet. I've been in this jungle for a while now, and at no point has it ever been this quiet. I look at Marin and he seems puzzled by it. Our answer comes soon enough.

Thirty or forty feet away from where we're camped out, I see a ripple of energy in the darkness. It starts at a single point at the top, but then extends on either side until it forms a doorway. Around the threshold, the shadow-painted jungle extends in every direction, but I can see the glow of the rivers of lava in the distance through the opening. Marin and I don't waste any time and glimmer through the gate, which closes as soon as we're clear.

Taking a moment to get my bearings, I turn around and I see the jungle several hundred feet behind me. In front of me I see the volcano, towering into the night sky, and the six rivers of molten fire extend all around the plateau. Nothing grows here, but there is no evidence that it ever did; not a single tree or plant sprouts from the surrounding stone. Between each of the rivers of fire, I see the giant runes emanating red light, but it's hard to make out what they look like. The more I look at the surrounding area, the more I can tell this was not a place forged by the natural world; this was the work of something else. The jury's still out on whether that something is good or evil, but I'm hoping for the former.

"Well then, onward and upward," I say, nodding towards the mountain.

"Well, you've got us this far, Winters, I'm not about to stop here. I'll follow your lead."

We walk towards the mountain in muted silence. There's something about this place. It radiates an unearthly silence and seems to demand everything else does. I can't hear the buzz of the jungle or even the night wind. It settles over us like a blanket, and I can't seem to summon the urge to speak. Whatever created this place was a power beyond humanity, or even the Court. There is old power here, and it demands respect, and silence. We're more than happy to oblige it as we walk. Besides, I need time to think.

We've been traveling, and I've known the destination, but as the mountain looms closer and closer, I don't feel remotely ready for whatever this test is. I've got no clue if I'm worthy or not, or even if I will make it passed this guardian I've been told about. Marin seems to think I'll be fine, but he's so easy going all the time, it's hard to tell if it's just a front. He might be internally freaking out, and I'd never know about it. I guess there's only one way to find out. I steady my nerves and keep walking. The mountain is close now, and with every step I can feel myself drawing nearer to whatever tests await.

Before I know it, I'm standing before the gate at the base of the mountain. In person, it's even more massive. Each pillar of the gate is at least fifty feet around, and a hundred high. It's similar in design to old Shinto gates I've seen in magazines from Japan. A long frame runs over the top of it, extending past the pillars, and from the edges of the frame two huge bells hang down on iron chains. There is nothing to stop me from walking through the gate, but as I near the entrance, a growing dread fills my chest. As soon as we near the threshold of the gate, the bells rings. It's a deep sound, dark and brooding, as though these were the bells that toll before the world ends. I nearly scream at the sound, because it seems so out of synch with this silent place. Their tolling echoes across the plateau for several minutes before breaking off.

After the apocalypse doorbell ends, I look at Marin and he seems as confused as I am. "Does it mention that in your friendly guide to the Path of Flame?" I ask him.

"Fresh out of helpful hints, I'm afraid. Most of the details I have pertain to the constructions of the Path and its origins. No bells, sadly."

I sigh. "What's the point in brining a wise magi tour guide if you can't even..." I don't have time to finish my witty retort as I'm interrupted by an explosion of hissing steam as molten lava bubbles up through cracks all around us. As soon as it boils up from the crevices, it forms into a small pool and then levitates into the air, eventually taking the shape of a woman.

"I greet you, seeker. Do you intend to face the Path?"

I think the being is speaking to me, but I'm having trouble concentrating. In front of me, hovering several feet in the air, is a replica of myself, or at least what it would look like if I was mostly constructed of rocks and lava. The height is about right, as is the hair length, even the facial structure. I don't have burning orbs of fire for eyes, but something is doing its level-best to look like me, and it's almost creepy how accurate it is. Even the voice of the creature sounds like me, albeit more fire and steam sounding, but it could probably pass for me at a bad karaoke bar.

"I'm assuming you're talking to me, so yes. I very much intend to face it," I say in response.

"Good. Then ready yourself, for only the worthy shall tread upon the path. Others die in flame and blood."

I look over to Marin for some guidance, but I realize that something has sealed the surrounding space off by rivers of lava. Two of the streams nearby have been diverted to form a circle around myself and the figure, and I see Marin trying to get in. He's casting every spell he can at the luminous lines of a magic barrier surrounding the circular river. He looks defeated, but I wave him off. He's not going to do either of us any good if he gets himself incinerated for poor behavior.

Before I can do anything else, the figure rushes at me and lunges. As it attacks, both of its glowing hands reform into claws that swipe at me with lethal intent. Everything I've heard about this test of worthiness is true; there isn't a second-place trophy. You pass or you die.

It takes several minutes of me evading the creature's attacks before there's a break. I'm sweating bullets, and it's not just the heat from all the magma; I've been running for my life, and I'm getting tired. This thing is showing no signs of getting winded, and I need to be on my game if I'm ever going to step foot on this stupid mountain.

My fiery doppelganger smiles at me. "Give in to your weakness. Give in to me," it says in a taunting sound. I've never been made fun of by living fire, and I have to say I'm not a fan.

"Just sit still and I'll put you out of both of our misery!" I yell as I start to incant on the run. I didn't learn much of frost-cult incanting, but I'm thinking flame-cult, my strong suite, isn't my best bet here. I hurl a few ice daggers at the creature. One catches it in the side, and the other misses. It hisses at me and renews its assault with twice the fury.

"You are imperfect! Give up and give in!" The creature screeches at me as it hurls several large fireballs my way. I glimmer across the circle at the last minute and the balls of flame shatter into the energy field right behind where I was. I turn and fire a beam of frigid ice magic towards it and it catches the creature in the gut. I'm feeling good with myself when I see the creature glance down, remove the spear, and grow bigger. By the time it's done, there's a twenty-foot-tall fiery Alex stomping around after me and I'm barely avoiding each stomp of its size XXXXL flame-boots.

I'm getting exhausted now. The strain of using a school of enchanting I'm not familiar with, coupled with the running for my life, is taking its toll. I don't know how much longer I can keep up.

"You are weak and insignificant. Give in to the inevitable!" The huge fire giant Alex shrieks as it begins what is likely to be its last assault. It's all I can do to glimmer out of the way, and I look to Marin. He looks desperate and exhausted himself. He's been trying to get through the field of energy surrounding our circle of death. As I turn to face it one last time, I get an idea.

Marin shakes his head vigorously and making large X hand signals as he tries to convince me out of what I'm about to do. I drop my guard and stand still, waiting for the angrier, fire-filled version of myself to do its worst. As it charges me, I have to admit that there's a large portion of myself that agrees with Marin, but I'm willing to bet he (and me to some extent are wrong). If I'm right, I win. If not... well, I hope I win. The giant fire-Alex brings its fist down on me and right before the moment of contact, the whole being disappears into an explosion of steam and smoke that knocks me flat on my butt.

Once I'm recovered, I look around and breathe a sigh of relief when I see an angry Marin sprinting over to me.

"What in the name of all the gods were you thinking? You half-frightened me to death!"

"Well, good to see you care. Makes a girl feel all warm and gooey inside. I took a chance, and it paid off."

"Well, the next time you feel like taking a chance, please let it be sometime where I can do something other than just watch you get roasted alive?"

"Deal," I say with a smile.

He pulls me to my feet and grumbles at me a couple more times. He's more concerned about me than he's willing to admit. It's cute. I collect myself as the post near-death experience euphoria wears off and I see my flame-clone standing over by the gate. Marin and I walk over to it.

"Well, do I get a ribbon for playing at least?" I ask the creature.

"No, but you have done something no magi or other being for a thousand years or more has done. You have shown yourself worthy of the path".

"How? I lost." I ask. I'll admit, in hindsight, it was a crazy gamble. I'm not fully sure why I did it.

"I need explain nothing to you for now; you may yet die. Come, the Path awaits," the creature says.

Turning, it points a single finger up the treacherous mountain path. I go to walk and turn to Marin.

"I have to do this on my own, don't I?" I ask him.

"Afraid so my dear, Miss Winters. Don't worry, you'll be fine. I'm at least eighty-three percent sure you won't die."

"Thanks. I love those odds," I say with an eye-roll. To be fair, they're probably the best odds anyone has given me of surviving anything since I arrived in Aquillon. I take one last look at Marin before turning to face fire-Alex and start up the mountain. I'm not sure if I'm coming down this mountain or not, but the fact I've made it here at all has to count for something, but hey, who's keeping score, anyway?

14

Kyria

B y the position of the sun in the sky, Kyria reckoned it wasn't quite mid day, and she'd nearly broken the spell three times. Once when she accidentally let Ahrun wander away, and nearly off a cliff and two other times, she wanted to berate him for insufferably naïve comments. He couldn't see what she was seeing; how hopeless everything clearly was.

They had begun the slow hike down to the crater where Braga was lying. The great mountain range of spines that formed his back rose and down as he breathed, but he hadn't budged from the spot all day. As they neared the ridge of the crater, the surrounding jungle died off, leaving only the black tendrils leading back to the creature. Ahrun was the lucky one, Kyria thought to herself as they walked. He didn't have to see the creature, or the vile corruption its presence had wrought on the natural world around them.

From the edge of the pit, the black veins consumed the land around where Kyria and Ahrun walked. The vantage point earlier hadn't offered Kyria a clear picture of the situation; it was much worse.

The veins she had spotted were big ones, but like roots of a great evil tree, smaller ones shot off from the sides. As she neared the black lines, she stifled a scream. Each of the large veins pulsed, and she saw black ooze snaking its way through the vein and into the other smaller offshoots, like tributaries in the world's most polluted river. The smaller veins had attached themselves onto anything that lived. Trees, plants, and some small animals had become stuck to the veins and were being slowly drained of life until they were nothing but sad husks. Kyria made a mental note not to step on any of them and had her hands full steering Ahrun around them.

Ahrun was doing well despite not having his sight. He seemed more alert than normal, and Kyria remembered seeing Old Guard soldiers who had lost their sight in battle gain a renewed sense of hearing. He could anticipate most obstacles before she saw them, and he had even alerted her to hidden pitfalls in the ground, and even some smaller tendrils that hid below the soil. Annoyingly, he was doing the talking for both of them.

"I can hear the foul beast approaching, and I feel confident that we will emerge victorious, don't you?" he asked her as they walked. She stopped and waited for him to figure it out.

"Ah. The spell deprives you of speech. It seemed quiet there for a while."

Kyria rubbed her eyes and punched his arm, pulling him away from a nearby rock he was about to stumble into, which would have sent him careening into a tendril.

"Still, I feel good about our chances, and you are as always a beacon of positive energy. I feel much better just having you here, m'lady."

She rolled her eyes and made a gagging motion, mostly to herself, but she still smiled at him despite his overzealous naivete. For a thousand-year-old knight, he wasn't nearly as jaded as he should have been, but that wasn't a bad thing. She let him prattle on to himself for a while, but as they drew closer to the edge of the pit, she put her hand over his mouth. They came to the edge now and more of Braga was visible.

As she looked down into the crater, she realized why Alex had kept her from looking back when they were escaping his nest with the waystone. Braga wasn't something humans were meant to see.

His torso took up nearly the entire crater, which Kyria estimated to be about five hundred feet across, and three hundred down. The opening in the earth wasn't natural; it looked as though Braga had carved it out with great claws. All along the craterous opening where Braga lay, gashes and gouges lined the walls, and most looked fresh. The outer shell of the beast was all bone, ancient and massive. A ribcage of different bones covered its torso and a great skull covered what should have been a head, with tusks extending down from the edges of the skull. Beneath the bones, a writhing mass of muscle and skin moved back and forth, as if trapped in places by the bones. Claws the size of small horses gleamed in the sunlight and rested at the end of powerful limbs. Each of the great veins was connected to a distinct part of the creature's anatomy and the black ooze vomited from the end of each vein onto the writhing flesh. Beneath the eye sockets of the skull two glowing orbs shone like the lanterns of the underworld, illuminating the surrounding rocks. There was no head beyond that, only flesh and muscle coated in the slick, black fluid.

Kyria gazed on in horror, her mind shredding as she tried to comprehend what she was seeing. It was an unholy amalgam of other creatures, all absorbed into the greater essence. In Braga's world, there was only him. Nothing else could exist; he was the beast that would consume the sky, the world, and everything in between. He wasn't just the eater of light; he was the devourer of worlds. Kyria felt herself walking towards the edge of the pit, pulled toward Braga as a tide pulls water to a shore; powerless and unconcerned with free will. At the last moment, she felt Ahrun pull her down to the ground and grip her head.

"I don't know what you're seeing, but look at me. You don't want to go down there. There is nothing down there but death and darkness," Ahrun whispered to her as he held her down. She shook her head and struggled against him. She wanted to go to Braga. She needed to go to him. Nothing else mattered, only the hideous compulsion to go to the great beast and surrender herself to him. Ahrun spoke to her again, but his words seemed distant and faded, like the echo of sound as she crashed beneath the waves of madness.

"You are stronger than this, Kyria Killburn. I have seen you fight demons, fight the odds, fight the impossible, fight the world. You're the fighter your father raised, and you will fight this. You hear me? You did not come this far only to give yourself to a mad beast. Be better than this. I know you are. Rex did too."

The sound of her father's name hit her like a bolt of lightning. She sat up, gasping for breath, and realized she hadn't been breathing. She had been so drawn into the creature's pull she had stopped. She looked at Ahrun and hugged him tightly, between hyperventilated breaths. After a thousand more deep inhales, she finally steadied herself. She clasped her hand tightly on Ahrun's shoulder and he seemed to understand her meaning.

"Think nothing of it. You would have done the same for me. Now perhaps it would be better to wait for night. Even if the creature will not leave its lair, it might sleep. If nothing else, the darkness will give us some cover. Is there a passable way down?"

Kyria nodded and made a circular pattern on the palm of Ahrun's hand. He contemplated it for a moment and then responded. "There is a path down the side of the lair in a spiral?"

Kyria nodded again. She did at least remember that much from her near brain-washing moment earlier. It was a narrow path, but wide enough for them, and Braga faced away from the path for the moment. Kyria poked one eye over the edge and took in a few more details, while not lingering her gaze on Braga. She was doubtful Ahrun could snap her out of Braga's intoxicating effect twice. His pull was powerful, and she still felt vulnerable to it.

They waited there in silence for a long time before the sun settled on the eastern horizon. There were no stars tonight, but Kyria idly wondered if the stars would even dare to shine on such a creature, for fear he might eat them too. There was a great crash, and the earth thundered beneath them. Kyria looked over top of the edge and saw that Braga had lowered his head and closed his eyes for the moment.

Kyria pulled on Ahrun's sleeve and they stood up. She guided him safely around the edge of the crater for a long while until they reached the path. Kyria noted more details as she walked. This nest was an ancient one. Nothing grew from the rocks around the pit, but she could tell by looking at the stone that it had been that way for a long time. Every few feet she glanced back towards Ahrun to make sure he hadn't fallen off, although she'd probably hear that.

It was an eternity to the bottom, but they finally arrived. There was little space to maneuver here as Braga's body took up most of the room. Kyria could barely breathe so close to the creature and being this close she got a terrifying view of the flesh of Braga beneath his massive Exo-skeleton. Braga's body moved like a million different pieces confined by the bony cage. It seemed like everything he had ever devoured had become part of him, trapped forever within his essence.

Kyria tried to focus on her footing as she and Ahrun made their way towards the front of the creature. There had been no sign of blood at the creature's rear, so Kyria figured (with a sinking feeling) that Braga kept the blood of the ancient ones in front of him for easy access and protection. They would have been dead a hundred times over if not for Fogu's spell. Braga's one weakness was that he thought his senses were prefect and believed nothing would slip by him. It amused Kyria that even as ancient and powerful a creature as Braga was, he had become arrogant. She would make him pay for that mistake.

Reaching the front of Braga, Kyria looked up and saw that he was asleep. The great skull moved up and down as he breathed, but Kyria tried not to look too closely at what was behind it. At the end of Braga's neck, the flesh stopped and a swirling ball of black energy floated listlessly inside the skull. It radiated pure malice and hatred. The air surrounding the skull was thick and made it difficult to breathe. Sitting in two small pools before each of Braga's tusks, Kyria saw the blood. She tugged on Ahrun's tunic and he stopped walking. She made a motion in his palm for him to stand down.

As Kyria approached the pools, she saw it wasn't just blood. The liquid was red, but that's pretty much where its similarities to blood ended. The red fluid moved about the pool, as if of its own volition. There was a gleaming glow that danced across the surface of each pool, and little waves of it rippled across the surface even though there was no wind to push it around. Kyria knelt down and drew a vial out of her pack. She placed the vial in the pool and it quickly filled up. A little of the blood splashed up on her hand, which tingled with energy. She felt a brief surge within her and for a moment; her nerves relaxed, and she felt calm, but then the moment passed. She capped the vial and walked back to where Ahrun was.

All around the edge of the nest, a long series of stone huts were carved into the wall. They were simple and rudimentary, but more than that, they were familiar. Kyria knew she had seen them before, and it took her only a moment to realize where, but it was already too late. She should have paid closer attention, should have been more cautious. She was the one with the eyes; this was her job, and she failed.

Kyria felt a knot of dread and panic twisting in her stomach as she looked over to Ahrun and saw the cultist standing behind him. Covered in black tar (or perhaps whatever vile substance ran through Braga's veins) the villager was standing silent, covered in scars and a terrible animal skull mask. Kyria saw the likeness now. The cultist raised a wicked-looking knife and prepared to strike Ahrun. There was no time, and Kyria was out of options. Even if she could have thrown a knife, Ahrun would be dead long before the knife found its target. She had no choice.

"Ahrun, look out behind ya!" she shouted at him. Her voice was a keen blade cutting through the unholy silence of the tainted ground around her. Even if Braga hadn't heard her, the spell wore off as soon as the words left Kyria's lips. It felt like a warm blanket slipping off of her, and she felt exposed. Ahrun knew the jig was up and opened his eyes, turning to meet the villager with his sword.

From the nostril holes of his skull, Braga sniffed the air and the same deep howl came from his mouth. Kyria remembered the unearthly sound; she had heard it before in the nest with Alex and the waystone. It chilled her just as much now as it had then, and Kyria turned to flee back to where Ahrun waited. All at once Braga shot to his feet and brought his great claw swiping across the end of the pit, crushing huts and stones as though they were made of thin paper. Each spike on the end of Braga's claw would have been enough to skewer three men in one motion, but when combined with the other four it was a living god of death, and Kyria and Ahrun narrowly ducked beneath it and the ensuing avalanche of rocks from the cliff above them.

"Pilfering thieves!" Braga screamed.

Kyria hadn't even considered the notion that he might have been able to speak. His voice was like his howl; a terrible sound of grating bones and shrill hisses that no human's ears should ever have heard. Kyria trembled at each word and ducked down beneath another swipe of Braga's claw.

"Did you think I had forgotten? I will not forgive this intrusion, and there will be a great pleasure as I digest you slowly. You will never leave this place!" Braga's blind eyes hunted about, and Kyria shivered as the glow of them passed over her. It wouldn't take Braga long to work out where they were hiding.

"Sorry I blew our cover, but I figured ya wouldn't mind," Kyria said to Ahrun.

"Decidedly not. I owe you my life once again, but that will have to wait. We need to be gone, and soon. My eyes are still adjusting. Do you see any viable exits?"

Kyria scanned the pit again. Braga was still sniffing around and each time he did, he got a little closer. She was about to give up looking when her eyes barely made out the opening in the wall. One of Braga's claws had opened up a sliver of a hole in the wall on the far end of the pit. It was impossible to see whether it led anywhere, but going back up the path they came down was out. It seemed a lethal run to cross the bottom of the pit, but it also seemed to be their only option. Braga was getting closer now, and he would be on them in moments.

"Nae time ta explain, just follow me an' don't get yerself killed."

"Sounds like a plan," Ahrun said with a grin.

Kyria stood up and waited. Every time Braga passed there was a momentary gap in his legs, and it would be just wide enough to pass through. She waited until the moment before Braga sniffed again.

"Now!" she said as she exploded into a sprint across the pit. Ahrun followed, just as fast, but he stumbled as he ran, having not adjusted to his eyesight. There was torchlight in the huts now, and dozens of cultists were making their way down rope ladders to join the hunt. Kyria jumped and cleared the gap in Braga's legs, and Ahrun followed closely just before they closed. Braga howled again and swiped across the pit, destroying more huts and slicing cultists that in the wrong place in half. He turned his massive body and faced the opening, giving the air one final sniff.

Kyria made it into the hole and turned to see Ahrun running towards her. She heard Braga before she saw it.

"Goodbye insignificant insect."

Braga opened the great jaws of his outer skull and a spine of bone, sharpened to a point, oozed its way out of the coiling darkness and flew forward. Kyria reached out and pulled Ahrun in, but she felt the impact before she saw it. Looking down, she saw Ahrun gripping the end of the bone spear, which had punctured his lower abdomen. Blood bubbled up from Ahrun's mouth and Kyria pulled him into the tunnel.

"So that's where you've gone. Well, if I can't have you, then you will die in a tomb of stone, and my face is the last thing you will ever see," Braga said, leering at Kyria who shouted several choice phrases at him in defiance. Bringing his claw into a fist, Braga slammed the wall above the hole and rocks came tumbling down, burying Kyria and Ahrun in darkness. Braga's chilling laughter was all Kyria heard as the last stone suffocated the moonlight and then she was alone, holding her dying friend as the world tumbled into darkness.

15

Alex

My evil fire twin and I have been hiking for what feels like forever before it stops at an overlook. I don't really have any frame of reference for what's about to happen, and really, what do you say to your evil fire clone? To be fair, I'm not sure she's evil.

We're stopped at a small overlook which points away from the volcano and towards the surrounding valley. It's easier to get a sense of what this place looks like from up here. Just like the plateau Sanctum was on, this one seems sheltered from the rest of the world. Hazy energy fills the air near the boundaries where encroaching jungle tries to sneak in and the entire plane is covered in a dome. Above us, the stars are hardly visible through thick clouds that cover nearly every inch of the sky.

I turn back to my fire-clone and ask, "so what am I supposed to call you?"

"What I am has no bearing on our task. Why do you want to know?"

"Seems awkward to go on a soul-searching, death-defying trial of epic proportions with a complete stranger, doesn't it? I'm Alex

Winters," I say, extending my hand for a handshake. I don't think I'm on hugging terms with fire-me just yet.

"I know who you are," the being says. If it had eyes, I think they'd be rolling at me. "If you must know a name, you may call me Andrassela."

"Alright, Andrassela, so what's the first test?"

"You ask a lot of questions. A lot more than the last Seeker did."

"Well, how'd that work out for him?"

Andrassela doesn't respond and seems to concede the point. "I was just giving you a break. You humans are weak, and I figured you would need it."

"That was nice of you, but I guess we can keep going..." I trail off when I see a glimmer of something in the corner of my eye. On a ledge below the platform we're standing on, I see a plump red gem shining in the moonlight. The ledge is below us and to the left, but there seems to be a simple path down to it. Andrassela notices my delay and stops.

"You see the gem?"

"I do."

"Good, if you hadn't seen it we would stop here. This is the first test. Retrieve the gem for me," Andrassela says.

"Can't you just get it yourself? Seems like a fairly mundane test."

"Do not question me, human. Get the gem. Without it, we cannot channel your inner potential."

"Fine," I say. I put my stuff down and make my way over to the edge of the overlook. The ledge the gem is balanced on is thin, barely the width of the stone, but sharp rocks jutting out of the side of the mountain form a stepping-stone path down to it. Still, one bad step and I'll be base-jumping without a bungee cord. Wait. I'm an idiot. I look at the lowest stone, just below the ledge, and focus on it. It shouldn't be hard to glimmer there.

I open my eyes and I'm still standing here. Andrassela has an amused look on her face.

"Thought it would be that easy, magus? The arrogance of your kind never changes. You will find your powers impotent on the Path. If you are nothing without them, you are nothing with them, and only the worthy will claim what lies at the heart of the Path."

"You could have just said so..." I say, grumbling. I lower myself onto the first stone step. I'm standing on it and it doesn't take my hands long to find crevices to grip onto. Lowering myself down, I sit on the edge of the step and place one foot gingerly on the next. There's more of a gap than I'd like there to be and I have to overextend to get both feet on the lower step. I sit on the next step and lower my foot again, and after nearly slipping twice, I'm now on the lower step, parallel with the ledge.

I must have misjudged the distance because it's at least six feet between me and the ledge where the jewel rests, and I've barely got room enough to keep my footing, much less make a running jump to catch the ledge. Once I'm there, there's not even room to pull myself up, or any obvious way of getting back on to the step I'm on. I look up at the overlook where Andrassela is watching me.

"So, this seems like a terrible idea. I'm no physics major, but I don't really see a way I'm getting across without magic."

"Figure it out. If this matters to you, you will do what it takes! No more hesitation." I can hear the urgency in her voice and I feel the call to action rising in my gut, but I take a moment and consider. I need whatever is at the end of this path, but I'm not going to throw my life away to get it.

"Nope. Hard pass. I'm coming back up. There has to be another way." I turn and jump, pulling myself up step by step until I'm back on the overlook.

"You have failed, human. Go home."

"I didn't fail," I say definitely, "the test was impossible. It was a bad test, and I chose not to take part. We call it opting out where I'm from."

"You're not listening. You will go no further on my mountain," Andrasella says, a flash of anger in her voice.

"I will go as far as I want, but I'm not quitting just because you said so. Now take me to the next test!"

Andrasella doesn't seem happy, but she relents. "Very well, human. I was trying to save you. From here on, there will be no turning back, and you will wish you had heeded my advice. Let us proceed."

We begin up the trail again, slowly circling our way to the top of the mountain. Andrasella doesn't seem to have anything else to say to me, so I just watch the mountain as we walk. The path is growing more narrow and the footing more tenuous. I hadn't noticed it until now, but my fire-clone isn't walking; she floats an inch above the ground. After an hour of silent marching, we arrive at the entrance to a cave.

The cave's opening isn't much over three feet across, but runs nearly double my height to the top. It looks as though it may have been a natural fissure at one point, but the edges are carved and smoothed to form an ornate lining. Runes cover the border of the opening; the same ones carved into the plateau behind me. They are beautiful and alien, and even with my newly gained linguistic powers (thanks magi powers, you rock) I can't make out what these say.

"Through this cave lies the next trial, but you will have to go alone. I hope to see you on the other side, but there is no return from this. Once you enter, you will leave victorious or you will not leave at all," Andrasella says. I nod and she shimmers before finally disappearing altogether in a puff of steam and smoke. I hope to see me on the other side too buddy, I really do. Steeling my nerves one last time, I walk past the threshold of the cave and into the gloom beyond.

As soon as my foot clears the doorway, the sound of stone grinding fills the cave and I turn to see the door rising quickly from the floor. Even if I had wanted to leave the door is too quick. Before I know it, my eyes are adjusting to the shadows of the cave.

From the narrow entrance, the path widens to match the wider frame of the surrounding tunnel. After a few moments, the same alien runes glow along the sides of the cave and I see lines of red energy light up either side of the tunnel. It's a little obvious, but I think I've found the Path of Flame. The runes and the lines lead me through the tunnel and I if I hadn't looked up a moment ago, I would have run smack into the mirror.

Stepping back to make sure I'm not suffering the effects of a concussion, I check to make sure I'm really seeing this. Yup, I am. Embedded in the rocks in front of me is a full size mirror. It's wedged into the rock too perfectly, and not at all naturally, as if the mirror was here long before the mountain, and the rocks had grown around it. It's also an unusually clean mirror; there isn't a spot on this thing. Not one blemish from top to bottom. It is, in all other respects, just a mirror. Well, that's until my image moves independently of me.

I watch my mirror image move around the other side of the mirror, watching me. It's deeply creepy. There's something about this version of me that's not right. It looks enough like me, and it's not on fire like the last clone of myself I bumped into, but this isn't me. I don't know how I know, but I know. It gives me a wicked smile and continues to pace.

Without further warning, the walls of the cavern beyond the mirror burst and magma floods the chamber. I see myself pull a knife from a nearby rock and wait. I don't like where this is headed. Suddenly, an image of Marin appears standing next to my clone. My clone grabs Marin and plunges the knife deep into his heart and drops his body in the magma. My stomach is churning watching this play out, but as Marin's body disappears in the magma, I see evil-Alex walk through a newly appeared portal and escape the cave before the lava fills the chamber. I've got a bad, bad feeling that I just watched the world's most messed up how-to manual.

I'm quietly hoping that I was wrong when I see the knife appear on the same rock, and soon after the lava fills the room from fissures in the wall. This time, though, I feel it. The heat radiates around me and I feel my skin burning. A small bubble of it nearly catches my boot as the island I'm on becomes smaller and smaller. On queue, Marin appears standing in front of me.

"No! I'm not doing it. Burn me if you like, but I'm not doing... that!" I yell to no one in particular. There is no response from the lava, except to keep filling the room at a more alarming pace. I try to wake up Marin, shaking him and slapping his face. There's a glazed over look on his face, and nothing, not me or the heat, is getting him to wake up.

The lava is nearly on us now, and I don't know what to do. I see evil-Alex smiling her wicked smile at me through the mirror, but I don't budge. "Do it" she mouths to me, but I don't move a muscle. If it weren't for the most intense heat I've ever felt, there would be tears in my eyes, but I also don't want to give whatever sick entity is playing this game the satisfaction. Closing my eyes, I take a deep breath.

"If this is how you measure worthiness, then I'm not worthy," I yell, and hurl the knife towards the mirror with all the force I can muster. I'm shaking and furious and terrified, but I'm not doing this. I'm done playing this thing's games. I've said my peace and accepted my fate.

The knife flies across the room and smashed into the mirror which cracks rather easily, and a flood of water fills the cave, dousing the lava and consuming me in steam. I feel myself trip over, but pleasantly enough, I don't fall into lava, or onto burning hot rocks. I look around and stand up. I'm on the other side of the mirror now, or at least I think I am. The glass is back to its original form - pristine, and I see evil-Alex smiling at me, but it looks more normal. She vanishes and I see Marin standing behind me, looking very confused.

"Where am I?" he asks before I wrestle him into a bear hug.

"Oh my God, I'm glad I didn't stab you," is all I can say, which I imagine is confusing without context, but I don't care. I'm thrilled I didn't stab him.

"I'm going to put the myriad of questions I have on hold and suggest that maybe we get out of the scary cave?" he says.

"No argument here."

We make our way out of the cave, which lets out onto another overlook, but this time we're inside the caldera of the volcano. The platform extends maybe fifty feet over the volcano's caldera from the cave's exit. The heat rising from below us makes it hard to concentrate on anything, but I take a moment to take in my surroundings. I'd rather not take a step onto something that looks like a rock only to plummet to my fiery doom below.

I look over the platform and it's a straight drop to the bubbling pit of fire below. I lean back with a gulp and focus on the less frightening details of my surroundings. All around the platform, large stone pillars reach for the sky. They look vaguely Egyptian and not like any architecture I've seen in Aquillon thus-far, but I'm not entirely sure I'm still on Aquillon, so there's that. From the top of each pillar (there are ten- I counted) a hand reaches out to the night sky above, and a small head of flame rolls around in the palm of each hand. More of the runes cover the ground beneath each of the pillars. I look to Marin.

"Any clue what the next step is?" I ask him.

He responds, but a familiar hissing sound interrupts him, and I see Andrasella forming in the center of the platform.

"Fear not, human, I have not abandoned you, yet," Andrasella says with a chittering laugh of smoke and steam.

"Thanks. Neat party trick in the cave back there. Care to explain?" I ask.

"All in good time. This way," she says as she points to the first pillar.

I follow her and Marin tags along. The first pillar we stop at is carved with the relief of a well on it. "Touch each of these shrines and we will see if you are worthy. I hope to see you again, but I'm not holding my breath."

"Great vote of confidence as usual," I say, but Andrasella is gone already into her usual screen of smoke and steam. I look back at Marin. "How about your books? Any insight into any of this?"

"Well, I can tell you that you're already farther than anyone from the Eastern Watch ever made it, so bravo to that, Alex," Marin says.

"Well, I guess here goes nothing," I say as I press my hand against the pillar.

Instantly the world goes black and I open my eyes and I'm somewhere else. Looking around, I'm in an alleyway in a city I've never been in. I see a man standing in front of me, leaning against a brick wall. He's dressed in a tunic and a wide-brimmed hat and looks up at me.

"So, how about it, kid? You want to go home?" As he asks I see my trailer in the woods come into focus behind him. I can't remember where I've been or how I got here. I want to go home. I've been away from home for a long time and I'd like to go back, but I don't think that's the answer he's looking for.

"No, I still have work to do, I need to get back." As soon as I speak the mage fades and I'm back on the platform. The pillar crumbles and falls into the volcano and nearly takes me with it. A small portion of the platform disappears. I will assume they don't remove part of the platform for passing a test.

"Well, I take it that could have gone better?" Marin asks, looking at the missing platform with a hint of concern on his face.

"Not so much. I'm hoping there's a low-cut score for this test."

"On to the next one?"

"I don't see any other choice," I say.

Walking over to the next pillar, I make a note to pay closer attention to it this time before I go touching it. This one has similar features, but the image carved into it is different. This one depicts a kneeling man before a crowd. The image is faded and worn, but I can make out the details on his face; there's a look of peace and contentment. I'm not sure how much that helps me. I extend my hand and touch the pillar.

This time I'm in a courtroom, or what looks like one, anyway. I'm standing in a box and there are angry people around me. An older woman in white robes approaches me.

"Do you believe he is guilty?" she asks, pointing towards a man sitting a ways away from me. He seems run down and defeated. Everyone in the court seems to think he's done something, because they're peppering the poor guy with some vile insults. As I look at him longer and anger boils in my chest, I try to focus. Something's wrong.

"No, he's not."

Howls of outrage erupt across the courtroom and I'm zapped back to the platform in the volcano. This time, the pillar doesn't move and Marin and I breathe a sigh of relief. I may not understand what I'm being tested on, but at least I understand the mechanics of the game. I go through each test one by one until I reach the last one. Each is a situation as random as the one before it. Once I have to run a race or sit, and another time I'm given the chance to give my money to a homeless man or a rich guy who needed lunch (I pick the homeless dude and failed so I don't have much to go on as far as what makes up a pass or a fail).

I've passed four and failed five, so the platform is looking like swiss cheese and Marin is standing on a small sliver somewhere near me, cheering me on. I don't really know what happens if I don't have a perfect score, but that ship definitely sailed a while ago so I'm just hoping that a fifty percent is good enough for a pass to whatever the next phase of this Path is. I work my way over to the last pillar, watching my footwork as I go, and look at it.

Like the rest, the image on it is obscure. I see a shattered chain on the ground. Not much to go on, so I look at Marin one final time. "Well, if this doesn't go so well…"

"It's going to be great," Marin says with a grin and a thumbs up. "Besides, I'd take dying in a fiery volcano over another hundred years with those stuffy old codgers. You've made my life more interesting, Winters."

"One of these days you're going to have to tell me why you bothered coming with me in the first place," I say with a nervous laugh.

When I first arrived at Sanctum, he just sort of befriended me, but I wasn't overflowing with friends or friendly faces, so I never really questioned it. I figure if he was up to no good, he would have split long before now. I remember my mother. My conversation with her seems like ten lifetimes ago. I still feel bad about how I left things. Here's hoping I get to see her again, if only to get some closure.

I reach out and press the pillar and touch it, and I'm standing in a dark void. I'm floating in mid-air (assuming I'm in air; I could float in Jello for all I know). I see a hooded figure approaching me and he stops and extends both arms. Two floating images appear and as they come into focus, I gasp.

On the left, I see my friends. Ahrun, Kyria, Marin, Sal, and others engaged in an epic battle with the Court. A great army surges around them and noble men and women are fighting against demons and Lord and Ladies of the Court in all out anarchy and chaos. I watch the tide of the battle turn and the humans fall. My eyes water as one by one my friends are cut down until it's just Ahrun and Kyria on their knees staring defiantly at someone. The crowd of victorious demons clears and the Lord of Long Shadows strides out before them. His black mane is flowing in the wind and the sun radiates off his flawless golden armor. He exchanges some words with them, and then he brings his scythe to their heads and brings down the killing blow. I know it's not real, but I collapse to my knees, sobbing hysterically.

The figure now gestures to his left and I see a new image. All of my friends are alive, but I can see they're not ok. They mill about a rain-drowned village as demons ride by them on horses. They all have familiar brands and the pride is harassing the villagers. As Ahrun and Kyria and Marin wander by me, they look at. Their eyes are downcast and they seem like broken shells of themselves. In the center of the village I see the Lord of Long Shadows surveying the scene with a grim smile on his face. Without warning, both images vanish and the old man is looking at me. He seems familiar, but I can't place it.

"Choose," he says brusquely.

"No, there has to be another option, another way."

"There is no other way this can end. Choose."

"There is no choice at all. I lose both ways."

"A girl is never without choice. Now choose!"

Without waiting to think, I point to the left. Neither option is good, but I have to choose one. I'm devastated, sobbing mess as I return to the platform and Marin catches me.

"What happened?" he asks, a tone of genuine concern in his voice.

I can't form the words to talk about it, so I just look up at the pillar.

The pillar is thankfully intact and I see the balls of flame work their way down onto the platform and combine to form an enormous bonfire out of which Andrasella walks. She is clapping quietly.

"Why?" I ask. "Why make me go through that?"

"Come and see," is all Andrasella says. She extends her arm and a stone bridge rises from the depths of the caldera and connects with a stone platform hanging in the air in the center of the chasm. It wasn't there a moment ago, so I'm assuming this is part of the test. She walks onto it and Marin helps me to my feet so I can continue. We work our way across the bridge in silence, and I'm grateful he doesn't press me for more details on what I saw. I couldn't talk about it if I wanted to. We finally arrive at the center of the caldera and the bridge falls away, leaving us on the stone platform in the center. Andrasella turns to me.

"I commend you on making it this far. You are the first of your kind to do so, but then again, you are the first of your kind. But now we will see if this was all for naught. Now comes the true test. Ready yourself."

16

Kyria

A t first the only sound Kyria heard was the shallow breathing of Ahrun who was slumped over in her arms. She felt the end of the bone spear and she was careful about how she moved. Ahrun wasn't complaining, but every time the spear moved even a little, his entire body shuddered. The cave in prevented her from seeing him, but he felt weak and cold sweat drenched his face. She needed to act, and fast, or her friend would be dead.

The cave opening wasn't huge and had gotten even smaller thanks to the avalanche caused by Braga. For a while Kyria heard chanting and howling outside, but now it was silent. She needed to find a way out, but she couldn't move Ahrun, and she definitely wasn't leaving him there alone.

After a while of listening and stroking Ahrun's head to keep him calm, Kyria heard something else. Water. It was a faint sound; barely distinguishable from the ambient noise of the cave, but somewhere deeper in the cave system, there was a trickle of water. One of the first lessons her father had taught her about survival in the wild was that if you were lost, find water. Water always flowed from somewhere, and at least that much of a sense of direction was better than nothing.

"Alright, Ahrun, how do ya feel about a quick jaunt down the cave?"

He coughed and his voice was weak and broken as he replied. "I can't think of a lovelier way to spend an evening."

"Well then, let's get up an' movin'. Can't let ya lollygag about all day. It's nae good for ya." Kyria fought back tears and her voice cracked as she spoke, but she kept the emotion out of her words. She had seen dying men before, and the more the people around them acknowledged their condition, the faster they went. If she could just get to some light, she could form a plan. Ahrun was not dying on her; she wouldn't allow it. She had lost enough people for two lifetimes.

Kyria stood slowly, cautious about the unseen ceiling, but to her surprise, she could stand to her full height. She reached down and grabbed Ahrun's arm and helped him up. He spasmed in pain as he stood, but said nothing. Reaching around the other side of him, Kyria felt the end of the spear in his lower abdomen and was relieved it had broken off short when Ahrun had fallen into the cave as it collapsed. Only the front of the spear was lodged in him, but that was still enough to go all the way through. Kyria had some limited medical knowledge from treating Old Guard soldiers and she knew that if the spear had nicked an artery or vital organ, Ahrun would already be dead, so he had that going for him. Still, by the sound of his breathing, he didn't have long.

Kyria walked gingerly, leading Ahrun down the path. It sloped down gently, but she had to guide him around more than a few rocks and holes in the floor. It was torturously slow going, and they both kept silent as they went. After a while of walking, Kyria felt the wall, and it seemed to split into a fork. She held her breath and listened as closely as she could for the water. Nothing at first, and she silently cursed. If she had lost the sound, they might wander for hours in this night-filled tunnel. She nearly walked down the path to the right before she heard the slightest sound of water running over stones. It was still barely a sound, but it was closer, and it came from the left.

She slowly directed Ahrun to the left, and they ambled on for a while in darkness. Some time later (it was impossible to judge time in the cave - it may well have been morning by now) the narrow tunnel opened up into a wider chamber, and torchlight flooded the end. It thrilled Kyria to see again, but torchlight meant people, and people in this region of the world meant trouble. Kyria pushed Ahrun against a wall and crouched down, peering cautiously out of the tunnel's opening.

The shaft opened out into a vast chamber, with rounded, high ceilings. Small dwellings of thatch and mud ringed the outer edge with a raised platform in the center. Torches burned on the wall and several larger tunnels opened on the far wall. All around the cave's walls there were primitive drawings of tiny figures worshipping Braga, and Kyria listened. It didn't seem like anybody was home, but she wasn't taking any chances. Looking around her, she found a broad stone and hurled it to the center of the cave. It bounced off another rock with a loud, echoing sound that filled the chamber. After several moments and no madmen charging her, Kyria led Ahrun into the chamber and helped him lie down on the center platform.

She looked down and smiled at him, and he tried to return the smile. His breathing was weaker now, and Kyria could see him slipping, even though he fought it.

"I have treasured your friendship, Kyria the Generous. I fear this may be my final..."

Kyria cut him off. "Don't ya say it. Don't ya even think it ya eegit. Yer not goin' anywhere without me, and yer certainly not dyin' in this dank cave."

"I am grateful for your optimism, but I have seen more than my share of this world, and if I die knowing I helped defeat the Court and

127

help you, it will not have been a life wasted, I think."

"Gods yer wordy, for a dyin' man. Now shut up so I can think." She turned away from him to hide her tears. Think girl, think. It took her a moment, but the thought came to her. She rifled through her bag for a moment before producing the vial of blood. Ahrun saw her and shook his head.

"No, Kyria… you can't. Too much rests on this blood making it back to the Mistress of Scales. I'm not worth it. Besides, we don't even know what that would do. It might not heal me, and then it would have been wasted."

They were all good points, but Kyria wasn't listening. She knew what he was saying was right. There were bigger things at stake here than one life. But in that moment, she remembered her father, and she remembered Thistle, and she remembered every other brave soul taken before their time. Enough she silently decided. She had lost enough, and would lose no more. She turned back and opened the vial, but Ahrun pushed her hand aside.

"I know what you're trying to do, but I can't let you do it. My life isn't worth it."

"But it is worth it, ta me," Kyria said, pleading with tears streaming down her face. She could no longer be strong, and she couldn't hold her emotions back any longer.

"Live well, Kyria Killburn," Ahrun said weakly.

Kyria turned away for a moment and collected herself. She quickly poured the vial into her mouth. It tingled, and she felt its power for a moment, but she was careful not to swallow any. She turned back, grabbing Ahrun and pulled him into a kiss. She pressed her lips tightly against his and even in his condition; he seemed surprised, but relaxed and returned the kiss. Before he could stop it, however, he felt warm liquid flowing from her mouth to his, and down his throat. It was like liquid fire, but as it passed down his throat and into his stomach, his entire body tingled. He felt more and more revitalized, and he reached down and pulled the spear from his gut.

Kyria sat back and watched in amazement as the gaping hole from the spear-wound not only didn't bleed, but it bubbled and steam and slowly the flesh and sinew worked its way back together, until all that remained was a hole in Ahrun's shirt. She looked at his face, which seemed healthier now; color had returned to his cheeks and his eyes were their old vibrant selves. Ahrun at up and looked around. There was still a hint of a glow inside his skin as the last of the blood's magic faded and he was back to normal.

"You shouldn't have done that!" Ahrun said in almost a yell.

"Yer welcome, ya eegit."

Ahrun gritted his teeth and took a deep breath. "I thank you for what you did, but I fear it may come back to bite us. Now about your method of…"

Kyria cut him off. "If ya ever tell so much as a soul about this, I'll make ya wish ya had let Braga gulp ya up in his great gullet," Kyria said, trying to keep her cheeks from burning. Now that the moment of desperation had passed, she was having trouble distinguishing her desperate attempt to save her friend from an actual kiss, but the more she thought about it, the hazier the lines got and the redder her face became. She turned away from Ahrun and tried to compose herself.

"I don't know if the cost of my life is worth it, but you have my thanks. I won't utter a sound of it to a soul," Ahrun said.

"An' wipe that great galootin' eegit grin off yer face!"

"Oh, right," Ahrun said, attempting to remain stony-faced and serious. Kyria began focusing on the tunnels on the far wall. She didn't have time to have lingering thoughts about a kiss. Nae girl, it wasn't even a kiss, she tried to tell herself. She got up and began inspecting the two tunnels before she had time to worry about whether she believed herself.

Both tunnels seemed identical in most respects, but it quickly became clear from moving torchlight and the echo of people speaking, which one they should go down. Kyria gathered her pack and supplies and hurried down the tunnel to the left, with Ahrun following her.

The tunnel sloped upwards toward a dim light, which Kyria desperately hoped was sunshine. The angle of the tunnel was gentle at first, but grew more steep as they walked. By the time the tunnel ended, Kyria and Ahrun were gripping small divots and stalagmites just to keep from tumbling backwards into darkness. With one last pull, Kyria launched herself out of the cave and into an ocean of sunlight.

It took a long time for Kyria's eyes to adjust to the dazzling light around her, but the world slowly came back into view. Ahrun was standing beside her, trying to catch his breath, and she took in her surroundings.

They were standing just outside the entrance to a thick section of jungle and it seemed Braga's nest was behind them, hidden by a large hill. Just clearing to top ridges of the trees Kyria could see Braga's spines rising and falling and she shuddered just looking at them, despite the heat.

"So, what now?" She asked Ahrun.

"Well, we've spoiled the enchantment that hides out scent, and used all the blood to avoid my untimely demise, and we can't go back to the dragon empty handed. I suppose we could..."

Ahrun never got to finish his statement as a shrill scream from the top of the hill interrupted him. Kyria turned and saw one of Braga's mad tribe, a young woman with black hair and bone-white skin, pointing and shrieking at them. There was an explosion of motion over the hill as cultists, hidden in the trees, surged towards them. The earth shook and Kyria looked at Braga's spines, which rose high over the trees as he came crashing over the hilltop. His blind eyes scanned the landscape as he sniffed, but it only took him moments to find them.

"Good. I'm glad you pestilent little fleas escaped. I was hoping for another chance to kill you." The hillside exploded as Braga brought his immense body over the top, crushing trees and cultists alike. His legs crashed down close to where Kyria and Ahrun were standing, and they turned and began sprinting away. It didn't seem likely that they could outrun the tribe of maniacs chasing them, much less Braga, but it didn't stop Kyria from trying. Her legs thundered over the plain and into the jungle with Ahrun on her heels.

Kyria burst through the undergrowth, her speed spurred on by the howling of Braga. The unholy beast tore up the countryside as he ran towards them, his great claws severing trees and uprooting entire sections of the jungle in single swipes. Each one got closer to them as they ran, ducking under spears and knives thrown at them by the madmen who still pursued them. Kyria ran until she couldn't feel her legs anymore, and then kept running, but finally her luck ran out. She nearly ran into a tall palm that blocked her path, and Ahrun stopped short next to her.

They turned to face the onslaught of madness and death from the exploding jungle behind them, and Kyria gripped her sword in one hand, and subconsciously gripped Ahrun's hand in the other, bracing for what she knew was coming.

Instead, there was a flurry of wind like a miniature hurricane overhead, followed by a blast of intense heat. The surrounding plants withered and Kyria felt herself losing consciousness. She knew this heat. It couldn't be...

"Back you sycophants and leeches, back!" Roared the Mistress of Scale overhead, following her proclamation with another fiery inferno. Some tribesman ran, but others screamed wild defiance at the dragon, only to be met with an unfortunate, sizzling end. Braga howled and swiped at his airborne foe, but she easily avoided his attacks. He even launched a wave of bone-spears from his mouth, but she melted them with another torrent of flame. Deciding he was outmatched for the moment, Braga retreated over the hilltop, screaming wildly at the dragon.

"Get on, food," the dragon commanded, lowering a wing.

Kyria and Ahrun didn't wait for a second invitation and climbed aboard the great creature's back. Once they were atop her, gripping onto horns, scales, or anything else they could find to hold, the dragon launched herself into the air and took flight. Even though they had risen from the jaws of death, Kyria maintained her iron grip on Ahrun's hand, as Braga, the pit, and everything else about the nightmare jungle quickly became a fading memory as they rose above the clouds.

17

Alex

By the time I've dodged the third lava monster's strike, I'm wondering what kind of person the Path of flame is looking for, and whether this is all just some ruse to lure perfectly nice magi (ok, there aren't that many of those, but bear with me) to their deaths. This thought is promptly cut short by another blast of lava from the fourth magma beast, and I'm running for my life again.

Moments after we arrived on the platform, the stone bridge fell away and Adrasella just said, "ready yourself". That was only moments before a gigantic hole opened in the center of the floating platform and four lava monsters rose out of it and started trying to barbeque Marin and me. I haven't made much progress figuring out what I'm supposed to do because of the aforementioned fire monsters trying to kill or eat me.

The four creatures look something like floating scarecrows. Well, if scarecrows were made of molten stone, oozing fire, and flames anyway. They don't have eyes, but it doesn't stop them from throwing very well-timed and accurate fireballs at me. Marin's not doing much better; he's been on the run for minutes now, glimmering in and out (his magic works just fine up here, go figure). Every once in a while, he finds time to fire a beam of ice magic back at one of the monsters, but mostly he's just running.

And there's the hole. What started as a hole the size of a plump tree trunk has been slowly expanding by the minute to its present size, which is somewhere between a Volkswagen Beetle and a small elephant. I can't really see it growing, but every time I check on it (between close brushes with a fiery demise) it's a little big, bigger. I can't really worry about that because the first fire-beast is readying an attack.

I jump backwards, the flame narrowly singes my cloak, and I re-balance just in time to avoid plummeting backwards into the volcano. I glance over at Marin, who's hiding behind a very thick wall of ice he's incanted out of the ground.

"What's the play here, Alex?"

"Your guess is," I side-step another fireball, "as good as mine, buddy. My magic isn't working right now."

"Well, I'm assuming this," he glimmers across the platform, "rapidly growing hole has something to do with something. Your little friend didn't warn you about this?"

"I'm afraid she forgot to mention it." I sidestep another attack, this one even closer. By now the hole in the center of the platform is nearly half its diameter, and I'm running out of both time and space. The fire-beasts aren't relenting, and I don't have any ideas about what I'm supposed to do.

Well, there's one idea, but it's a terrible idea. Like Custard's Last Stand bad idea. I keep thinking back to when Adrasella was trying to stomp me to death (as opposed to just leading me to my death) and I'm remembering what she said. Give in. I thought she meant to give in to her, but maybe she meant something else...

As I'm continuing to dodge the flame blasts of death and consider my terrible, no good idea, I really don't see any other way out. To quote my favorite T.V. character, "Sometimes, you have to roll the hard six." I'm pretty sure this is a seven.

"Hey, Marin," I yell across the now gaping hole in the middle of what's quickly become a stone ring.

"Any ideas?" he asks. "I'm running out of useless attacks over here."

"Well, I have one, but you're not gonna like it. Look, if this doesn't work…"

"It'll work, and I trust you. Now shut up and do it, whatever it is." His voice doesn't waver and gives me just the boost of confidence I need to do something really stupid.

I stop dead in my tracks and close my eyes. I know it seems like a losing strategy when deadly fire-beasts are involved, but stay with me. Taking a deep breath, I let jump.

Yes, I jump. Granted, it seems crazy from anyone else's perspective, but I feel good about this. Or that's the rush of euphoric chemicals headed to my brain shortly before my untimely demise. As I'm falling, I feel the heat around me growing, but I feel something else too. It's like a layer of frost leaving me and the further I fall, the calmer I feel. By the time I'm near the bottom, my mind is clear and still; everything else is just burning away. I'm feet above the bubbling lava and there's only me left. Not my fear, not my guilt, not my worries, nothing. Just me.

I've reached the point where I'm fairly sure there should have been lava and unpleasant death. At the moment before impact, the molten fire parts and opens to reveal what looks like a latchkey, hovering between two ancient metal rings embedded in the stone below the bed of lava. None of this should be possible, but I should also be dead, so I'm not going to be filing any complaints with the department of magic volcanos any time soon.

Once I'm near enough to the latchkey I'm pulled through, and the world reorients itself upright and I'm thrown onto my feet. After taking a moment to adjust to the fun-house mirror physics of whatever pocket-dimension I'm currently standing in, I look around.

Behind (above?) me the latchkey is still active and I can barely make out the stone circle closing up. As a bonus, the fire-beasts seem to have stopped trying to kill Marin, so that's a plus. I seem to be standing on a metal cube floating in space. A never-ending void of night and stars stretches around me, and their twinkling light reflects in the chrome-like metal of the cube. Near the other end of the section I'm standing on, I see Andrasella sitting on a throne. There are four others, two on each side, surrounding her, but they're all empty. The thrones are simple in design: stone carved without gems or gold or any other adornment. The only feature on them are the strange runes that I saw on my way up the mountain.

As I approach Adrasella, I see other latchkeys surround the cube. Some are open and lead to places I've never seen before, but others are closed, the iron rings the only evidence that they ever existed. I've reached the thrones now and Andrasella is smiling at me and doing her annoying slow clap. I've come too far to risk it all by punching her in the face, but man, it's tempting.

"Welcome to my realm, human. You are the first to set foot here. Well done. I'm sure you have questions."

"To begin with, Andrasella, what was the point of all of this? I know it's a test of worthiness, but how are you supposed to judge me?"

"I am not the one who judges. You are. The name Andrasella is one I adopted to placate your human need for naming things. I cannot stomach it anymore. Please do not continue to use it."

I sigh and attempt to not roll my eyes. "So, what should I call you?"

"I find the human need to assign titles to everything amusing, and your obsession with giving permanent labels to impermanent things even more so. I do not have a name as you understand it. Some have called me The Lady of Magic, and others have called me the Queen of Open Doors. You need call me neither."

"Ok, so what do you mean I judged me? That doesn't make any sense."

"It was your own doubts and fears that created the trials you faced. I facilitated you through them, but I did not create them."

"So, what would have happened if I failed?"

"That's where I step in and kill you."

"Very helpful, thanks." I say.

She nods enthusiastically as my sarcasm sails very far over her.

"So, I created these challenges for myself. Why? I Wouldn't it have been easier to see how many hotdogs I could eat or something? And why hasn't anyone else completed this path?" I ask.

"The Path has only ever been sought by wicked men and women, eager to boost their power for less than savory reasons. As soon as they began the path, their own inadequacies of spirit consumed them. Then, after the Fall, they stopped coming altogether."

"Why?"

"The leader of their order, Falstaff struck a deal with the Court. They exchanged their souls for immortality, and a pledge of non-interference. They gave up their humanity and stopped seeking the path for fear or true death."

My head is spinning with questions. "So, when you told me I was the first of my kind, you meant the first human."

"Yes. Your mother is a magus, through and through, but she took your father as a lover and the child they produced had substantial power. Therefore Falstaff fears you. You had the potential to do what so many magi cannot; to ascend the Path of Flame. When he learned of your birth, he sought to kill you, but your mother instructed your father to take you somewhere the Grand Esoteric couldn't find you - a world without magic. He tortured her for years to get the location, but she never broke."

"So, my dad is from Aquillon too?"

"Yes. He was a slave, traded to Sanctum by Court and given long life by the Eastern Watch."

I feel like someone just ran me over with a truck. I'm not sure what's worse - the crippling sense of existence crisis, or the overwhelming guilt I feel about how I treated my mom. I put that aside for now, because I still have questions.

"So why bring me back? If she went through all that trouble to hide me, why bring me back into the thick of all this nonsense."

"She believes she did it to save you. Your father's death was not an accident. Over the years, Falstaff was tracking ley lines and arcane energies, and he was getting closer. He thought he found you, but the incant found your father instead. Your mother knew his next incant would not miss."

My voice is quivering with rage as I respond. "Falstaff killed my father?"

She nods. There's a firestorm of rage swirling around me, but that will have to wait. I still need more answers. There will be a time for my anger though.

"So, what was the point of all of this? The Path, the trials, all of it? I appreciate the information, but I don't feel any different."

"The Path is not about gaining anything," she says, "it is about losing things. The path burns away those things that keep you from your true potential. All beings are capable of magic. Some have enough of an innate ability to foster the talent. For most, magic is like lightning, gone before they ever really see it. But even if they wanted to do something with it, there are too many things blocking their ability to focus on it. Greed, anger, doubt, malice, fear. The list goes on. The Path isn't about proving your worth to me. It was about proving your worth to yourself. Overcoming your greatest weaknesses to obtain your greatest strength."

"But I'm telling you, I don't feel any different."

"Really?" Andrasella points to the center of the cube and I see an orange hovering in place. "Destroy that," she commands.

I turn and look at the orange and picture it sitting on the floor, sliced into pieces. No sooner does the image come into my mind than I see a spectral blade dissecting the floating fruit. I turn back to Andrasella. "How did I do that? I didn't incant anything, it was just like instinct or something? It's never been that easy."

"Now that the barriers in your mind have been removed, the connection between the magical ley lines that flow through the universe and yourself is uninterrupted. You think, and magic acts. There are still limits. Do not overdo it or the strain will kill you. You are just a human, after all."

"Noted. Well, it's been a pleasure, your majesty. One more question."

"Yes, human?" She seems annoyed, but I feel I've more than earned a decent Q and A.

"What's this prophecy my mother told Falstaff about? I heard Ahazi mention something about it."

"I cannot tell you anything else about that, save for that the wheels are turning. I have done my part. Now go. I tire of your presence, and I must rest. You humans are very taxing."

"The feeling is mutual, trust me," I say with a grin. "Well, it's been fun I guess. I don't suppose we'll see each other again, huh?"

"Perhaps. Until then, Alessandra Falkrest, don't die."

"What did you call me?"

"Your given name. Ask your mother, Tamil, if you see her again. Now go."

She doesn't give me much choice as I feel the latchkey pull me backwards and the entire scene dissolves into torrents of arcane energy. I thrust backwards through the portal and thankfully I don't end up face down in lava. I'm deposited on my butt on the stone platform. Where Marin is waiting for me. As soon as he sees me, he rushes over.

"God's alive, Alex, you scared me." He's gripping my shoulders and I can see a genuine worry in his eyes.

"I've only been gone for a bit, but I can see why you would worry, given what I did last."

"A bit... Alex, it's been three days," he says with a confused look on his face.

"You're kidding, it only felt like a few minutes."

"Well then, thank all that's holy that you didn't stop to have tea. I'll have to hear about it later, though. This place has been getting less and less hospitable since you left. "

I look around, and he's not wrong. The lava below us is rising rapidly, and there are gigantic cracks in the mountainside. I also see fire-beasts rising out of the caldera, and I'm in no mood to deal with them again, even with my new super magic.

"Agreed. Let's eighty-six this popsicle stand," I say back to Marin.

He looks like he now has several more questions, but we need to go. I have an idea. I hold out my hand.

"That's cute, Alex, but it's hardly the time," he says with his normal amount of snark.

"Shut up and take my hand," I say. I'll admit holding his hand is awkward, but there's also a part of me that doesn't mind too much. I focus on the idea of flight, and it's enough, I'm launched into the air and we're gone. I'm not holding Marin's hand that hard, but he's flying with me as if he's just an extension of me. We soar over the rim of the volcano and slowly float down the side of the mountain until we arrive at the gate. I understand Andrasella's warning now; this powerful magic takes a greater toll on me. I'm out of breath and I feel like I've run a marathon by the time we set down beyond the gate.

It's still night around us, but I see daylight streaming through the portal at the other end of the opening. Whatever time field is in play here isn't affecting the outside world. We walk the rest of the way and I take one last look at the peak. By now it's collapsing into itself and the entire plane is erupting into tidal waves of lava as fire consumes everything. The message is simple; you're done, now please vamoose. We take the hint and jump through the portal.

As soon as we're through, I hear a popping sound and the latchkey is gone, with nothing showing that it was ever there. Looking up, the sun seems to be in the same spot in the sky and it seems like no time at all has passed, although without some kind of date-book it would be impossible to say for sure. We gather our belongings and start back through our trail in the jungle. Marin had enough foresight to etch marks into the trees as we were walking, and it paid off. We have a path back to the Den, and from there the waystone (which has been remarkably quiet; I'm not complaining) will take us back to Sanctum.

As we're walking, I'm mostly lost in my world of information overload and Marin is leaving me alone, and I'm very grateful to him for it. I can barely wrap my head around all the information Andrasella gave me, and I keep swinging violently from one mood to the next (which may be why Marin is keeping his distance). From my correct name (I'm sticking with Alex - I don't care what the Queen of whoever said) to my father's death, to my mother's role in protecting me, it's all too much. It's fair to say my life's been chaotic since I arrived a few months ago, but now I just feel like I'm living someone else's life.

We finally arrive back at the Den. I'm pleased to see that Bob and Steve have become excellent farm hands and aren't murdering anyone so gold stars for them. I thank everyone in the village again for their help and Marin and I open the portal to sanctum and step through.

On the other side I'm staring up at the tower and there's a cold resolve flowing through my veins like ice water. I look over to Marin.

"I promise I'll share everything I've learned in time, and thanks for not pressing me," he nods, "but I have some unfinished business to attend to first."

18

Kyria

Kyria slept for most of the way back to the Mistress's mountaintop. It wasn't entirely clear if she was sleeping, or the taxing emotions of the day had taken their toll on her and she had collapsed. In either case, she awoke bleary-eyed and unsure of her surroundings. After rolling several directions (and nearly rolling off the dragon's back - a helpful tug from Ahrun prevented this) she sat up, pushed her auburn hair out of her eyes, and blinked until the scene came fully into focus..

Nearly screaming when she realized where she was, she looked around in a panic and saw Ahrun, who had propped himself up comfortably on one of the many spines of the dragon. He smiled at her and she grinned awkwardly back at him as the memories of the past day flooded over her like a river. The hole in Ahrun's black tunic flapped about in the breeze and reminded her of it all - their escape from Braga, the wound that nearly killed Ahrun, and the kiss that saved him. Well, not a kiss, Kyria decided. Definitely not a kiss. She was just saving her friend. The fact that the last thing she remembered was holding his hand as tightly as she had ever held anything was an irrelevant and annoying detail.

Once she had worked up the nerve to look over the side of the dragon, she wished she hadn't. Kyria had never been overly fond of heights, and flying on the back of the ancient beast wasn't improving her opinion on the subject, and the alarming speed at which they shot through the air was fuel on the proverbial fire. Kyria did all she could to settle her stomach and hold on for dear life at the same time. As she looked over at Ahrun and realized she was blushing, she briefly considered leaping over the side of the dragon and taking her chances, but thought better of it. Ahrun either sensed her embarrassment or was too nervous to chance moving atop the flying creature, but kept his distance either way, and Kyria was grateful for that, at least.

Thankfully Kyria felt the dragon descend slowly, and she said a silent prayer while swearing fervently to never ride a dragon (or anything larger than a horse) again. She felt her ears pop as the dragon drifted onto the mountaintop with a thud and became still. Kyria wasted no time jumping down to the ground and walking as far away from the creature as her legs would carry her and promptly began vomiting behind a rock.

When she finally regathered herself she looked over to where Ahrun was and saw that he was conversing with the dragon who had plopped its vast body back down into its cave. The expression on the Mistress's face seemed to be a mixture of irritation and amusement.

"I can't say that I expected much from you, food, and yet somehow you've still let me down. Impressive," the dragon said, each word rumbling the surrounding stones.

As Kyria neared the dragon, she felt her skin slowly singing as the heat of the beast's mouth grew, and it reminded her how the wrong word would reduce them both to a pile of ashes.

"We did our best m'lady, but they were circumstances beyond our control. We lost the blood."

"And you won't be getting any more of it, that much I can tell you.

By now Braga will have burrowed deep, where even Fogu can't find him, and he will have taken his blood with him. You've wasted a great opportunity, food. I hope it was worth it," the dragon said with an annoyed grumble.

"Aye, it was," Kyria said. "Look, I'm sorry we didn't bring back tha' blood, but I had ta use if for somethin' else, an' it was plenty important."

"And that was? If you've come all this way back empty-handed, you could at least entertain me with a story."

"I was savin' my friend, an' I'll leave it at tha'."

"Noble, but foolish. Well, begone with you then. As usual, you humans have disappointed me, but I will do you one last courtesy and not eat you."

Ahrun bowed and Kyria turned to leave, but her gumption got the better of her before she could stop herself.

"Then why save us?" she demanded angrily.

"Because I was bored. Now get going before my stomach rumbles," the dragon said with a sneer. She opened her massive jaws and let a small patch of smoke waft out as if to emphasize her request.

"Yer lyin'," Kyria said, planting her feet firmly in the ground before the dragon's snout. The heat from the creature's mouth was intense and despite her outward display of defiance, her heart was thundering like wild horses in her chest.

"Kyria, I really don't think this is the wisest…" Ahrun began, trying to intercede.

"Greater beings than you have been incinerated for saying less, tiny creature. You are nothing but shivering meat wrapped around brittle bone, and yet you would speak to me in such a manner? I feel your fear, human. Do not feign bravery to me, it will win you nothing but death," the dragon roared. Falling rocks nearly crushed Kyria, but she held her ground, not moving an inch.

"Fine, eat me an' my friend, but I'll still be right. I'll not be lied ta by anyone, even a great fire-breathin' lizard such as yerself. Ya weren't bored, ya rescued us because ya wanted us ta succeed. Ya were too much of a coward to face Braga yerself, but ya wanted us ta, real bad. Ya were happy enough ta send us off ta die, and when ya saw us from above, ya swooped in ta save the day because ya want yer children back, like any mother would. But yer too proud to admit it."

Kyria was standing face to face with the dragon and the scorching heat from its mouth dried out her eyes, but she refused to blink. Each of the dragon's fangs could have run her through a half a dozen times, but she stood silent and stoic, hoping her gamble would pay off.

The dragon drew its head back and opened its mouth. Kyria braced herself as she saw the glow of the fire within, and she closed her eyes and waited. After moments of considering though, the Mistress lowered her head back down and laughed a deep, rolling laughter, like thunder in the distant hills.

"You are clever for such a tiny, spongy thing. I have been alone for a long time, and it is many centuries since anyone surprised me. You stand correct, and I cede the point to you. I want to see my children, more than anything. I allowed myself to hope again when you came, but the weight of defeat I feel now is more than I can bear. That is why I wanted you gone. Seeing you is a reminder that I will never see my young again." There was a deep sadness in the Mistress's voice as she spoke. Kyria imagined Alex would have hugged her if she had been here.

"So, there isn't any other way," Ahrun asked.

"Well, there is one thing that might work, but it would come at a substantial cost, and it must be given freely. I did not ask because I did not believe you would give it," the dragon said.

"What? Tell me and I will consider it, at least," Ahrun said.

"Even though the power of the blood has dispersed throughout you, a portion of it yet remains. There is another magic within you, Ahrun of the Seventh Dawn. Old magic, long forgotten to the world."

"My immortality," Ahrun said.

"How do you think your brothers and sisters were granted such a long life? They used the blood of another ancient. If I were to take them both from you, I might have enough of its power to open a portal to where my brood has been held. Again, it must be given freely. If I could have taken it from you, know that I would have," the Mistress said in a grimly factual tone.

Kyria walked over to Ahrun.

"Ya can't, Ahrun. If yer mortal won' ya lose all yer memories?"

"Yes, but it would be a minor price to pay for a victory over the Court. You were willing to trade your chance for my life, and I have lived many lives. I am ready to walk among men again, as one of them. You have given me a gift I can never repay, but I think this should at least allow me to live it to the fullest, and I thank you for that," Ahrun said to Kyria. Turning to the dragon, he continued, "Do what you must."

"Very well, hold still, or this may well kill you." As the dragon said this, she reached out one of her claws and poked the tip into Ahrun's shoulder. He grimaced with pain, but waved Kyria off when she surged forward to help.

Pulling back her claw, there was a tiny, iridescent strand of light that came from Ahrun's body, like a glowing string. She pulled and pulled, extracting the glowing substance until there was no more, and it sat coiled in her claw like a call of iridescent yarn. As she extracted it, Ahrun winced and his eyes fluttered as he murmured a steady stream of unintelligible speech. Ahrun collapsed into Kyria's arms and the wound from the dragon's claw resealed itself. Kyria cradled Ahrun's head in her lap and stoked his head until finally his eyes fluttered open.

"Good, I thought I might 'ave lost ya, and tha' would've been a might inconvenient for…" Kyria never got the chance to finish her sentence as Ahrun reached up and pulled her head into his and kissed her. This time Kyria kissed him back, and it wasn't out of desperation or fear, but out of feelings that crashed on her like a wave. For a moment in time, there was no Court of Hours, no war, no dragon; nothing but a girl kissing her knight, lost in a moment of pure bliss.

Then the moment ended, and Kyria stood in a haze, helping Ahrun to his feet. She pulled him in to her and they both looked up at the dragon who had been somewhat forgotten in the moment.

The Mistress of Scale (oblivious to the blossoming romance beneath her) lifted the ball of energy high into the air and breathed fire into it. Even from a distance, Kyria felt the heat of the dragon fire and put her hand up over her face to shield herself from it. When the dragon had finished, Kyria and Ahrun looked up to see a large glowing portal, where the ball of energy had been.

Without further ceremony or warning there came a great stirring of winds and a chorus of roars as dragon after dragon burst from the open portal. They varied in shape, size, color, and age. Kyria lost count somewhere in the low two hundreds. The younger ones swarmed to the Mistress while the older dragons found rocks to perch on. Before long there was hardly an inch of mountain top left to stand on that wasn't filled with dragons. As the last dragon wandered lazily through (a plump yellow one with a large jovial grin on its face) the portal fizzled into nothing as quickly as it had appeared.

Kyria felt a scurrying passed her legs and looked down to see tiny baby dragons running about and playing, causing a large uproar among the elderly ones. A small purple dragon has nestled itself in a coil around Ahrun's leg, but he seemed unbothered by it, and Kyria couldn't help but chuckle at him.

As Kyria studied him, Ahrun seemed different. There was a vivaciousness in his eyes and a bright spot in his laugh that she swore she had never seen. He seemed less reserved and full of energy. He even looked younger; the marks of care and worry had washed away, leaving his face youthful and energetic. For whatever longevity it had provided, the blood of the ancient one had taken something from Ahrun as a young man, almost as if it had frozen him in time. He seemed to have whatever it was back now, and Kyria had never seen him looking happier.

The deep, rolling voice of the Mistress of Scale interrupted Kyria's musing (she was definitely not staring, she told herself). "I cannot tell you how good it is to have my children back. Thank you, humans. I cannot repay this debt".

"You could start by sending your brood back to Aquillon," Ahrun said, "we could sorely use the edge in our struggle against the Court."

"That is a favor I cannot grant, I'm afraid. It has been too long since I was reunited with my children. I will not risk their lives now, I am sorry." She seemed sorry, but it did nothing the quell Kyria's temper.

"Ya mean ta say we did all this, an' Ahrun gave up his immortality, just for ya ta betray us when ya got what ya wanted?" Kyria yelled with a voice of unchecked anger.

"We are grateful, and we will grant anything else you request of us, but alliances between our kinds never end well. I will not force my brood to go where they will be at risk," the mistress said.

Kyria looked around at the host of dragons and then said something very unwise.

"Then yer all cowards, the lot o' ya. Is there not one o' ya slimy, snivelin' reptiles that will help us? After all, we've been through on account o' yer scaly hides!"

The dragons collectively looked more uncomfortable than enraged, sensing that she was right. But being right when arguing with dragons doesn't make you any more fireproof. After a long, awkward, and incineration-free pause, there was some shuffling near the back of the cave, and out wandered the fat yellow dragon who had been last out of the portal.

"I'll help! My name is Larm!" The dragon spoke in an excitable, high-pitched tone of voice that made Kyria think it might have once been a golden retriever in a past life. There was a general rumble of chuckles and Kyria spotted the Mistress doing the dragon equivalent of rolling her eyes.

"Now, Larm, I don't know if this is the best idea," the Mistress cautioned.

"Nope, as my friend Alex likes ta say, nae take-backs. Larm volunteered," Kyria said.

"Careful, human. I owe you a great debt, but you are dancing on the last thread of my patience," the Mistress growled.

"It is fine, Mother. I am happy to go with them. They save Larm from a scary, evil place. Larm no like. Larm go with them. Pay back mother's debt. It will be fun!" As Larm spoke, his tongue lolled out of his mouth to one side and his eyes lit up as though he really believed it would be fun.

Kyria sighed, he might have been odd, and he wasn't the fastest, but one dragon was better than no dragons, and it seemed like those were the only two options.

The mistress seemed irritated, but did not debate the point further.

"Very well, he may go with you if that is his choice," as she said this she eyed him and Larm was reduced to a pile of shivering dragon-jelly, "but if one of his scales is harmed, I will visit my wrath on you personally."

Kyria nodded and turned to Larm.

"Ya ready, Larm? We've got ta be gettin' back ta meet my friend."

"Larm is ready. This will be an excellent adventure! Larm likes new friends!"

Kyria sighed and looked at Ahrun, who shrugged as he pried the tiny baby dragon off his leg with promises that he would be back, eventually. Larm lowered his wing and Kyria rolled her eyes. So much for not riding dragons, she thought to herself with a grimace. She jumped up onto Larm and pulled Ahrun up in front of her and wrapped her arms around him.

"Don' get any ideas ya eegit, I jus' don't enjoy flyin' on these scaly beasties."

"Of course not," he replied with a chuckle.

"Let's jus' get this over with. Larm, we'd like to go now, thank ya kindly."

"Ok, let's fly. Flying is fun. Hold on tight, friends! If you fall off Larm, you will die. Dying is not fun!" Larm said in an enthusiastic voice, as though he was presenting fresh information. Kyria had to concur, though. Dying was not fun.

With a fair amount of effort, Larm lifted himself off the ground and they were quickly leaving the mountaintop. Kyria waved goodbye to the dragons and turned back to face Ahrun and her new dragon-friend Larm, who was already panting heavily with the effort. They were soon back over jungle and somewhere in the green depths below. Kyria could have sworn she saw Harold crashing around the underbrush.

"So where can Larm take new friends?" Larm asked.

"We're going back to Sanctum. This stone the Eastern Watch gave us should guide you back," Ahrun said, retrieving a small waystone from his pocket.

"I thought yer memories lost ta us." Kyria said.

"The memories of my brothers and sisters that I kept watch over are, but my memories are my own."

The magi had begrudgingly given it to him shortly before their departure, presumably on the assumption that they would get themselves killed. It couldn't teleport them, but it shot out a beam of energy that led back to Sanctum and would get them through the barrier once they arrived.

"Larm follow pretty, shiny light. Larm find!"

"Good, err, boy?" Kyria said, while giving Larm's hind quarters a scratch which he seemed to enjoy.

She sighed. As they slowly made their way back towards sanctum, Kyria mused what a long, emotional journey it had been. Especially since all they had to show for it was a fat, overeager dragon that seemed severely in need of cardio. Still, at least he was friendly. A friendly fat dragon seemed less likely to eat them.

19

Alex

I'm standing in front of the doors to Sanctum, and I feel like anyone in a five-mile radius could hear my heartbeat. I'm sweating despite the chill in the air, and it's hard to stay focused, but I have to. Marin's waiting quietly at my side. I've never been more grateful to have him here, and I'm even more thankful that he hasn't insisted on asking too many questions since I got back from mystic cube-world.

Looking up at the doors, all I feel is rage and shame. Rage at the coward behind them and shame for the words I said to my mother. Whatever prophecy nonsense she told Falstaff about, I know the reason she sent me away, and the reason she brought me back. And I will have more than words with Falstaff about it.

I start by knocking. I figure it's the polite thing to do.

Nothing.

I continue my knocking, and a similar, and equally annoying amount of nothing happens.

"You don't think they all went out to lunch?" I ask Marin with a grin.

He glances around at the empty plateau. "Unlikely. I imagine they're all pretending to be busy."

"Well, then I suppose I'll have to knock a little louder."

I take a few steps back and focus on the door, pouring all my anger into it. I feel the magic flowing freely, without pause or distraction. It's as if I think, and magic responds. Before it was like doing algebra in my head, but now it's more fluid - reflexive. I can see what Andrasella was saying. But it's also more taxing. Because each incant required so much prep and concentration, it restricted how many spells I could cast. Now it's like I'm standing in the middle of a quick river and I'm directing its flow. It's a lot of power, but I'll drown myself if I'm not careful.

It doesn't take long for the energy to form a tangible result. A pair of deafening booms ring out across the starlight bathed plateau, shaking the surrounding rocks, and nearly knocking poor Marin off his feet. When everything settles, there are two giant fist impressions on the doors. Invisible Hulk-Hands. Nice.

Nothing. Ok. Let's try something a little more... direct.

I focus my mind on the doors themselves and then the image of glass shattering and direct a torrent of arcane energy. I haven't had long to figure out this souped-up version of my abilities, but it does the trick. The doors shatter like taking a sledgehammer to a mason jar and I quickly put up a field of energy to deflect the oncoming shards of wood (very smart, Alex; who knew blowing up the wooden door would, in fact, produce splinters?).

Once the debris clears and the last of the doors are just hanging like rag-dolls on their hinges, I see a scurrying hive of magi in blue robes trying to be anywhere but there. I need to be careful. I feel drained already, but there's no stopping now. This only ends one way.

Marin and I make our way to the nearest latchkey. I'm not sure how, but I know where this one goes. Looking around, I can see snaking blue lines of energy weaving in and out of the walls, connecting latchkeys throughout Sanctum. This one leads up to the floor where the Trials were held. I have a gut feeling that's where Falstaff will be. Before I can step through the portal, I feel Marin grab my wrist.

"You know where this road leads. I don't know what you learned on the Path of Flame, but I assume you know how this story ends?"

I can't meet his gaze, but I nod. I feel like he's judging me somehow, or maybe that's just me getting jumpy.

"Alright," he says, "just wanted to make sure you were prepared for... whatever comes next." He says nothing else, but steps through the latchkey, and I follow.

There's an odd quiet on the other side. The hallway outside the trail chambers are deserted, but I see energy in the air. There's an illusion at play; this is a trap. I tug at the arcane sparks with my mind, and it melts like water falling over a small group of magi. I don't recognize the first few, but then they part and Caiaphus strolls out. His sneer has gotten none more charming since I last saw him. He's playing guard dog for the Grand Esoteric; everything about that makes sense.

"I'm going to be really reasonable here, Caiaphas. You and your thugs get out of my hallway and let me and Marin by, and I won't embarrass you," I say.

"Oh, so the wench has learned a few new party tricks since she's been gone with her boyfriend? I'm sure the privacy helped with those late night study sessions. Didn't know you had it in you, Marin. Good for you, I suppose."

Gross. I don't know if he's bluffing to buy some time, or he's really just this stupid. I'm betting the latter.

"Look, you need to listen to her, Caiaphas," Marin says in an uneasy voice, "something's different. She changed."

"No more talk. I will not listen to some harlot and her whipping boy! You want to get back to the trial chambers, you go through me," Caiaphas says, chuckling. He readies his stance and I can feel energy swirling to him and he starts to incant. His buddies spread out and begin incanting.

The world will never know what great incant Caiaphas was working on. Before he could finish I readied my mind and the air temperature spiked around me. Scorching fire blazed from my hands and whipped around me, swirling into a column behind me, which I sent at full speed towards the group of magi. They put up a half-hearted shield, but the tower of fire burst on them, throwing them back against the wall, hard. Several of their robes caught on fire, and the force of it seemed to knock Caiaphas out cold (well, hot, but you get the idea).

As soon as the room clears, Marin has to catch me before I collapse. I feel like I've been running marathons all day, and my mind is even more unsteady than before. I'm still focused, and I feel a direct connection to the rivers of magic energy around me.

After a few more minutes, I'm able to stand and steady myself and I see the trial chamber. I can feel the energy surging on the other side of the door, and I know Falstaff is there. The door opens slowly and I walk in, Marin behind me.

I walk down the long bridge to the center of the platform. Magi fill the stands and in the center of the platform, off his throne, I see Falstaff. He's gripping his staff and there's a wildfire in his eyes.

My mother is sitting in the crowd. Even from here, I can see the bruising and the swollen eye. I guess I should be happy he didn't go further, but I feel anger welling in me like the tide pulling away from a beach before a tsunami.

"I tried to be civil about this, girl," Falstaff says, spitting the word at me like it's the dirtiest word he can come up with. "If you had just left, and gone back to Aquillon with your bag of tricks, we could have avoided all of this."

"Well, sorry to inconvenience you, but we have a business. I know everything now." As I speak, I'm fighting a losing battle to hold my anger back. I wouldn't worry about that normally, but there's something in my head screaming for me to set off a bomb in here and I need to contain that.

"You don't know anything. I was here long before you crawled into this world, and I will be here long after."

"You're a coward. I know the deal you made. I know why you fear death so much." There's a stirring in the crowd and I hear what sounds like a confused murmuring. "You never told them?"

"They didn't need to know. I had their memory sealed away. I was responsible for their safety and I assured. I gave us life!"

"At what cost? He's hiding something from you! He took something from you!" The crowd seems to turn.

"Enough of this. I don't have to explain myself to anyone, never mind some half-breed from another world!" As he says this, he unleashes a torrent of electricity from his fingers, Sith-Lord style. Glimmering is even easier for me now, and I avoid it with no issue. I send a bolt of freezing energy his way and he sidesteps, but he's slower now. When I faced him before, he was a step ahead of me, but now I have the edge.

Taking the offensive, I let the magic pour through me as my anger towards him builds. This coward killed my father, and made my mother hide me, denying me the chance to grow up with her; he will pay for that. I don't even know if I'm incanting anymore, but energy pours through me and my anger gives it form. Fire, ice, electricity, it takes many forms, but all with lethal intent. Falstaff is still dodging me, but barely. He's spent himself casting shields, but I'm getting through. One last fire blast, and his shield breaks, leaving him a crumpled mess on the floor.

Gripping him with my mind, I raise him to meet me, binding him in a gale of wind that surrounds him like rope. He's bruised and broken, but his eyes still flash defiance at me.

"It's over. The truth now," I say in a voice that's not entirely my own. It's the other me, the one from the place of dust and shadow, that lives behind my waking moments. I know now why the Path of Flame tests your merits, and what Andrasella meant when she said that I was the architect of my own trials. My greatest fear wasn't that I wasn't worthy, but of what I would do with the power inside.

Falstaff glowers at me. "I have done what I have done. I will say no more."

"Fine, then I'll tell them." I turn to face the group of seated Magi. "When the Court came, a thousand years ago, Falstaff feared for his life. He struck a deal with them and traded your souls for immortality. He keeps you hear because if you die, there is nothing else. He took that from you. Every one of you who joined them, he took your soul when you joined. I'm sure he failed to mention that detail."

Outrage is stirring in the crowd now. I turn back to Falstaff, who is still silent. I want to kill him, and there are so many reasons I should, but I can't do it. As much as he took from me, he took more from them.

"I give him back to you. You can decide what to do with him," I say.

By now the Magi are on their feet and many have glimmer down in front of me. There's a stream of apologies and ashamed looks as they approach me. I bind Falstaff's mouth and feet. I can sense he is drained. He couldn't conjure any more incants if he wanted to. From the back of the crowd, I see Marin walking up to me. There's still a look of concern on his face, but mostly relief.

"I wasn't sure how that would go, but I'm glad I've made a habit of not betting against you, Winters."

"I couldn't have done this without you, old buddy."

"So, what now?"

"What do you mean? What now?"

"Well, the Grand Esoteric is the title given to the strongest Magi. I think we all know who that is."

"Yes, we do," I say. But it's not me. I make my way through the crowd to where my mother is standing. "This is my mother, Tamsil Falkrest. Without her, I would have died a long time ago. He tortured her for years to give me up, but never did. You want to know who the strongest Magus here is? You have your answer."

"But she's a..." I hear one idiot pipe up in the back.

"By all means, finish that sentence. Let's see how that goes for you." I say. "I leave you in the hands of Grand Esoteric Falkrest, and I'm sure she has more than a few changes in mind. She can figure out what to do with Falstaff and do some other... housecleaning." I let my last phrase go off like a bombshell as my mother is swarmed by nervous-looking Magi who are processing what I mean. I can catch up with her later, but for now we exchange a look. I couldn't even formulate the words to say everything I feel right now anyway, even if she was available. I make my way to the back of the room where Marin is waiting for me.

"Well, that should shake things up around here. About time, too. These old farts have gotten a bit too comfortable with the status quo, if you ask me."

I smile. It's been a long, strange, trying time since I got here, but through it all Marin has just been... Marin. "It's good to know that some things don't change," I say. "Now if you could give a hand getting to my room, I believe I'm about to pass out."

I then passed out.

I wake up an unknown amount of hours later in my room. I never spent much time here, but it's nice to have a room somewhere. It's the closest thing to home I've had since I got to Aquillon. I'm still in my clothes, so I get up and change back into my robes. They still don't fit right, but at least I don't hate them as much anymore. Leaving my room, I make my way down to the ground floor where my mother is directing a small legion of magi.

As soon as she sees me, she wraps me up in an enormous hug that lasts a very long time. I'm sobbing when she lets go, and I take a few minutes to compose myself enough to speak.

"Mom, I'm so sorry. I didn't know, I didn't know..."

She strokes my hair and hushes me.

"My darling girl, it's fine. I wanted to tell you as soon as you arrived, but I had to act like I knew nothing. If Falstaff had suspected who you really were, he would have killed you on sight. I masked your energy, so he knew you were powerful, but not why."

"What about that prophecy you mentioned?"

"Just some hogwash about a jackal and a sparrow I found in an old book. Just needed to convince him that you were special enough to let in."

The words shoot through me like lightning. I've heard them before, when I saw the Lord of Awakenings in my vision. I keep that to myself and continue.

"So, I hope you'll get this place turned around now."

"Yes, we've severed Falstaff's connection to magic, so he's harmless. For now, he's in the dungeons, but we can find a place for him later. And I've opened up the studies of magic to all initiates, regardless of gender. There was some grumbling about it, but I told them if they had a problem, they could take it up with my daughter." She chuckles as she says this. It was good to see her smile and laugh. After what she had been through, she deserves it. "I was also able to get an old friend out of a lifetime sentence in the archives," she says.

"I'm glad you found your way here, young Alessandra. You've done your mother proud!"

I turn and see an old man in faded blue robes. I take a second, but I recognize him.

"You! You're the one who brought me here!" I run up and feign a punch, and he flinches, but then I wrap him into a hug. He doesn't seem to know what to do with himself.

"Grandsatff helped me when nobody else would. I wouldn't have been able to save you from Fallstaff if not for him, and his apprentice," Tamsil said.

"Who?" I ask.

"Well, I told you I'd explain why I took you on eventually, didn't I?" I hear Marin's cheerful voice as he steps out from behind Grandstaff.

"You helped bring me here?" I ask, shock resonating in my voice.

"Well, the magic needed to create portals between worlds is very ancient, and required many components, who young Marin here was helpful in obtaining. He didn't know what he was doing, because we kept him in the dark to shield him from blame. Once you arrived here, we told him to seek you out and help, but didn't tell him why. He's been an outcast here, so it made enough sense and didn't draw too much suspicion."

My mind is swimming with all the new information. I suppose I can't be that mad at Marin for holding back on info he never had. I still punch his arm a few times, just on principal.

"So where will you go now? I can't imagine there's much we can teach you now." My mother says, switching topics.

"Back to Aquillon. You all could come with me. We could use your help with the war," I say.

"I would love nothing better," my mother says with a sad smile, "but it will take time to sort things out here. Just because I am the Grand Esoteric, I can't force the order to leave. They've been here for a thousand years. It will take time to convince them to risk everything for a cause they know little about. We will send aid as soon as we're able, you have my word on that. You can take Marin here as a down payment!"

He shoots her an annoyed glance, but then looks back at me. "Well, I wasn't relishing the thought of another five hundred years in the book study. So, when do we leave?"

"Well," I begin, "we just need to wait for my friends to get back. They should arrive..."

As I'm speaking I stop as a small flying speck enters my vision. By the time it grows big enough for me to see what it is, I'm jumping up and down, and run out to meet them. The tiny image of Ahrun and Kyria grows more and more visible as they drift on a fat, yellow, dragon. I'll admit, I was expecting a slightly bigger dragon, for all the effort they went through.

I'm sure they'll have an interesting story to tell.

I know I do.

II

Part Two

20

A Meeting of Old Friends

It had been hours and Kyria was more than ready to be rid of her new friend, Larm. Her rump hurt (the dragon's back was roomy, although not comfortable), she had no interest in making eye contact with Ahrun; she was feeling green around the gills, and every now and again the wind would catch a bit of drool from Larm's lolling tongue, which only occasionally missed her.

After a second exposure to it, Kyria was definitely not a fan of travel by dragon.

Still, she couldn't argue with the speed.

Despite not seeming to move quick, they cleared regions rapidly and in what seemed like less than half a day, the looming visage of Sanctum darkened the horizon. It was hard to make out the distance to the tower, but it seemed like they would be there in no time. Kyria shifted her gaze to Ahrun, who was peacefully watching the skyline. It seemed like the same old Ahrun she had known for months, but again, there was something slightly different now.

"So," Kyria said, cutting the silence abruptly. "We'll be needin' tha' mini stone before too long, if ya wouldn't mine gettin' it out of yer pack."

"Of course," Ahrun replied with a smile. Kyria realized she was staring and looked away as her face turned several shades of crimson. Even with hours of silence on her hands, she didn't quite know what to make of the kiss. Despite her best efforts, she couldn't convince herself it had been one sided, and whenever she stole a glance at the knight, there was a slight fluttering in her chest that hadn't been there either. She had no idea what to do with that. Her life had been a long series of running and fighting, and nothing like this had ever crossed her mind. There wasn't room in her life for anything but strife, or at least that's what she had been telling herself. She wasn't sure of anything anymore.

She realized that Ahrun had been holding out the stone for some time, and grabbed it from him, and mumble-grunted "Thank ya" in a tone that human ears would have trouble identifying.

Once she had the stone, it gave her something to focus on and she pointed it out over the horizon. It cast a beam of blue energy in a line extending outward, but it became stronger when it was pointed towards Sanctum.

"Ooooh, shiny. Larm likes shiny," Larm declared as he banked left, nearly dislodging his passengers (he had done this early when he chased a bird for lunch.) He adjusted his flight-plan to follow the line of energy until finally they had come to the shield. According to the magus who had given the stone to Ahrun (he refused to give it to Kyria as he thought the responsibility of holding it was beyond her "faculties"), the barrier wouldn't be visible unless the stone was there. The blue line touched the shimmering wall of energy and slowly cut a hole just big enough for Larm's plus-sized torso. The hole sealed back up with a pop as soon as they had cleared it.

The plateau on which Sanctum rested had changed little, and took them no time to fly through. As they drew closer, Kyria squinted against the eastern horizon and barely made out a tiny figure with blonde hair jumping up and down. Kyria chuckled to herself. It seemed Alex had gotten no less excitable in the last few weeks. There were other details that seemed puzzling to Kyria, like the giant splintered hole where great doors used to be. She figured she'd ask when they landed.

Larm put them down a few dozen yards away from the door, after lazily drifting down in a spiraled flight pattern. Once they were within a few feet Kyria jumped off the dragon's back and landed with a thud. It wasn't the most pleasant landing, but she didn't want to spend one second longer on the beast's back than she had to. She heard Ahrun grumbling from above about breaking her legs, and she smiled to herself. Anything Ahrun didn't approve of was probably worth doing. A dozen feet ahead of her, she saw Alex running towards her.

Alex and Kyria collided somewhere around the midpoint at full speed in what could only be described as a tackle-hug. The two friends squeezed each other until it hurt and didn't let go for a long time. Alex knew it had only been a few weeks since she had last seen Kyria and Ahrun, but it seemed like a lifetime and more to her. Alex and Kyria reluctantly let go of one another, and Kyria was the first to speak.

"Quite a grand mess ya made o' the place," Kyria said with a raised eyebrow, eyeing the still-steaming doors of Sanctum. Alex shrugged.

"I figured we could use a new set of doors. The old ones were… stupid. So, I blew them up." Alex's answer didn't seem to satisfy Kyria's raised eyebrow one bit. "Ok, so there might be more to the story than that," Alex conceded with a sheepish grin.

"I figured as much. There'll be enough time for tha' later. For now, my behind aches and I need a bath an' a bit o' grub. We can catch up…"

Kyria never finished her sentence as Ahrun enveloped both of them in a giant group hug. Alex returned the hug happily enough, but Kyria wiggled her way out, trying her best to hide the complicated emotions on her face. Alex raised an eyebrow of her own.

"So, I'm guessing I'm not the only one with an interesting story? What's going on with you two?" Alex asked.

"I'll explain later, for now I'd just as soon go inside," Kyria said.

Alex wanted to ask more, but she saw a desperate look in her friend's eyes, and she dropped it for now. Ahrun's face was a stone mask, not revealing any more details than Kyria's.

"Alright, keep your secrets then, for now. Come on in and I'll catch you up on what's been happening."

Alex turned and walked past what remained of the doors with her friends in tow. As they made their way into the tower Alex told her friends everything that happened. By the time she was done, they had arrived at the banquet hall.

"Well, it sounds as if everything worked out for the better. And these new powers of yours?" Ahrun asked Alex.

"Not new exactly, just… enhanced. From what they explained to me, there just aren't really limits on my power anymore. Not physical limits anyway."

"What do ya mean? Ya have always had incredible abilities an'… sweet mother o' mercy," Kyria said, trailing off. Alex realized Kyria had stopped in her tracks by the sight of a large roast. Her friend wasted no time finding a knife, plates, forks, and began carving up the meat and serving it. "Are ya daft, ya eegits? We can talk later. For now, we eat!"

Alex realized how hungry she had grown and didn't lodge further protest.

After a mostly silent meal, Alex ushered Kyria upstairs to her room. As soon as they closed the door, Alex turned to Kyria.

"Ok, what is going on with you two? I know you're both weirdos, but you're both acting stranger than normal."

"It's nothing, nae thing worth speakin' about anyway," Kyria said, turning several shades of scarlet.

"Nope, I'm not buying that. Spill," Alex demanded with her arms crossed.

Kyria exhaled and crossed the room to sit on Alex's bed and began sharing the details of their journey. By the time she was done, Alex had joined her on the bed, a look of perplexed amusement on her face.

"So, you two..."

"Shut it."

"And that makes you..."

"Nothin'. Now shut it yer nae good guttersnipe."

"Ok, fine. I'll drop it. But you two make a cute..."

"I swear ta gods Alex, if ya speak one more blazin' word I'll gut ya like a fish, funny powers or nae," Kyria warned, waggling an angry finger at Alex, who figured she'd gotten about as much information out of Kyria as she was going to, so she switched topics.

"So, Ahrun's mortal now?"

"Aye, it seems tha' way. I'm not for sure on how it all works, but he says he has nae memories of his order, just his own life. He seems at peace with it, but I feel like he might hidin' somethin' from me. We 'aven't talk a whole heap since well... ya know... for, reasons."

"Right," Alex said. It was Kyria's turn to switch topics.

"So, now tha' we have yer ladyship's powers upright an' shiny, what's next?" She asked.

"Well, I put my mother in charge of everything around here, and she says when she can get things more organized, she'll send reinforcements. For now, we're on our own. Well, with one fat dragon anyway," Alex said, letting a question mark linger over her last remark.

"Don't ask," Kyria replied, a hind of exasperation in her voice.

"Well, between the fat dragon I'm not allowed to ask about, and the budding romance that I'm definitely not allowed to ask about, it seems you've come back as something of an exotic woman of mystery. My little Kyria, all grown up," Alex mused, affecting her most endearing voice.

Kyria's punch to her arm was swift and hard, but it was worth it, and Alex burst out laughing. Kyria held back as long as she was able, but it was no use. She broke down into hysterical giggling with her friend, and for a moment they were just two friends laughing about a fat dragon and, of all things, a boy.

After the moment passed Alex felt the day's events wash over her and apparently Kyria was in the same boat as she had begun lightly snoring next to Alex on the bed. Alex got up and rolled Kyria's legs onto the bed and gently removed her boots. Alex lay down next to her and the world faded to darkness.

Alex's dreams that night were restless and frightening. She awakened all at once as she felt her body racked with shivering from the cold. Looking around, she saw that her room's hearth was out, so she concentrated on a warmth and a small, snaking trail of fire found its way to the logs. Before long, her room was chirping and popping with warmth and she was feeling slightly better.

Looking beside her, she saw that Kyria had already left. Putting on her traveling clothes and cloak, Alex made her way out into the corridor and down to the banquet hall. As she passed magi in the halls, their reactions to her seemed to vary between nervous smiles and abject terror. Alex figured she couldn't blame them.

As she entered the dining hall, Alex noticed Kyria and Ahrun near the wall, in deep conversation, and definitely closer than a platonic distance to one another. She focused on the ground next to them and glimmered over.

"God's alive!" Kyria shrieked, "Yer gonna kill me with fright long before the blazin' Court can get their grubby paws on me."

"Morning, friends," Alex beamed, blatantly ignoring Kyria's comment. "What are we talking about?"

"Nothing of any importance," Ahrun said.

Alex wasn't sure, but she thought she saw him blushing, and she definitely saw Kyria glaring at both her and Ahrun, presumably for separate reasons.

Alex decided not to press her luck any more and moved on. "So, I figure we should form a plan. We need to get back to Aquillon and meet up with the guard. I don't know if it's enough, but between my new abilities and the dragon we…gained, it should help tip the balance a little."

"I agree," Ahrun said, nodding. "Our best point of contact would be Felwind. I don't know what's gone since we left, but the guard had a powerful presence there before we left, so it's a place to start."

As he spoke, Alex watched Ahrun. What Kyria had told her last night seemed true. There was a youthful energy about him, and even the tenor of his voice had changed. It was as if by taking the blood of the ancients out of him he had a new lease on life. Even his eyes seemed to shimmer in a way that that hadn't before. Despite his physical appearance, Alex had always regarded Ahrun as a wise teacher, or an elder to be looked up to. Now, he seemed more on the same page as her.

"Well, we best be makin' our way there soon," Kyria interjected. "I cannot imagine the Lord of Long Shadows was happy when we escaped, an' if I know one thing about tha' infernal cat, I know he takes his displeasure out on humans. If Felwind still stands, it won't last for long."

A shiver of icy fear passed over Alex as she realized the awful truth of Kyria's words. While she had been away in the Wyld Places, no matter how hard her life had seemed, she had remained somewhat detached from Aquillon, and the Court. Even Thistle's death seemed far away. Now, it all came flooding back.

"Right. We leave within the hour," Alex said, her voice filled with resolve. She turned to leave and with a thought glimmered into her room. She put together her few possessions (her red baseball cap, her sword, and she even packed her robes) and closed the door on her room. It hadn't been much, but for a few short weeks, it was like a home. As she turned from the door, she saw Marin leaning against a wall.

"So, we're off then?" he asked.

"Yup, back to Aquillon," Alex said.

"I haven't been there in more years than I can count," Marin said. His voice was wistful but not overly affectionate.

"You don't sound thrilled to be back," Alex said as she walked with him to the nearest latchkey.

"I was a boy when I left with the Watch. I hardly remember it, but I imagine it won't be much the same place as I left it. Just a strange feeling, I guess. Like stepping into another memory, another life."

"I guess I can relate. It hasn't even been a year, but I feel like Earth is a distant memory. I can barely remember anything about my old life."

"Do you miss it?" Marin asked as they reached the latchkey.

"Well, I guess I don't miss not being chased by demons or angry lava monsters, but as far as my life? Jury's out. I'll let you know when they reach a verdict," Alex said with a sad smile, stepping into the portal. She felt the energy tug her inside, and a moment later she was standing at the entrance of Sanctum. Marin came through the portal moments later.

Kyria and Ahrun were waiting for them near the doors, and Larm was a few dozen feet outside, chasing something up a nearby hill.

"Alright, well, that's everybody," Alex said. Kyria walked up to Marin and thrust out her hand.

"Kyria Killburn, good ta know ya," she said.

"Marin, and the feeling is mutual," he said.

"I appreciate ya takin' care o' Alex, here. I figured she'd need a chaperone, what with the responsible people off chasin' dragons," Kyria said, sounding smug and haughty.

Alex rolled her eyes and stuck her tongue out at Kyria, who returned the favor.

"Now now children play nice together." Alex's mother emerged from a nearby room. Her sleeves were rolled up, and she looked tired. Alex pulled her in for a hug and had trouble letting her go. She was still racked with guilt, but that was a conversation for another day.

"So, you have a plan then?" Tamsil asked.

"We do, we're going to meet up with the Old Guard in Felwind, so if you can convince some magi to enter the fight, that's where to send them," Alex said.

"I'll do my best. Alessan... I mean, Alex. Stay safe out there. The Lord of Long Shadows has never been humiliated as badly as he was when you escaped him. His vengeance will be swift once he finds out you have returned."

"We will, thanks Tam.. I mean mom." The group said goodbye to Tamsil and left Sanctum behind. Once they had corralled Larm back from his hunt (he was hunting a grub) they all found room on his back and the dragon lifted into the sky.

Alex smiled as the wind caught her hair, and they lifted farther and farther away from Sanctum. She waved to her mom until she couldn't see her anymore, and the tower slowly became a vanishing speck on the eastern horizon. They passed through the barrier and before long they were making good time over the jungle.

Despite the mixed response from her group (Ahrun was fine, Marin seemed terrified, and Kyria had already vomited over the side of Larm twice) Alex enjoyed flying. It felt freeing to leave her problems behind on the ground, at least for the moment. After several hours, they had reached the edge of the Wyld Places and she saw the Heart of Storms approaching, and the problems she left behind in Aquillon came roaring back into focus.

21

The City of Free Men

Crossing the lightning infested skies of the Heart of Storms turned out to be the least of Alex's problems. Sure, they nearly died a half-dozen times. The flying had gotten so rough that Kyria had passed out (landing directly into Ahrun's arms, Alex noted), and Alex could have sworn she saw a very familiar shadow following them in the waters below, but on balance it wasn't so bad. It wasn't until they cleared the Aquillonian coastline that things got grim.

The first thing Alex spotted was Daemonfall, the tiny village they had departed out of with Sullas, nearly a month ago. Alex was fairly sure that was where it had been, anyway. All that remained atop the rocky bluff was a smoldering ruin of charred timbers and burnt out skeletons. Seeing the place brought back painful memories, but it was compounded by the guilty feeling that Alex was responsible for the village's unfortunate fate. By now, Kyria had pulled herself from her groggy stupor, and clasped her hand firmly on Alex's shoulder.

"Ya can' no' beat yerself up about this. The Court is evil, an' they're gonna do evil things, nae matter what."

Alex said nothing, but she nodded, and they flew on.

As they passed further inland, nothing seemed better. Alex had forgotten how bleak everything was. Every village they passed over was deserted, or looked even more miserable than Alex remembered Vandlehaven. They cut a wide arc around the Wastes, as even Larm didn't seem interested in flying over the toxic area. Alex wondered how the Mirefolk were doing, but there wasn't time to stop and check. If they arrived in Felwind before the Court, it would be a minor miracle.

As they flew, small bands of roaming demons attempted to attack them, but Larm just flew higher. He seemed different up here to Alex. On the ground he had seemed juvenile and immature, but there was a power and grace to him in the air that Alex found stunning. She couldn't even imagine what an older, more mature dragon would be like.

By the evening, they had flown far inland and in the distance, Alex could barely make out the silhouette of Felwind. As they drew closer, Alex breathed a sigh of relief as it seemed nothing was smashed, smoldering, or otherwise on fire. Kyria (who had mostly adjusted to flying, it seemed) rifled through her back and produced a small mirror.

"Odd time to be checking your hair," Marin said with a coy smile.

"Shut up, ya great eegit. I know what I'm about," Kyria responded. They hadn't interacted much (mostly because of Kyria's vomiting) but Alex had a feeling they would get along just fine.

Without further comment, Kyria pointed the mirror towards the city, and caught the last rays of the setting sun, flashing light in patterns. It wasn't Morse, but Alex got the idea. They put down a few hundred feet outside the city, and because no one was firing arrows at them, Alex figured the mirror trick had done its job.

As they jumped down from the dragon, Alex rubbed her rump.

Dragon riding might have been the fastest way to travel, well, not counting glimmering, but it definitely wasn't the most comfortable.

Alex squinted towards the gates and saw a small party of soldiers riding out to meet them. It was hard to make out much, but she didn't see any fox masks, so that was good enough for her. They pulled up their horses and dismounted, and Alex smiled at a familiar face.

"Great galloping gods alive, I never thought I'd be seeing your ugly mugs again!" Sal roared as she pulled Kyria in for a hug. "And you brought a pet back!"

"Larm is not pet!" Larm proclaimed energetically. "Larm is friend. No eat humans!" Larm seemed especially pleased with himself for sharing what he seemed to feel was critical information.

"Well Larm - good to meet you," Sal said. "I'm Sal, and if you are friends of my dear friends here, you're welcome in Felwind. Now come on you lot, we'd best be getting in the gates. We've a lot to discuss." Nobody else had much to say, so they followed Sal inside the gates, which closed behind them with a massive crash. They looked like the guard had upgraded them since Alex had last been in Felwind.

The evening sun was setting on Felwind by the time they made it into the city proper, onto the high street, and Alex was at once grateful to be back in the city. It had seemed like a vibrant place before, but it was at night that Felwind truly came alive, it seemed.

A sea of lanterns emerged moments after the last rays of sunlight glimmered below the horizon, and it bathed the high street in an enchanting sea of firefly light. The same lively collection of vendors Alex remembered were busily packing up for the evening, and an entirely new collection were just beginning their evening of hawking and bustling. The lantern light flickered off the multicolored buildings as they walked the streets and Alex took the city in. Despite the fear and chaos of the world around it, Felwind was still the same eclectically human city it had been when Alex left it, and she was at ease just being back in the commotion.

"So, it looks like you got rid of your fox infestation?" Alex asked as they walked.

"Yes ma'am," Sal said. "We're not sure what your team did when you were away, but it got the Court stirred up something fierce. The Foxes Guild also had a bad implosion around that time, so we took advantage and sent them packing. I can only hope you had something to do with all that?"

"Nae comment," Kyria said with a smirk which drew a chuckle from Sal.

"The city's never been happier, but it's not all good. The Court has been pushing back hard. Our operatives report that every day it gets worse out there. They've only been hitting us here with small raiding parties, but we're expecting a sizeable force any time now," Sal said as they rounded a bend into an open circular cul du sac. At the center of the circle was a large manor from which murals of snarling foxes glared down at them.

"Another plus, what with the Foxes taking a collective hike, the Guard got some spruced up accommodations. I'll fill you once we're inside. We're fairly sure we got the last of their spies out of town, but you can't ever be too careful," Sal said. Alex and her friends followed her inside, while Larm found a nearby rooftop to perch on.

"I kind of figured a dragon would be a bigger deal? Why aren't people running around screaming about it?" Alex asked.

"Nobody in living memory has ever seen one," Marin said. "They probably just think it's an enormous lizard. As for why that's not strange, you've got me there."

Alex shrugged and continued in passed the foyer. The inside of the building was exactly the decadence she figured it would be. Orange bannisters cascaded down to marble floors and every part of the walls were covered in gold and precious stones. Just like in the Den, there were painting of foxes everywhere. As the group entered a dining room that was three times the size of Alex's entire trailer back on earth, she noted several guardsmen along the far wall removing panels with what looked like crowbars.

"We're selling the place off, bit by bit. Plenty of merchants in the city with good coin for this sort of nonsense," Sal said, rolling her eyes.

It didn't surprise Alex to learn that Sal wasn't one for ornate decorations. She didn't seem to have changed much since they last met. Her grey hair was orderly and her eyes were just as sharp.

They all sat down on one end of an enormous dining table and Sal called a nearby guardsman over, whispering something into his ear. Moments later he reappeared from another room with a large plate of cold meat and several smaller plates of fruit and cheese. Alex didn't wait for an invitation and dug in. "They may have been evil, but they had excellent taste, and they stuffed their larder to the roof," Alex said between bites.

After a satisfying meal, Sal debriefed the situation. "As I said outside, something a while back sent the Court into a panic. Raids across Aquillon are up, and it seems the territories still under direct control of the hands are suffering mightily. I heard tell they executed an entire village in the Lethalan's just last week. But more than that, the demons seem nervous, scared even. I'm guessing there's a story to tell there."

Alex filled Sal in on the events of the last month. Her voice broke a little when she recapped the events at Daemonfall. Thistle's absence still hurt. She finished her story and Sal squeezed her hand.

"I'm sorry for your loss. He was a good and honorable man."

Alex couldn't find the words to respond, so she nodded.

"Well, that all makes enough sense. From what we can gather, the Lord of Long Shadows has united all the hands again under his banner, like he did in the Fall. The only reason they'd be willing to work together is if they felt threatened. So, you've done something nobody had managed in a thousand years, Miss Winters."

"Bully for me," Alex said. Somehow serving as the driving force behind a gigantic family reunion of demon lords and ladies wasn't feeling like a win in her book.

Sal continued. "It seems they've been biding their time, just exacting revenge on the people under their heels, but it's not all bad. Pockets of resistance have been springing up. A couple weeks back we got reports of a village near Shelhyle that rose and threw the lesser demons out of town. They had to abandon the village and go into hiding. But the stories of your exploits have traveled, and we've never seen people like this. We've only ever been able to convince them to hide us and give us supplies, never fight back. You're giving people hope, Miss Winters, and that's a lot more than they've had in a long time."

Alex smiled a little. The thought of people rallying behind her was both exhilarating and terrifying. She had never even been an assistant manager at the diner, so being a rallying symbol of hope and rebellion was a new hat for her.

A dull blast of a horn in the distance cut the conversation short. Kyria and Sal both perked up and looked at each other.

"Tha's no' good," Kyria said.

"They'd only sound that horn for one reason. It seems the Court of Hours has sent a welcome party for you, Alex," Sal said with a grim smile.

"They really know how to make a girl feel special," Alex said.

"Come on, we need to get to the Western Gate," Sal said.

Running outside, Kyria cracked the night air with a sharp whistle. Larm came wafting down from the rooftops. He had a chicken in his mouth.

"Ah, now where did ya get tha' chicken ya scaley galoot?" Kyria asked with an annoyed voice of a mother whose child had just gotten into some trouble.

180

Larm gulped down the chicken. "Larm found chickens in nice man's backyard. Larm like chicken. Nice man gave some to Larm. Not sure why, but chickens are tasty." He punctuated his statement by licking Kyria's hand. She yelped and did not engage the dragon with further questions. They all hopped on Larm's back, including Sal, who seemed more than skeptical. Larm lifted into the air and they deposited them on the ramparts of the western wall in no time.

As soon as they looked out beyond the walls, a bucket of icy fear doused Alex. Beyond the walls, demons filled the valley leading up to the city. Glowing portals near the rear of the army spewed forth more by the minute, and at the rear of the army, several Hands were gathered. A huge golden ox with glowing green eyes stood two hooves and held a great scepter in two hands. Alex recognized him as the Hand of Four, Lord of Idols. His golden host stood in front of him in perfect rows. Next to him, a swarm of locust buzzed about and formed the figure of a man. She figured this to be the Hand of Ten, Lord of Plagues, given the horde of zombies in front of him. Next to the Hand of Ten was the Hand of Two, Lady of Deep Waters. Her muradae stretch before her as a vast, unchecked army of chittering madness.

There was no time.

The Court of Hours had come.

22

The Siege of Felwind

As the last of the demons poured from the portals, a silence settled over the valley like a thick blanket, saturated with darkness and accented by fearful breathing. It seemed to last forever, and Alex was hearing her own heartbeat reverberate in her head when a distant trumpet blast shattered the silence. There was a flurry of movement from within the demons' battle lines. The center of each line of warriors broke, and the Hands moved forward, within shouting distance of the walls.

Once they were close enough to be seen in the torchlight from the walls of the city, Alex shuddered at their appearance. The Lady of Deep Waters was much like Alex remembered her, only bigger now. It seemed they could manipulate their size to suit their purpose, though Alex doubted it was anything more than an illusion. Next to her stood the swarm of locust, acting as one being. Thousands of insects formed each limb, and from the center of the being's face, black eyes that swirled with black energy peered out into the world. Taking up the right flank was the Lord of Idols. The giant anthropomorphic ox was covered in gold jewelry and fine linens, and the torchlight danced off the gems in his scepter. Beneath him a small army of humans formed a litter, carrying the weight of the Lord. Alex's stomach churned at the sight.

"Well now, my dear thrall, I was so hoping we'd run into each other again," the Hand of Two preened in her horrible voice.

"That makes one of us, snake face, but if you're looking for more of what I served you back in Vandlehaven, step right up," Alex shouted back. Her voice carried a borrowed confidence, as she lent it as much as she could spare. Even if her abilities had been greatly enhanced, this was still looking like a fairly one-sided fight.

"I regret your time in our world has made you no more respectful of beings of more worth than you. A pity. Still, we did not come to parley with you. We came to bargain with the people of Felwind." She stopped speaking and the Hand of Four spoke from his throne.

"We do not seek your destruction. We have known of your city for some time, but always we have left it alone. Give us the girl, and we will maintain this truce. No one needs to die tonight." His voice was thick and smooth, and even Alex had trouble focusing. It was also louder somehow and seemed to echo through the dark streets behind her.

Clever, Alex thought to herself. They knew they'd never convince the guard to give Alex up, but common folk were more easily swayed. Alex heard a stirring in the streets behind the walls she and her friends were standing on.

In the streets below, a large group of townspeople had gathered. They all held torches and a variety of simple weapons. Alex had seen this in more than a few Frankenstein movies, and she had a bad feeling she knew how it would end. Sal, Kyria, and Ahrun were tensed up, hands on their sword hilts. Marin was quietly standing in the back, but looked as though he was reading a few incants. A young woman came forward in the crowd.

"Which one of you is Alex Winters?" she shouted up.

Alex came forward and raised her arm. "I am."

"The things they say about you, from Alcrest, is it true? Did you really escape?"

"I did. We made it out. And we killed more than a few demons on our way out. I know you don't owe me anything, and I can't ask you to take up my fight."

The young woman cut her off and threw up a small necklace.

"It's not just your fight. My husband died in Alcrest. This necklace was all I could get back from him, from smugglers. If you're really the girl who stood against the Lord of Long Shadows, and won, then we won't be sending you anywhere. We're with you, Alex Winters, so no more wives have to get necklaces back for husbands, or fathers. Come on, lads!" The young woman had whipped the crowd into a frenzy, and Alex called out to them.

Alex waved back to them and turned back to the lords and lady.

"It seems the people of Felwind have no plans on falling for your garbage. This is a city of free men, so if you want to get me, you'll have to come and take me," Alex shouted back.

"So. Illogical. Thralls. Are. They. Will. Be. Perfected. We. Can. Still. Save. Them." The buzzing from the locusts that made up the Hand of Ten was almost so chaotic it was hard to catch the words.

"My dear Lord of Plagues, when will you ever learn? All you have to do is take their minds!" The Hand of Four said nonchalantly.

"You two can do what you want with your share of the thralls. I'm killing mine," The Hand of Two replied. "Muradae! Attack!" As soon as the cry went forth from her lips, the Muradae descended on the city like a crashing wave, and the rotfiends and golden hosts charged in after them.

As soon as the demons came within range, the archers on the walls launched a torrent of arrows into the valley below and cut down a swath of demons in the first volley alone. The lords and lady seemed to wince a bit as the archers destroyed them, but it was momentary and the demons reformed at the end of the line and charged back into battle.

The first wave hit the walls, and they shuddered. The rotfiends came first in wave after wave, forming a platform for the golden hosts and muradae to climb on. The archers fired again, but their arrows merely picked raindrops out of an ocean. Alex and Marin climbed up onto the ramparts, apparently thinking the same thing. Alex turned back to Ahrun and Kyria.

"You two man the gate below. It won't hold forever. I'll cast a warding incant on it, but even that won't keep them out for long." Neither of her friends seemed pleased to leave Alex, but they obliged and disappeared down the steps into the street below. Alex turned to Marin. "On three."

He nodded.

Alex focused on quieting her mind, and it came easier than she figured it would have. The demons had nearly reached the top of the wall under a surging pile of rotfiend zombies. Despite the panicked shouting of guardsmen around her, Alex remained calm, and the world was quiet. She focused on the sensation of heat and channeled her thoughts below. Extending her palms, a font of liquid fire poured from her hands and onto the demons. There was a screeching sound as it reached them and they dissolved. On the other side of the wall Marin was blasting the demons with a stream of frozen energy and their ascent slowed.

Boosted by the temporary setback, the Old Guard troops around them rallied and began fighting with renewed energy, cutting down any eel demon or golden host that neared the top of the wall. Alex continued her rain of death from above, as did Marin, but they were still losing by the numbers. As fast as they could melt or freeze a demon, they seemed to reform at the far end of the battlefield near their respective lord and charge back into battle. Alex wasn't slowing down, but she felt herself draining.

On his end of the rampart, Marin was barely keeping up. He had to stop every so often and re-cast his incants, and in the delay, several demons broke onto the top of the rampart. They were cut down immediately, but Alex could see the writing on the wall. This was a battle they had already lost, they just hadn't lost it yet.

From somewhere in the back of her peripheral vision, Alex noticed a large, yellow object hovering. Turning for a moment, Alex saw Larm hovering in the air behind the wall. She had somehow forgotten that they had a dragon.

"Larm help? Friends need help?" the dragon asked.

"Yes," Alex shouted back, trying her best not to sound irritated. Larm was not the most observant creature.

"How Larm help?"

Alex again tried not to sound snippy, figuring it was best not to look a gift dragon in the mouth. She couldn't see in the street below, but it sounded like the gate was nearly breached. Demons had popped over the tops of the wall where a defender had fallen, or when Marin had to stop and recast his incant.

"Ok, see the not human things?"

"Yes! Larm sees."

"Just burn them or eat them, or get rid of them somehow. That'd be great!" Alex said.

"Yes. Larm can do that."

With that, Larm vanished as he shot skyward. For a dreadful few minutes Alex was very concerned that he had literally gone to chase a wild goose, but a moment later there was a flash of yellow and then an explosion of heat. Larm shot back down and pulled up at the last second, avoiding the ground, then turned his head and unleashed a pillar of the most intense fire Alex had ever seen. Even from up on the walls, the heat seared her face, and she had to look away. The dragon's fire instantly incinerated the base of the zombie-ladder, and the demons fell backward into a pit of roasting zombies. Looking up, Alex saw that the Hands were all stunned, and the demons were reforming slowly nearby, but not nearly at the rate they were.

As the demons who survived the initial onslaught slowly recovered and stood, they paused the attack, looking back to their lines for orders. The Hands screamed back to them in a language Alex didn't recognize and they renewed their assault, this time focusing on the gate. Alex looked over to Marin who was exhausted, but seemed to get what she wanted, and they glimmered to the street below.

The situation on the ground was much worse than Alex had thought. Everywhere, guardsmen and women sat in oppressive silence, recovering from wounds and fatigue. As Alex arrived at the gate, her heart sank. The gate was a shattered mess, torn with holes and splintering everywhere. In fact, if not for the warding incant still holding it together, the demons would have flooded the city.

"Nice o' ya ta join us common folk down here." Alex heard Kyria's voice and turn with a smile, but it vanished as soon as she saw her friend lying against a nearby wall. Ahrun was kneeling beside her, clutching her hand. Her voice was strained, and she seemed pale in the moonlight. Sweat matted her auburn hair, and she leaned her head against Ahrun's chest.

"Oh god, are you ok?" Alex asked in a panic as she ran over.

"I'm fine, don' ya go blubberin' over my corpse just yet," Kyria said with a scoff.

"What happened," Alex asked.

"The ward fell for a moment and a muradae spear made it through," Ahrun said. "I think she'll be alright, but if the ward falls again, we're all doomed. We heard the dragon outside, but once the demons breach

187

the walls, the dragon won't be able to attack them in the city."

Alex nodded. She needed a plan. She heard Larm swoop through and felt the heat of his attack, but she heard fewer shrieks. "Stay here," she told Ahrun and Kyria.

"I wasn't plannin' on goin' anywhere," Kyria said with an eye roll and chuckle.

Ahrun nodded.

Alex wanted to heal her friend, but she was feeling drained and she needed to save her strength.

Alex turned to Marin.

"So hear me out," she began.

"I'm not going to like this, am I?" Marin asked. He still sounded exhausted and looked like he only had one or two more incants in him before he collapsed.

"Probably not, but shut up and listen. What if we did a frost fire nova incant?"

"You mean that spell that neither of us have ever studied, and that's only been cast experimentally, and killed everyone who took part, and was then subsequently banned? That frost fire nova?"

"Well, when you put it like that..." Alex said. "All of that aside, do you think it could work?"

"I mean, frost fire is an unstable, unnatural element that should prevent any demons it touches from reforming, at least for a good long while, so yes, assuming we could cast it without dying horrible, painful deaths, it should work. But I'm the only one who knows how to cast it, and I'm not nearly powerful enough, even on a day when I haven't been freezing hordes of demons."

"Well, I had an idea. But I'm not sure how well it'll work. Do you trust me?"

"I'd say it's about sixty, forty in your favor at this point."

Alex frowned at him and found the strength to punch his arm. He chuckled.

"Of course, I trust you, dummy. I followed you into a volcano."

"Ok, well come on then." Alex pulled him up and into the center of the street. She had never ever thought of trying something like this, and she wasn't sure magic would do it, but it was something. And something almost always beat nothing. She focused her mind on him, everything she knew about him, and let her power stream into him, and before long she let go. It had worked. Alex raised her right arm, and Marin did.

"Ok Alex, what exactly did you do?"

Marin was talking, but it seemed only to be in Alex's head.

"I'm not sure, but I think I did a Vulcan mind meld? I'm not really sure if this has another name, so I'm gonna go with that."

"You mean we're..." Marin trailed off.

"Yup."

"And do you have any idea how to sever this connection?"

"Not really. I was hoping to learn as I went. On-the-job training."

"Delightful. Well, let's go then. How did you intend to get out there anyway to cast this thing? If we glimmer out there, we're dead. If we go out the gate, we're dead, as is everybody else."

"I've got an idea for that, but I don't think you're going to like that either."

As they flew high above the battlefield on Larm's back, the steady stream of unmentionable curses flowing from Marin's mind to Alex's was indeed confirmation that Marin did not like Alex's idea. Or riding dragons. Or heights. Still, Alex hadn't been able to figure out a way to get them where they needed to be without getting killed, so here they were.

"So, can we review this hair-brained scheme of yours?" Marin's thoughts flowed through Alex's mind.

"We jump off the dragon and glimmer into the center of their army right before we hit the ground and cast the frost fire nova before we get killed by angry demons?"

"Perfect. What could go wrong?"

"That's the spirit, buddy!" Alex grinned her most genuine smile at Marin, but it didn't seem to make him like the plan any more. Alex had her reservations too, but she didn't see any way around it. If they glimmered into the demons from the ground, it wouldn't take them long to figure out what happened and overwhelm Alex and Marin, but glimmering from a dead fall would transfer over the momentum and stun whatever demons were around them, which should provide them with enough time to cast the incant.

Hopefully.

They had reached what Alex had noted in her head as the drop point and she dug her heels into Larm, who stopped and hovered over the battlefield. They were high enough to be out of the range of spears, arrows, and other projectiles, but Alex wasn't about to wait around and see what kind of demon magic the Court could hurl up here.

"Ready?" She asked Marin in her mind.

"No."

"Great. On the count of three. One, two…" Alex pulled them off the dragon, and they began their impromptu sky dive. Alex thought Marin had exhausted his supply of curses on the flight over. She was wrong.

As they fell and picked up speed Alex searched through Marin's mind. This was a new incant, so she didn't quite know how it all worked. Marin wasn't putting up any resistance, and she could move through his mind until she found what she was looking for. She saw the incant for the frost fire nova, and she prepared his mind to cast it. There was something else poking around in the edges of Marin's mind, but whatever it was was highly guarded, even from Marin himself. It intrigued Alex, but there was no time to focus on anything but

THE SIEGE OF FELWIND

the spell. She opened herself to him and she felt her power flowing into him. The ground was growing close now, so she focused on the glimmer, and left the nova to Marin, turning the reigns back over to him.

The ground was close now, and she focused on a spot near a group of demons who were hoisting a battering ram. At the moment before they hit the ground she opened her mind and focused on that spot, until they glimmered there, flattening ever demon nearby. As they got up Alex saw Marin working through the incant and opened her mind to him completely, letting power flow without limit into Marin. At the moment before it overwhelmed him, he unleashed the nova.

Alex didn't remember much of what happened next. The nova went off with a screeching hiss of steam as the mage fire and frost combined into one chaotic force, each trying to destroy the other. With Marin as the epicenter, the nova exploded out and the destructive frost fire consumed everything. Demons evaporated with a chorus of screams and did not reform at the edge of their lines. The nova spread out onto the battlefield and the demons broke rank, retreating to the portals that were now re-opening. All three Hands abandoned the field and most of their troops jumped into the portals after them. They closed behind the demon lords, leaving a portion of the lesser demons stranded, until the nova of frost fire reached them and consumed them. Alex slumped over and darkness took her.

By the time consciousness returned to her, Alex didn't know how many hours had passed, but the sun shining over her provided some idea. As she tried to move, she felt herself being lifted. She peered up at Marin, helping her rise into a sitting position.

"Hey, buddy. Did we die?" Alex asked hazily.

"Nope, no death, although if you ever pull a stunt like that again, I might kill you. You nearly did yourself in as it was, but you pulled through. I'm not sure how much magic you channeled, but it wasn't healthy. Don't do that again. Ever." From Marin's tone, he wasn't joking.

Alex tasted blood in her mouth and she ached all over. She was inclined to take his advice. Alex looked around and saw Kyria hobbling over, supported by Ahrun.

"Always have ta outdo me, eh? Showoff," Kyria said.

"You know, I'm all about the big show," Alex said, making her best attempt at jazz hands. She then realized nobody knew what jazz hands were and felt fairly dumb. Kyria looked better, but still seemed pale.

"Did we win?" Alex asked. Her head still felt like someone was doing a twenty-one gun salute inside of it.

"For now," Ahrun said. "But according to Sal, the demons will be back. This is the fourth attack they've repelled."

"So even with my powers, and a dragon, we still didn't get rid of them?" Alex asked. Her feeling of victory had been short lived. "So how do we win, if we can't even kill these things?"

"That's the question," Sal said as she walked over from a nearby medical tent. "We've been winning some battles across Aquillon, but every time it's the same. We kill them, they reform somewhere else in a few days, then come back. Even if we win the battles, they will win the war."

"There has to be someone who knows how to beat them, doesn't there?" Alex asked.

"Well, no one remembers anything from before the Fall, so nobody has any real insight on where the demons came from, or how to send them back," Sal said.

"Even you?" Alex asked Ahrun.

"Well, I lost access to my order's memories when I gave up my immorality, but even before that, no. I have some memory of the Fall itself, but nothing that would provide a clue of how to defeat the Court. When the Court of Hours came to Rakara a thousand years ago, it was like a wind of destruction. They came without warning, and left nothing in their wake, with no hint of their motivations or origin. We only know they are not of Aquillon." Alex realized she had never heard him talk about his life before becoming a paladin, but that was a conversation for another day.

"So, what's the play then?" Alex asked, exasperated.

"I think I might know a lead, but it's dangerous," Marin said, speaking up.

"We're in," Kyria said, without missing a beat.

"You might want to hear my idea first, before agreeing to it?" Marin said skeptically. "There's a reason I didn't suggest it earlier."

23

The Seaward Cities

Alex had to admit, even by the normally insane standard with which she now judged plans, this one was extra-strength crazy.

"You know the Seaward Cities? Or what's left of them, anyway?" Marin asked. They all nodded.

"The Seaward Cities were part of the ancient Aquillonian Empire, and while I remember no more than anyone else, I thought it might be a place to start. There's just one catch."

"I'm assuming it has something to do with the fact that they're underwater?" Ahrun asked with a wry chuckle.

"Well, not all of them, technically. The top half of them almost killed me when I first got here," Alex added.

"Not even close to the top half, actually. I've been to the Seaward Cities, and they extend far into the depths," Marin said.

"I don' care how deep these blazin' ruins are, what possible reason could we have ta go there?" Kyria asked.

"Well, I know that when the Court conquered Aquillon, they destroyed most of the records of, well, everything, but I'm guessing they didn't bother with whatever was in the Seaward Cities since they sank during the Fall. I'd bet my last imperial marc that there'd be some usable information down there."

"Down in the sunken city where we can' go since we're no' fish?" Kyria asked.

"Yes. Well, yes, that it's in the city, but we can go. I believe I know an incant that should serve our purposes, and I even think I know which of the Seaward Cities the lost Archives are in. Besides, even if we don't get what we need, there's a veritable treasure trove of information down there and we could…" Alex and Kyria both gave him a dirty look and he waved them off. "It was just a thought!"

"And the ghosts?" Ahrun asked. Even he didn't seem sold on the plan.

Alex remembered seeing them as they passed through a sunken city on Sulas's ship after their encounter with Ahazi.

"Oh, right. The ghosts. I think I might know a way around that too. Alex, think you could work up an invisibility incant?" Marin asked.

"Well, I've never done it before, but I could practice on the way?"

"And if it doesn't work?" Kyria demanded.

"Well, then the ghosts will rip us apart, or drown us. Or both," Ahrun said with a grim look on his face.

"Look, I know it's not the best idea, but unless anybody has another one. These might be the only archives on Aquillon that weren't destroyed with the coming of the Court. If there's an answer there, we have to look for it!" Marin sounded convicted and Alex sighed. As usual, the insane plan was the only viable one.

"Well, I for one am on board with the insane plan!" Alex said.

"Comin' from the girl who is most often the author of an' just completed caryin' out an insane plan," Kyria said skeptically with a wheezing cough. Ahrun caught her for support.

"Easy there. That's enough sass from you," Ahrun said with a smile.

"Well, if you are intending to follow through with this insane plan, I'd suggest you get moving," Sal said. "Not that I don't enjoy hosting you all, but I think they knew you would be here and sent a force to match. If you're moving on anyway, I suggest you do it soon, for the sake of my city."

Alex felt a little put off by the comment, but she understood. Sal had more to worry about than Alex and her friends.

"She's right," Alex said. "If the demon lords are targeting us, we need to be scarce."

No one seemed to be in the mood to argue the point, so they shuffled back to the former lair of the Foxes Guild. Once they arrived, they packed their belongings and met outside where Larm had made a new friend.

Alex smelled who it was before she saw them. Only one person on Aquillon had so perfectly married the unpleasant odor of day-old fish with the stink of week old liquor. Horace was outside, playing with Larm, who seemed to get great amusement out of trying to lick him. Alex put a stop to it as it worried her that Larm might succeed and become sick, and they sort of needed their ride.

"Horace, it's so… to see you," Alex called out to him. He looked up and seemed a bit puzzled at first, but then returned the greeting in the form of an affectionate grunting sound. He saw Kyria before it was too late and ran over and hugged her. She pried him off while gagging.

"Eee gods, Horace, ya drunkard. What are ya playin' about?" Kyria asked, still attempting not to hurl.

"I just heard that you lot were in town and I wanted to say hello!" Horace beamed.

"Aye, well consider it said, we're gettin' out o' town as we speak," Kyria said.

"Leaving so soon? Why? Did something happen?" Horace asked.

Kyria and Alex both rolled their eyes and pointed back towards the pillar of smoke coming from the western gate.

"Oh my! I must report at once! I wouldn't want anyone to think I was shirking my duty as a member of the Old Guard!" Horace exclaimed while running (well, more like hobbling) towards the gate. Alex and Kyria exchanged a glance and laughed.

"It's nice that some things don't change," Alex said, between laughs.

"Aye, tha' it is," Kyria agreed, wiping tears from her eyes.

The rest of the group was gathering downstairs with their belongings, and Sal walked outside.

"Look, I hate to kick you out like this," she began.

"Don't mention it. We understand," Alex said, clasping a hand on her shoulder. She turned to her friends. "Everybody read?"

They all nodded, so Kyria gave a sharp whistle, and Larm, who had been chasing birds on the rooftops, slowly descended. The group climbed on his back, and they were ready to leave.

"Now, just because I'm giving you the boot, doesn't mean I don't want to see your ugly mugs again. Don't go getting yourselves killed now!" Sal called out to them as Larm climbed skyward.

"We'll do our best," Alex yelled back down to her. In all honesty, she wasn't sure she could keep that promise. Once they were over top of the city's roofs, they picked up speed. In the streets below, a cry went up, and Alex looked down on the entire town lining the streets, cheering for them. Small children ran about with colorful streamers, and people of all ages were cheering them on. Alex wondered if they realized how much danger she and her friends had brought to the city. Still, it was nice to be cheered on by someone. Being a hero had to have at least a few perks, every now and again.

As they passed over the lake and banked left to continue west, Alex sat back and enjoyed the simple pleasure of the wind blowing through her hair. Looking back at her friends, Marin was reading through scrolls from his pack, and Kyria had curled up in Ahrun's lap, fast asleep. Alex smiled despite herself. They seemed an odd couple, but whatever they had been through in the Wyld Places had brought them together, and she couldn't be happier for them.

She turned her attention back to the landscape. Her airborne position offered a much different perspective on Aquillon than trudging through it. As they passed from one rolling hill to another, Alex couldn't help but notice the beauty of the land. Subtle hues of green and yellow painted the landscape, and every so often a small farm or settlement would pop into view. Some were abandoned or destroyed, but others were not, and she could see small dots of people going about their daily lives. Small groups of roaming demons (Golden Hosts, by the look of them) noted their presence, but did not attack them. Alex dug her heels into Larm every so often as they would pass a ruined castle full of enemies, and Larm rose higher in the air to avoid them.

High above the land, Alex noticed a large series of ruins and she banked Larm closer to them. From the looks of it, it seemed like it had once been a city, but the place was crawling with demons now. Even from this high up, Alex could see hundreds of humans in white robes, bowing down around the city to large golden statues of an ox. In the center of the city, the Hand of Four himself sat on a large throne before a crowd of worshippers.

"I know what you're thinking." Marin's voice startled her, and she tried her best not to fall off Larm. She turned to him.

"No, not like that. The mental link incant fizzled when you lost consciousness, but I know you well enough to know you want to go down there and rescue those poor souls."

Alex remained silent. Sometimes she hated how well he seemed to know her. Despite the mission, that was exactly what Alex wanted to do.

"It wouldn't do any good. Those people's minds have been lost for a long time. They're little more than husks, sustained by the dark energy of the Lord of Idols. Even if you were to kill him somehow, they would all die. He demands absolute devotion from his flock and doesn't give them reprieve even to sleep or eat. The best thing we can do for them now is to defeat the Court somehow, so that fate doesn't befall anyone else."

Alex didn't respond. She was angry, but she knew Marin was right.

"How do you know so much about Aquillon, anyway?" she asked, changing the subject as they drifted clear of the ruined city and back on course.

"I didn't always live in Sanctum. Five hundred years ago, I lived in a small village, close to here. My parents got caught under the sway of Four, so I ran away. One day when I got cornered by some hosts, I made them explode with my mind. Shortly after that, a Magus found me, and took me to Sanctum?"

"So, the Eastern Watch comes to Aquillon?"

"Rarely, and only to recruit people with the gift. Outside of children born to a magus, one in ten thousand people have the gift, so when someone shows it, they find them."

"So, what will happen to you, now that you've left Sanctum?"

"I'll age, like the rest of the world. We don't really know how Sanctum works, other than that it resulted from Falstaff's deal with the Court, but I don't even know if they built it. It's been there far longer than humans have. There are still many mysteries that even we haven't worked out."

"Well, that makes me feel better, I guess," Alex said. She was about to speak again when a drop of icy rain slammed into her face. The chilly rain woke up Kyria, who shot up with a collection of creative exclamations. Looking up, she realized they were about to leave the lowlands and enter the Drowned Coast. In the months Alex had been gone, the place hadn't changed much.

A line of steel grey thunderheads formed an almost tangible wall between the regions, and as soon as Larm dipped down into the coast, the landscape changed abruptly. The rolling hills were replaced with rocky terrain and sparse vegetation. Lonely pines swayed in the salt breeze and were lashed by howling gusts of wind, and the rain got worse as they flew. Everyone had packed traveling cloaks, so they all pulled them out and braced them against the rain, trying to stay as dry as they could.

Fortunately, they had reached their destination and Alex saw the ruins of the Seaward Cities jutting up out of the crashing surf like the fangs of a sea monster. Alex spotted a clearing close to the beach in a small group of trees and they put down there.

As she jumped off Larm, Alex's boots sank into the sand and the rain lashed her face, but she didn't notice any of those things. What caught Alex's attention was the group of angry men in red coats wielding cutlasses, all pointed at her and her friends. She had nearly forgotten about the Red Fleet, but it seemed they hadn't forgotten about her.

24

Old Acquaintences

"We were hopin' ya might drop by, Miss Winters," was the first thing their leader said to Alex and her friends. He was a man of medium height and age, with wispy brown hair covering a balding head. His eyes were grey and scars covered his face.

Ahrun's sword was out, and even in her injured state, Kyria looked like she was ready for a fight. Marin looked like he was preparing several incants, and Larm seemed to debate between eating the pirates and making friends with them. Despite being outnumbered, Alex felt, for once, that they had the upper hand. She doubted the pirates knew that, though.

"Look, if you're spoiling for a rematch, you picked a bad time, and a back crew to try it on. This won't end well for you," Alex said. Her voice was as sharp as the wind howling through the trees, and she meant every word. There were few things she hated worse than the Court, but humans who worked with them willingly were among them.

"As interestin' as that might prove ta be, lass, I've come to parley.

We'll negotiate in good faith, so long as yer lizard here doesn't get jumpy," the leader said.

Alex was wary of trusting him, but she also wasn't looking to start fights she didn't need to.

"We're listening. Talk," she said.

"Well, we was given orders ta take ya back to the Lady o' deep waters, but I've got a better idea. I'm thinkin' that if I help ye, ye can bring her down and give us our seas back. What says ye?" the captain asked.

"I thought you were working for the Lady? Why sell her out?"

"Look, we're not good men, and don't make claim ta be, but we don't like bein' under anyone's boot heel, no matter how wealthy it makes us. Besides, it was me brother she killed when you escaped Vandlehaven. Granted, I would 'ave killed him if we met up, but he was my brother ta kill. No one else!" The surrounding pirates murmured in agreement, as if the statement made all the sense in the world. Alex supposed it did, to a pirate anyway.

"Let's say I agree. What do we get out of this?" Alex asked.

"First, we don't kill ye. I've heard tell of yer fightin' skills and as formidable as they are, I've six more ships in this area and if I send up this flair, they, and the Court will know where ye are. I don't have ta kill ya ta win," he said.

Alex said nothing and ceded the point.

"If ye agree, I can provide safe passage in this territory, and smuggle ye and yer friends about on me ship. The muradae won't look there."

"And what do we have to do? This seems like an easy bargain on our part?" Marin asked, sounding skeptical.

"Ye just 'ave ta keep fightin' the Court o' Hours, so I think ye still 'ave the tougher end of the bargain."

"Can I confer with my friends?" Alex asked.

The pirate nodded.

Alex turned and huddled up her friends. Larm shoved his enormous head into the circle. She wasn't sure how much use his input would be, but Alex couldn't find the heart to exclude him from the discussion.

"So, what's the move?" Alex asked.

"I know these devils," Ahrun said, spitting on the ground as he spoke, "and I wouldn't trust them with anything. Even if their offer is legitimate, they'll turn on our backs as soon as a better offer comes calling."

"On the other hand," Marin said, "a ship would make getting to the ruins a lot easier. They also know these waters and might get us where we're going faster. I'm not saying the Red Fleet aren't scum, but there might be an advantage to be gained."

"I'm with Ahrun. I don' trust these yellow-bellied dogs for one lick o' a second," Kyria said.

"I think their red coats are very nice. We should trust them!" Larm added, seeming very pleased with his contribution.

"Well, I don't feel great about trusting these idiots, but I don't see as we have much choice, and we have the upper hand. Better the devil you know," Alex said with a resigned shrug. She turned back to the group of pirates. "Very well, we accept your offer. And we'll be needing your ship."

Everyone put their weapons away, and they walked from the clearing to the shore. The landscape hadn't changed much from the last time Alex was in the region, and the weather definitely hadn't improved; it was lousy. By the time they reached a series of questionable row-boats tied up along the beach, Alex was soaked and freezing. She was half tempted to light a fire in her hands to warm up, but she didn't want to show her cards to the pirates any earlier than she had to. She didn't trust them, and wasn't altogether certain about the deal she had made, but it seemed the lesser of two evils.

They got in the boats and pushed off into the choppy, iron colored sea. The only sound that Alex heard over the waves and wind was the grunting of the crew as they pulled the oars. Larm flew alongside them, keeping a cautious distance. The pirates didn't love it, but it was hard to tell a dragon where you preferred for it to be without being barbecued and eaten; a fact that even these dim-witted pirates seemed to respect.

They pulled up to the ship, which bobbed listlessly in the surf's churn, and Alex made her way up a rope ladder and onto the main deck. It reminded her of the one that had pulled her out of the sea all those months ago. It felt strange, like walking into a memory from another life. So much had changed in the span of months, that Alex hardly felt like the same person.

The last of the crew climbed aboard and they pulled up anchor. The captain turned to them.

"Alright, where are we bound for?" he asked.

Marin, who seemed prepared, had already produced a scroll with old maps and markings that no one (other than him) could decipher. "Well," he said, "if we are where I think we are, we need to due east until we come on a statue that looks like a large goddess being swallowed by a sea monster."

"An' this great beasty is…?" Kyria asked.

"Just a myth… probably," Marin said. He tried to sound convincing, but it mostly seemed like he was trying to convince himself as much as anyone else.

"Ok, then we make for the creepy statue. Onward, Captain!" Alex said with conviction. The pirates mostly rolled their eyes and waited for the actual captain to give the order, but then sprang to action once he had. Crewmen scuttled up the mast, and the sails dropped, catching the wind and propelling the ship forward with a shudder. Alex nearly lost her balance, but caught a railing at the last second.

The ship picked up speed, and before long, they were breezing past ruin after ruin. They were just as Alex had remembered; forlorn and beautiful. Graceful columns and sculptures pierced the sky, and Alex wondered what they might have looked like in their former glory. She looked down in the water and the depths extended far below what she could see, plugging down into an everlasting night. Occasionally a shimmer would catch her eye, and she had the distinct feeling that they were not alone. She shivered and pulled her cloak closer to her.

"Ya really got faith in this insane plan o' yer friend's?" Alex turned and saw that Kyria had joined her on the railing.

"I'm afraid I do," Alex said with a sigh. She understood Kyria's hesitation. Her friend wasn't quick to trust, and this was an admittedly crazy plan.

"So, I take it ya trust this eegit then, do ya?"

"Guilty again. We went through a lot when we were looking for the Path of Flames, and I feel like there were a hundred good chanced to abandon me. And he never took them. I've found that's a good mark of whom to trust around here, don't you agree?" Alex asked with a grin.

"I can' argue tha'." Kyria said, staring vacantly off to the shore.

"So, are we ready to spill some more details about this situation?" Alex asked while nodding towards Ahrun.

"Look, I'm no' even sure if there's anythin' there, alright?"

"I mean, you didn't fall into anyone else's lap to take your snooze on the ride over," Alex muttered.

Kyria punched her in the arm, but didn't argue the point.

"We just... we went through a lot, an' I guess I had never seen him like... tha' before. Well, I hadn't seen anyone like tha' before, and something jus' changed. Tha's all. I can' explain it any better than tha'."

"I get it. I'm happy for both of you. I mean it. I don't know what tomorrow's bringing at this rate, but just enjoy it while you can. There seems to be enough misery on Aquillon to last us all till doomsday and beyond, so it's nice to see a little happiness. Besides, there's not an overabundance of cute guys as far as I've seen, so you know, you could have done worse," Alex said with an impish smile.

"I can' argue with ya there," Kyria said.

"Can't argue about what?" Ahrun asked, sliding up to the railing. Alex stifled a giggle and Kyria's face exploded in a deep crimson blush. Thankfully for her, a horn cut through the awkward silence and the shrill voice of a lookout cut down through the howling wind.

"Target spotted off the starboard side!"

All three of them looked up, and Marin rushed to the side of the ship. Rising from the depths was exactly what Marin had described. The statue, depicting some long-forgotten goddess, stood at least three stories tall, and given that it was only exposed from the shoulders up, it was easily the most impressive structure Alex had laid eyes on since her arrival. Coiling around the neck of the graceful figure were the tentacles of what appeared to be an octopus, though the head wasn't visible. Several tall structures surrounded the statues, forming a ring, watched over by the pale eyes of the goddess. It was a haunting image, but Alex realized that something else had stirred the crew to a frenzy.

Alex looked down at the water around the statue. It appeared to move in a downward circular pattern. The seas around the ring were rough, but seemed to move randomly, but this was a specific pattern of water being pulled downward. The captain called out, and a crewman dropped the anchor, bringing the ship to a halt, just before it entered the whirlpool. Even from their anchored position, Alex could feel the currents pulling at the ship.

"Well, the entrance won't be doing us any favors," Marin said with an exasperated sigh.

"Does it ever?" Ahrun asked. Marin looked like he wanted to say something, but he just shrugged in apparent agreement.

"So, how do we get down there now?" Alex asked. "I'm assuming just jumping in would be a terrible plan."

"Well, I have an idea, but it's not a very good one," Marin said. Alex just sighed. She was getting sick of the run of not very good ideas, but staring down at the whirlpool of doom wasn't inspiring her with anything helpful, so she nodded at Marin.

"I know an old incant that might help us. It wasn't ever used much, mostly because nobody saw a use for it, but it's stable enough. It's a tornado incant. It might pull the water in the other direction, cancelling out its motion, and slowing the water long enough for a diver or two to get down there."

"I'm sensin' a but comin'," Kyria said.

"Well, someone would have to stay here to tether the spell or the tornado will just move wherever it wants, like, well, a tornado."

"I think Kyria should stay," Ahrun mumbled with no prompting.

"Like hells I am. There's no way I'm stayin' up on this leaky ramshackle tub, while yer off playin' mermaids! I'm goin'! I don' need ya doin' me any grand favors!" Kyria shot back with a fire lighting in her eyes.

"I'm not," Ahrun yelled back, his deep voice rising above the howl of the wind. "With your injury, I don't know if you would keep up, and you're no good to anyone dead and we need someone to tether the spell to up here."

Kyria was nearly to Ahrun's face to continue shouting when she slipped, barely catching herself. She clutched at her side where the spear wound didn't look all the way healed. She glared at Ahrun and her eyes were dripping with anger, but she said nothing else. It was an argument she knew she would not win, but Alex was grateful that she didn't have to step in.

The three gathered near the edge of the deck. Marin looked at Kyria. "You don't need to do anything other than not move. I'm tethering the effect to you, so if you move, it does too. Got it?" Kyria gave him an angry glare and a curt nod. Marin turned back to Ahrun and Alex.

207

"Alright, Alex, I'll work on the air bubble, you work on the invisibility spell, ok?" Alex nodded. She had thought of it on the way over and had made her left arm shimmer out of sight a few times. How much harder could three full size humans be?

They were just about ready to make the dive, and Marin turned and began chanting. In no time, a large twister filled with arcane energy rocketed out of his palm and into the water. Alex watched as the arcane winds dissipated throughout the whirlpool and the vortex slowly came to a halt. Marin turned and grabbed Kyria's palm, leaving a small ball of energy.

"Ok, now just don't move or… everybody dies," he said.

Kyria gave him a death stare and rolled her eyes. However annoyed she was, Kyria followed the order admirably and plopped down on a nearby barrel. Marin turned to Alex and Ahrun and cast another spell on them. At once, Alex's vision blurred, and it became hard to breathe.

"Don't fret, it'll all even out underwater. Now for that invisibility spell?" Marin asked, before casting his spell on himself. Alex concentrated and felt the power flow over her and her friends. Slowly the rest of the crew and Kyria seemed to vanish. Alex looked around, but she could only see Ahrun and Marin.

"Um, where is everyone?" Alex asked, the smallest panic gripping her voice.

"We're still out here, it's you eegits who've gone an' disappeared." Alex realized how the spell was working. The trouble with her new powers, as opposed to proper incants, was that her powers always seemed to do what she wanted them to, but not always in the way she wanted them to. Her spell had made her and her friends invisible, but it had also made everyone else vanish, at least to her anyway.

"Alright, well then I guess we're ok!" Alex said. Turning to Marin, she said, "Ready to dive whenever you are."

"Ahrun, if yer listin', mark me. If you go an' get yerself killed without me, I will hunt down your ghost and beat it up. So, ya know, stay safe." Kyria said.

"Ok, we need to get going, now. The tornado won't last forever, we need to get diving." Not waiting for further invitation, Marin took a running start and jumped over the side of the ship into the dark waters below. Ahrun was the next to follow suit, leaving only Alex. She collected her breath and jumped over the railing, plunging headfirst into the black, freezing waters.

25

The Archive Beneath The Waves

The water hit Alex's body like cold lightening as she came up to the surface, shivering. She concentrated on warmth and slowly a soft blanket of warm energy passed over her She looked around to find her friends. Even though she could hear yelling from the ship, she looked up and didn't see anyone. Several seconds later, Marin and Ahrun surfaced. Alex could feel the drain that the invisibility spell was putting on her, and she knew they had to hurry.

"Alright, follow me. We need to stay close or this underwater incant won't work. I know it seems counter-intuitive, but as soon as you get under the water, open your eyes and mouths and take the deepest breath you can."

Alex and Ahrun nodded and followed Marin below the waves as he dived under.

Alex opened her eyes, and she looked around. It was dark, but she could see as well as on land and everything seemed somewhat illuminated, providing improved visibility. Even though it was just dark shadows and silhouettes, she could make out the floor of the ocean. Turning, she saw Ahrun and Marin had swum towards the ruins. Even from this distance, she could see the lines of unstable wind magic holding the whirlpool at bay. She paused and despite her body fighting her not to do so, she opened her mouth and sucked in as much seawater as she could.

Marin's spell worked. Even though it didn't do much for the flavor, breathing in the water was like breathing air. As she swam, she took deep breaths of it and by the time they reached the outer edge of the ring of structures she had become an accomplished fish. Marin's spell also seemed to do something to her swimming abilities. Each movement through the water was easier, and more powerful than it should have been.

Marin reached the first ruined tower and paused, finding a handhold. The details of the structure came into clearer view as Alex neared it. It was just as beautiful as above the water, but down here it was more preserved. Algae and coral grew overtop of it, but the stunning architecture still shone through. The structure got progressively bigger as it reached the ocean floor. Some rooms still seemed like they could be entered, though time and tide had destroyed others.

"Alright, if I read that map right, the entrance to the archive should be at the base of the statue," Marin said. Alex and Ahrun looked over in surprise at Marin. "That's the last component of the spell. We can talk to each other, but I'd recommend keeping the chatter down. I have seen nothing yet, but we are definitely not alone down here."

Alex and Ahrun nodded, and they continued their descent.

Despite her spell, Alex was nearly numb by the time they reached the bottom. She had extended it to her friends, but the cold was pervasive and unrelenting. She also felt the pressure of the surrounding water, but Marin's spell seemed to keep it at bay, at least for the moment.

Once they reached the bottom, Alex could assess the size and scale of the statue and the surrounding structures, and they were mesmerizing. The statue was by far the biggest thing she had seen on Aquillon, and the towers that surrounded it were equally impressive. Surrounding the statue, a flat surface of white stone and tile connected the statue in what appeared to have been an open square during the time of the empire. Sea plants had overtaken the regal stones, and it was now just a watery memory of grander times gone by.

"We should fan out," Marin said when they touched down at the bottom. "It's near the statue, but we'll have a better chance of finding it if we split up."

Alex didn't wait for further instructions and kicked off the bottom of the platform, swimming left. Even with her enhanced underwater vision thanks to Marin's incant, it was still hard to see down there. Layers of centuries-old silt and debris clouded the water and got progressively worse as Alex moved about the water. She was nearly finished when she noticed a small glimmer. How the object was catching any light down here was anybody's guess, but Alex swam over to investigate, regardless.

The glimmer was at the base of the statue, nearly to the left foot. Alex pulled off some seaweeds and algae and revealed an iridescent pearl knob. She was about to touch it when she felt the water get even colder than it already was. She looked up and saw that two figures were floating a short distance above her head. The light passed through their ethereal shapes and she could barely make out their faces, but it seemed to be a man and a woman in strange clothing. Ducking down, Alex swam under a nearby boulder, waiting for them to pass. She had no idea where Ahrun and Marin were, but she just hoped that they would see the ghosts before they were discovered. Alex didn't know much about this invisibility spell that she had created, but if she could see ghosts, they could probably see her.

The two specters had nearly passed by completely when Alex felt a sharp pain and yelped, letting out a cloud of air bubbles. She looked down, realizing that she had caught herself on a sharp piece of coral.

Alex silenced herself, but she knew it was too late. She looked up from under the boulder and saw that the two spirits had stopped and were now frantically looking around, trying to find the source of the noise. They floated downwards and probed the area.

Alex pressed herself against the backside of the boulder and pressed her hands against her mouth. The cut on her leg still stung, but she had a feeling it would feel better than whatever those creatures might do to her. She felt the water grow colder and colder as one ghost passed by the boulder and stopped, only a foot or two from where Alex was hiding. It began to turn and Alex braced herself for a fight, but at the last moment a series of shrieks from the other ghosts drew its attention and the figure floated back up to its partner. Alex looked out and saw that they had resumed floating in the same direction as before.

After waiting a short while just to be on the safe side, Alex swam out from under the boulder and went back to inspecting the pearl knob. She gripped it and turned it in various directions. After some jostling and gentle persuasion, she got it to turn all the way around and she fidgeted with it.

It felt like forever and a day had passed, but Alex was finally starting to make some headway. The knob seemed to turn and push inward, but only in certain orientations, and Alex deduced this to be the tumblers on the lock. It took a while longer, but she finally worked the combinations until finally, the lock clicked and sunk deeper into the wall. There was a deep rumbling sound as lines formed on the wall behind the pearl knob, and eventually the outline of a door was visible. The door lowered itself into the floor, revealing a dark tunnel of spiral stairs leading deeper into the base of the statue.

Alex turned and saw Ahrun and Marin swimming down to hear, having heard to noise.

"Well done, Alex! We need to move quickly," Marin said, "that noise will not go unnoticed."

"I know. I nearly ran into two of the spookies a little while ago," Alex said. The three swam inside and moments later the door closed behind them. Marin grabbed their hands and chanted a few more words, and there was a colossal explosion of water as a giant air pocket materialized and surrounded them. They fell a few feet but landed on the top stair.

"I figured this would be easier, once we found the archive," Marin said, producing a soaked torch from his pack. He held it out to Alex. "Do you mind? I'm nearly at my limit of casting."

Alex nodded. Marin looked dangerously drained, and the living wind incant was still working outside to keep the whirlpool at bay. Alex focused on flame and a soft cone of mage-fire appeared, which she transferred over to the torch. Normal fire wouldn't have caught it, but mage-fire didn't play by the rules, or so Alex had noticed. Marin produced two more torches and lit them off the first, and they walked down the stairs, deeper into the archive.

As they moved, Alex saw that the air pocket pushed the water back and as the air contacted the ruins many of them hissed and dissolved. The structure of the building seemed to remain intact, but she figured she'd monitor the situation. They reached the bottom of the stairs, which opened onto a long bridge, and Alex audibly gasped when she saw the other side.

The bridge extended out several hundred feet over a large open chasm. The wall on either side of the chasm was lined with shelves beyond counting and the ceiling extended upwards, covered with stunning frescoes and mosaics of scenes from the ancient empire.

"This place wasn't buried..." Alex mumbled to herself.

"What's that?" Ahrun asked.

"This archive. It wasn't buried. This used to be a building that extended high into the sky. You all used to have skyscrapers! See,"

Alex said, pointing to the windows. Every fifty feet there was a great window on the wall separating the shelves. The glass had all been broken out, but the opening looked out onto the depths. "This is incredible!" Alex continued. "What we thought was the sea floor must have been a layer of debris and silt. Who knows how tall this building is?"

"As impressive as it, and believe me, I could stand here all day, we need to get moving. I have no idea how we're going to find what we're looking for. There must be a hundred thousand records here, or more!" Marin said, sounding equal parts exasperated and impressed.

"Well, we'd be looking for something recent, well relatively. Any records they might have had of the Court's arrival would have been published right after the fall, so they might be somewhere near the top?" Ahrun said. As he said this, the water became freezing and Alex felt a shiver of fear. She saw the ghost as it passed into the air pocket. Alex braced herself and readied a few incants in her head. Ahrun whipped around, drawing his sword.

"Calm yourselves. I do not wish to harm you," the ghost said. Its voice was a distant echo, and it reverberated. Alex tried to make out some of his (from the voice she guessed this to be a man) features, but they shifted and shimmered in and out too fast.

"Ok, how are we supposed to know you're not just buying time and secretly signaling the others with your... mind or something?" Alex asked. She realized that it sounded like a bit of a silly question, but since this was the first ghost she'd ever had a conversation with, it seemed fair to establish some ground rules.

"No," the ghost said, almost sounding exasperated. "I can't talk to the others with my mind. Besides, I've known you were here since you opened the door. If I wanted to alert anyone, I would have. So now that we have dispensed with the pointless questions, would you mind telling me what you're doing here? You are the first living creatures to visit my archives since they sank."

Marin spoke up this time. "We seek information on the Court of Hours. I believe they have recorded some of it in the last days of the empire. All other records were destroyed."

"I know what you are looking for, but your quest has been in vain. The court destroyed our records. After the Fall, when we first awakened, there was an unrelenting assault by the muradae and the Lady of Deep Waters. As Eternal Guardians, we swore a lifetime of service to protect these places, and the memory of our people. Only once we gave them the records of the Fall and our information on the Court, did the assault cease. It was loathsome to us, but we did what we had to do to protect what we have sworn to protect."

Ahrun nodded. "I understand your vows. I am a Paladin of the Seventh Dawn, and I have taken similar oaths, but surely you can help us. What do you remember of the Fall? Perhaps you can provide some insight that might lead to the Court's destruction? Surely after all this time, you still desire that?"

"I have the memories that you seek, but I would not help you. You have no memory of the Fall, but I do, and worse that the demons, I remember the mainland imperials abandoning us. We begged for more ships to evacuate the cities, but our cries fell on deaf ears. The emperor felt it more prudent to use the imperial fleet for military applications. The last sound I remember was this complex sinking, and the screams of the thousands who would die. I do not hold you responsible, and so I will not call the other guardians."

Ahrun seemed crestfallen, but did not press the issue further.

"Now, please. Take you leave. If my more zealous brothers and sisters discover you, I will have no choice but to help them kill you," the ghost said. Marin and Ahrun turned and left, but Alex didn't move.

"Come on, man. We came a long way, and I'm not even from this world, and I'm sorry for what the empire did to your people. I am.

But hurting our chances of bringing down the ones responsible for your destruction out of spite isn't much different from helping the Court." Alex braced herself since she only saw the conversation going one of two ways, and one of them was terrible for her and her friends.

The specter flared and seemed ready to sound the alarm, but then paused.

"You may have a point. I will not break my vow, but let me tell you this; no living creature, save the Court, can give you what you seek," the ghost said.

Alex looked confused. "I don't understand. How does that help us?"

"You weren't listening, girl. I said no living creature. We are not Aquillon's only dead. And others may be more helpful than we. Journey far north and seek snow unsullied by the footsteps of man or demon. They are what we once called the Silent Banks, and within them, the Halls of Silence. Perhaps you will find your answers there. Now go; I hear something…"

The specter never finished its sentence as three ghosts burst through the door behind them.

"Intruders! You dare befoul this place with your filth? You will not see the surface again." The ghosts burst through the air bubble and produced spectral swords, swiping at Alex. They missed, barely, but Alex felt the air part as the blades passed by, and she wasn't about to wait around to figure out if they would really hurt or not. She and her friends turned and ran back towards the entrance, rushing past the armed wraiths. They barreled up the stairs, their enemies in tow, and rushed through the doors and out onto the sea floor.

Looking around, Alex could tell the situation had deteriorated since they had been inside. Aside from what looked like an angry army of ghosts forming on the outskirts of the top of the archive, the living wind incant was on its last legs, and barely kept the waters of the whirlpool at bay. On the edges of the arcane tornado, the water snapped and snarled like an angry sea serpent, trying to break back in. Alex looked back, and it seemed like they had lost the three guardians for the moment.

"Ok, we need a quick out here, but if we glimmer up to the surface, the change in pressure would probably kill us. Any ideas?" she asked.

Marin looked too exhausted to speak, still trying to keep the wind incant alive. If that broke, they would all be dead in a hurry.

"Well, do you know any water incants? Perhaps if we could ride a wave upwards, it would be slow enough?" Ahrun suggested.

"I'll see what I can do," Alex said. She felt pretty rested and felt bad about Marin carrying the load. She remembered the reverse-gravity incant she had used on her journey to find the Path of Flames, and she had an idea. She looked at Marin. "Can you keep this air bubble going for a little while longer?"

He didn't respond, but gave her a shaky thumbs up.

Alex pulled Marin over to her with one arm and Ahrun with the other. She focused on flying upward and remembered her lessons with Marin. She was reasonably confident she could pull it off, but with her powers unlocked to their full potential, she had to make sure she didn't blast them all into space. She took a deep breath and let go with her mind.

She felt a surge of energy beneath her, and soon enough they were rocketing through the water at a fair speed. The air pocket held and Alex looked up and saw the surface and noticed the shimmer of ghosts charging behind her through the water. At the moment they nearly had her, Alex and her friends burst through the surface and rocketed into the air. At the moment they were over the ship, Alex released her grip and they all collapsed onto the deck. The last thing Alex saw was Marin collapsing unconscious onto the deck, and she wasn't far behind him. The world grew black and Alex faded into oblivion.

26

A Land of Frost and Bone

Alex wasn't sure what time it was when she woke up, or even where she was. Sitting up in a cot, she took a moment to assess her surroundings. The dank interior of an old-style wooden ship jogged her memory, and the crash of the waves against the hull and the salty sea air completed her fragmented recollection. She was aboard a Red Fleet ship, bound for the north of Aquillon, and the Silent Banks.

She rolled out of bed, and the chill of the cabin enveloped her skin. It felt cold, and she looked down and realized why. She was standing stark naked. Alex quickly pulled the sheet of her cot around her, despite being alone in the cabin. She only hoped Kyria was the one responsible for her disrobing.

Alex looked around and spotted her clothes. Her traveling clothes, a green tunic, brown pants, boots, and a long cloak were spread out to try on a nearby table, but they were still soaked. Fortunately, someone (hopefully Kyria) had hung up her blue robes, which she threw on, and pulled her blond hair back into a braid. Her skin still felt damp and clammy, but her robes were at least warm.

Alex exited the cabin and made her way onto the main deck where the stink of frigid air bit at her face. She shuffled past two crewmen and made her way against the railing to get a better look of where they were.

The scenery had transformed since she was last conscious. The tempestuous waters of the Sea of Tears had calmed, and the water they sailed through was still as glass, and black, perfectly reflecting the stars back at her. The moon was nowhere to be seen, and the nearest land was at least several miles from their current course. Every so often, the ship would push past a chunk of ice in the water, and strange creatures followed the course of the ship, gliding through the ebony sea like phantoms. Their bodies were sleek and elongated, and their heads looked like dolphins. Their skin was nearly translucent and their eyes were pale blue pearls dancing in the night. Every so often they would breach the water and fall back down in it, barely making a splash.

"Night Angels, or so my father called em." Alex turned and saw Kyria walking up behind her. Alex ran to her and the two friends hugged a long while. When they finally separated, Kyria and Alex walked back over to the railing.

"He always wanted ta see one before he died," Kyria said, her voice catching.

"Well, I know he'd be proud of how far you've come, that's for sure," Alex said, patting Kyria on the back. "So, how long was I out?"

"Four days. I didn't know if, or when ya were comin' back ta us, and to be honest, those clothes o' yers were startin' ta stink, so I stripped ya down an' washed em'. I hope ya don' mind," Kyria said with a cheeky smile.

"Sure, that's not awkward or anything," Alex said, trailing off. "How's Marin?" she asked, hoping to change the subject. Kyria's jovial smile vanished.

"Nae good, if I'm bein' honest. He's not woken up once since ya three rocketed out o' the spray, and he don' look so good."

Alex nodded. It made sense, even if she didn't like it. The amount of magical energy Marin channeled was more than enough to kill someone. She'd probably spent a lot less by a large degree, and she had been out for four days. "And Ahrun?" she asked.

"He was fine by the next day, although he was worse for wear. He's alright now though," Kyria said with a quiet smile. "Thank ya for bringin' 'im back ta me. I don' quite know what he is ta me jus' yet, but I mean ta keep him around a good longtime, while I figure it out."

Alex nodded, and the two friends took in the silent water, and watched the night angels for a while longer. The first traces of sunlight had shimmered over the western edge of the water, and Kyria looked beat. She mumbled something about going off to bed and fell asleep on the railing, nearly tumbling into the water. Alex caught her, helped her into a bunk below in a deserted cabin. When she arrived back up top, Ahrun was waiting for her.

"Did you finally put that wild-woman to bed?"

"I did," Alex said, taking a modest bow.

"Good! She's been up almost every waking hour monitoring you two. Maybe now that one of you is awake, she'll finally sleep," Ahrun said with a soft chuckle. They stood together in silence for a while, watching the sun rise above the western horizon, showing the ocean with rays of dancing light. The sun felt luxuriously soft and warm on Alex's face, which was a pleasant departure from the biting cold. The ice was growing thicker in the water, and the night angels had disappeared with the rising of the sun.

"So," Alex said, "what happened when Marin and I were asleep?"

"Well, from what Kyria told me, the guardians chased the ship for a while, but never broke the surface, and once we were safely out of their waters, left us alone altogether. It's been quiet sailing since then. We spotted a few muradae in the waters yesterday, but since we entered the north, there haven't been any sightings of them. I think this might be the only place on Aquillon proper that the Court fear going, although for what reason, I cannot say."

"Hey, I'm all for a gift horse at this point," Alex said.

Ahrun was about to speak when Alex felt a sudden jolt that nearly threw her overboard. She looked around frantically for the source of the disturbance. The ship had come to a sudden halt and Alex saw crewmen lowering the anchor. She looked for the captain, but found that he was already walking towards them.

"This is as far as we go," the captain said.

Alex was about to ask why, but saw something out of the corner of her eye that seemed to answer the question. A large pillar of ice jutted up out of the water, nearly the height of a three-story building, and it was unclear how many hundreds of feet it extended down into the water. If the tower of ice wasn't imposing enough, the front of it was carved as a near perfect replica of a human skeleton. Nothing about the thing seemed to stress strangers being welcome.

"Yeah, I can't imagine the giant ice skeleton will do much for your suspicious pirates," Alex said.

"That, and the ice flows are too thick. The Sea's Vengeance is a mighty fine ship, and I'm not losin' her on some fool's errand. I'll have my men take ye ashore, but you're on your own from there. And take your lizard with you," the captain said, pointing up to the crow's nest where Larm was apparently trying to make friends with the lookout who looked both terrified and amused at the same time.

"Well, I can't thank you enough. You're doing the right thing by helping us," Alex said.

"Don't go takin' a shine ya me, an' mine. We'll be enemies as soon as ya step foot back on land," the captain said bluntly.

"Fair enough, but you have my thanks all the same," Alex said, and extended her hand. The captain shook it and smiled.

"Well, enemies or no, give the Court what for. Gods know they deserve it," the captain said.

"Never got your name," Ahrun said.

"Argus Bartholomew. Now get off my ship; that thing is givin' my crew the spooks."

Ahrun and Alex wasted no time collecting their things and making ready to leave. Kyria woke up and after only a mild amount of cursing and grumbling, she was dressed and ready to leave. Marin could barely get out of bed, and Alex had to support him heavily. They loaded him into a boat and lower it into the ocean, at which point Marin passed out again. They pulled the oars, and they were away from the ship in no time.

As the rowboat cut across the still ocean, the howling wind cut down from the hills beyond the shore and Alex shivered. It was a cold like she had never felt since arriving on Aquillon, and while it seemed a welcome change from the oppressive heat, there was something sinister in the frigid air. It was a presence, both unsubstantial and overwhelming at the same time. It was as if the air she breathed was incensed at her presence.

By the time the rowboat bumped onto the rocky shoreline, Marin had regained consciousness. Alex exited the boat and helped Marin out, propping him up on a large boulder close to the water with a blanket.

"Hey there, buddy. We made it! Welcome to the creepy north pole of death!" Alex said, giving Marin's shoulder a squeeze.

He smiled back at her and gave her a shaky thumbs up. "So now that we're here, do you have any idea where we're heading?"

Marin riffled through his pack and produced a scroll.

"This is the only map the Eastern Watch had of the Silent Banks. It's just dumb luck that I have it. Grabbed every map we had in the archives. I don't even know who made a map of the Silent Banks, since nobody has been here in the last several hundred years."

"What in the blazin' abyss are ya talkin' about? I've never heard of these banks," Kyria said.

"Neither have I, or at least I don't remember if I have," Ahrun said. Alex remembered that he lost access to the memories of his order when he gave up his immortality.

"All I know are legends," Marin said, "and half remembered stories passed down through the Watch. It's a land where nothing lives, and nothing grows. A land of ice and death, where the dead of the realm go for their eternal rest. Although the guardian's description of the Halls of Silence was the first time I'd ever heard of such a thing."

Ahrun and Alex nodded, and Kyria didn't seem too lost, so Alex figured that Ahrun must have at least partially caught her up to speed.

"Well, seems like a friendly place. Do we know where these Halls might be?" Alex asked.

"I have only one guess, but it's a long shot. From the very limited reports we have of this area of Aquillon, the air is rife with spirits passing through to the halls. If you've felt unusually strong, and aggressively cold gusts of wind, that's them, or so the stories go. It stands to good reason that we should be able to follow the gusts of wind to their eventual destination. In theory," Marin said, qualifying his statement.

"And if yer wrong? What then?" Kyria asked.

"We wander the frozen wastes until we run out of food and die of exposure to the elements," Marin said with a grin. Alex wasn't sure if he was being cheeky, or if he was still delirious.

"Well, we've come this far, and we have a dragon," Alex said.

"Do we?" Marin asked, nodding towards the shore. Larm was sitting on his back legs, and had a concerned look on his face, or what Alex thought might be the look of concern. He had made no motion towards them and hadn't even tried to lick anyone in last several minutes. That definitely wasn't a good sign.

"What's goin' on, Larm? What's the matter?" Kyria asked in a soft, plaintive voice.

"Larm no like this place. Cold. Too cold for young dragon to fly. Older dragons fly in cold, but not Larm. Wings too weak. Besides, too many people."

"Larm, it's just us," Alex said.

"No, many many humans, only not like you. Shimmering and angry, lost and sad. They howl, and it hurts Larm's ears. Please don't make Larm go. I can wait here, fly you back once you come back from Halls."

Alex felt a chill run down her spine, and it wasn't from the temperature. There were spirits here, all around her, even if she couldn't see them. She hadn't really thought about the fact that dragons might see things she couldn't.

"Larm, can you tell us where the spirits are going?" Alex asked.

Larm didn't answer, pointing his left claw upwards, following a path over the hill. A large cliff face surrounded the shoreline, but there was a small path that opened up at the bottom, and zig-zagged its way to the top. Now that Alex knew what to look for, she noted that the gusts of wind seemed to meander their way up the path.

"Well, alright then. It looks like we're going up," Alex said. Marin got up and onto his feet, while Ahrun and Kyria went through the supplies. "Wait, what are we going to eat?" Alex asked. Kyria grinned at her and opened her pack, which was stuffed with loaves of bread, jars of things, and cured meats.

"The Red Fleet's larder was lookin' a mite heavy, so I relieved em' o' some provision I deemed non-essential to their voyage," Kyria said as her grin grew bigger.

"The pirates were fat," Ahrun said in a matter-of-fact tone, and Alex burst out laughing. It seemed like such an out-of-place comment to make that Alex couldn't help herself but chuckle, which caused Kyria to burst into giggles. Even Marin gave a few quick laughs, despite still seemed woozy and out of it.

"Onward and upward, as Thistle would say," Alex said. They shared a moment for their fallen friend and the climb began. Larm seemed intent to sit on the beach and chase small sea birds. Alex was more than a little uneasy leaving their ride home there, especially when their ride seemed just as likely to fly off and chase seals, assuming Aquillon had seals.

Despite being a fairly straightforward climb, it took Alex and her friends until mid-day to climb to the top of the seaside cliff. As they climbed higher and higher, Alex got a better look at the frozen sea, and it became easier and easier to see why the pirates had dropped them off. The ice flows grew thicker and thicker the closer you got to the giant ice skeleton, and beyond it there was very little water, and most of the sea had frozen over.

As she climbed, Alex kept her mind on what she was doing. The footing was tenuous and as they walked the rocky ground became more and more covered with ice and permafrost. There were also times when it seemed the angry wind was trying to direct her feet straight off the path. While it wasn't the Haunted Mansion in Disney World, Alex had no interest in becoming the one thousandth happy haunt.

Alex was wondering if they had perhaps died at some point and this climb was the Aquillonian version of purgatory when she heard Kyria shout that they had reached the top. She was so excited to see something other than the stupid icy rocks that she double-timed up to the top of the path to see what the north of Aquillon offered.

More rocks, and more ice, was as it happened, all the north offered. Alex wasn't sure what she was expecting, but before her at the top of the endless cliff-side path was a tundra of snow, frost, and desolation.

It seemed to extend for miles in every direction; a blinding white expanse of death and ice. Snowbanks piled high and the wind up here was twice as biting and all the sun's warmth had been sapped from the air. It was as close as Alex had ever been to the arctic, and it was definitely reinforcing Alex's lack of any desire to go there.

If the ice and the snow weren't bad enough, there were the towers. Every mile or so a sharp tower of what appeared to be bone shot up out of the ice. The bone pillars were ringed with strange blue runes. Alex couldn't read them, but she knew she had seen anything like them before, at the path of flames.

"Well, on the bright side..." Alex said to her friends, before trailing off. "Actually, I got nothin' ya'll." She was having trouble finding a bright side, figuratively or literally. The sun was hiding behind some delightfully dark and morbid clouds.

"At least it seems the Ha..halls won't be hard to find," Marin said, stammering from the cold. Alex was worried about him, but they had to press on. She looked where he was pointing and saw what he was talking about.

In the far distance, deep into the snow and ice, was a small ring of what looked like mountains, and in the center of the ring, a large series of towers pierced the skyline, even above the mountains. It was the only structure within eyesight for miles.

It had been easier than Alex thought, but they had found the Halls of Silence. Now she just had to worry about the fact that it was too easy. It was always something.

27

The Keeper of the Dead

T he next two days proved to be the Aquillonian equivalent of the phrase, 'objects in the mirror may appear closer than they actually are.'

At first the Silent Halls seemed close enough to walk to in the space of an afternoon, and by the end of the afternoon, they seemed no closer. Alex trotted along, putting one foot in front of the other for hours on end as the wind howled around them. The temperature was dropping and by the end of the first day and it forced them to make camp because as soon as the sun disappeared below the eastern edge of the world, the cold went from unpleasant to lethal.

They established camp and, with the help of Alex's magic, established a roaring flame that seemed undeterred by the wind, and didn't need wood. Kyria mildly grumbled that her smokeless fire would have been hotter, but moved as close as she was able all the same.

There was little conversation around the campfire that night, as everyone was mostly concerned with staying warm. Kyria pressed up against Ahrun, who put his arm around her. It still seemed strange and out of place, but they seemed happy, and Alex was happy for them.

Alex hadn't had much time, or interest in guys back on Earth, and they had been the furthest thing from her mind since arriving on Aquillon. Still, she felt lonesome. She looked over at Marin and smiled to herself. Maybe someday. Not today, though.

That night they split the watch evenly, although Ahrun and Kyria spend theirs together, and in the morning, they broke camp to make an early start. The daylight hadn't lasted long yesterday, and Alex figured they were in whatever Aquillon's shortest daylight season was, so every moment of light was precious since the night was a shadowy void of ice and death. Any attempt to travel at night would have been foolhardy, bordering on fatal.

It was hard to stay focused as they traveled through. The wind blocked any attempt at conversation, and all there was to see was snow and ice. Towering snow banks rose on either side of the path they traveled on, and Alex occasionally would lose sight of the towers, causing a momentary panic. More unnerving was the knowledge that if anything upset the snow on either side of them, they would be buried alive and no one would come looking for them. It was growing very apparent to Alex why no one had any interest in visiting this region of Aquillon. If the snow and the ghosts didn't kill you, boredom would.

Mid-day brought a welcome break from the doldrums of travel. The path opened up into a large circular area that seemed to have been hollowed out. The snow leveled out on either side of the circle, offering a better view of the tundra. In the center, stood one of the strange bone-spike towers they had seen from the top of the cliff, and all around it, something had etched blue runes in the ground. They glowed with a pale light and even though the snow was falling lightly, not one snowflake landed on the runes. Even the wind was quiet for once and passed through the center of the circle as a whimper.

"What do ya suppose it is?" Kyria said, wondering aloud.

"I don't know, but this has been here a very long time," Marin said.

"How can you tell?" Ahrun asked.

"These runes predate anything in the archives. We have records of everything after the fall, and these don't show up anywhere. Whatever they are, they're older than the Fall, the Court, and they probably pre-date the empire."

"I've seen these before," Alex said. "You have too," she said to Marin.

"I have?"

"Outside of the Path of Flames, on that plateau in the Wyld Places."

"Ah, yes. They look similar. Didn't you say you spoke to a being in the heart of that volcano?"

"Yes, Andrasella, I think was her name. She called herself the Lady of Magic. I'm not sure we were even on Aquillon, to be honest. I think we were somewhere outside it."

"Then we might be outside of it now?" Ahrun asked.

"I'm not sure, but this sure doesn't feel like a place anybody visits on the regular," Alex said, looking up at the bone tower. When she looked closer, she realized the tower was covered in intricate carvings of grizzly and macabre scenes of dead souls being led in chains by specters. The images were haunting and terrible, and it was hard to stare at them for long.

"I think we need to get moving. I don't think we should be here." Alex said, a twinge of fear in her voice.

"Aye, no argument here. Let's plod on," Kyria said. No one else had an argument to make, although Marin looked like he wouldn't mind staying to study the tower for a hundred years or so. Alex tugged him along and they set out again.

To Alex's relief, as they left the circular opening and embarked on the path, she spotted the towers again, but they seemed much closer this time. By the time the sun set that night and they made camp that night, the towers swallowed up the horizon.

"So, when we get there, who are we looking to talk to?" Alex asked as they ate dinner.

"We will need to find the older spirits who dwell in the halls," Marin said. "I don't know who exactly, but if the guardian at the archive was correct, every spirit from Aquillon will be down there."

A somber pall passed over the group as they realized the implications of Marin's statement. It reminded Alex of when Odysseus visited the underworld. She wondered if Thistle was down there, or Rex, or someone from Ahrun's past that even he didn't remember anymore.

"And how are we supposed to get into these halls?" Alex asked, trying to break the dreaded silence that gripped them.

"Well, I guess we just walk up and knock?" Marin suggested.

"We'll just have to hope these ghosts are more hospitable than the ones we dealt with back in the Seaward Cities," Ahrun said glumly. Alex wanted to say something to lift everyone's spirits, but she was coming up empty. This place seemed to sap their spirits, as much as it sapped the warmth from them. Alex would be happy to be in and out of the halls tomorrow. This was not a place for the living to dwell in.

That night, Alex's dreams were fractured and horrible. Angry faces shifted in and out of fulminating darkness and when Kyria woke her up for her turn at the watch, her heart was racing and she was sweating, despite the cold.

She sat up and tried to shake off the jitters as Ahrun and Kyria rolled over and went back to sleep. The warmth from the fire felt good, but there was something watching her in the darkness. Just beyond where the light died, Alex could have sworn she saw movement, and felt the oppressive weight of eyes on her. The forlorn howl of the wind didn't help matters. She didn't wake the others, because she was only partially convinced she saw something, and she wanted to let them rest.

The sun's pale rays finally showered the tundra, and Alex woke the others. Even though the sun was up, she was still deeply unsettled, and wanted to be out of this part of the world as soon as possible.

They set out and by midmorning they arrived at the outskirts of the first tower. Now that they were closer, Alex could see the place in better detail.

The first thing that Alex noted was the incredible scale of the place. To be honest, she had never felt smaller. A large semicircular ring of mountain cut its way out of the tundra and carved into them was the largest stone building Alex had ever seen. It made Alcrest look tiny. Infinite windows and doors covered the surface of it, along with more grim illustrations of death, similar to the ones they saw on the bone tower yesterday. At the top of the multi-tiered building were two gargantuan bells. On every layer of the structure, doors opened and closed at random, creating a racket that carried on the wind, even several hundred feet away.

The towers themselves were two massive blocks of obsidian glass that pierced the sky. They were featureless black monoliths that reflected nothing; light and Alex's own reflection were swallowed up, and the longer Alex looked at the tower, the more dread filled her heart. Between the two towers was a road that lead into the halls themselves. The road was lined with the blue, glowing runes and a pair of statues depicting what Alex could only guess was Aquillon's version of the grim reaper. They were large skeletal figures, holding spears and wearing crowns that were broken in the middle. Their eyes were hollow, black voids.

Alex and her friends walked on the road towards the halls. No one, not even Marin, seemed in the mood to explore. As they made it passed the first set of statues, green flames materialized in their eyes and there was a deep rumbling in the ground. Alex looked around.

"Alright, who set off the booby trap?" she asked.

Nobody said anything, but the rumbling became deeper and deeper, and Alex looked up and realized where it was coming from.

From the top of the tallest peak of the mountain range, a large embankment of snow and ice was moving. It shifted around for a while before standing up. It took Alex a few minutes to figure out what she was looking at, but eventually the shape of the giant man came into focus. He wore black robes and carried a staff that was nearly the length of the towers that flanked the group, and he turned to face them.

His features were that of a gruff older man. His head was covered in a helmet with the likeness of a human skull, and he had an icy blue and white beard that extended to his chest. His eyes, which peered at them through the skull-helmet's eye sockets, were milky white. Before anyone could react, he spoke, and his voice barreled down the mountains and rumbled in Alex's chest.

"Living interlopers! Mortal vandals! Pilfering thieves that come to the land where no man draws breath. Your footsteps will no longer soil this sacred ground!" With that, the giant leapt off the mountaintop and landed in front of Alex with such force, she and her friends fell to the ground. Once they picked themselves back up, Alex looked up and saw a sword the size of a small house inches from her face.

"Whoa now, big fella. There's been a bit of a misunderstanding now. Take it easy," Alex said. She had no idea who, or what this thing was, but if she didn't play nice, she'd be dead in a heartbeat.

"There is no misunderstanding," the giant said. His voice was the terrible shattering of mountains, and the grinding of bones. For all of Alex's powers, she felt weak and insignificant compared to him. "You are living men. You have come to the kingdom of the dead to steal. You are more agents of the court. You will die, and I will see to it your souls are properly punished."

"We're no' allies o' the Court. Trust me, if we had a hankerin' ta die, we could 'ave done that jus' fine back in a warmer part o' the world," Kyria said.

"Yes, and I can tell you we're no friends of the Court. We came here seeking knowledge of how to destroy them," Alex said.

"A likely ruse any carrion rogue might use to best me. I am eternal, and I have seen such tricks before. My mind is made up. I will not commit the sentence of your trespass."

"Wait! There must be some way for us to prove ourselves to you?" Alex asked, throwing her hands up.

"There is a way, but it would not... perhaps. I can see you have been touched by an Eternal. If you survived that encounter, perhaps you would survive," the giant said, scratching his beard. As he did, icicles and bones fell from the billowing tufts of hair.

"Yes, I passed through the Path of Flame and spoke with Andrasella, the Lady of Magic. I'll do whatever you ask," Alex said, bowing slightly. The giant had put away his sword for now and seemed deep in thought as he considered her statement.

"Very well. I will grip your soul and see if you are who you say you are. But," the giant paused and held up his hand. At once, Marin, Ahrun, and Kyria's eyes went white, and they floated slightly above the ground, going limp. "If you are lying to me, your friends will die first. You are powerful, but you cannot save them. Do we have an accord?"

Alex gritted her teeth. She didn't like dealing with hostage takers, but she had nothing to hide, and seemed to be all out of better options at the moment. "Fine. I'm Alex Alex Winters. If I'm dealing with you, I'd like at least your name."

"I am Kelebar, keeper of the dead, and the servant of death. In his absence, I am the keeper of the Halls of Silence."

"Well, good to meet you. I'd offer to shake your hand, but you might crush me, so let's just do this thing."

Kelebar said nothing further, but opened his palm and a small orb of frost shot out of it, and hovered several feet away from Alex. She was about to ask what was next when a thin beam of blue energy shot out of the orb and pierced her chest, and the world went black.

When Alex came to, she was floating in space. All around her the stars shone and she could see into the endless void for eternity. Far in the distance, she could see planets orbiting stars and all the cosmos stretched before her. She looked around and realized that she wasn't floating, it just felt that way. She was standing on an enormous cube, very similar to the one where she had spoken to Adrasella. This one was white and looked uncomfortably close to being made of bone. Alex made a mental note to ignore the three second rule, if somebody wanted to have tea.

All along the bone cube were the same runes as she had seen back on Aquillon; strange and beautiful alien language that glowed blue into the endlessness night sky. At the very edge of the cube was a throne of bones and black cloth, and a dark figure in tattered robes sat upon it.

"Hello?" Alex said. It was more a question than a greeting.

"Come forward, Alessandra Falkrest," the figure replied. Its voice was living ice and fear, and it hissed on the air like trapped steam and grinding bone. Fear washed over Alex and she felt paralyzed by the figure, whose details weren't clear. It took an immense force of will to reply.

"Uh, my name's actually Alex Winters, but ok," Alex said. She realized that was her given name, but the last few weeks had been so crazy, she hadn't really gotten around to dealing with her pending identity crisis just yet. Definitely the top of her to-do list.

"Speak only truth here. There are no lies that hide from death."

"So, Kelebar sent me here to see you. Something about proving myself or some such?"

"He was right to do so. Forgive his gruffness, the Court have deceived him many times. You are fortunate he granted you this audience at all."

"Audience with whom might I ask?"

"You know me. You have known me for all the breaths you have taken, and you will know me until your last. I am Death, the King of Broken Crowns."

"So, you know about the Court?"

"I know more of that detestable lot than they know of themselves. They are abominations that exist outside the natural law."

"So, why don't you give me the information I need on them and I can be on my way. No need to go into your spooky Casa de los Muertos," Alex said.

"I will not tell to the living what only the dead may know. If they share it with you, that is their affair. My job is only to judge your merit, unworthy as you are."

"Alright. Judge away then, my man," Alex said with a sigh.

The King stood from his throne and walked towards her. His shadow seemed to consume every trace of light that hit it. The closer he got, the more she felt like running away, but there was really nowhere to run to. He finally stopped several feet from Alex and she could feel the cold radiating out of him; a being of living darkness and winter. Even standing this close, Alex had trouble making out his features because they constantly shifted from the physical to the ethereal. He extended his hand, which appeared as bone in one moment, and shadow in the next. It gripped her head and Alex screamed as a cold so intense it was like freezing fire engulfed her body. Happiness fled and joy faded, and all hope retreated like leaves on the wind.

Alex stood paralyzed as she felt the cold essence of death pass through her. It seemed to probe through her soul, and it gripped every moment and every memory of her entire life. She saw every moment from her earliest memories and the pale specter of the King's hand passed over the memory, weighing each and passing on to the next. The feeling crept deeper and deeper until finally Alex felt like it plunged her into a frozen lake. Downward and downward she sunk, until she felt like she was at the bottom of a lake, drowning in ice and sorrow.

Then, as soon as the feeling started, it ended. Alex gasped and took in air as fast as she could, clawing at her throat. It was the feeling of dying and being reborn, all at once and Alex sat shivering and sobbing in the wake. The King withdrew his hand and sat for a moment in silence before speaking.

"You are worthy enough. You are no spy of the Court, of that much I am sure."

Alex couldn't speak, but merely nodded.

"You are free to return to the world, and you have my blessing to enter the halls. Beyond that, I will not help you."

Alex nodded her head and walked backwards. A small portal had opened up at the edge of the cube and she walked towards it, eager to leave. She felt nothing and wondered if this was what it was like to be dead. She hoped not.

"We will meet again, Alessandra. Like all things that draw breath, you owe me a debt, and I will collect. For today though, take your life, and that of your friends, and be grateful." Tears were streaming down her face when Alex dove into the portal, and at once she found herself in the howling wind outside the city of the dead. Kelebar looked up, and her friends rushed over to her.

"Where were you? And what happened to your hair?" Marin asked.

"What do you mean?" Alex said. Marin conjured up a spectral mirror, and Alex saw herself. She hadn't realized how long it had been since she last saw herself, but sure enough, a large streak of white ran through her otherwise runny blond hair. She guessed it was the price for being touched by death himself, although she doubted that was the debt he was talking about. Taking a moment to look at the rest of herself, she noticed that her eyes looked older, but given what she had been through in the last several months, she was lucky not to look worse.

"You've been gone a day, and we were getting worried," Ahrun said.

"Time is not a welcome member of the King's court. It does not flow through his realm," Kelebar rumbled. "But the King had given you his blessing. You may enter the Halls of Silence, but first I must rend your souls."

"What? What! Yer not rendin' nothin' ya great eegit," Kyria said.

"How did you expect to get in? Do you see any doors you could access?" Kelebar asked.

"Nae, but... well. What does this entail?" Kyria asked.

"I will remove your souls from your bodies. Your corpses will stay here, and you will go inside. Once you come back out, I will put you back in and you can be on your way. Soon, I hope." Kelebar replied with a deep grumble. "Besides, even if you could get yourselves in with your mortal forms still attached, the Keepers would find you, and even I couldn't help you then. As it is, you will have to be careful, lest they discover you as false spirits."

"What are these Keepers?" Ahrun asked, the edge of concern in his voice.

"They are among the oldest spirits in this world. They kept these lands long before the King of Broken Crowns built this place. They abhor the living, and will shred your souls to scattered fragments if they discover you skulking about the halls. The dead know their own. Keep your presence known to only what souls are beholden to the completion of your task. The more souls you interact with, the more your presence will cause ripples."

"Anything else we should know?" Alex asked.

"Yes. Your bodies will decay if you leave them without souls for too long, so do not spend more time than you need," Kelebar said with grim certainty.

"Look, as much as I'd love to settle down in a charming little place like that for my retirement," Alex said, "we'll be quick. You have my word. Rend away, good buddy."

Kelebar drew his sword so quickly that none of them could react, and he cleaved it through them. Instead of an impressive amount of blood and dying, however, Alex saw it pass through her and saw herself fall to the ground. She turned to ask Kelebar several colorfully worded questions, but the sound in the world around something muted her. She could see Kelebar, but she couldn't quite hear him. Turning to see her friends, Alex screamed. Or she would have if she hadn't been a ghost.

She saw Ahrun, Marin, and Kyria nearby looking at her, but it was hardly her friends that were directing her attention (although they made good looking ghosts). Between her and them, floated a torrential river of spirits. Ghosts shimmered and floated past her on their way to the halls. Alex turned and saw that they moved in rivers towards the many doors in the strange stone building. For the moment the other spirits seemed to take no notice of them, but Alex wanted to hurry, in case that fact changed anytime soon. One thing became increasingly clear as Alex watched the spirits around her float past; she was now solidly in the land of the dead, and she needed to hurry.

They were running out of time.

28

Into the Halls of Silence

E ven though the snow whipped around her, Alex heard no wind. Even though she saw the ice, she felt no cold. Even though her friends mouthed words, she heard nothing. All her senses were muted, and every sound was an echo of a reverberation, and it was difficult to hear anything, or focus on anything.

On the plus side, she could fly.

Well, not fly exactly, but float. At first, she did it without meaning to, as she tried to walk. Alex put one foot in front of the other but instead of solid ground, her feet just sort of hovered above it . With a concentrated effort, she managed to move forward, and without realizing it, she was floating upwards at an angle. Looking around, she saw her friends were nearby.

"Well, this is fun," Kyria said.

Alex turned and saw that her mouth wasn't moving.

"How am I hearing you?" Alex asked.

"I think it's some sort of vibration of emotion. The dead don't speak, but they can communicate thoughts and feelings with each other." This time it was Marin who was speaking.

"Well, let's not sit around all day chit-chatting," Alex sent back to them. "We need to get to the Halls."

"A point I must agree on," Ahrun said as he floated up to them. "I'm sure you feel the effect of the strain this separation is putting on us. The body is not meant to be separated from the soul and live."

Alex felt what he was talking about. Even now, moments after the sundering, she felt drained - more and more separated from her body. She looked down and saw her body, and the bodies of her friends lying in the snow. It was surreal, looking at her body. Her blond hair cascaded across the snow, and her skin was pale as winter ice. She looked older, somehow, than twenty, or twenty-one. She was pretty sure she had a birthday at some point in the past few months, but time wasn't exactly the easiest thing to keep track of on Aquillon.

The group didn't waste any more time chewing the fat of their literal existential crisis. Alex led them forward towards the halls. All around her the river of spirits floated in both directions. Where the spirits floating away from the Halls were going was anybody's guess, but Alex wasn't about to stop and ask.

As they neared the structures the details of the Halls of Silence came into clearer view. The building front, which extended several dozen feet from the mountain out of which it was carved, comprised of two enormous spires which were connected by a large rampart and a wall below. Every inch of the wall, and both spires was covered with ornate wooden doors which opened and closed, letting spirits in or out. Alex turned and looked at her friends.

"So, anybody want to venture a guess as to which door we need to be entering?" she said in her ghost speak. As she did, she saw several spirits nearby them stop and turn, observing her group. Their faces shimmered so frequently, it was hard to tell what they were looking at, but it certainly looked like suspicion. Alex made a mental note to keep communication brief and emotionless, as it seemed the spirits were attracted to emotion, as well as thoughts. She passed her observation along to her friends in as few words as possible.

"I guess it makes sense to start at the bottom and work our way up?" Marin suggested.

No one had any better ideas, so they proceeded forward. As they passed the river of souls flowing into the Halls, Alex took a closer look at them. They seemed to be all shapes, sizes, and ages. She shivered as the spectral forms of children floated past her, next to the shade of several soldiers. The dead didn't seem to interact with one another, but flowed to their intended destination with solemn determination.

They neared the Halls and Alex returned her attention to the task at hand. Now that they were close the Halls the scale of the structure was mind-bogglingly immense. Looking up, Alex guessed that they must have extended several hundred feet in the air or more. The surface of the building was a shining alabaster which seemed to move and swirl. The doors themselves were dark brown timbers, ancient and sturdy with the same strange blue runes around their frames. Despite their size, the doors gave off no sound when they opened or closed.

Alex and her friends stood before the nearest door for a while and it began to open. A dark figure began to emerge and Alex instinctively pulled her friends back behind the door. The figure came into full view and Alex realized it must be one of the keepers that Death had told her about. In contrast to the bluish white figures all around them, the keeper was a figure of shadow. Dark robes, black as night radiated a fulminating sea of obsidian energy and two green eyes searched the landscape from under a dark cowl. In its left hand, the keeper gripped a long staff of bone, wreathed in green flame, and as he moved, it pointed the staff at various spirits. As it did the spirits stopped moving and began to flow white before moving on.

Alex didn't know if she and her friend would glow the right color, but she definitely wasn't about to try it out. Alex waited until the keeper was fully turned around and made her move. Moving quickly, or as quickly as she was able given the circumstances, Alex guided her friends behind the door just as it was about to shut.

"What in the blazes was tha' thing?" Kyria asked.

"It's a keeper. Kelbar is cool with us being here, but I'm pretty sure if one of those things catches us, we're pretty much cooked," Alex said.

"Well, let us attempt to avoid being cooked then," Ahrun said with what Alex thought was a grin. Ghost faces were pretty hard to read. Alex made a mental note not to get engaged in any poker games for the duration of her stay. She noticed the door moving again and began floating deeper into the Halls.

Now that they were clear of the doorway Alex took in her surroundings, and it was pretty hard to not stare. The interior of the halls was one massive chamber, stretching upward towards a pitch-black void. The floor, which stretched for hundreds and hundreds of feet towards the far wall was split in two by a large chasm from which spirits floated upward, and all along the chasm large statues of Death kept watch.

On the far wall, large openings had been carved out and groups of spirits sat and mingled with each other. Looking upward towards the vaulted ceilings, Alex realized the entire mountain was hollow. She waited for a group of spirits to pass and then floated over to the edge of the chasm.

As soon as she looked over the edge, she wished she hadn't. The chasm extended down into the darkness for an eternity, illuminated only by torches every so often. Along both sides of the ravine, black chains snaked their way out of the walls and held spirits in a vice-like grip as they writhed in agony. The deeper down Alex looked, the more numerous the keepers became. She pulled away from the edge just as one looked up at her.

"It's not very wise for spirits to look down into the abyss, especially ones who aren't even dead," a gruff voice behind her said.

The entire group turned in alarm, and Alex reached for her sword instinctively, although she wasn't sure what she would have done with it, even if it were there. She relaxed when she realized that she recognized the spirit, albeit with a deep sense of sadness. It took Alex a moment, but she eventually realized she was speaking with the innkeeper from Vandlehaven. He had been one of the first people to show he kindness when she arrived in Aquillon.

"What happened to you?" Alex asked. "It's only been a few months since I left you and your people in Vandlehaven."

"Has it? Time is fuzzy down here. There are souls who swear they've been down here a week, and they're the oldest ones here, and folks that act like the ancient ones who just showed up yesterday. As for me, the village and I had another run in with the Red Fleet. I held them off while the others escaped."

"That's noble, but..." Alex trailed off.

"Don't start shedding tears for me. Being dead isn't exactly a thrill, but I get to see my girl again, and that matters more to me than anything. So, what brings living souls to a place like this?" he asked.

"How can ya tell we're livin'?" Kyria asked.

"Something about the energy you put off. Ain't quite right, like you're a half-step out of synch with the rest of us. It was harder to tell from far away, but close up, it's simple enough to work out. I'd stay away from the keepers if I was you. You saw them folks down in the ravine?"

Alex nodded.

"They're doomed souls that met with the harsh judgement of the keepers. Death's been gone a long time, from what I hear tell, and the keepers been running the show. Nobody's been real happy with the way they've been running the place, but we're dead, so we're not in much of a position to argue."

244

"Well, then maybe you can help us get out of here quick enough to avoid them?" Marin asked.

"Sure, any friend of Alex Winters is a friend of mine," the spirit said.

"Well, we need information on the Court of Hours, but from before the Fall. We need to know more about them so that maybe we can stop them for good," Alex said.

"Well, the good news is I know exactly who you need to talk to," the innkeeper said.

"There's bad news, isn't there?" Alex said, trying not to send too many annoyed emotions out along with her thoughts.

"Yes. He's in the lowest reaches of the abyss, where only the worst souls are kept. From what I hear from the others, he's been down there for a very long time. Even had the chance to join us here in the Halls, but he refused."

"That seems strange," Ahrun said. "From ever legend I remember, the emperor was a kind and noble soul."

"Well, I'll be sure to ask him which parts of those legends were a bunch of cow dung if he ever gets out."

"So, souls can escape the abyss?" Ahrun asked.

"Not exactly. They earn their way back, over time. After they've spent enough eons suffering, they are allowed to join us here," the innkeeper said.

"And how would we go about finding the emperor? There's bound to be more than one soul down there, I imagine," Marin pointed out.

"Yes, but he's the oldest, so he's at the bottom. There are no souls here from before the Fall. I guess they must be wherever we're going someday."

"But I don't get it," Alex said. "You said that condemned souls can join you here? Join you for what? Where are you going?"

"We're all just waiting. Nobody seems to know for what, but someday, we're all leaving here. This place wasn't built to be a home, or a prison, but a waystation. A place between places. That's why it's so jealously guarded. Only the dead may know what lies beyond the Halls of Silence."

"Well, we'd best be getting along, so how do we get down to the emperor?" Alex asked.

"Assuming you left your sanity back with your bodies, there's an entrance along the far wall. A set of stairs. Don't try floating down or the Keepers will catch you," the innkeeper said.

"Well, thanks for the information. I'm sorry you died, but I'm glad you're with your daughter again. I hope you get wherever you're going, eventually." Alex replied.

"I thank you, Ms. Winters, but these days, I think you should pity the living." With that ominous message, the specter faded.

"Alright, well down we go," Alex said.

"How do we avoid being seen by the Keepers?" Marin asked.

"I've got an idea, but I don' think yer gonna like it," Kyria said with a grin.

Kyria was correct. Alex did not like her idea.

"This is insane," Alex protested.

"Alex, I love ya like a sister, but I'm a disembodied spirit, floatin' around with a bunch o' dead folk, and I only came here because of the recommendation o' another dead eegit. I think we passed insane sometime last month."

"Well, how do you plan to escape the attention of the Keepers, once you have?" Alex asked.

"I can be stealthy, when I please ta," Kyria shot back.

"Alright, well, I guess if you think you have it handled, I trust you. Lord knows we've been through enough." Ahrun still seemed skeptical and only agreed on the condition that he go with Kyria, although Alex wasn't sure what he planned on doing if they got caught.

"Ok," Alex said, "Well we all meet back by the entrance, and get out of dodge once you see me pop out of the spooky canyon."

"Spooky canyon. Really Alex?" Marin asked with a sigh.

"Eh, Abyss was too creepy. If I have to go down into it, it's the spooky canyon." Nobody argued with Alex and they all made their way to the spooky canyon. As they neared it, Kyria and Ahrun split off and floated away to another part of the Halls. There had been a lot of ghost-talking, but the spirits in the Halls seemed less interested in them on this side of the doors.

Alex and Marin reached the edge of the staircase leading down into the Abyss and all Alex wanted to do was run. The Abyss was the worst place Alex had even been on Aquillon, topping even Alcrest in terms of suffering and pain. Raw agony radiated out of the pit in waves of black tendrils that snapped at her heels as she floated by. Alex peered down the staircase.

The stairs dropped off rapidly, and were so steep they gave her a sense of vertigo, even though she would be floating down them and there wasn't any danger of falling. The deeper Alex looked, the thicker the Keepers became, floating past tormented souls. The first several floors seemed to be clear, so Alex and Marin began making their way down. Kyria and Ahrun hadn't set off the distraction yet, but to a head start couldn't hurt.

As Alex and Marin made their way down the stairs the gloom of the Abyss took over. Even one flight of stairs down, the lights of the Halls had all but faded and were replaced with an omnipresent darkness that radiated fear, regret, and loneliness. Even though Marin's spirit floated right behind her, Alex felt alone and terrified. On her left the maw of the abyss opened wider and wider, and the farther down she looked, the more despair crept into her heart.

The wall to her right wasn't much better. Every inch of it was plastered with hopeless souls who were tethered to the walls by the black energy. They writhed in agony and their faces were contorted in a never-ending scream that Alex couldn't bear to look at. The tortured souls didn't seem to be aware of them, so Alex pressed on, even though she felt hopeless. She knew it would be a long way to the bottom, and only the need for quickness motivated her. Once Kyria made her grand ruckus, there wouldn't be a whole lot of time until she was found, and Alex wasn't letting that happen.

They had reached the lowest point of the Abyss that was Keeper free, so they paused and waited in a recessed alcove of the wall of souls. Marin didn't look much happier than Alex, and they floated in silence, waiting for the sign, which came with a crashing whoop above.

"Oye! Ya shifty spectery types! Aye, I'm talkin' to ya. My name's Kyria Killburn, and I'm the woman who cheated death. Come and claim my soul, if yer able!" This brash announcement was followed by a long string of obscene gestures, and some general screeching. Alex couldn't see her, but just hearing her friend's lighthearted jesting made her feel a little better.

At first it wasn't entirely clear that the Keepers had heard Kyria, or if they had, whether or not they cared. For a long, hideous moment, it seemed as though the bait hadn't worked, and the Keepers simply stared up at the area from which the sound had come. Then came a crash of screaming and hissing as several dozen keepers rose with alarming speed from the Abyss and rushed into the Halls above. Several still lurked in the deeper parts of the chasm, but Kyria had done her part, now Alex needed to hurry.

With a concerted effort, Alex pushed herself from the ledge and began floating downward with Marin in tow. It was slow at first, but she seemed to be able to will herself to fall faster. Looking down, she saw the grim outline of a Keeper occupying the center of the Abyss, but she managed to duck back onto the staircase and into one of the alcoves that honeycombed the walls. Alex watched as the glowing eyes of the Keeper moved over the wall, but Alex and Marin remained hidden. Once the creature had moved on to another section, Alex resumed her freefall.

As she plunged into the darkness, it became harder and harder for Alex to remember why she had even come into the Abyss to begin with. The light from the Halls above was as distant as the stars, and down here the souls of the dead were sparse, each with their own area of the wall. Their torment was worse, and Alex avoided lingering her gaze on any of them. Even though they were probably bad people in their life on Aquillon (Alex figured a large contingent of the Foxes Guild was down here) she couldn't imagine that anyone deserved this. Just being down here for a little while was bad enough.

After a long while of floating, Alex and Marin finally reached the bottom. The chasm's walls had been empty for some time now, and the walls met in the middle of the Abyss, forming what appeared to be a dry river bed running for endless distance. Nothing existed this far down, and no light penetrates the depths of the Abyss. It was a place of unending night, and only the ethereal glow of Marin's shade cast the smallest amount of illumination.

The sense of sadness was a palpable sea in which Alex was trying not to drown in. She felt as though she would never leave, and that this was the end. After all these years, she finally understood the description in Dante's *Inferno* - "Abandon hope, all ye who enter here." Hope had fled long ago, with the light, and the world. Here there was only darkness and regret.

"We need to keep moving," Marin said. His thoughts sounded brave, and untainted by fear. Alex marveled at his strength. She nodded, and followed where he led.

As they floated forward, the silhouettes of a ruined throne room slowly began to materialize. They had no detail or substance, but were shadows given form, like the ghosts of a mind. In the center of the room, chained to a massive throne, Alex saw an old man in a dusty suit of armor. He looked up and regarded them from milk-white eyes.

"You are very brave, or perhaps very stupid to have come so far into the kingdom of the dead. Why have you come here?"

Even though the snow whipped around her, Alex heard no wind. Even though she saw the ice, she felt no cold. Even though her friends mouthed words, she heard nothing. All her senses were muted, and every sound was an echo of a reverberation, and it was difficult to hear anything, or focus on anything.

On the plus side, she could fly.

Well, not fly exactly, but float. At first, she did it without meaning to, as she tried to walk. Alex put one foot in front of the other, but instead of solid ground, her feet just sort of hovered above it. With a concentrated effort, she moved forward, and without realizing it, she was floating upwards at an angle. Looking around, she saw her friends were nearby.

"Well, this is fun," Kyria said..

Alex turned and saw that her mouth wasn't moving.

"How am I hearing you?" Alex asked.

"I think it's some vibration of emotion. The dead don't speak, but they can communicate thoughts and feelings with each other." This time it was Marin who was speaking.

"Well, let's not sit around all day chit-chatting," Alex sent back to them. "We need to get to the Halls."

"A point I must agree on," Ahrun said as he floated up to them. "I'm sure you feel the effect of the strain this separation is putting on us. The body is not meant to be separated from the soul and live."

Alex felt what he was talking about. Even now, moments after the sundering, she felt drained - more and more separated from her body. She looked down and saw her body, and the bodies of her friends lying in the snow. It was surreal, looking at her body. Her blond hair cascaded across the snow, and her skin was pale as the winter ice. She looked older, somehow, than twenty- or twenty-one. She was pretty sure she had a birthday at some point in the past few months, but time wasn't exactly the easiest thing to keep track of on Aquillon.

The group wasted no more time chewing the fat of their literal existential crisis. Alex led them forward towards the halls. All around her, the river of spirits floated in both directions. Where the spirits floating away from the Halls were going was anybody's guess, but Alex wasn't about to stop and ask.

As they neared the structures, the details of the Halls of Silence came into clearer view. The building front, which extended several dozen feet from the mountain out of which it was carved, comprised two enormous spires, connected by a large rampart and a wall below. Every inch of the wall, and both spires, was covered with ornate wooden doors which opened and closed, letting spirits in or out. Alex turned and looked at her friends.

"So, anybody want to venture a guess as to which door we need to be entering?" she said in her ghost speak. As she did, she saw several spirits nearby them stop and turn, observing her group. Their faces shimmered so frequently, it was hard to tell what they were looking at, but it looked like suspicion. Alex made a mental note to keep communication brief and emotionless, as it seemed emotion and thoughts attracted the spirits. She passed her observation along to her friends in as few words as possible.

"I guess it makes sense to start at the bottom and work our way up?" Marin suggested.

No one had any better ideas, so they proceeded forward. As they passed the river of souls flowing into the Halls, Alex inspected them. They seemed to be all shapes, sizes, and ages. She shivered as the spectral forms of children floated past her, next to the shade of several soldiers. The dead didn't seem to interact with one another, but flowed to their intended destination with solemn determination.

They neared the Halls, and Alex returned her attention to the task at hand. Now that they were close the Halls, the scale of the structure was mind-bogglingly immense. Looking up, Alex guessed that they must have extended several hundred feet in the air or more. The surface of the building was a shining alabaster which seemed to move and swirl. The doors themselves were dark brown timbers, ancient and sturdy with the same strange blue runes around their frames. Despite their size, the doors gave off no sound when they opened or closed.

Alex and her friends stood before the nearest door for a while and it opened. A dark figure emerged and Alex instinctively pulled her friends back behind the door. The figure came into full view, and Alex realized it must be a keeper, one of the guardians that Death had told her about. In contrast to the bluish white figures all around them, the keeper was a figure of shadow. Dark robes, black as night, radiated a fulminating sea of obsidian energy and two green eyes searched the landscape from under a dark cowl. In its left hand, the keeper gripped a long staff of bone, wreathed in green flame, and as he moved, it pointed the staff at various spirits. As it did, the spirits stopped moving and glowed white before moving on.

Alex didn't know if she and her friend would glow the right color, but she definitely wasn't about to try it out. Alex waited until the keeper was fully turned around and made her move. Moving quickly, or as quickly as she was able given the circumstances, Alex guided her friends behind the door just as it was about to shut.

"What in the blazes was tha' thing?" Kyria asked.

"It's a keeper. Kelebar is cool with us being here, but I'm pretty sure if one of those things catches us, we're cooked," Alex said.

"Well, let us attempt to avoid being cooked then," Ahrun said with what Alex thought was a grin. Ghost faces were hard to read. Alex made a mental note not to get engaged in any poker games for the duration of her stay. She noticed the door moving again and began floating deeper into the Halls.

Now that they were clear of the doorway Alex took in her surroundings, and it was hard to not stare. The interior of the halls was one massive chamber, stretching upward towards a pitch-black void. The floor, which stretched for hundreds and hundreds of feet towards the far wall, was split in two by a large chasm from which spirits floated upward, and all along the chasm colossal statues of Death kept watch.

On the far wall, large openings had been carved out and groups of spirits sat and mingled with each other. Looking upward towards the vaulted ceilings, Alex realized the entire mountain was hollow. She waited for a group of spirits to pass and then floated over to the edge of the chasm.

As soon as she looked over the edge, she wished she hadn't. The chasm extended down into the darkness for an eternity, illuminated only by torches every so often. Along both sides of the ravine, black chains snaked their way out of the walls and held spirits in a vice-like grip as they writhed in agony. The deeper down Alex looked, the more numerous the keepers became. She pulled away from the edge just as one looked up at her.

"It's not wise for spirits to look down into the abyss, especially ones who aren't even dead," a gruff voice behind her said.

The entire group turned in alarm, and Alex reached for her sword instinctively, although she wasn't sure what she would have done with it, even if it were there. She relaxed when she realized that she recognized the spirit, albeit with a deep sense of sadness. It took Alex a moment, but she eventually realized she was speaking with the innkeeper from Vandlehaven. He had been one of the first people to show her kindness when she arrived in Aquillon.

"What happened to you?" Alex asked. "It's only been a few months since I left you and your people in Vandlehaven."

"Has it? Time is fuzzy down here. There are souls who swear they've been down here a week, and they're the oldest ones here, and folks that act like the ancient ones who just showed up yesterday. The village and I had another run in with the Red Fleet. I held them off while the others escaped."

"That's noble, but..." Alex trailed off.

"Don't start shedding tears for me. Being dead isn't exactly a thrill, but I get to see my girl again, and that matters more to me than anything. So, what brings living souls to a place like this?" he asked.

"How can ya tell we're livin'?" Kyria asked.

"Something about the energy you put off. Ain't right, like you're a half-step out of synch with the rest of us. It was harder to tell from far away, but close up, it's simple enough to work out. I'd stay away from the keepers if I was you. You saw them folks down in the ravine?"

Alex nodded.

"They're doomed souls that met with the harsh judgement of the keepers. Death's been gone a long time, from what I hear tell, and the keepers been running the show. Nobody's been real happy with the way they've been running the place, but we're dead, so we're not in much of a position to argue."

"Well, then maybe you can help us get out of here quick enough to avoid them?" Marin asked.

"Sure, any friend of Alex Winters is a friend of mine," the spirit said.

"Well, we need information on the Court of Hours, but from before the Fall. We need to know more about them so that maybe we can stop them for good," Alex said.

"Well, the good news is I know exactly who you need to talk to," the innkeeper said.

"There's bad news, isn't there?" Alex said, trying not to send too many annoyed emotions out along with her thoughts.

"Yes. He's in the lowest reaches of the abyss where only the worst souls are kept. From what I hear from the others, he's been down there for a very long time. Even had the chance to join us here in the Halls. But he refused."

"That seems strange," Ahrun said. "From ever legend I remember, the emperor was a kind and noble soul."

"Well, I will ask him which parts of those legends were a bunch of cows dung if he ever gets out."

"So, souls can escape the abyss?" Ahrun asked.

"Not exactly. They earn their way back, over time. After they've spent enough eons suffering, the keepers allow them to join us here," the innkeeper said.

"And how would we go about finding the emperor? There's bound to be more than one soul down there, I imagine," Marin pointed out.

"Yes, but he's the oldest, so he's at the bottom. There are no souls here from before the Fall. I guess they must be wherever we're going someday."

"But I don't get it," Alex said. "You said that condemned souls can join you here? Join you for what? Where are you going?"

"We're all just waiting. Nobody seems to know for what, but someday, we're all leaving here. This place wasn't built to be a home, or a prison, but a waystation. A place between places. That's why it's so jealously guarded. Only the dead may know what lies beyond the Halls of Silence."

"Well, we'd best be getting along, so how do we get down to the emperor?" Alex asked.

"Assuming you left your sanity back with your bodies, there's an entrance along the far wall. A set of stairs. Don't try floating down or the Keepers will catch you," the innkeeper said.

"Well, thanks for the information. I'm sorry you died, but I'm glad you're with your daughter again. I hope you get wherever you're going, eventually." Alex replied.

"I thank you, Ms. Winters, but these days, I think you should pity the living." With that ominous message, the specter faded.

"Alright, well down we go," Alex said.

"How do we avoid being seen by the Keepers?" Marin asked.

"I've got an idea, but I don' think yer gonna like it," Kyria said with a grin.

Kyria was correct. Alex did not like her idea.

"This is insane," Alex protested.

"Alex, I love ya like a sister, but I'm a disembodied spirit, floatin' around with a bunch o' dead folk, and I only came here because of the recommendation o' another dead eegit. I think we passed insane sometime last month."

"Well, how do you plan to escape the attention of the Keepers, once you have?" Alex asked.

"I can be stealthy when I please ta," Kyria shot back.

"Alright, well, I guess if you think you have it handled, I trust you. Lord knows we've been through enough." Ahrun still seemed skeptical and only agreed on the condition that he go with Kyria, although Alex wasn't sure what he planned on doing if they got caught.

"Ok," Alex said, "Well we all meet back by the entrance, and get out of dodge once you see me pop out of the spooky canyon."

"Spooky canyon. Really, Alex?" Marin asked with a sigh.

"Eh, Abyss was too creepy. If I have to go down into it, it's the spooky canyon." Nobody argued with Alex, and they all made their way to the spooky canyon. As they neared it, Kyria and Ahrun split off and floated away to another part of the Halls. There had been a lot of ghost-talking, but the spirits in the Halls seemed less interested in them on this side of the doors.

Alex and Marin reached the edge of the staircase leading down into the Abyss, and all Alex wanted to do was run. The Abyss was the worst place Alex had even been on Aquillon, topping even Alcrest in terms of suffering and pain. Raw agony radiated out of the pit in waves of black tendrils that snapped at her heels as she floated by. Alex peered down the staircase.

The stairs dropped off rapidly, and were so steep they gave her a sense of vertigo, even though she would be floating down them and there wasn't any danger of falling. The deeper Alex looked, the thicker the Keepers became, floating past tormented souls. The first several floors seemed to be clear, so Alex and Marin began making their way down. Kyria and Ahrun hadn't set off the distraction yet, but to a head start couldn't hurt.

As Alex and Marin made their way down the stairs, the gloom of the Abyss took over. Even one flight of stairs down, the lights of the Halls had all but faded and were replaced with an omnipresent darkness that radiated fear, regret, and loneliness. Even though Marin's spirit floated right behind her, Alex felt alone and terrified. On her left the maw of the abyss opened wider and wider, and the farther down she looked, the more despair crept into her heart.

The wall to her right wasn't much better. Hopeless souls plastered every inch, tethered by black energy. They writhed in agony and they contorted their faces in a never-ending scream that Alex couldn't bear to look at. The tortured souls didn't seem to be aware of them, so Alex pressed on, even though she felt hopeless. She knew it would be a long way to the bottom, and only the need for quickness motivated her. Once Kyria made her grand ruckus, there wouldn't be a lot of time until the keepers found her, and Alex wasn't letting that happen.

They had reached the lowest point of the Abyss that was Keeper free, so they paused and waited in a recessed alcove of the wall of souls. Marin didn't look much happier than Alex, and they floated in silence, waiting for the sign, which came with a crashing whoop above.

"Oye! Ya shifty spectery types! Aye, I'm talkin' to ya. My name's Kyria Killburn, and I'm the woman who cheated death. Come and claim my soul, if yer able!" A long string of obscene gestures, and some general screeching followed this brash announcement. Alex couldn't see her, but just hearing her friend's lighthearted jesting made her feel a little better.

At first it wasn't entirely clear that the Keepers had heard Kyria, or if they had, whether they cared. For a long, hideous moment, it appeared the bait hadn't worked, and the Keepers stared up at the area from which the sound had come. Then came a crash of screaming and hissing as several dozen keepers rose with alarming speed from the Abyss and rushed into the Halls above. Several still lurked in the deeper parts of the chasm, but Kyria had done her part. Now Alex needed to hurry.

With a concerted effort, Alex pushed herself from the ledge and began floating downward with Marin in tow. It was slow at first, but she seemed to be able to will herself to fall faster. Looking down, she saw the grim outline of a Keeper occupying the center of the Abyss, but she ducked back onto the staircase and into one alcove that honeycombed the walls. Alex watched as the glowing eyes of the Keeper moved over the wall, but Alex and Marin remained hidden. Once the creature had moved on to another section, Alex resumed her freefall.

As she plunged into the darkness, it became harder and harder for Alex to remember why she had even come into the Abyss to begin with. The light from the Halls above was as distant as the stars, and down here the souls of the dead were sparse, each with their own area of the wall. Their torment was worse, and Alex avoided lingering her gaze on any of them. Even though they were probably bad people in their life on Aquillon (Alex figured a large contingent of the Foxes Guild was down here) she couldn't imagine that anyone deserved this. Just being down here for a little while was bad enough.

After a long while of floating, Alex and Marin finally reached the bottom. The chasm's walls had been empty for some time now, and the walls met in the middle of the Abyss, forming what appeared to be a dry river bed running for endless distance. Nothing existed this far down, and no light penetrates the depths of the Abyss. It was a place of unending night, and only the ethereal glow of Marin's shade cast the smallest amount of illumination.

The sense of sadness was a palpable sea in which Alex was trying not to drown in. She felt as though she would never leave, and that this was the end. After all these years, she finally understood the description in Dante's Inferno - "Abandon hope, all ye who enter here." Hope had fled long ago, with the light and the world. Here there was only darkness and regret.

"We need to keep moving," Marin said. His thoughts sounded brave and untainted by fear. Alex marveled at his strength. She nodded and followed where he led.

As they floated forward, the silhouettes of a ruined throne room slowly materialized. They had no detail or substance, but were shadows given form, like the ghosts of a mind. In the center of the room, chained to a massive throne, Alex saw an old man in a dusty suit of armor. He looked up and regarded them from milk-white eyes.

"You are very brave, or perhaps idiotic, to have ventured so far into the kingdom of the dead. Why have you come here?"

29

The Last Emperor of Man

I t was a long moment before Alex could muster the spirit to say anything. The feeling of dread and despair this far into the abyss sapped her like frigid water, and she felt her willpower leaving her as she spoke. They needed to get out soon.

"We need information on the Court of Hours. We were told that you might provide some idea of where they came from, or how we can get rid of them for good," Alex said.

"The Court is still in power? I'm hardly surprised. Yes, I can give you what you seek, but tell me. Who are you to have come so far into the dark? This was not a journey for the faint of heart," the emperor said. His voice was the slow wheeze of a dying pipe organ and rattled with dust and the passing of a millennium. All around him the scene of his castle shifted from time to time, always outlined in the swirling shadow. Even the throne the emperor sat on seemed immaterial and fleeting.

"I am Alex Winters, and this is my friend, Marin."

"I see. It is not every day that someone from another world visits us. You have come a longer way than most on your road to this pit of shadow. Why should I help you?"

"Well, we came a long way," Marin interjected.

"Besides, we can't get you out of here, but we can help you get revenge on the Court," Alex said, hoping to stoke some fire that remained in the old man.

"You are children, playing at a game of gods in a time gone by. You know nothing. Begone," the emperor said, waving his hand.

"I mean, you can't really force us to go anywhere, and we're persistent," Alex said. The last bit was true, even if she didn't feel it.

"There is nothing you can do to me that has not already been done, and there is nothing you can give me. What I know will stay with me. I cannot let it leave. Now for the last time, get out!"

"We're not leaving," Alex said evenly, "and I don't even really think you want us to. You've been down here for so long, I think we're the first people who've ever come down this far. I think you're thrilled to see people, or well, spirits again. I know you remain down here willingly. Why?"

"Because this is what I deserve. You seek the source of the Court of Hours? You have found him." The emperor sounded broken as he spoke, and his shade shifted in and out.

"What do you mean?" Marin asked.

"So you seek information to treat the Court as if it were a disease, or some pestilence, but that is not so. The Court is the symptom, not the ailment."

"So, what is the ailment?" Alex asked.

"There is a reason I wanted you to leave. I wanted to spare you. We are the disease. Humanity. Our sins, our corruption, our greed. You seek the culprit for the Court of Hours? You need look no further than a mirror."

"I don't understand. The Court came here to conquer Aquillon, to

261

rule it," Alex said.

"It would be easy to think that, but it is not so. But if you would seek the truth, I will tell it to you, though it will cause you much ruination and despair." The emperor paused and composed himself before speaking again.

"I am Emperor Caelum Septarum the III, the last of my line. I ruled over the Aquillonian Empire in its heights. We had climbed for a thousand years and conquered all but the Wyld Places. Our power was unmatched, but so too became our avarice. As I watched the empire grow, the people of the empire changed. I suppose it had been brewing for some time, but they became entitled and elitist. The rich flourished, while grinding the poor into the ground, who responded by fighting each other. Compassion and mercy became shows of weakness and liability."

"Sounds oddly familiar," Alex said with an eye roll.

"But your people followed the gods, didn't they?" Marin asked.

"Yes, but telling people you are a follower of the Court of Virtues and showing that to be true are seldom the same thing," the emperor said.

"Wait, what's the Court of Virtues?" Alex asked.

"The people of Aquillon do not remember the names of their gods, but they were once called the Court of Virtues, with twelve lords and ladies, each governing a particular aspect of virtue and morality. It was through their guiding principles that the empire could reach such heights. But the people forgot. Sure, they continued to pray and purport themselves as pillars of virtue, but really they had become hollow jackals. I should have seen it coming. The priests had warned me for years that the lords and ladies of the court had grown distant, but I would not listen. The Fall was the only thing that could have happened."

"So, the Court of Virtues sent the Court of Hours, as punishment?"

Alex asked. It stunned her.

"Indeed. Each of the Court of Hours is an inversion of one of the Lords or Ladies of Virtue. The Lord of Long Shadows is the mirror image of the Lord of Freedom. The Lord of Plagues is the shadowed reflection of the Lord of Health. We twisted the virtues and used them to serve our own ends, so the gods sent us the Court of Hours. They are the gods we deserve."

"But if the goal of the Court of Hours was to punish humanity for its sins, then why didn't they leave? A thousand years of suffering seems extreme. Besides, no one alive today is responsible for the sins that led to the fall." Marin said.

"All that you say is true. I do not know what the intention was by the Court of Virtue, but if the Court of Hours is still there, I expect they have outstayed their original mission by a good margin. They are twisted beings, so it is likely they believe their work is yet unfinished," the emperor said.

"But why can't anybody remember this? If the goal is to make humanity repent, then why seal their memories away?" Alex asked.

"Because the Court of Hours did not seal the memory of humanity. I did," the emperor said stoically.

"What? Why? How could you do that to your own people?" Alex demanded, her voice rising to a crescendo of anger.

"Because I did not think people could bear the guilt that I had. If people remembered that they were to blame for the Court's evil, they would surely have given up the fight long ago. We prayed to the gods for years after the fall, but there was no reply. I knew they had abandoned us. After that, I made sure the information I knew stayed with me. I worked a spell so powerful that it destroyed what was left of Rakara, the capital. It covered the land, and all who walked on it and sealed their memories. When I was done, I took my life, and the secret died with me."

"You worked a spell?" Marin asked.

"Yes. My lineage were gifted in the arcane arts. It allowed my ancestors to take power. In ancient times there was a quarrel in the family. One side thought that magic should be studied, and the other thought we should use it for the benefit of humanity. They split, and one became the Eastern Watch. The other, my ancestors, used their power to unite the warring tribes of man under one banner."

"But even with the power of a magus," Alex said, "how did you work a spell that powerful? It should have killed you."

"I found a large supply of the elixir used by the Paladins of the Seventh Dawn in their rituals. It kept my sustained why I cast the spell. It also obliterated what was left of Rakara, and every one of the people still there."

"You're a monster," Alex said bitterly.

"I have paid for my crimes, and I pay for them still, here in this pit of despair. Every moment I am chained in this chair, I re-live the pain of those I killed with my spell, and those I doomed by my inaction. I saw the decline of my empire, and I did not act. There are many thousands of guilty souls in the Abyss, but none more so than I."

"And what about the rest of them?" Alex said. "The good ones waiting up there?"

"They are waiting for a day that will never come, when the Court of Virtue arrives to take them home."

"So, their entire existence here is a lie?" Alex asked, her voice quivering with rage.

"Better than them knowing the truth. That is a burden that I must bare alone."

Alex shook her head. She didn't know what she had hoped to find out exactly, but now she felt more hopeless than ever. Maybe the emperor was right. Maybe this was a truth that no one needed to know. If a thousand years of the suffering Alex had seen during her time on Aquillon wasn't enough to convince the Court of Virtue that they had repented, nothing would.

"So, there's no hope? There has to be something we can do." Alex asked, despite the tsunami of despair crashing on her.

"Unless you could find a way to speak with the gods directly, no. They created the Court of Hours, so only they can truly destroy them."

"There must be some way of doing it? Some way of getting there?"

"Well, perhaps there is. You are a child of two worlds. I can see that in your spirit. If anyone could travel to their world, it would be you, but I know nothing more than that. I have told you all I can. I can feel the Keepers getting closer to your friends up there."

"Thank you, Caelum," Alex said. "I hope you find peace, eventually."

"Hope is something I gave up long ago. Now go!"

Alex and Marin turned and left, as the shadows of the Abyss slowly consumed the emperor.

"That was a lot," Alex said as they floated away.

"I want to hate him, but I can't," said Marin. "He did what he thought was right, and I don't know if I could have done anything different."

"Maybe. Well, let's blow this creepy popsicle stand. I'm sick of the spooky canyon." Alex said, mustering up a smile.

"That makes two of us, kid," Marin said.

She smiled back at him. Throughout all of this, he had been a guiding light. If she had to descend into a place so horrible, Alex was eternally grateful for her Virgil.

They rose slowly from the Abyss and didn't notice any Keepers on the way up. Kyria's excellent diversion had drawn them away. Alex was feeling dangerously optimistic about how things were going until she popped her head over the top of the Abyss, and her stomach dropped.

Kyria and Ahrun had their backs against the wall (so to speak) and were surrounded by a horde of Keepers, while an enormous collection of spirits looked on from a distance.

30

The Judgement of the Dead

Before Marin could even think to stop her, Alex surged forward out of the Abyss and into the crowd of spirits. She moved more quickly than she even realized she could as her panic and urgency to get to her friends shot her forward like a ghost cannon. Before the keepers could do anything about it, she had rushed into the middle of the group and took her place by Kyria's side.

"Nice o' ya ta join us," Kyria said with a grin. "I was wonderin' if ya were plannin' on retirein' down there an' buildin' a blazin' summer home."

"Better late than never," Alex said, rolling her eyes and sticking her tongue out at Kyria.

"Well, we are glad to have you back, even if we're all doomed," Ahrun said. He seemed to be in fairly good spirits, considering the situation. "You shouldn't have come back for us."

"Look, I just learned some crazy stuff, and the world isn't going to save itself, and I'm not doing it without you losers," Alex said.

"Silence, interlopers," came a shrill voice from behind Alex. She turned and saw that one Keeper in particular had floated out of the crowd. It was bigger and taller, but otherwise looked the same as the rest. It's glowing, lidless eyes burned into Alex. "You are intruders and thieves here. And we will judge you as such."

"Um, well, oh boy, this is awkward," Alex said.

"Does the thief have anything to say before we pass sentence?" The keeper asked her.

"Well, it's just that your boss, Death, gave me a hall pass to be here. He's going to get mad at you when he realizes how you're treating his guests. I'm seeing a desk job in your future," Alex said.

"Impossible. The King of Broken Crowns wouldn't do that. He had never allowed a living soul within the Halls of Silence. You are lying, and you will be judged and punished."

"Fine, call him. Bring him here," Alex said, trying to call the keepers' bluff. "He's going to be really annoyed, but you just call him here. If I am lying, he'll tell you, and you'll be good to go, what with the judging and whatnot. If you're so sure you're right, you've got nothing to worry about."

The Keeper paused and looked around at the others, seeming almost nervous. Then the moment passed, and it looked back at Alex.

"We need not check with anyone. Our master has given us sole dominion over these halls, and we are the ones who will pass judgment. You will speak no more," the Keeper said, and it pointed its skeletal finger at Alex and her friends. Suddenly she felt as though something sucked the wind out of her lungs. She couldn't speak, and when she looked at her friends, their mouths had vanished.

Alex braced herself for the inevitable end and whatever unpleasant fate awaited her, but they were interrupted by a speak, booming voice in the back of the crowd of spirits.

"You are not the dead, and you are not the judges here. We have had quite enough of you!"

It was a deep voice, rich with the warmth of memory; an impossible voice that Alex thought she would never hear again. If she had been breathing, she might have stopped, but echoes of longing and sadness reverberated through her soul as she heard each word spoken.

"Now get the hell away from my kid!" The crowd of ghosts that had gathered parted, and a form drifted through them until it was close enough to make out. It had been years since she had seen him, but every detail of his appearance was burned into her memory. Her dad hadn't changed a bit (well, aside from being a vaguely translucent ghost).

His form resembled the way he looked right before his death. He was in his mid-forties, and reasonably fit, despite a small beer gut that came from an over-zealous admiration of Boston-area beverages. He had short brown hair, cut to a military-looking crop, and a trim beard that shadowed his neckline, and sported a Chara Boston Bruins jersey. Even in death, his emerald green eyes sparkled at Alex.

"Da... Dad?" Alex asked, choking up on the question.

"Good to see ya, kiddo," he said. Every word radiated warmth and love, and Alex felt weak, despite being a disembodied spirit. Alex's dad turned to the Keepers.

"Listen hear, ya creeps. This is my daughter, and she's got more heart and soul than I ever had, and I'd vouch for her to the gods themselves. You're not touching a hair on her head, or you go through me."

The lead Keeper seemed incensed and was about to speak when the innkeeper spoke up.

"And me. This woman's a kind soul, and you'll not harm her if I have anything to say about it!" Several other spirits floated next to him and sounded off their allegiance. She vaguely remembered them as being patrons on the night of the Red Fleets attack, all those months ago. Another soldier stood out from the crowd.

"Aye, I remember when she took the field against the Court at Felwind. I died in the assault, but she saved my city, and my son," she said. "You'll not harm her while my platoon and I stand here." At this, several other spirits in armor gathered around the woman who spoke.

There was a sickening pause and finally the keeper relented, seeming to resign itself to the situation.

"Very well," came the shrieking hiss of a voice, "if this is the judgment of the dead, we will abide by it, but we will hold you personally responsible for her conduct until she returns to where she belongs." The creature glowered at Alex, who waved it a cheerful goodbye as it floated away. The moment it did, most of the spirits dissipated, but Alex's dad was still standing there. She moved to him as fast as she could and threw her arms around him. They passed through him, but she still felt close.

"Dad, what are you doing here?" Alex asked.

"I mean, I'm dead, so shouldn't I be asking you the same thing?" he said with a chuckle. Alex smiled bigger and bigger with every word he spoke. His voice was a wind of memory and affection that wrapped her up.

"Well, we came here to get information, which we did, but seriously, how did you end up here?"

"Well, I may have lived much of my life on Earth, but my soul is Aquillonian, so when I died, I just sort of ended up here. I kind of wish I ended up somewhere else, though. The food is terrible, and the entertainment is only so-so. I even tried to get a bingo night going, and that was a train-wreck. At least I might have been able to pick up a Sox game here or there in Earth heaven..." he trailed off, shaking his head. "Where are my manners, or yours, kiddo? You haven't introduced me to your friends! I'm Charlie Winters. I hope my kid hasn't gotten you into too much trouble."

"Not at all, good sir," Ahrun said. "She is the most honorable woman I have..." he paused as the temperature dropped a few degrees and he looked back at Kyria, who was giving him an icy stare. "One of the most noble women I have ever met."

"Well, she did almost get me killed by a lava beast," Marin grumbled, "but we're past that now."

"Aye, she's a good lass. Ya raised a good one, Charlie. I'm Kyria Killburn, an' this bumblin' fool who did no' bother ta introduce himself is Ahrun Valheim. Alex has told us nothin' but good things about ya. I'm honored ta meet ya, and thanks for savin' our collective rumps, I might add."

"Well, that's good to hear. And not a problem at all. Nobody likes those creepy jerks anyway, so it was nice to stand em' up for once," Charlie said. "How does the struggle against the Court? I've been hearing things since you arrived, Alex, but it's choppy. I only get news when somebody dies, so it's not exactly WCVB around here."

Alex gave him the cliff-notes of what had happened since her arrival. He listened intently.

"I'm sorry about your friend, Thistle," Charlie said. "The Court has ruined many lives, but it sounds like you finally have a beat on stopping them for good. And I'm glad you've come to terms with your mother. She's an excellent woman, and she did what she had to, to keep you safe."

"Yeah, she is. I can see why you liked her," Alex said.

"Well, you need to get going, kid. You've got lots to do, and I don't know how much longer the Keepers will tolerate your presence, and I'm all out of inspirational speeches."

"But, Dad, it's… it's not enough time," Alex said with a broken voice.

"Kid, with you, ten thousand years wouldn't be enough. This is still more than I ever thought I'd have again," Charlie said, sounding close to tears himself. They embraced one more time, and Alex and her friends turned to leave. Kyria turned back.

"Charlie, can ya do me a favor?" she asked.

271

"Sure."

"If ya see a man named Rex, tell him I said I love him. He was a bit o' a hellion so he might be down in the Abyss workin' himself out for a while, but if ya see him, tell him his Kyria said hello." Kyria sounded broken and defeated as she spoke, and Alex felt a pang of guilt as they turned to leave.

Alex lead them back down the hallway they came through, and they passed several Keepers who gave them lethal looks, but did not move to strike them. As they reached the doors, Alex turned back to see her dad waving at them in the distance. She waved and rushed out the door as it opened. If she stayed a minute longer, she'd never leave.

Outside, the barren tundra of the north had changed little. The river of souls still floated towards the halls, and a larger contingent of Keepers floated on the air, watching each spirit who entered intently, determined not to let any more intruders in. The group made their way from the halls quietly, with no one saying anything.

They finally arrived back at where they had left their bodies, which seemed to be no worse for wear. Kelebar turned to them.

"I see you have arrived, and in time. I would not have been able to keep your bodies warm much longer." With this he cut the surrounding air with his sword and Alex felt herself being ripped back into her body, and she woke up with a gasp as frigid air rushed into her lungs like a torrent of ice. It took several long minutes for her to regain her composure fully.

"So, I vote never to do that again," was the first thing out of Marin's mouth. "Like, ever."

"Agreed. That was not a place where the living were meant to go and return from," Ahrun said.

Alex and Kyria said nothing. Alex wasn't sure how she felt. Her mind was a confused mess of emotions, and she refocused on the task at hand.

"Well, we got the information we came for, we'd best be getting out of here. I'm not sure what the next step is, but I know it's not here," Alex said.

"I must agree," Kelebar rumbled. "You have disturbed the dead enough for several generations. Begone and please don't return until you are good and dead." The giant said this not in the menacing tone of a threat, but in the cadence of a kind request.

"Don' ya worry, ya big galoot. We will no' be back soon. Too many frozen spookies for my taste," Kyria said, trying to project confidence. She still sounded broken and defeated.

"Thanks for not killing us, Kelly!" Alex said.

Kelebar didn't look as though he enjoyed his nick-name, but Alex turned and marched south before he could react. As she did, Kelebar thundered the earth with a great leap that put him back atop the mountains which loomed over the Halls of Silence. Alex grimaced as she looked back at them, as she tried to fight the nagging feeling she had left some part of herself in the Abyss. She was back in her body, but nothing felt quite the same. The wind wasn't as cold, and the air wasn't as crisp. Even the colors of the world seemed muted. Even if the colors returned, Alex wasn't sure she'd be seeing them out of the same eyes.

They spent the next days and nights of marching across the tundra in small amounts of sparse conversation, but mostly tense silence. The landscape had not changed as one ice-filled vista blended into the next, and before long, even the bone towers were ghosts on the northern horizon.

Despite growing up in Boston winters, Alex felt she was done with ice and snow for the foreseeable future, and just when she was considering throwing herself off a nearby snow embankment, she heard the piercing shriek of a seagull and the pale blue of the ocean was before them. They descended the cliff side to the stony beach and

273

looked around.

The sun shimmered in blinding light off the still waters of the bay, and in the distance, the monolithic skeleton continued to breathe out frost onto the water and ice of the frozen sea. Still, there was a rather large something missing from the otherwise beautiful scene.

"Guys, didn't we leave our dragon parked here?" Alex asked.

"I swear ta all the gods, if tha' no account, flea-bitten, scaley beasty has gone off an' run away on us, I'll be makin' myself a fine set o' dragon hide armor," Kyria said, shaking a righteously angry fist into the freezing air.

"Is there like another plan for getting out of here? Because the pirates are gone, and so is most of our food," Marin said.

"I don't think Larm would have come this far just to abandon us, although I think he might chase a tasty-looking seagull to the ends of Aquillon. Just chill, it'll be fine," Alex said, trying to reassure them, despite not feeling great about the situation.

They made camp and sat around a small fire that Alex conjured up for most of the day. Nobody had much of anything to say, and everyone nervously scanned the eastern horizon looking for any sign of their dragon companion. It was nearly mid day when Alex was losing hope, that she heard a distant sound coming from the cliff line. She turned to see Larm flailing about one of his claws in what she could only assume was his version of a wave. It mostly looked like he was having a small seizure, but the effort he was putting into it was sweet.

Alex beckoned him down, but he turned and wandered back over the cliff. Alex turned to her friends.

"I'll go see what he's on about," she said.

"I'll come with you," said Marin.

Alex nodded. In three glimmers they were atop the cliff line, although Alex felt sapped by the end. Glimmering was a much easier, exact science when it was on a diagonal plane, just forward and backward. Up and down were harder.

Once they had gotten their bearings, Alex and Marin wandered over to where Larm was. He lumbered over to them and tried to lick Alex, who sidestepped it and gave him a side-hug and neck scratch. Marin wasn't so lucky.

"What are you doing up here, buddy?" Alex asked, trying to maintain her patient tone. However simple and child-like Larm acted, he was still a two-thousand-pound, fire-breathing dragon. She didn't want to scold him in case he threw a temper tantrum by barbecuing her.

"Spent too much time in cold. Larm can't fly right now. Dragon fire being. Cold takes strength. Just walk. Larm knew he couldn't fly friends home, so he walked until he found nice humans to take friends home." Larm moved and revealed a small contingent of soldiers approaching from the south on horseback. They pulled up to a cautious distance from the dragon and dismounted.

"Hail and well met, Alex Winters, Hero of Felwind," one soldier said to Alex. "We're glad you made it back."

"That makes two of us. You are?" Alex asked.

"My name is Captain Samuel Kartra, and The General has sent me to retrieve the Heroes of Felwind, and escort you out of this frozen waste."

"Say no more. We'll be right back," Alex said.

After a series of glimmers down the cliff side, Alex explained the situation up top to Kyria and Ahrun who broke the camp and the four friends made it back up the cliff. It took a while, but as soon as they made it to the top, they were mounted up and on their way.

"Where are we going?" Marin asked Captain Kartra as they rode south.

"The Old Guard has a fort close to here, just at the base of the Wrathfall Mountains. You can rest and resupply there."

They rode (as Larm trotted along next to them) the rest of the day, and Alex was wondering if they would have to break camp for the night when she spotted the outline of a small fort on the southern horizon. It was constructed of large grey stones and sturdy timbers, and firefly torches dotted the ramparts all around it. In the distance beyond a gigantic series of mountains blotted out the landscape beyond. They were imposing, ice capped titans that pierced the southern sky, and reminded Alex of the Himalayas back on Earth.

The sun had gone down by the time they reached the fort and rode inside, and Alex was grateful to be away from the snow as the temperature had dropped considerably in the last several hours. They turned their horses over to a stable boy who took them inside a barn. Larm followed, on the general assumption that he could eat the horses since nobody was using them anymore. Alex was too tired to correct him and figured she'd leave that to the stable-hand.

They followed the captain inside into a large dining hall where the soldiers of the fort had gathered for the evening meal. They were all ladling steaming hot stew out of a large black cauldron, and as the smell of the tender beef and vegetables hit Alex's nose. She was convinced it was the best thing she had ever smelled. She hopped in line behind her friends and happily grabbed a bowl and followed them to a nearby table. Kyria didn't make it though as she stopped dead in her tracks and dropped her bowl on the floor, nearly causing Alex to collide into her and drop her stew. She was about to snap at Kyria when until Alex looked up and saw what had caused her distraction.

Standing at the back of the room, looming over everyone else by a considerable margin, was Rex. He looked older, and there were several scars on his face, just above his beard that Alex was sure hadn't been there before, but his eyes hadn't changed. They flickered in the firelight like small jewels set above a massive sea of scruffy beard.

"Well now ya have gone an' made quite a mess for the pages ta clean

up. What kind o' mannerless heathen did I raise?" Rex asked with a
gigantic grin.

31

The Northern Outpost

F
ive seconds after Rex had spoken, Kyria flew across the room and tackled him with a violent hug, much to the chagrin of several guardsmen and their toppled over bowls of stew. None of that mattered to Kyria, who planted her face in Rex's chest and sobbed uncontrollably while punching him as hard as she could.

"Ya great eegit," Kyria said between sobs. "How could ya leave me like tha'?"

"It was no' my intention ta leave ya, lass, but I'm back now, and so are you so let's sit and talk. I imagine ya have much ta discuss."

Kyria raised her puffy red eyes from his coat and nodded while choking back a sniffle. Rex beckoned the group over to his table and he made room for them with a deadly glare at several guardsmen who shuffled away to new seats elsewhere.

"So, how did you get out of that bind back at the stonemoot?" Alex asked. It thrilled her to see Rex again, but it didn't add up. The last time she had seen him there were several very large, furious Pride demons about to make mincemeat out of him.

"Well, ya see they were goin' ta kill me, but they stopped at the last second, as if on orders from some higher up and took me prisoner instead. From there they took me ta a large slave camp a long way away and let me rot for the better part o' two months. Fortunately, the cats they had guardin' the place were about as bright as they were kind, and I made good my escape. From there, I made my way north. I met up with Sal in Felwind, who told me all o' the grand adventure ya lot have had, an' I came here with a contingent o' guardsmen. I figured ya'd end up here eventually."

"Fine. Well, I guess I can forgive ya for not meeting us sooner," Kyria said, punching his arm one last time. "I should introduce ya ta my friends. This is Marin," she said, and he made a quick bow. "And this is Ahrun, former fancy pants knight, and paladin o' some shiny order." There was an odd pause between her words and Rex speaking. Alex felt a slight moment of tension pass over the two men.

"It's good ta meet ya, sir," Rex said, clasping Ahrun's hand in his.

"You've raised a fine daughter. I owe her my life many times over. She's an incredible young woman." Rex seemed to grip Ahrun's hand longer than was needed, and Alex spoke up.

"Well, ok, now that everybody's acquainted, why don't we eat?"

Everyone was too hungry to object, and they settled in at a nearby table. Kyria mouthed a silent, 'thank you' to Alex, who grinned at her. After everyone had enjoyed their fair share and a half of piping hot stew, Alex turned toward Rex.

"I'm so happy you made it out, but why do you think they didn't just kill you?"

"I wondered tha' myself for a time. I suppose they wanted information, or maybe the cretins just got their jolly's torturing me. Gods only know. I'm just thankful to 'ave made it out at all."

"Tha' makes two o' us," Kyria grunted with a mouth full of stew. Alex didn't consider herself much of a dainty lady, but Kyria's table manners were outright atrocious.

"So, now as ya have yer information, where do ya plan on goin'? The Old Guard stands ready ta assist ya," Rex said, thumping the table. Several groups of nearby soldiers raised their mugs and gave a hearty agreement.

"We need to get through to where the old gods live," Marin said.

"How in the blazin' abyss do ya suggest yer gonna accomplish tha?" Rex asked.

"We don't have any promising leads, honestly. I figured we'd make a plan in the morning. It's been a long day," Alex said. From the yawning of her friends, she took it she wasn't the only one who felt this way.

"Well, I've already set up accommodations in the barracks. Follow me," Rex said.

The group stood and followed him out into the snow-filled courtyard and into a doorway on the opposite side of the fort. Most of the soldiers had turned in for the evening, and only a small contingent served on the walls as night's watch.

When they were inside, Alex made the executive decision that girls got top bunk and wiggled into hers before anyone could argue. Rex directed Ahrun to a bunk as far away from Kyria's as he could, with a cheerful smile. Before long, everyone was in bed and snoring away.

Alex tossed and turned for what seemed like hours before finally fading off into sleep. The roiling churn of her subconscious played out in a million terrifying ways, and when she awoke in the morning, her eyes burned as if she hadn't gotten a wink of sleep. She rolled out of her bunk groggily and stumbled her way down to a washroom.

One perk of being a magus was not having to deal with Aquillon's lack of indoor plumbing. A simple incant gave her a basin full of steaming water and she splashed it on her face. The warmth perked her up somewhat and once she felt cleaner and more awake; she left the barracks and entered the courtyard. She noted that her friends had all gotten up before her.

As soon as Alex stepped foot in the courtyard, she knew something was wrong. Soldiers ran about frantically, grabbing weapons and strapping on armor. Marin sprinted up to her with a manic look on his face. His robes were disheveled, and he was breathing hard.

"Good, you're up. We were about to come get you. Come on."

Alex followed him up several flights of rickety wooden stairs to the top of the southern wall. Ahrun and Kyria stood at the top looking over the ramparts with nervous looks on their faces. Rex was there in full armor, with a hammer the size of his old axe gripped firmly in his right hand. Alex could almost guess what lay over the horizon before she saw it.

Once she got to the top, she peered over the southern rampart, and her heart sank. In the silent, frozen morning air, a hundred banners waved along a battle line filled with Akari goat-men, Pride, and Golden Hosts. In the center of the army, the Lord of Long Shadows waited atop a massive serpent which served as a mount. His golden armor caught the sunlight streaming over the western horizon, and his single red eye burned in the distance. Alex's chest tightened, and her heartbeat quickened tenfold. The battle line extended half a mile in each direction, cutting off any retreat from either side of the fort.

The Court of Hours had come, and this time, there could be no escape.

32

A Field of Frozen Death

Alex counted the demons along the battle lines, but gave up somewhere in the low two hundreds. They outnumbered the Guard by a margin of at least twenty to one, and that was being generous. She was about to ask Rex how an entire army of demons had snuck up to the fort overnight with no one noticing, but then she saw the portals behind the war machines of the Akari. They shimmered with black energy and cut circles of night on the otherwise cloudless southern horizon.

"Why aren't they attacking?" Alex asked Rex.

"Yer guess is as good as mine, but I imagine tha' ole black cat wants something. I've seen his forces kill a thousand women and children for nae reason, so if he's holdin' back his hand, it's for cause."

Alex nodded and just then the great serpent the Lord of Long Shadows rode on slithered closer to the fort. It was a beast of nightmarish proportions, and as Alex watched it approach, she realized with surprise that it was no beast at all but a great whirling machine of cogs and metal. Each polished metal scale folded into the next in perfect symmetry, and the light of the sun danced on its hide.

Great, glowing emerald eyes watched the fortress and steam poured from its mouth. Once he was close enough to shout, the great lion spoke.

"We meet again, Alessandra Falkrest," he said. His voice still had all the rich layers of smooth seduction as before, but Alex knew the evil that lay beneath it.

"My name's Alex Winters, idiot. Did I give you brain damage from our last fight or something?"

"Your humor may play well with the insects you call friends, but do not snipe words with me. It is only my patience and my wish to speak to you that holds my hand."

"Got nothing to say to you, evil Simba. Bugger off and leave us alone."

The Lord did not respond except to motion one of his paws towards the fort. With a great screaming hiss, one of the Akari trebuchets launched a flaming boulder towards the wall. It struck the earth and burned its way deep into the snow. Alex could tell it was not an errant shot. It was a message.

"Fine. I'll talk, but don't throw any more of those at my friends."

Alex glimmered down to the ground outside the fort before any of her friends could talk better sense into her. She didn't like dealing one on one with the demon king again, but she didn't see any other choice. She looked back at Marin and made a circular gesture, hoping he would get her meaning. If she could buy him enough time, he might shield the place from assault, and that would force the army to come to them. It had worked at the Alamo, Alex figured. Well, for a while anyway.

Once she was sure Marin understood her signal, she made her way out onto the center of the open field. The permafrost crunched under her boots and she could smell the flaming pitch of artillery wafting on the morning breeze. As she neared the halfway point, the hissing whir of servos and gears of the mechanical serpent pierced the relative silence of the battlefield. Once it was close enough, the demon jumped off and landed several feet from her.

"What happened, chief? Run out of slaves to carry your fat butt around?" Alex taunted.

"Our time apart has made your insolence no less tiresome. I called you here to offer you your friends' lives. Come with me and there is no need for them to die. I see no point in slaughtering them if we can come to an arrangement like civilized creatures."

Even though Alex knew they were outright lies, his words pulled at her, snaking their way into her brain like insidious worms of deceit.

"Right. Civilized. Like when you attacked Felwind and tried to kill thousands of unarmed men, women, and children? If that's the civilized you're talking about, I'll just as soon go back to being a savage with my buddies over there."

The Lord growled and Alex saw him grip his scythe tighter.

"Do not be a fool, girl. It impressed me to learn of your powers at the battle of Felwind, but neither you nor your friends will stop us here. We will obliterate you. Be reasonable."

"Not enslaving humanity would have been reasonable. Not killing my friend would have been reasonable. Not trying to kill me and the rest of my friends would have been reasonable. We're way past reasonable, so let me give you my answer," Alex said. Her voice was a low, venomous growl, and she reached out with her mind, sending all her anger and hatred towards the Hand of Seven. He swiped away the surge of fire that erupted from her hand.

"Girl. Did you really think you could wound me again in the same manner? You taught me that trick already."

"No, I didn't think it would work. But I figured it might keep you distracted long enough for that to happen," Alex said, smirking, as she pointed to the great mechanical serpent.

Alex concentrated on the mechanical monster, and it convulsed for a moment before it spewed fire out of its mouth and collapsed into a molten pile of metal.

The demon king roared and swung at Alex, but she was a step ahead and glimmered back fifty feet and turned to run. The Lord wasn't foolish enough to pursue within the range of her friends, so he began back towards his army, signaling to begin the assault. The first flaming missile howled through the air as Alex neared the walls of the fort. She watched it and waited, holding her breath. It slammed into an invisible wall and broke apart.

"Atta boy Marin," Alex said to herself, smiling. She was close enough to glimmer now, and she focused on an open spot on the rampart and appeared there. She turned and saw Kyria and Ahrun running up to her. Marin was still focused on maintaining the shield.

"If ya ever do somethin' tha' daft again, I swear I'll," Kyria said before Alex cut her off.

"Kyria, you know the drill. Stupid, insane, world-saving heroics is what we do. It's kind of our thing."

"The woman has a point," Ahrun said. Kyria punched both of them in the arm.

"Well, whatever ya said ta tha' idiot cat got them all stirred up in a hurry," Kyria said, pointing.

Alex turned and saw the demon army had begun to march, or in the Akari's case, charge recklessly. Even though Marin's shield had put the war machines out of commission, they were still heavily outnumbered, and down one magus. The moment he let the shield down, Alex knew the trebuchets would resume the bombardment and then they were really sunk.

All the Guard had deployed around the walls and Alex took her place beside them and waited for the coming storm.

The ground rumbled.

The wind howled.

The smell of fear hung thick in the air, mingling with the smoke of the flaming debris from the projectile. Then there was a moment of calm, and the sun shone down on Alex and she took a deep breath. Just as quickly, the moment ended, and the sun hid its face behind dark clouds, as if hiding from the slaughter to come.

The first wave hit the walls like a crashing tsunami, and Alex had to brace herself to keep from falling over the rampart. Other soldiers weren't so lucky and fell screaming into a sea of chittering madness.

"Loose your arrows," a commander screamed. and the guard fired the first round of spike death into the enemy. Dozens of the demons fell, but just as before, they reformed on the far side of the battlefield. Alex took a deep breath and unleashed her powers on the evil below. A wave of molten fire erupted from her outstretched palms, liquifying every demon it touched. She poured all her anger, all of her fear, all of her anguish into her magic and it flowed as a river of glowing red death. As she watched her enemies fall, the dark side of her took hold and with each demon she felled, her malice grew.

There was a scream on the opposite rampart, and Alex turned to see what it was. The Akari had surged over the walls by stacking on themselves and forming a living ladder. Despite the best efforts of the guardsmen, they were losing ground.

"I have this," Alex said, in a voice that wasn't quite her own. "Go."

Ahrun and Kyria didn't argue, and they ran down the stairs, bounded across the courtyard, and ran up the stairs, cutting demons down as they went. Alex knew she should feel more worried for them, but all she felt was rage. She turned her attention back to her enemies.

After a while longer of melting the demons in front of her, they retreated, and regroup near the main gate of the fortress. Alex sprinted along the ramparts, getting as close to the gate as she was able, but she didn't have a good vantage point to continue her assault. As Alex looked around the edges of the fort, the demons had mostly abandoned the assault on the walls, in favor of attacking the gate. She glimmered to the center of the courtyard where a large contingent of the guard was gathering.

As she reached them, Alex looked around and realized with a sinking feeling how many casualties they had suffered. Bodies of guardsmen and women littered the ramparts, and the number of soldiers had dwindled. She saw Ahrun and Kyria running through the crowd of bruised and bloodied defenders, and she grabbed both of them in a hug. Alex's battle rage seemed to have subsided for the moment. She was about to speak to her friends when a shatteringly loud thumb rang out from the gate.

A large imprint of what Alex assumed was a battering ram sent splinter flying in every direction as a dozen soldiers pressed against the gate, trying to secure it. It would only be a matter of time before the gate fell, and the few defenders on the walls were barely keeping the demons who were still attacking the rampart at bay. Alex wanted to believe they could still win somehow, but the end was coming, and that fact seemed increasingly clearer.

"What is going on?"

Alex, Kyria, and Ahrun turned and saw that Larm had left the stables and was standing next to them.

"Nice of ya ta join us," Kyria said.

"Larm tried to get warm so Larm could fly friends away, but it is too cold. Larm is sorry he has let his friends down. Larm is a bad dragon. Other, better dragons could have helped friends, but Larm is weak. Can't even fly or breath fire in the cold."

"Larm, you were the only dragon who would help us, and that alone makes you the best and the bravest. It should honor me to fight alongside such a brave creature," Ahrun said. Larm's face lit up, and he focused on the gate with a determined stare. Alex figured he couldn't breathe fire, but he could still fight. Still, the odds didn't seem to be in their favor.

"Well, this might be it, guys," Alex said, prepping a half a dozen different spells in her head. As she spoke the battering ram slammed against the gate, and an enormous crack ripped down the middle of the gate. Demonic hands and swords reached inside the crack, trying to hurt or kill anything that was close enough. The door looked one more assault away from giving in for good. Alex heard a cry and saw that the demons were overwhelming the defenders on the ramparts. A group of golden hosts was advancing on the stairs and on the other side, a swarm of Akari were cutting down the remaining soldiers as more climbed over the top.

"I did not wish to die today, but if I must, I cannot think of better company than my good friends, and the woman I love," Ahrun said. Before she could protest, he scooped Kyria up into a long, passionate kiss. Kyria resisted at first, but then embraced it and returned the kiss.

Rex, who parted the crowd and walked towards them, cleared his throat. "If ya survive this, I'm goin' ta kill ya."

"Fair enough," said Ahrun. "But I'm honored to love your daughter all the same."

Alex looked up and saw that Marin was gone from the ramparts, and her heart fell. She felt a tap on her shoulder and turned to see his playful green eyes looking into hers.

"You weren't about to have all the fun without me, right?" he asked.

"No, buddy. I saved you at least seven hundred demons. And if I don't have time to say it, thank you. For everything. I know it might not mean much, under the circumstances, but I'm glad I met you."

"Don't go getting all mushy on my now, kid. It'll ruin your reputation," he said with a smirk. Then Alex kissed him. She didn't quite know why she did it, but it felt right, and she figured she didn't have much to lose as she'd most likely be dead within the hour. The kiss was long and warm and soft, and if it was the last good thing that Alex felt in her life, she was ok with that.

"Marin, I..."

Whatever Alex was going to say was cut off by the thundering strike of the battering ram, which tolled like a funeral bell across the courtyard. The gate burst open and the remaining guard were planting their feet and waiting for the sea of demons.

33

The Last Stand of the Old Guard

T he battle erupted from all sides of the courtyard as the gate collapsed and a stream of screaming demons rushed past the soldiers who had been trying in vain to hold the gate. Demons rushed over the wall as the last of the defenders abandoned their posts and fell.

Alex put everything else out of her mind and focused on the battle. She poured fire towards the opening where the gate had stood. Demons fell by the dozens but were replaced nearly as quickly, and Alex was already drained from the magic she had spent earlier.

Next to her, Larm roared as he slashed and clawed through dozens of demons. Gone was the passive dragon who spoke in simple sentences and just wanted to lick things. He was replaced with a creature of living, scaled death. The guardsmen kept the demons away from Larm while he struck from a range with his spiked tail and gleaming claws.

On Alex's left, Kyria whirled like a tornado of steel as her blades cut down any demon who came even remotely close to the line of defenders, and Ahrun threw his sword out and watched it cut down demons on its way out and back. Alex was almost starting to feel a glimmer of hope when she saw a vast shadow darken the line of defenders.

Looking up, Alex saw the Lord of Long Shadows bestriding the edges of the southern rampart. His scythe gleamed in the sunlight and his red eye burned, taking the place of the sun his massive figure was blotting out.

"Your resistance was admirable, but ultimately futile. The end now, I think," he said in a deep rumble. His dread voice spread along the circle of defending guardsmen like an insidious wave and they broke long before he lept into the air and landed, swinging his scythe in a circle and cutting several guardsmen down. In moments the line was shattered and the Lord of Long Shadows whirled his scythe around, a living cyclone of death and ruin. Alex retreated quickly and threw several fireballs to distract him from the others.

He turned and charged her, bringing his scythe down inches from her feet. Alex glimmered away and responded with a salvo of flame, but the demon extended his paw and chanted something, and the flames bounced harmlessly off of him.

"I told you those tricks would not work on me. Enough of this. Come with me, and I will spare these pitiful wretches." He paused his attack and motioned around the inner courtyard.

He didn't need his foul magic to persuade Alex that she was on the losing side of the battle. Less than a handful of guardsmen still stood, and they were all surrounded by demons. Ahrun, Kyria, and Marin faced outward, forming a formidable triangular defense, but Alex watched their attacks and it was clear they didn't have much left. Rex was still playing the part of a one-man wrecking crew, but he was cornered and outnumbered and eventually some demon or other would get a lucky strike. Alex knew the truth with no coercing; this battle was over.

"Fine. Tell them to back off. I'll go with you."

"A wise choice." The Lord of Long Shadows held up a paw, and the demons paused. The defenders dropped their swords and even Ahrun dropped his, as he attempted to restrain Kyria who had no interest in going out quietly. A calm passed over the body-filled courtyard, but in one corner the fighting hadn't ended.

Alex turned to where the sound was coming from. A small group of Akari had surrounded Larm and gotten inside of his striking range. He snapped them but in small numbers they were too quick to be caught by his lumber claws and teeth. The Hand of Seven saw them and growled.

"I gave you idiots an order. Drop your weapons."

One turned and looked at the demon king. "You are not the true bringer of war. You are weak, and we will take the blood they owe us. Kill the dragon and take his head brothers! We will be much gloried in the Halls of Blood!"

"No," the Hand screamed. "You do not know what you are doing, you must not…"

He leapt to them, but he came too late. The Akari who spoke brought down his axe, and it cleaved into Larm's chest. Larm collapsed with a yelp and didn't move.

"You mindless goats! Do you know what you have done?" With a swift motion, the demon king charged and cut them down, but a deep roar pierced the still air before he could do anything else.

"I have tolerated your filth for long enough, and now my flesh lies bleeding on the ground for my inaction. Run if you wish. Hide if you wish. Your cities will burn. Your ilk will burn. You will burn. And when I have charred every piece of all that you are to ash, I will burn the ashes."

Alex looked to the sky where the voice came from and shielded her eyes against the sun. When her vision returned, she saw the most beautiful sight she had ever seen; glowing portals and a sky darkened with the wings of hundreds of dragons.

34

A Fire in the East

"Run an' hide," was the first, was all Kyria shouted, and the beleaguered defenders didn't wait for a second warning.

Alex glimmered backwards into a small covered outcropping of the wall as she saw a huge red dragon diving for the fortress with its mouth opened. The Lord of Long Shadows waved his hands, and a portal appeared, into which he escaped, but he closed it behind him, leaving his soldiers to die. Before the demons could react or run the entire courtyard was charred with flame from the dragon above. The fire was molten death, and it incinerated everything it touched to smoldering ashes.

Alex felt the stones behind her shake as the dragon above pulled out of the dive at the last second and swept over the battlefield. Alex ran out to the courtyard, careful to avoid the parts that were still on fire, and glimmered to the upper rampart to see what was going on.

As she looked out over the walls, the scene was utter chaos. Dragons of every shape and size and color prowled the battlefield, burning groups of demons alive and snatching clumps of them up in their claws and dropping them to their deaths. The demons attempted to fight back, but their attacks were neither accurate nor strong enough to cause any actual damage. Alex spotted several Akari trying to ready a war machine, but before they were anywhere close, the entire machine was caught up in flames from several passing dragons. The Lord of Long Shadows had long since abandoned their footsoldiers, and it took only minutes for the host of dragons to clear the field.

Alex felt a hand on her shoulder and turned. It was Marin. His shock of white hair floated in the breeze and his green eyes took in the carnage over the battlefield.

"I'm glad you're alive. It'd be kind of rude to kiss me and then get yourself killed," he said with a hazy grin. The toll from keeping the shield alive was etched into his face, and he wore exhaustion like a heavy coat.

"That makes two of us," Alex said, trying her best to fight off a rising sea of nervousness. Marin said nothing else, and the two walked in silence to where the rest of the guard was forming up.

The dragons had cleaned up the last of the retreating demons and formed a circle around the large red one who had landed in the center of what used to be the demons' battle lines.

"So, what do we do now?" Rex asked.

"The dragon's an old friend," Kyria said. "We need ta take her son ta her."

Rex nodded and barked orders at the guardsmen closest to him. They hustled down the stairs and gently lifted Larm's body and began carrying it out. Alex ran down the stairs with her friends in tow, and each one grabbed a part of Larm's body.

The walk was long and silent, and Alex focused on her grim task. Larm was still breathing, but it was choppy and weak. She could tell they didn't have long. They finally arrived before the great red dragon and slowly lifted Larm down on his back so he could see her.

"Mother?" Larm asked in a quiet voice.

"Yes, my child, I am here."

"Larm sorry, Mother. Larm not strong like you. Larm wanted to make you proud."

"You have made us all proud. You were the strong one, my child. You took action while the rest of us cowered in our caves. You have shown us the meaning of courage."

"Larm's friends are here?" he asked.

Alex and her friends rushed over to him.

"We're here, ya brave sod," Kyria said. Her voice broke as tears welled in her eyes.

"You did real good, kid," Alex said, stifling back a sob, "we were all proud of you. You fought like a champ." She turned away and choked on the tears. When she turned back Larm smiled weakly at them.

"Do not be sad for Larm. Larm only ever wanted friends, and to make friends happy. Larm has done what Larm wanted to..." his voice faded as the light went out of eyes and his head slumped over. Kyria collapsed into Ahrun's arms in fits of uncontrolled sobbing, and Alex's eyes stung with tears. Even Ahrun seemed misty eyed.

The red dragon raised her head and utter a cry that shattered the stillness of the battlefield. It was a deep, mournful cry that sent chills down Alex's spine. When it ended, the dragon looked down at the humans.

"My son is dead. He is the first dragon to have died in Aquillon in a millennium, but he will not die in vain. As the gods are my witnesses, his death will mean something. It will be the fire that begins the inferno of revolution and burns the plague of the Court of Hours out of this world. But now is not the time for such talk. I wish for my son to be buried with honor, and there are many dead of your kind that should be afforded the same courtesy. Once that is done, we will see what this new alliance, bourn of grief may bring." With that, she turned and took flight, taking Larm's body in her claw.

Rex rallied his soldiers. "We will begin pickin' up what bodies we can an' placin' 'em below cover, at least them as was untouched by the dragon's fire, anyway. No man or woman shall rest before his brothers and sisters are safe from the reach o' the carrion bird. Now get to it." The soldiers looked strained to their end, but they took a breath and got to work with determined looks on their faces. Rex turned to Alex and her friends.

"I must go an' help collect the bodies. I think the commander's quarters were unharmed. Ya should get what rest ya can."

"We should help," Alex said.

"Nae. Ya need strength for the journey ahead. I don' know what yer plannin', but I know yer not done yet. No' even close."

"Thank you, Rex. You're right, we should get a rest," Marin said.

Rex looked at him for a long while before responding. "Yer a powerful sod, I'll give ya tha'. Thank ya for what ya done for my men." He shook Marin's hand, walked back towards where the soldiers were gathering bodies.

Alex followed her friends back to the fort, feeling utterly drained, physically and mentally. Her feet trudged through the snow and the world felt mute of color and feeling. She barely remembered making it back to the commander's quarters, but once she did, she collapsed into a dreamless slumber.

She awoke some time later. Hours, days, minutes - it was hard to tell how long she had slept, but it felt a little less like a semi-truck was running over her brain, so Alex figured that was a good sign. The commander's quarters were empty except for Marin, who had his nose deep in a book about Aquillonian slug farming. Why he had thought to bring that particular book from Sanctum, Alex would probably never know. It didn't matter. Alex had several more pressing issues on her mind.

"So, about that kiss," Alex said.

"Do you mind?" Marin shot her a playfully annoyed glance. "I was just getting to the good part."

"About how to get the most out of your Aquillonian slugs?"

"Exactly! Well, now you've broken my train of thought, and I can't enact my master plan of running away to become a slug farmer, I guess I have to talk to you." It was uncanny. As he spoke Alex could see hear her friend's warm tone, and familiar sarcasm, but there was something new in his voice.

"Look, people do crazy things in battle, and I'd forgive you if you didn't have any interest in me now that the adrenaline is wearing off but I..."

Marin never got to say anything else as Alex lept from her bed and collapsed onto him in a deep, warm embrace, wrapping him up in a passionate kiss. When she was done she sat in a comfortable silence next to him, holding his hand. He had a shell-shocked look on his face and seemed to try to find his words. Alex spoke up in a soft voice.

"I don't have much experience in this area, but that seemed easier than talking."

"No argument here kid. So what does this make us?"

"Can we sort that out tomorrow?" Alex asked. "I like you because things are simple, and I know this," she held up their hands as she spoke, "makes things less simple, but for today can it just stay simple?"

"I like simple" Marin said. "I might even..." Alex looked up and saw that Marin had dozed off. Alex said nothing else and curled up into him and enjoyed the silence. Before long she was asleep, nestled in his arms.

Alex got up several hours later and crossed the room. She left Marin snoozing. She knew this would complicate things, and that scared her a bit, but the more she thought about it, the more right it felt. She could figure everything else out later. For now, she needed breakfast. Or lunch. Or possibly both at the same time.

35

The Burning of the Dead

T he next two days passed as mostly a blur for Alex. She gave Marin some space, since it seemed fair to give him some quiet time to think.

It took Alex almost the entire next day to regain her strength. In the adrenaline-fueled heat of battle, she had underestimated how much energy her incanting would consume, and it was taking its toll.

The remaining soldiers spent their time repairing the fortress. Once her strength was back in full, Alex pitched in, if only to keep her mind off everything else.

"Tha's nae way ta sling mortar." Alex heard Kyria's voice and turned. Alex had been working on putting the bricks back in this section of wall for an hour now, and while she was annoyed with the critique, she had to admit Kyria had a point.

"I'd like to see you do better."

"Fine. I'll show ya then." Kyria went to work next to Alex repairing a nearby section of wall. The two worked in silence for a while before Kyria spoke.

"How are ya feelin'? About everythin'?"

"That's a complicated question."

"Fine. How are ya feelin' about Marin?"

"Like I said. Complicated. I don't really know what to do with it, so here I am, slinging mortar."

"Fair I suppose. And about everything else?"

"Overwhelmed. Hopeless. Heartbroken. Take your pick."

"I know. Larm was a goofy eegit, but he did no' deserve ta die like he did."

"I just feel guilty. I know I shouldn't, and I'm sure that dragon would have melted us all into piles of flaming goo if she thought we were responsible. I can't shake the feeling that it's my fault somehow. And all of those soldiers? They wouldn't have died if I hadn't come here, or if I had given myself up."

"Yer a good lass, an' I feel for Larm," Kyria's voice broke as she talked. "But ya can't go takin' everyone's death on yer conscience. War is awful. People die. Fathers, mothers, brothers, sisters. But ya have ta keep yer head up an' fight. It's the only thing that makes any o' it mean anythin'."

"How are you doing having your dad back?" Alex asked. "Have you spent any time with him?"

"A little. He's mostly overwhelmed with all the work of cleanin' up. An' he's been preparin' like crazy for the meetin' this afternoon."

"What meeting?"

"Ah, right. I forgot the wee lamb was dozin' while all the rest of us were hard at work," Kyria said with a giggle as Alex took a swipe at her. "The Mistress o' Scale called a meetin' ta discuss our mutual futures."

"I thought she wanted to bury the dead first?"

"I don' know why she changed her mind, but if I know anythin' about that old bat, it's that she never does anythin' without a reason. The meetin' is in a half-hour."

"Alright, well we'd best quit our chit-chat and finish this wall missy!"

Alex wasn't sure why, but she enjoyed fixing the wall. In the sea of complicated messes that had become her life recently, there was something simple about it that she found refreshing. By the time they were done, Alex saw a group of horses being brought to the hole in the wall where the gate used to be, and she walked over with Kyria in tow.

Rex approached them, and Marin and Ahrun weren't far behind. Rex saluted Alex. "I'm glad ta see ya made a full recovery from yer witchin' and sorcerin.'"

"Likewise. Can we come to these talks?" Alex asked.

"I wouldn't have them without ya," Rex said.

Without further conversation, everyone mounted a horse, and they left. Marin glanced over at Alex but said nothing. Whatever this was between them wouldn't get better with talking, Alex decided.

As they rode across the frozen tundra, Alex's nostrils burned with the overwhelming stench of dead demon. There weren't any bodies left, just stains from where the black ooze had seeped into the ground. Alex refocused her attention on the large group of dragons ahead of her.

The dragons were all grounded, and they sat on their haunches, but uprightly so that it seemed they were standing. Every shape and size and color was represented among the flock (were dragons called a flock, Alex wondered) and the sunlight gleamed off their scales. They formed a crescent atop a small hill, and in the center was a pyre on which Larm's body sat. Behind him, the great red dragon loomed, nearly as tall as the mountains behind her, or so it seemed.

"Welcome, humans." Her voice was the roar of the ocean crashing on the still morning air, and the rumble of an earthquake followed each word. Alex felt chills run down her spine, and it wasn't the morning air.

"We are honored ta be speakin' with ya. Our condolences for yer

301

loss," Rex said.

"And ours for yours, but we are not gathered here to speak on the past. I would talk of our future. We share the enemy that we have always shared: The Court of Hours."

"Well, I speak for all the guard when I say that we'd be honored ta join in an alliance with ya towards defeating them."

There was a murmur of growls among the dragons.

"The dissent you hear in the Scale is not your fault, human. We dragons have very long memories and have always been wary of alliances with humans. While my memory was sealed away long ago, with everyone else's, theirs were not. They have spoken to me of many alliances between our kind and yours. They never last long or end well. What assurances do we have that if we win, things will not fall apart as they always do?"

It was Kyria who spoke this time. "I canno' speak on behalf o' the dead, but ya have my word, and the word o' the Old Guard that any agreement we make here today will be honored, as long as one human stands breathin'."

"Ah, I remember you, little one. I like your fire, and I trust you. Help me understand why I should trust the rest of your species."

"Because these people have nothing," Alex said. Her heart thundered in her chest as she spoke. The wrong word or phrase would not end well for her or her friends. "I've been all over this world, and I've met these people. They are honest and true. They have been beaten a hundred times, but they're not broken. I can promise that they're the most loyal allies you could ask for. They won't let you down. They haven't let me down yet, and I wouldn't be standing here if it weren't for them."

"You are a child of two worlds?" The Mistress of Scale asked.

"I am."

"Your words have the ring of truth about them, and I suppose if you humans cannot live up to our expectations, we can always eat you. You lot are rather pathetic." There was a ripple of chuckles throughout the flock. It didn't sound to Alex like the Mistress was joking. "Very well. We will partner with you until the filth of the court has been eradicated. We will work out the details in three days, when we bury my son."

"As ya wish." Rex seemed frustrated by the delay, but even he wasn't foolhardy enough to argue with an enormous dragon. As the human contingent turned to leave, Alex waited behind. Her friends paused with her, and she turned to the Mistress of Scale.

"What do the tiny humans want now? I am tired and my nostrils burn of your stink," the dragon said in a low growl.

"Ya lot don' smell particularly grand yerselves," Kyria shot back.

"Ah, the bold little creature speaks again," the Mistresses' nostrils flared, but then the ghost of a smile crept across her mouth. Several other dragons shifted nervously. "I am never sure if I want to keep you around, or eat you. For today, you can speak your peace."

"I seek a way to reach the old gods in their world," Alex said.

"Why would you want to do that?"

Alex paused. If she shared the whole truth of the Court's existence and their origin, it might be a devastating blow to the moral of the Old Guard, and she needed them to keep up the fight. She hated the emperor for sealing away the memories of his people, but she saw the wisdom in it, now that she was burdened with the truth. "My reasons are my own, but it is important to me, and the people of Aquillon."

"Very well. I will help you, even if you cling to your secrets. It is little help to begin with. The only creature who may know of a way is the Hand of One, Lord of Awakenings. It was he who banished my children during the fall, and his skill with portal magic is unmatched. I have also heard whispers that he feuds with the Court and does not keep his council with them. I do not know if he will help you, but if he does not, your quest is doomed. Whatever it is."

"Where can we find him? There are no records of him, and he has no lesser demons to press for information," Marina asked.

The Mistress gave her a quizzical look, but continued without comment. "There again, I will help, though you may wish I hadn't. He keeps his hall in Stormfall, far to the south of here."

Alex looked around and saw her friends' looks fall sour and hopeless. "What gives, guys? Where is Stormfall?"

"It is the southernmost tip of Aquillon, just below the Wastes," Ahrun said. His face was etched with a grim frown.

"Well, we've been everywhere else in Aquillon; why not Stormfall?" Alex asked.

"It's a land where nae one returns from. Even the foul minions o' the Court cannot venture there," Kyria said.

"Why not? The Wastes were just awful, but we got in and out of them fine."

"After the fall, the Lord of Awakenings surrounded his territory in a field of energy. Those that try to bypass it become trapped in it. Never aging, never dying, trapped in a living death for all time. Only the Hand of One knows how to traverse the field," Ahrun said.

Alex's heart sank. To come all this way just to come up short at the end. But then she remembered something.

"What about my dream?"

"What dream?" Marina asked.

"Aye, I remember. She had a vision where the Hand o' One spoke ta her."

"Well, that is an interesting wrinkle. I don't know if he'll speak with you, but you're more than welcome to make the journey," the Mistress of Scales said.

"Could we enlist the aid of one of your children?" Alex asked.

A storm cloud passed over the Mistresses' face. "I do not entirely blame you for Larm's death, but I will not risk another child's life for your fool's errand. No human will ever again ride a dragon's back. This is my will, and it shall be obeyed." Her tone was bordering on lethal, and Alex didn't argue the point. She bowed and took her leave, and her friends followed.

It was mid-afternoon by time Alex and her friends arrived back at the fortress. Rex and his men had been busy. They stacked the bodies of the men and women lost in the battle on pyres outside the fortress. The bodies had been prepared as best as simple fighters could, and Alex could tell by counting that many of the bodies had been ruined beyond recognition, or had not been recovered.

Rex walked out to greet them.

"How did yer meetin' with the lady dragon go?"

"I think we have a direction to go in. The funeral is tonight?" Alex asked.

"Aye. We'll burn our dead an' they there's. I'd be lyin' if I said I trusted that lot o' skalies."

"Dad, we have ta try, otherwise the court wins," Kyria said, her voice soft. "Besides, if it weren't for tha' big skaly lyin' on their pyre, we'd all be dead. He was our friend."

"Well, I can't say nae ta their power, and I suppose trust will follow. Ya should get some dinner. The funeral will begin soon."

Alex wasn't feeling in the mood for a meal, but she knew he was right. She followed her friends into the fort, and they found their way to the mess hall. She was somewhat mystified by the fact the hall and the kitchen seemed to be the only structures in the fort that seemed unharmed by the siege, but she wasn't about to question a bit of good luck.

Alex's friends ate in silence and she barely tasted the meal. Her mind was in every other place but the present. There was an overwhelming crush of somber tension growing in her stomach. Her quest had never seemed more hopeless. Everything she had gone through all boiled down to an audience with the Hand of One, which he might or might not grant, and if he didn't, it was over. Alex knew the guard and their new allies would fight bravely, but eventually the court would win. Even dragon fire could only delay the inevitable. All they could do was hold the line until she could find a way to speak with the Court of Virtues. And if she didn't, the world was doomed, and everything she and her friends had gone through would be for nothing.

Alex stole a glance at her across the table. Marin caught her eyes between bites of stale bread and smiled a quiet smile. It was the same one from the night before and Alex returned it. They shared the moment but made no more effort to speak.

A horse thundered in the distance, and Alex looked up from her stew. Why is it always stew? She wondered to herself. Thankfully, she didn't have to figure out her emotional quandary about the stew, as Rex strode through the makeshift doors at the end of the mess hall.

"Rise. We go now ta honor the dead what gave their lives for us."

The soldiers rose and Alex with them. They shuffled out into the frigid darkness. Alex and her friend stuck together, and they all walked out to the field where the pyres stood. A long ring of torches was set up and illuminated the dozens of funeral platforms on which sat the honored dead. In the dancing echoes of the firelight, Alex saw the Mistress of Scale. She had set Larm's body on a gigantic pile of wood at the center of the soldiers.

Rex called the humans to attention, and the flock of dragons that hovered behind the Mistress bowed their heads. The Mistress merely nodded.

"Tonight, we come together ta honor our dead. These heroes here, of flesh and of scale, gave the last true gift anyone can - their lives. We honor 'em for their lives, an' we thank them for their deaths, so tha' we might see another dawn ta fight." The men and women around

306

Rex let out a roar that pierced the blackness of the night. It was a primal sound of loss and rage, as only the living left behind by the dead can produce. The dragons followed, howling their sorrow into the frozen night and bellowing flame upwards. The display lit up the night and for a moment it was as though day had broken early. Then the moment passed, and the beast of night swallowed them whole again.

In the darkness, the Mistress of Scale's eyes glittered and danced in the ghosts of firelight. "Your words touch and move the heart of an old wyrm, human. I salute your honored dead as I do mine, and I make now a pledge of loyalty to your kind. We would have blood, and vengeance, and death, and we will help you bring it. I do not know what the future holds for our kinds, but for this day, and all the days to come until the scourge of the Court of Hours is removed from this world, I know this; there will be blood and killing until the score is paid a hundred thousandfold." At this, she tilted her head to the starless sky above and roared. It was a sound unlike any Alex had heard before, or would ever hear again. It was all the rage and sorrow of a thousand years and the anguish of a mother, amplified by the primal power of a titan of death and fire.

Alex grabbed the nearest hand, which was Marin's and squeezed it tight, all at once being moved to tears, and terrified beyond words. Looking out beyond where the firelight died, Alex felt a presence watching her, and slowly two white eyes, burning like fire, appeared. As the figure moved into the light, Alex saw they were attached to a strange figure under a long black robe. His hands were guarded in gloves that shimmered in the firelight and seemed to reflect the surrounding light. He stood for a moment until the humans he stood next to noted him and drew their swords.

"Who are ya, creature o' night come skulking about ta mock our mournin'?" Rex said in a dangerous growl. He pulled his great black war hammer from his shoulders. Ahrun had his sword in his hand, and Kyria's daggers were at the ready.

"Now, now. There's no need for hostility. I am no friend, but do not count me as an enemy. I am here to give something and take something." His voice was a ripple in time. A sound which no earthly creature could utter, and it reverberated through the world as though it was the first sound, and the last.

"You have the stink of a demon on you. Speak your name, so I may know which of the Court's wretches I am sending to a fiery end," the mistress growled. Even from a great distance, Alex could feel the heat radiating from the dragon's mouth, and she knew it wasn't an idle threat.

"I always liked you, Karaval," the figure replied to the Mistress. "Even as a whelp. I would give you something else, but since you press beyond position, I will give you only my name. I am the Hand of One, Lord of Awakenings."

The sentence exploded like a firebomb in the ranks of soldiers and dragons. They all surged forward to strike, but the figure held up a hand and the world paused. Nothing moved, nothing stirred, and even time held its breath.

"Now that I have given you something, I will take what I came for." He held out his hand and Alex collapsed. Kyria and Ahrun strained with all their might against the invisible force holding them in place, but not a single fiber of muscle moved. The world was still as the Lord of Awakenings willed it. He raised his hand and Alex's body hovered towards him, her blond hair floating in the air. The Hand turned and spoke a word which rippled in the fabric of existence and a portal opened, into which Alex's body disappeared.

As it did, he turned to the captive audience.

"Do not worry yourself, she will be well. She is perhaps the first being in a thousand years to arouse my curiosity, and so I would have words with her. If you should wish her return, prove yourselves and find me in Stormfall. I caution you though, her return is not free. I would have you bring a vial of pure contagion from the Lord of Plagues."

He turned towards the portal but stopped a foot shy of it. "And I will give you another gift, free from the asking of it. Do not go around the mountains, but through them. The Lord of Long Shadows amasses an army unlike this world has ever seen, and he will destroy you unless you go through the mountains. Your draconic allies may have caught him off guard once, but he will be prepared for you when next you meet. Go through the mountains. There is a power there that even he will not defy."

With those words, the Lord of Awakenings turned and walked through the portal, which closed with a violent explosion that snuffed out the torches. The stillness ended and Ahrun, Kyria, and Marin rushed towards where the portal had been, but it was too late.

Alex was gone, and all that remained was the bleak darkness, and the howling of the wind.

Also by M. Anderson

The Lord of Long Shadows
In *The Lord of Long Shadows (Knights of the Fallen Realm, Book 1)* **Twenty-year-old orphan Alex Winters' quiet life is shattered when a chance encounter transports her to a world beyond her imagination and into the adventure of a lifetime.**

Praise for *The Lord of Long Shadows:*

"For young fans just beginning their journey into the fantasy genre, *The Lord of Long Shadows* by M. Anderson is an excellent place to start. Following in the footsteps of so many legendary fantasy worlds, this first installment of a new series hints at a creative and bold vision, as well as a gifted mind for storytelling and a true love for the genre."
   - Self Publishing Review

"The Lord of Long Shadows is the Young Adult book you'll wish you had as a kid—but the one you're happy to return to at any age. With magic, loss, bravery, and epic battles, this first book in the Knights of the Fallen Realm series comes out swinging—and hits."

- Independent Book Review

www.ingramcontent.com/pod-product-compliance
Lightning Source LLC
Chambersburg PA
CBHW020251200626
46816CB00001BA/244